ANGELS IN DISGUISE
THE GLORIOUS VICTORIES OF ELEANOR MACLEOD
VOLUME TWO
by Ashley Mayers

First Printing: 2019
ISBN 978-1-943918-18-8
International Print Edition

Grass Roof Publishing
P.O. Box 14908
San Francisco, California, 94114
www.GloriousVictories.com

Also by Ashley Mayers:
THE SITA CHRONICLES:
   Red Sapphire
   Violet Sapphire
   White Sapphire
   Golden Sapphire
   Cerulean Sapphire
   Green Sapphire
   Black Sapphire
THE ADVENTURES OF EDMUND AND ELEANOR:
   The Cursed Baron
   Angels in Disguise
   Damsels and Demons
   Eastward Beyond the Sky
   Before Midnight Ends
THE RIDDLE

Notes from the publisher:

The Glorious Victories of Eleanor MacLeod is a new five-book epic that adds another layer to the rich fantasy world created by Ashley Mayers and first published in 2015-16 in her seven-book modern multicultural epic, *The Sita Chronicles.*

Angels in Disguise, the second book of Eleanor MacLeod's story, begins epistolically right after the ending of *The Sita Chronicles,* and quickly returns the reader to the 1920s, when Eleanor MacLeod's personal epic began in earnest. As an homage to the genres that Ashley Mayers found most fascinating as a young reader herself, each book in Eleanor's epic plays with elements of a classic genre. *Angels in Disguise* incorporates elements of an art deco spy novel with a unique Ashley Mayers twist.

Throughout this series, it is the author's intention to give enough background for an uninitiated reader to develop a relationship with the world of *The Sita Chronicles,* while introducing them to several new heroines whose stories haven't yet been told. Both series fit together as puzzle pieces, creating unique insights into characters who are lovingly developed over the combined set of twelve books. All five books of Eleanor's story are intended to be read in order.

This series, like *The Sita Chronicles,* is a completely original, multicultural saga with roots in Hindu mythology. It exists in a world not dissimilar to ours, where Avatars (deities on Earth), Rakshasas (shapeshifting demons originating on Venus), and Yakshas (shapeshifting nature spirits) are real. While knowledge of Hinduism is not required to enjoy this series, a short glossary is provided in the back of the book to offer readers more context on Hindu cultural references.

TABLE OF CONTENTS

PROLOGUE

Dearest Ellie,

I hope this manuscript finds you well. I can't believe it's been three months since we saw you last, but we've all been so busy that it feels like time is just slipping through our fingers! Perhaps we should all have a picnic in Mélusine's crystal cave and take a few days without the clock ticking to relax and enjoy the pleasure of each other's company. In the meantime, though, there is a lot to catch up on!

Your father and I were excited to see the raving reviews of your newest photography exhibit; although, I can't say that either of us were surprised. Perhaps now you will finally believe that Edmund's glowing praise of your artistic talent wasn't rooted solely in a doting father's blind love. Now it seems like all of Edinburgh is going mad about it, or all the world, really. The Scots just get to be in the thick of it with your hordes of adoring fans gathering on Princes Street. Welcome to the limelight ;).

Kuveni has been kind enough to send us a daily collection of all the press about you. It just pops right onto the breakfast table out of thin air while Edmund is drinking his coffee in the morning.

It's become a bit of a game, because even when he's expecting it, Kuveni manages to startle him as soon as he lets his guard down. I'm still not sure how she always knows where we are as we gallivant across the globe in disguise, but I'd hate to think that she spends her entire life lurking invisibly in our vicinity. Edmund and I have both asked her about what else she has to do, and she insists that she is not simply following us around all day. We've decided that she must have a unique Yakshini talent that she hasn't admitted to yet, since she seems to know where you and Neha are all the time too. In any case, Edmund and I have both been grateful for her help in keeping us up to date on your impressive accomplishments.

I do hope that your audience is appreciating the artistry of your work, rather than just gawking at your alien art. I'm sure it's some mixture of both, just as it is with the resurgence of public interest in Edmund's paintings, but your work certainly stands on its own merits, regardless of the reason for their popular interest. Edmund has come to believe that one divine reason for his artistic talent is to inspire human interest in the arts, and I'd say that you have taken his torch and run with it. Like father, like daughter ;).

Speaking of Edmund's art, did you see the footage of what happened when we visited the new exhibit of his paintings at the Louvre? If not, you should definitely look up the footage online, because many bystanders recorded our spectacle on their phones. Neha can't stop laughing, no matter how many times she watches it.

It all started when your father and I were living in a lovely hilltop village in Bohemia for a few weeks while we helped build several hospitals in the countryside. When we saw the news footage of the long lines for his exhibit at the Louvre, we couldn't resist popping by to observe the curious public's reaction firsthand. He was convinced that their interest had very little to do with the artistic merit of his work, and so we decided to test his theory (in disguise, of course).

As you know, your father's conspicuous height always makes stealthy Rakshasa farces difficult for us to pull off, and this time was no exception, even when he used a very well-practiced form. As soon as we got in line, everyone around us began pointing and whispering and hoping, and we lasted about an hour chatting with our neighbors in the queue under the guise that we were Aussie students studying abroad at the Sorbonne, until we reached the inside of the gallery. I have to say, we almost pulled it off. *Almost.*

We made our way around the room as slowly as we could manage with the proctors yelling at us to keep moving (they weren't very happy about having to keep the gawking crowds under control), when Edmund noticed that the labels on some of the paintings did not credit your mother (I'm not sure whether he's ever told you that they painted a few together over the years. If you haven't seen them, you should ask Kuveni to pop you in there after hours some time). As you can imagine, he simply couldn't let it go.

He attempted to alert the proctor and asked discreetly to speak to the management (my heart went out to him as he tried his hardest not to make a scene), but after a few infuriatingly unhelpful responses, he told the proctor who he was, and as the man refused steadfastly to believe him, he lost his senses and gave everyone in the gallery the show of their lives.

With one especially flourished movement, he dissolved his disguise revealing not only his recognizable human form, but his sparkling golden falcon wings! The proctor practically fainted with surprise, and the crowd went absolutely wild. At that point, I figured there was no reason to keep up my farce either, and so I revealed my identity, and they went even madder.

But your father was a singularly focused man, and as they whipped out their phones to record our every move, he pulled a pen out of the hidden pocket in his form and wrote your mother's name right onto the placards himself. He then commanded the crowd to be quiet and set about explaining in great detail the history of each piece, the styles used, and your mother's contributions.

By the end, our wild crowd was thoroughly entranced, and with a mischievous bow of good sportsmanship, he winked at the proctor and told him that he would be keeping an eye on the accuracy of the placards from now on, returned the pen to his pocket, took my hand, and strutted right out of the gallery with his wings still flagrantly on display. The gobsmacked crowd, of course, followed us right out the glass pyramid into the Louvre's courtyard, and I joined him with my own wings so that together we could make a particularly memorable public exit.

I don't know if I've ever seen him as pleased with himself as he was when we landed back in Bohemia. I think your mother's fiery spirit may have temporarily possessed him ;).

Now, speaking of your mother's fiery spirit, I'd best get onto the real point of this letter before I re-think sending it to you at all.

It has been six months since your mother transcended the great barrier between life and death to ask for my help—for me to connect you with her memories so that you can truly know her—and I've fallen shamefully behind in fulfilling my solemn vow.

I know that you are reluctant to take her memories into your head, and your concerns are not unfounded. I still do not fully understand how I'm able to function with so many other people's memories muddling my mind. I don't know how much my comfort with my unique talent lies in my divine abilities as the Guardian of Memories or as the Avatar of Lakshmi, and so I cannot fault you for avoiding the unknown, irreversible consequences of a memory transfer. With that in mind, I have decided to fulfill my vow to your mother in a different way: I have written you a manuscript.

It is always difficult to decide what to share and how to share it, and so I have made a humble first attempt. My hope is that through this manuscript, you can begin to know your mother as she truly was, and from this starting point, you can guide me about the level of detail that interests you for future installments. Perhaps, when you know more about the context, you will feel more comfortable taking the related memories from my mind, but I will leave that up to you.

Feel free to take your time—there is absolutely no rush. I must, however, reassure you that the story is a happy adventure, despite their many moments of darkness, danger, confusion, and hopelessness. Your parents overcame so many tribulations, and each time they became stronger, Ellie. It is that strength, above all, that your mother wanted me to pass along to you so that you can, perhaps, break away from the natural tendency towards avoidance that you inherited from your father. Your mother helped him mightily in that capacity, and she hoped so dearly that she could help you too.

We are planning to fly over to Edinburgh next week for a visit. Let us know when it suits you, and whether you'd prefer us to come in disguise or to bring the fanfare of our attentive public along with us. Edmund has been working on a few more forms that have been mildly more successful at hiding his identity. I'm sure you will find them as hilarious as the last few attempts he presented to you.

Be well, and say hello to your lovely sons for me.

With all my love,

Supriya

xoxo

P.S. Apologies for the level of detail in the romantic scenes. I know you probably don't want to think of your parents in that way at all, but your mother was very clear that she wanted you to know what a healthy romantic relationship looks like, and for better and worse, the physicality of the relationship is important. If it's any consolation, this is nowhere near as detailed as my mother's manuscripts were; she was the goddess of fertility, indeed! Her descriptions even shocked Neha! I had to slash and burn those scenes before I handed them over to Azi for publication. Now only Neha and I know every detail about her affairs, and that is certainly how things should remain… for eternity ;).

PART ONE
THE ENGAGEMENT

CHAPTER 1 – THE MORNING AFTER

January, 1923 – London

Eleanor stirred in the cold arms of her sleeping fiancé as a beam of sunlight landed on her face through the frosted window pane. The pounding headache of an epic hangover almost sent her right back into a disjointed dream, but as her foggy memories of the prior night flowed into her brain, a sudden excitement wrested her from her physical plight.

It had happened. The confession she had waited three long months for Edmund to make had finally happened. An entire web of deceit was now mercifully in tatters, and now Eleanor only had to worry about that other web... her web... the web Edmund's divine guardians had sucked her into within twenty-four hours of their fateful introduction.

At the request of Mélusine—whom Eleanor saw as Edmund's mysterious, shapeshifting auntie (for lack of a better term)—who had hastily revealed herself to Eleanor during their harrowing quest to solve the gory murder of a young scullery maid, Eleanor had patiently waited as her gentle, shell-shocked, half-human soldier bumbled his way through months of half-truths about his long, secret past and his plethora of otherworldly abilities until their rendez-vous with his oldest friend, Edward Rutherford (the only friend he'd ever had who knew his secret), pushed him right over the edge.

Even with everything she knew about him, her beloved soldier still had a knack for surprising her. She hadn't expected in the slightest that he would demonstrate his superhuman healing ability right there in a public cocktail lounge! And without the excuse of giddy intoxication that she and Edward could claim! She had already seen plenty of evidence that Edmund was never affected by alcohol, and despite his hasty revelation, she did not believe that the excessive amount of cognac they'd consumed throughout the evening was the culprit. Now, the hours they'd spent in the company of Edward Rutherford's grotesquely shrewish wife before they'd retired without her to the cocktail lounge in peace… that perhaps had more to do with it.

She had barely been able to contain herself as the woman hemmed and hawed over the most minor mishaps, and so she assumed that observing the contrast between the irrational, controlling relationship that Margaret Rutherford had with Edward, and the friendly, mutually-respectful one that she herself had with Edmund must have been as impactful for him as it had been for her.

With a completely sober mind, in the dark corner of the smoky bar, Edmund had squeezed his cognac glass until it shattered and cut open his hand to reveal the utterly alien violet metallic plasma that served as his body's primary healing mechanism. She had to admit, it was a bit more alien than she'd anticipated.

She'd expected some sort of unique self-healing ability in her gentle English soldier ever since Mélusine had casually dropped the interesting factoid that she herself was two thousand years old. After all, Edmund had managed to survive four hellish years in the trenches of Belgium without a single, miniscule scar to show for it.

10

She knew this for certain, as she had already spent many delightful hours on many separate occasions inspecting every lovely crevice of his naked body.

Then, of course, there was that moment in the dark, in the Baron of Heathfield's cursed home during their wretched murder investigation, when Edmund had pushed her out of the way and taken on the full brunt of an ill-conceived dagger attack. The power outage had conveniently allowed him to hide in the dark shadows while his Rakshasa plasma completed its work on his human flesh. She'd worked ever so hard to contain her curiosity as she'd respected his wishes and kept her distance, listening helplessly to his pained whimpers until the agonizing healing process was complete, and ever since then, she had wondered from time to time what the strange process would look like.

But, the intelligent movement of the bizarre foreign substance that disappeared right back into Edmund's body when it had completed its task—*that*, Eleanor hadn't expected. She was glad, in the end, that she'd had three months to prepare herself. She'd managed to hide the temporary discomfort his revelation had evoked, and now she was already reaping the rewards.

She'd had no idea how much more pleasurable their intimacy could be with Edmund basking in the novelty of their newfound honesty, and now she was thoroughly entranced. She was glad, in some ways, that she hadn't known it sooner; it would have made the wait feel that much more interminable. But now there was another problem. A new problem. The problem of the secrets that *she* would be forced to keep on behalf of Edmund's guardians who had given her far more information about his unique origins than he knew himself.

She wished for a fleeting moment that Mélusine had not revealed herself. Then she reached over to stroke the soft cheek of her sleeping soldier, and she let the thought go. They were engaged now. They were going to be together. She knew exactly what she was getting herself into, perhaps even more than he did, and she was grateful. If Mélusine hadn't revealed herself, Eleanor knew that her tenacity would have pushed Edmund too fast. She might have lost him completely. But now... *now* they were going to revel in the joys of fully knowing each other until death they do part. Or, at least until she died. The Grim Reaper would surely knock on her door before he knocked on Edmund's, if he could even get close to Edmund. She'd already noticed Mélusine's careful deflections on the topic of Edmund's mortality more than once.

Her mind wandered as she contemplated the other revelation of the evening that had truly surprised her—Edmund's centennial. She knew he was special the day that they met, but somehow through all of his half-truths and all of Mélusine's nuggets of useful information, she had not let herself acknowledge the possibility that he was already much older than he looked. Mélusine had called him 'Young Edmund' for god's sake! She had assumed that he was at the beginning of a very long journey, not already in the middle! She smiled as she realized her human logical folly. To someone two thousand years old, one century on Earth *was* still young.

She wondered how exactly it all worked. Mélusine had perfectly emulated a variety of human forms during their revelatory conversation... Would Edmund someday be able to do the same? Would he be able to make himself entirely into someone else? What would happen as he continued to age? Would he simply wake up one morning and be a young man again? Or even a young woman! The idea seemed utterly absurd, and a bit disconcerting. She loved him exactly how he was.

She relegated the thought to the back of her mind as he began to stir. She wiggled into the nook of his cold arm and waited for him to open his eyes.

"Good morning, old man," she said as he took in a deep, awakening breath.

He looked down at her and smiled. "I was afraid last night that you might not remember what happened. You and Edward drank more cognac than I've ever seen anyone drink… anyone other than me, of course."

"There is a footie match being played with my eyeballs," Eleanor admitted. "But I remember everything, old man. You're stuck marrying a wild Scottish thistle now. There's no way to weasel your way out of it."

He kissed her forehead, and then worked his way down to her lips. "I couldn't be happier, my dearest thistle. It is like the weight of the world has been lifted from my shoulders."

"I'm glad." Eleanor returned his embrace.

She fought back a pang of sadness that she didn't feel the same. Happy, yes. Unburdened, no. Alas, she was grateful that one of them could feel that way, and there were ever so many benefits that balanced out the great burden of the unusual destiny she had accepted…

As she leaned in for a deeper kiss, her headache's pounding exploded, and she pulled away.

"Are you alright?" Edmund asked concernedly.

"Perfectly fine," she lied as she reached over to the bedside table and drank down an entire glass of water. "The cognac is catching up with me, that's all. I suppose I should be more careful from now on not to pace you. My meagre human temperament isn't up to the task."

Edmund was startled by her reference. "Do you really think that I'm not human then?"

Eleanor struggled for words as she noticed the expression on his face that indicated she'd given herself away. She knew him well enough already to recognize when he smelled her fear. It was a rather annoying ability of his, if she was going to be honest. It made the years she'd spent perfecting the art of hiding her emotions utterly useless.

"Darling, you have violet metallic blood that heals you within moments of injury. I don't think that my medical background is necessary to diagnose that you aren't entirely human. Do you think that you're human?"

He paused for a long moment as he considered her assertion. "There are many things about me that aren't human... You have experienced most of them now, but not all of them. I suppose without more context about the source of my abnormalities, I must think of myself as mostly human."

Eleanor leaned in and kissed him gently on the lips. "I love you, Edmund. I love all that you are. Human and whatever else you happen to be. The violet blood does seem rather alien, don't you think? If I didn't know any better, I'd guess you were part Martian, but that is a rather silly thought."

It suddenly occurred to her as she spoke the words that Mélusine had not, in fact, told her anything about the original homeland of the Rakshasa people, only that they had been on Earth longer than humans had existed.

"Martian is better than demon," he murmured. He startled as he realized he'd voiced the thought out loud.

Eleanor became serious as she took his hands tightly into hers. "I do not believe for one second that you are a demon, Edmund, and you should not let yourself even entertain that possibility. Demons are superstitious creatures made up by religious zealots to trick humans into being afraid of anyone or anything different from them. Do not ever let their ignorance change the way you see yourself."

"I love you so much, Eleanor. After a hundred years, I finally know what love is," Edmund whispered as he kissed her again.

He gently invited her to settle back into his arms, and he sighed contentedly as she began running her warm fingers across his cold chest in gentle patterns.

"A hundred years..." Eleanor murmured. "It actually makes sense now that I think about it. I assumed that each of the adventures you mentioned over the last few months had been rather short, but it makes more sense that they were spread out over an extra fifty years."

Edmund shifted uncomfortably. "I'm sorry I lied to you about so many things, Eleanor. I hope you can forgive me."

Eleanor continued on with her soft, soothing strokes. "There is nothing to forgive, darling. You told me that you were lying to me practically as soon as we met, remember? That was rather honest of you when you think about it."

"Yes… I suppose… but still… It has been very painful keeping things from you. I know how much you detest men lying to you."

"I love that you have thought so much about it. You are nothing like any other man in this world, Edmund, and I love you so dearly for it." Eleanor moved her gentle attention to his nipples until they hardened, and a fresh round of goosebumps exploded across his skin. "Someone once told me that it is a most profound act of love to withhold information until the appropriate time. If you'd revealed all your cards to me the day we met, we wouldn't have been able to enjoy the slow unraveling of your web of lies together."

She hoped that her forgiveness would be returned to her if ever he discovered the ugly web of lies that she was spinning.

"You are a bastion of understanding, my dearest thistle," Edmund said as he sat up and gathered her into his arms.

After a few minutes of licking each other's tongues, Eleanor straddled her gentle soldier, and as a fresh burst of desire exploded deep within her, she set about enjoying another round of the new sensual pleasures afforded by Edmund's unburdened happiness.

"There is one thing that I haven't been able to figure out," she said as she nestled into the nook of his arm for a post work-out rest. "If you are over one hundred years old, why do you look like you are only middle-aged? Do you age slower than humans do? Or is there something else happening entirely? If you aged slower than everyone else, then certainly your old army acquaintances would have noticed by now."

"Are you sure you want to know?" Edmund asked with a fresh batch of nerves.

"I already know your deepest, darkest secret, darling," Eleanor reminded him. "Unless… unless the process is gruesome…"

Edmund shifted uncomfortably as he struggled to decide how exactly to describe the painful details.

"Good lord, you don't have to kill anyone, do you? Like a creature out of a penny dreadful?" Eleanor asked as she felt a pang of anxiety about Edmund's foreign nature for the first time. "That would be just my luck… proving my mother right for kissing on the first date…"

Edmund smiled as he brought the palm of her hand to his mouth to kiss it. "No, I don't have to kill anyone."

"You see, my imagination is always worse than reality." Eleanor sighed with relief. "It's best just to tell me straight, Colonel, on this and every other shocking secret, before my mind has a chance to wander too much."

Edmund took a moment to choose his words carefully. "When I am mortally wounded, the healing process returns my body to its strongest state. All of a sudden, I end up looking and feeling as if I'm about twenty, and then I age normally until it happens again."

"Good lord… That means that you have been mortally wounded? You poor thing! That must have felt wretched!"

Edmund gently intertwined her fingers with his. "I have re-set twice. Once in 1840 and once in 1895. Both times I was stabbed through the abdomen with multiple swords."

"Good lord." Eleanor worked to push the horrific image from her mind, and then another thought occurred to her. "What horrible luck! It happened the exact same way twice? What were the chances of that?!"

Edmund smiled. "The first time it was an accident. Two drunken soldiers were aiming for someone else, and I stepped in the way. The second time I did it to myself." She gasped, but he was unfazed by her predictable reaction. "I was grotesquely old and dreadfully uncomfortable. I was afraid I might die of old age, so I… er… catalyzed the process myself. Luckily it worked, but it was far more painful than the first time. Stabbing oneself with two swords at once is extremely unpleasant."

"I can imagine…" Eleanor murmured. She fought back the mental image. "Does that mean, then, that you were never mortally wounded in the war? You'd look much younger if you had been?"

Edmund nodded. "I was shot six times, but never so badly that it caused my body to re-set. I was rather lucky, I think. I don't know what those wicked army scientists would have done if they'd discovered my secret. Their chemical weapons were ghoulish enough, and I hate to fathom the experimentation that must have gone into those…" He grimaced. "I was more terrified of being captured by our own bloody doctors than I was of death itself. Who knows how many more men I could have saved if I hadn't been so bloody afraid of revealing my secret, but I just… couldn't. So many men died because of my selfish fear, Eleanor… too many to count."

"You were right to be afraid. I'm sorry, Edmund. You must have felt very alone in your fear."

That was the first time that Eleanor truly understood the complicated source of Edmund's unique brand of guilt-ridden shell shock.

"Yes… yes, I did."

"You are not alone anymore." Eleanor kissed him gently on the lips.

"There was something else…"

She felt his heart race as he prepared for his confession.

"You can tell me anything, Edmund. *Anything*."

Edmund's grimace grew as he let himself give into the memories that he'd avoided for so long. "The mustard gas... it infused me with power, and I hated myself for liking it, but I couldn't help it. It brought pain and death to my men. It caused such horrific injuries. I dreaded its consequences, but I craved it all the same, Eleanor! Sometimes I still dream about it, and my stomach growls with hunger."

Eleanor squeezed his hand. "The way you are describing it, it sounds like how humans respond to certain drugs. Perhaps your unique body chemistry has some sort of special compatibility with the substance."

Edmund brought her hand to his lips and kissed her fingers. "I've never considered that possibility. It sounds so mundane when you put it like that... almost natural."

"I'm sure that it was natural, darling. Everything in the world is. The things we think of superstitiously only seem that way because we don't know enough about them yet... your unusual talents included."

"But over time, Eleanor... over time the mustard gas made me hungry for other things. For ghoulish, monstrous, unspeakable things. I never acted upon the urges, but they were there more and more, taunting me at every turn. I don't know how much longer I could have held out if the war hadn't ended when it did. It was those urges I was fighting the weekend we met. The smell of the bloody corpse brought them back for the first time in four years. It was like nothing had changed. It made me terrified that I would never outrun it."

Eleanor thought for a long time before choosing her response. "In the trenches you were practically bathing in blood, Edmund. You were constantly faced with unimaginable gore. You were starving and malnourished, and all the while, you were taunted by a euphoric substance that made you feel good while those you loved were dying. Those are horrific circumstances for the strongest of men."

Edmund looked away. "I am not a man, Eleanor. It awoke something evil within me, something that now I have to control at the slightest provocation. There is no telling how dangerous I could be if I fully lost control."

"Darling, you are many things, and I can attest to the highest court that you are certainly a man." She winked, but he did not find her facetious comment funny. She hunkered down and returned to seriousness, noting for future reference that the inappropriate humor that worked so well with her other patients was not a useful tool with her own shell-shocked soldier. "Edmund, I have treated several soldiers over the years who didn't have the self-control that you had. One even tried to eat another soldier. When he realized what he'd done during a psychotherapy session at the army hospital afterwards, he killed himself the same evening." Edmund cringed at the image, and Eleanor took both of his hands into hers. "You have known a darkness that no one else can truly comprehend, but you triumphed. You didn't give in! Even when you were trapped in the thick of it, you didn't give in! And in Basingstoke, all it took was some focus and determination on your part, and you got over your urges, didn't you? Have they troubled you again since then? Since you escaped the stimulation that triggered your war memories?"

"No," he admitted. "I haven't struggled with them since."

Eleanor smiled. "You are mostly human, darling. And these struggles are entirely human. They may be compounded by your unusual composition, but they are not unique to you. You are strong enough to overcome them, and I have already seen you make great progress since we met. I couldn't be prouder, really."

Edmund kissed her on the forehead as he fought back tears. "I love you, Eleanor."

She let him give in to his joyful melancholy for a few more moments, and then a mischievous grin spread across her face, and she forcefully pulled him out of his misery and attacked him with tickles. "So, you'd better stay on the up-and-up, Colonel, because

I am too much of a wild Scottish thistle to become a glorified nurse-wife. Got it?"

He burst into involuntary laughter, and she continued her light-hearted offense until his face turned red and his eyes teared up.

"Now, what should we do today, my dashing, mostly-human fiancé? I'm down here for two more days before I have to return to Scotland to settle my affairs. There's a lot to do when a modern woman agrees to be married, you know. And don't even get me started on the mess of trouble I'm going to face trying to get anyone to employ me down here in the land of sassanacks. But whit's fur ye'll no go past ye."

"I'm sorry, what?"

Eleanor laughed. "It is an old Scots phrase, I think. My father used to say it when I was just a wee lass. But, Colonel, we have just reached a milestone! I've just reached the boundary of your superhuman linguistic talent!"

She tickled him playfully again, and he returned her jab with his own until they were both rolling on the bed with laughter. She couldn't remember the last time she'd laughed so hard that her stomach muscles hurt. In fact, she wasn't sure it had ever happened before in her life.

As he wiped the happy tears from her eyes, Edmund sighed with contentment and returned to their conversation.

"I often have trouble with idioms, unless I use a language often enough to understand them in context. I've never heard that one before."

"I suppose it's a bit like *que sera sera*. I'll have to leave my fate and my career to destiny, because the British Army isn't going to help."

"You can't just request a transfer?" Edmund asked naively. "With your experience? There are five veterans' hospitals in London alone."

"Darling, it is strictly against army policy to employ a married woman. I will be lucky if anyone on Earth will employ me after the deed is done. But, I'm a rather tenacious thistle in the side, so I am going to assume that somehow I'll manage. *How* is not something I'd like to think about at the moment."

Joy and sorrow battled fiercely in Edmund's expression.

"Please, darling, don't let it get you down. We are both very resourceful. I'm sure we'll be able to make something work. I've never been able to sit around and wait for fate. I'll start coming up with a whole mess of plans before I pop back down here in a few weeks. I'm sure by the time we're married, I'll have everything all worked out."

"I can't believe you'd agree to marry me knowing that it would cause you such problems!" Edmund exclaimed. "You love your work!"

"And I love you, darling," Eleanor said as she hopped off the bed and pulled him up into her arms. "I'm not willing to concede on either of my great loves. I will find a way to make both of them work."

Edmund twirled her around and pulled her into a passionate embrace, and Eleanor couldn't stop herself from giggling at the romance of the moment.

"What shall we do today, old man? We've already danced naked in each other's arms. That's a fine start!"

Edmund snuck another kiss, and then grinned as a bewitching idea that he had only ever fantasized about in his wildest dreams entered his head. "Would you like to see what I looked like as an old man? Would you like to know what's in store for you in twenty years?"

Eleanor's heart began racing as she contemplated whether or not Edmund had already managed to stumble into some ability that Mélusine didn't know he had.

"Show me, Edmund!" Eleanor agreed with anxious excitement. "I'd love to see!"

"The pictures aren't here. They're at my house in Basingstoke. It's mine, by the way, and it has been since I bought it in 1848. Every reference I made to my 'grandfather' when we were there before was really to me. I lived there for forty-seven years in the nineteenth century, making my living as an artist."

"Forty-seven years! Yes… yes, of course… Many more things make sense now!" Eleanor exclaimed. She couldn't believe she hadn't put that obvious reality together in her head sooner.

Edmund pulled her into one final, delicious, naked embrace and then naughtily slapped her bum. "Come on, my wild Scottish thistle. More revelations await!"

When they arrived at the station in Basingstoke, Eleanor's heart was racing with excitement. She'd been anticipating the many fascinating secrets that Edmund would eventually share with her for months, but still, the act of experiencing it was far more thrilling than she'd let herself imagine.

"Welcome to my home," Edmund whispered as he pulled her into another romantic twirl right there on the platform. She squealed with surprise and then laughed.

"How will we get to the manor this time?" Eleanor asked as she observed the empty station. "We don't have the thoroughbreds to help us!"

"Hrm…" Edmund's posture deflated. "You're right. I hadn't thought about it. When I lived here, my butler would always collect me from the station with the carriage. This village is not really big enough for taxis… I suppose I've been living in London for too long."

"Well, we do have our own legs to carry us," Eleanor said resignedly. "I didn't really wear proper shoes for a long country hike, though."

"Excuse me, Colonel!" A plump, middle-aged man with a red face and jolly countenance, sporting an impeccable chauffeur's uniform, called over to them from the end of the platform. "Are you Colonel Marriner?"

Edmund looked to Eleanor with surprise, and then he looked down at his well-fitted civilian suit.

"Yes?" he called back. "I am Colonel Marriner."

The mysterious man ran to greet them at a faster pace than Eleanor expected to see paired with his wide legs and jiggling belly. "Mr. Valov called me. He said you'd need a chauffeur when you arrived from London, sir?"

"Why yes! Jolly good on Mr. Valov!" He leaned in to whisper into Eleanor's ear. "That man is the best butler I've ever encountered."

"Yes... yes, I agree..."

Eleanor wondered which of Edmund's shapeshifting guardians had taken the form of Mr. Valov. She was sure he wasn't Mélusine (she'd interacted with him enough to pick up on a distinctly different personality), but he was impressively good at anticipating Edmund's needs... too good. She hoped that Mr. Valov wasn't the woman who'd raised him in Bath, as Mr. Valov had already provided them many breakfast coffees while they were lounging about Edmund's London townhouse in nothing but their bathrobes.

"I'm Mr. Quince," the chauffeur said cheerfully as he reached out his hand to shake theirs. "Do you have any luggage?"

"We didn't plan our little excursion," Edmund explained. "We came on a bit of a whim to take a look at my old family estate."

"We won't need any clothing, anyway," Eleanor whispered into his ear in Gaelic. "I for one plan to be naked from the moment we are inside the house until the moment we leave."

24

Edmund's eyes bulged with shocked excitement, and she giggled at her triumph.

"Very well, sir. Follow me. The car is waiting outside the station," Mr. Quince declared.

Eleanor was certain that she caught a twinkle of understanding in Mr. Quince's eye at their secret exchange.

"So, is there any special occasion for your visit?" Mr. Quince asked casually as they tumbled into the spacious back seat of a pristine new Rolls Royce.

Edmund squeezed Eleanor's hand. "We're engaged! I can still hardly believe that this wild Scottish thistle agreed to marry an old army man!"

Mr. Quince looked like he might explode with excitement. "How wonderful! Love is in the air!"

Eleanor almost fell into Edmund's lap as Mr. Quince started the car with a speedy screech.

"Good lord!" Edmund exclaimed. "These motorcars do go fast these days, don't they?"

Eleanor silently repositioned herself and naughtily brought Edmund's hand onto her leg. He squeezed her thigh, and then they both settled into their scandalous intertwined position to look out the window at the passing scenery.

"It was prettier with the snow," Eleanor admitted. "It's a bit dreary now with everything brown and dead, don't you think?"

"Ah, but in summer… in summer, it is unmatched!" Edmund swooned. "The rolling hills explode into so many colors of green, your eyes can hardly process it. And the wildflowers! Oh, the wildflowers, Eleanor! They smell divine! In March there will be so many daffodils that the hills will be entirely yellow and white."

"That sounds lovely." Eleanor stole a gentle kiss. "Edmund, do you think it would be lovely enough for our wedding?"

She melted into his arms as a look of pure, childlike joy entered his expression. "Are you really considering it, Eleanor? You don't want to have the ceremony in Scotland? I assumed that you'd want to be close to your family, since I don't have many people to invite."

Eleanor thought about the idea seriously for the first time. "To be honest, I'd rather do it here. My sisters and I are bastards in the eyes of the church anyway. I'd rather not have some judgmental minister throwing us the evil eye while we declare our undying love for each other. Their ceremonies are rather puritanical anyway. I don't suppose we can get out of a church wedding completely, though... Do you?"

"I suppose I've never thought about it... It is the twentieth century!"

"All you need is a registrar, two witnesses, and a building that has been designated with the Registrar General as religious," Mr. Quince interjected. "There are some ancient ruins in the woods of your estate, are there not, Colonel? Perhaps you can get that site registered; although, you'll have better luck saying it's Christian, I reckon. They might raise an eyebrow at anything that sounds too pagan."

"You don't think we can have it declared a Hindu temple?" Eleanor quipped.

"You are welcome to try," Mr. Quince replied without acknowledging the joking nature of Eleanor's question. "But the local vicars might beat down your door on your wedding night. They are dastardly attached to their own notion of God, if you know what I mean."

"Well, they'd certainly get more than they bargained for there, don't you think, darling? Those vicars would never forget our pagan celebration of lust... They might even learn something useful!" Eleanor suddenly became concerned about Edmund's silence. "Is something wrong?"

"No..." Edmund said distractedly.

"Now I know something's wrong," Eleanor said seriously. She squeezed his hand and switched into Gaelic. "Tell me, Edmund. What is going through your mind?"

26

He finally looked down at her and offered her a melancholy smile. "I'm sorry. It's just… it's too good. All of it. You. This. Us. It is unlike anything I've ever experienced, and coming back here with you, to share with you honestly the many secrets I've been hiding… it makes me worried that something horrible is going to happen. I can't say why. It's like how I feel right now is too good for me. It is not a sustainable feeling. I'm worried I will wake up, and this will all be gone, but I will still know what I've been missing for all these lonely years. It will be utterly unbearable."

Eleanor reached forward and stroked his cheek lovingly. "We're awake, Edmund. This is all real, and it isn't going anywhere."

"Yes… yes, I'm sure you're right," Edmund agreed half-heartedly as he refocused on the beautiful reality before him. "We're reaching the gates of my estate."

"It's beautiful," Eleanor sighed. "I wasn't really in a position to appreciate it before. The woods look rather magical, don't they? Even though we're in the dead of winter. Almost primeval." Eleanor turned her attention on Mr. Quince. "Did you say that there are ancient ruins in those woods?"

"Oh yes. I like to hike in the natural spots around here, and I've stumbled across the site many times. It's in a clearing surrounded by ancient lindens. Druidic, no doubt, but possibly taken on by Christians since then. I can take you there some time if you'd like to see it."

"There's no need. I know exactly where it is," Edmund declined. "It is lovely. I've painted it many hundreds of times. I never dreamed I'd be getting married there, though."

Eleanor kissed him on the cheek. "Some dreams do come true, Colonel. Let's not ruin the rare experience with worry."

"Yes… yes, you're right," Edmund said as he more seriously gathered his wits. "So, we'll plan to go into the Hampshire Registrar General's office on Monday morning to register a Druidic temple for our pagan ritual?"

Eleanor smiled at Edmund's return to humor. "Should we do our handfasting first? Or perhaps we should bring an animal sacrifice as a peace offering? Perhaps a stuffed goose?"

"We might as well roast it beforehand, you know, to make it easier to transport," Edmund played along. "Ah… and there it is," he said as the car pulled up the long drive and stopped right in front of the imposing steps of the stone manor.

"It's bigger than I remembered it." Eleanor tried not to let the idea that Edmund was wealthy enough to afford such a grand estate overwhelm her. "I suppose we were comparing it to the Baron of Heathfield's garish castle before."

"I find mine to feel much cozier than his. Perhaps it is just because I know it. I like thoroughly knowing my surroundings. It makes me feel at peace."

Edmund helped Eleanor out of the car.

"Shall I wait in the carriage house for your orders, sir?" Mr. Quince asked expectantly.

Edmund reached into his pocket and handed Mr. Quince a large bill. "That won't be necessary. Tell Mr. Valov that we greatly appreciate his foresight, but we will not need another ride until Monday morning. Perhaps you can return then?"

"As you wish, sir," Mr. Quince agreed. With a happy wave and another loud screech of the tires, he sped off.

Edmund took one long look around, and then without any warning, he swooped down and collected Eleanor into his arms. She squealed with the thrill of the surprise, and her squeals dissolved into a fit of laughter as he carried her up the front steps of his manor as if it was their wedding day.

"Colonel, we're not even married!" Eleanor protested jokingly. "What will the vicar say?"

"Eleanor MacLeod, I love you, and I'm going to marry you!" Edmund declared as he reached the top step.

"Edmund Marriner, I love you, and I'm going to marry you," Eleanor smiled. "But I think you're going to have to put me down to cross the threshold."

A mischievous grin spread across Edmund's face, and with one swift movement, with Eleanor MacLeod still in his arms, he kicked open the imposing wooden door to his own house.

He laughed giddily as the door flew off its hinges and landed many meters deep into the foyer.

"I suppose I didn't need so much force," he said sheepishly as he finally put her down. "I will fix it later."

Eleanor pulled him into a delicious embrace. "You know, Colonel, in ancient Scotland we'd be married now. Our vows were all it would take... well, vows and consummation."

As Edmund's entire body perked up at the delightful thought, Eleanor took his hand and led him into the parlor. "This room seems nice. We didn't try it out when we were here before."

She reached forward to remove Edmund's coat, and he followed her lead and helped her remove hers. They flung them across the room with giddy laughter and then set about ripping the rest of each other's clothes off, one item at a time.

"Marry me, Colonel," Eleanor said as she lay down on the old persian carpet and presented her naked body invitingly.

Edmund kneeled down and straddled her, but as she prepared for the delightful sensation of feeling him enter her, he changed his position and began kissing her thighs, working his way tantalizingly into her most sensitive areas.

"Good lord," she murmured as her gentle soldier began eliciting a more frenzied orgasm than any she'd ever felt in her life with his skilled tongue.

Without another word, only satisfied sighs and feverish moans, she gave in completely to the unexpected pleasures of Edmund Marriner's continuous surprises.

"Edmund, darling, where did you learn that? I've never experienced anything like it," Eleanor asked an hour later as she nestled into his cold, naked arms.

An intense blush worked its way onto his face. "My tutorials included some aspects of human sexuality."

"How odd. I can't fault them, I suppose. I am reaping the rewards of their excellent tutelage."

"We didn't *practice* any of the techniques during the tutorials," Edmund clarified awkwardly. "They were focused on theory... in the event that I would need the techniques in an appropriate setting, with an appropriate partner."

"I see. Well, I'm glad I qualified! How long ago was that? Your tutorials? You've kept the knowledge quite close to you."

"Almost a hundred years ago. I was in the orphanage in India, then I went to apprentice with a painter in Hyderabad until 1829, and then I was brought to a lovely little farm just outside of Bath, where I stayed quite contentedly until the unpleasant experience of my first re-set in 1840 forced me to start another societal life. I moved to London for a bit and studied western styles of painting, but the utter filth of Victorian London was too much for my unaccustomed temperament, and so I moved back to the country. To here."

"I see..." Eleanor began gently running her fingers across Edmund's chest. "And what made you decide on this particular house? Of all country houses in England?"

Edmund paused as he thought about her question. "You know, I haven't thought of it in so many years, I hardly remember! I suppose... let me think... I came out to Hampshire for a commission... a local lord wanted me to paint one of the many pastoral waterfalls in the South Downs, and I transferred trains in Basingstoke on my return trip to London. I hadn't smelled air so fresh since I'd lived in Bath, and a great longing to return to the country absolutely bewitched me. There was a real estate pamphlet in the train station, and when I saw the listing for this house, I hopped over to take a look. It was a wonderfully warm day in late spring—the perfect circumstances to fully appreciate all that it had to offer. The green grasses were just sprouting from the yellow fields of daffodils, and the property had its very own series of seasonal waterfalls. Since painting waterfalls had been my specialty for many years already, I justified the decision as a professional one, while, of course, secretly all I longed for was to escape from the dreadful scent of death that wafted off of the wretched Thames."

"I'm surprised you ever moved back to London," Eleanor said as she continued her gentle stimulation of his cold skin.

"Well, it's much better than it used to be," Edmund said as he gave into a quiet sigh. "I kept my townhouse when I made my move because I was too afraid to make such a drastic change without something familiar to fall back on. That townhouse is the one you know, and I used it when I needed to be in London for various artistic and cultural events that I still enjoyed attending from time to time. I didn't move back into it full time until four years ago when I came home from the war. I suppose then I needed the hustle and bustle of the city to keep me from going mad. I've been thinking, though, of someday returning here full time. I still prefer the country, although, I would, of course, defer to your wishes, Eleanor. There are many benefits to either situation."

Eleanor's heart raced with excitement at the strange idea that they were actually, for the first time, planning their future together. Suddenly possibilities she had never dared to consider rushed into her mind. She worked hard not to get ahead of herself.

"I'm not really a city girl myself," Eleanor admitted. "I grew up in a village near the Musselburgh racetrack, and I was thoroughly spoiled by my childhood days of riding my father's horses in the countryside. They weren't really his, of course. They belonged to various aristocrats and business magnets who had entrusted them into his care. The owners would have been livid if they'd learned that I was riding them… but, it turned out that *that* was the least of my father's worries…"

Edmund squeezed her hand in solidarity. "I'm sorry."

Eleanor shrugged and then changed the subject as she looked around the entirely covered walls of the parlor. "I can't believe all these paintings are yours; although, I suppose fifty years is a long time to be painting. You must have made tens of thousands of them."

"I lost track around 1880. There were certainly thousands of them, each one as ordinary as the next."

"I don't think they're ordinary! The sheer volume alone makes them extraordinary!" She smiled teasingly.

"Quantity over quality was certainly the motto of the Victorian Era," Edmund laughed. "My approach was no different."

"I was just teasing you, darling. I really do think they're better than you realize. I can't wait to take a closer look, now that I know that they're yours and not your estranged grandfather's. I was really working to fit him into the story of your secret past with the orphanage. I assumed that he must have been the kind relative you mentioned who set up your tutorials in Bath."

"No, that was someone else. I don't know how that man is related to me, actually. He doesn't age, as far as I can tell, so in that way, perhaps he is less human than I am. His name is Mr. Johnson, or so he claims. I have often wondered if he is my father, but I've never had enough courage to ask."

"You've met him in person, and you've never asked?!" Eleanor exclaimed. No wonder Mélusine and her fellow guardians had had such an easy time keeping their secrets!

Edmund was taken aback by her strong reaction, and she worked hard to calm herself.

"I'm sorry, I didn't mean to chastise you, darling."

"The risk has never seemed worth the reward," Edmund said quietly. "I have never been willing to risk saying anything that

32

might lead him to leave me alone for good… As it is, I have not seen him nearly as often as I saw him as a boy. When I was in Bath, I talked to him quite regularly when he would stop by to check in on my progress with the tutors. After I moved to London in 1840, I didn't see him again until the end of the war. He came to me once, in my townhouse in London, to see how I was doing. I put on the best show of my life to convince him that I was fine. I sometimes wish that I hadn't, that perhaps if I'd been more honest, he might have stayed longer. I just didn't want him to be disappointed in me."

"Oh, darling." Eleanor leaned in to kiss him gently. "I'm sure that he would be proud of you. Look at all you've accomplished since you escaped from that wretched orphanage! In only a few years you were debating Ovid with a Roman!"

As soon as the words came out of her mouth, Eleanor hoped that she hadn't given too much away, and then she hoped that Edmund hadn't tasted her anxiety on the matter.

"You really were paying attention to everything I told you, weren't you?" Edmund asked with surprise. "I was sure that I was boring you."

"You intrigued me from the moment we met, Colonel. Remember?"

"Yes. I do remember," Edmund agreed as he relaxed again and began running his cold fingers across Eleanor's naked breasts. "I'm glad my lies were interesting enough to keep your attention. This might be the only time in my life when they've benefitted me."

"Your lies must have been so lonely," Eleanor said as she sighed with pleasure at his touch. "I think your loneliness came through in your art, far more than you realized."

"Yes, I think you're right," Edmund agreed. "You were strikingly astute about many things when we were discussing my painting in the Baron's home. I had gone rather blind at the point that I'd painted that painting. Shortly after I painted it, I gave in and got spectacles. That added a few extra years to my career, although my subject-matter remained intensely mundane. That waterfall from the painting is just outside the back of this house, on the edge of the woods. It only runs in spring."

"So, your violet blood does not keep your eyes in tip top shape?" Eleanor asked curiously.

"I find that detail strange myself," Edmund admitted. "Most of the time, I think I'm a bit stronger than an average human, and perhaps a bit faster, but when I reach a certain age, I suffer from all of the typical human maladies. This last time around, when I reached about seventy, I began to suffer from a painful case of arthritis, and by seventy-five I was not in very good shape. I think perhaps my height was a factor, you know, with my joints supporting my Victorian posture and whatnot…"

"Fascinating…" Eleanor murmured as she ran her fingers along the subtle crow's feet at the corners of his eyes.

"My eyes, even now, are not nearly as good as they used to be, although I think modern lighting has slowed their degeneration this time around. They are not nearly as bad as they were when I was in this same physical state in the 1860s."

"I believe everything you've told me, but I still have a hard time picturing you back then," Eleanor admitted.

"Would you like to see the pictures?" Edmund asked with a hint of timidity. "I hope they don't disappoint you."

"Nothing about you could possibly disappoint me, old man," Eleanor reassured him as she hopped up from the floor and gave into a shiver.

"I'm sorry," Edmund said self-consciously as he gathered her coat up from the floor and bundled her up. "The heat from the coffee at breakfast has long fled me. I have some old kettles in the kitchen. I will pull up some water from the well to heat over the fire. I might have to drink it straight to warm me up, unless Lord Blakeney's staff happened to leave any tea in my kitchen."

"You don't have running water here?" Eleanor asked with surprise.

"I haven't lived here since 1895... and to be honest, I wasn't particularly enthusiastic about changing with the times, so many of the features in the house were outdated, even for that era. When I lived in London in the 1840s, the public water system was so abhorrent that the idea of bringing it into my home here was very unappealing. The well-water here was fresh and completely free of rats."

"Good lord..." Eleanor murmured. "Times have changed, haven't they?"

"More than you can imagine," he agreed. "But I will invite an engineer out next week while you're in Scotland. If we're going to host a wedding here, we'd better have modern conveniences."

Edmund pulled his coat on over his naked body.

"Tea or pictures first?" he asked cheerfully.

"Definitely pictures!" Eleanor exclaimed.

Edmund grinned and took her hand into his, and together they scampered with guilty squeals past the wide-open front door, through the foyer, past the formal dining room, and into the old-fashioned kitchen.

Eleanor shivered again and tightened her coat around her arms. "It's so much colder back here!"

"The front rooms are always nice and warm on sunny days, even in winter," Edmund explained. "They always feel a bit like a hot-house, and oh, how I love it! The humid sun keeps my temperature up. I'm sure I would have been much colder these last few hours if it weren't for the humid warmth of the room."

"I suppose we'll have to figure something out before tonight, now that the front door is missing. I hope the boiler still works."

"Oh, there is no boiler," Edmund said casually. "The house is only heated by the fireplaces."

Eleanor paused to take in the surprising intel. They had just spent hours on a winter's day in the perfectly warm parlor, despite the fact that the front door to the house was letting the chilly wind blow straight in. Surely, all of the nice heat should have found its way out through the opening.

"I'm sorry. I suppose I should have thought more carefully before I kicked in the door." Edmund took Eleanor's contemplative silence as disapproval.

"Well, I think the damage was worth it for the thrill," Eleanor reassured him.

"So do I," Edmund agreed.

Edmund stood back to observe a small iron stove, and before Eleanor could figure out what he was doing, he lifted it right up and placed it several feet over, out of his way. Eleanor subtly made her way over to it to assess its excessive weight for herself, while he carefully inspected the brick wall behind the stove's former position.

"Yes!" Edmund exclaimed as he pushed in one of the bricks, and the wall swung forward on a hinge, into a dark secret passageway. "I love secret passageways! I knew Lord Blakeney's staff wouldn't suspect a thing!"

He glanced around the kitchen, landing his gaze on a paraffin lantern that hung by the door, and then he excitedly lit the wick with a match that someone had left nestled just inside the lantern's frame in a clever moment of foresight.

He crouched down to avoid hitting his head on the low stone ceiling as he took her hand and guided her down an ancient stone staircase into the dank, damp darkness.

"Don't tell me you're the phantom of the opera, too," Eleanor quipped. "I don't think that story ended very well, at least for him."

"Never fear, my dearest thistle. I would never torture you with the *horror of my singing voice!*" Eleanor giggled as Edmund jokingly sung the last few words of the sentence with his best impression of an operatic baritone. "Besides, I'm far less human than he was, if I remember correctly. I think he was simply a disfigured madman who'd taken up residence in the catacombs below the Paris opera.

I'm surprised you've heard of the story at all. It's a rather obscure novel, isn't it?"

"One of the nurses in the VAD had a copy," Eleanor explained. "She'd actually hand-written her English translation into the margins of the French publication. English books were so hard to get in France, we all passed it around anyway."

"Yes... Yes, I suppose I've never thought about that constraint... How annoying that there would be books around that you couldn't read simply because of the language! What torture!"

Eleanor laughed. "It is a very human problem, I suppose. But this place, Edmund, this place does seem quite ripe for some sort of witchcraft. It's a good thing the villagers don't know you have it. They'd be beating down your door with pitchforks!"

Edmund became serious, and Eleanor regretted her callous remark.

"The thought has crossed my mind from time to time," he admitted. "That is one reason I didn't return to Basingstoke at all between 1895 when I skipped out of town a freshly-healed young man in the dead of night, and our weekend excursion in October. I was afraid someone might recognize me, and an angry peasant mob wouldn't be far behind. Mr. Banning's assumption, which he apparently shared with the county's newspaper, that I am the grandson of the man they all knew has made things much easier for me."

Edmund continued to crook his neck as they reached a very old wooden door.

"Are you ready to enter the phantom's lair?" Edmund asked with an unusual air of melodrama in his voice.

Eleanor nodded her agreement and hoped that he wouldn't sense the unusually fast beating of her heart.

As he pushed open the door, a surprisingly large room with dirt floors, stone walls, and tall, arched ceilings was covered from top to bottom in old, dusty junk. Clothing, old furniture, and many more of his paintings were sprawled out haphazardly across every inch of the space. The sound of trickling water echoed from somewhere beyond, creating a strange, peaceful contrast to the chaos before them.

"Blimey! My pet poltergeist ruined my lair!" Edmund exclaimed. "I knew I should have fed him before I left for India!"

Eleanor was momentarily speechless, as she debated whether or not Edmund had meant the comment seriously, wondering not if poltergeists really existed, but whether Edmund had come up with his own silly explanation for his guardians' magical intrusions.

Edmund's look of serious concern morphed into a wide, mischievous grin. "I'm sorry, I shouldn't tease you. It is an old vice that I haven't enjoyed in many years. I left this mess after I re-set myself. I'd been too weak to keep my house reasonably tidy for months at that point, and after the deed was done, I was in a rush to hide everything incriminating before I locked the house up. I'm normally not so messy."

Eleanor burst into laughter, as a great wave of relief washed over her. Not only was she free from an annoying extension of her web of lies, but she had never in her life met a man who could trick her so thoroughly. She had just seen in that moment a full glimpse of the carefree prankster Edmund had been before his torment in the trenches, and she shivered with excitement. This version of her gentle soldier, she loved even more.

"Please do not stop, Edmund. I love being teased," she said as she opened her coat to remind him that they were both naked under their outerwear. "I hope you realize, though, I enjoy a good prank from time to time. Are you ready to be teased?"

He opened his coat and pulled her into his arms, and they stood together, locked in a naughty naked embrace for many minutes until their frenzy enticed Edmund to push Eleanor up against the wall, and he tripped over a canvas and almost hit the floor.

"It's not really the most romantic of locales, is it?" he laughed.

"I've seen better," Eleanor agreed.

She tied the belt of her coat loosely around her, and reached forward to collect the offending painting.

"The paintings weren't interesting enough to be particularly incriminating." He tossed it nonchalantly to the side. "I had simply run out of places to put them in the house, and I couldn't bear to throw them away. The clothing on the other hand..." He reached forward and swept up a dusty set of trousers and then looked around the room and hopped carefully across the mess to gather up a matching jacket and vest. "The clothing was quite old. I wore this suit when I attended the celebration of Prince Leopold's first birthday at Windsor Castle in 1854."

"Windsor Castle!" Eleanor exclaimed. "Did you *meet* Queen Victoria?! How did that possibly come to pass?"

"One did not so much meet Queen Victoria, as be inspected by her," Edmund laughed. "It was a rather stodgy affair, to be honest. The court was absolutely obsessed with putting on a perfect show. A friend of mine from the Royal Academy had painted a portrait of the young prince, and he'd gotten it into his head that the royal family might like me to paint some pastoral murals for the castle. Somehow, he managed to both finagle an invitation for me to the royal party, and convince me that going to such an event was a fine idea."

"It wasn't? What happened? Something shocking?" Eleanor asked excitedly.

Edmund chuckled. "I'm really very ordinary, Eleanor. I know why you'd think the opposite, but I don't want to disappoint you. Nothing shocking happened in the slightest. It was really a dull evening marked by mindless conversation and occasional hushed admonishments from Prince Albert to his subtly misbehaving children. I suppose it wasn't the worst idea in the world to attend, it was an experience that perhaps would interest historians, but the entire do was rather painful, and I didn't, as it turned out, end up painting any murals for them, which was perfectly fine in my book."

"Why did you keep the clothing?" Eleanor asked as she reached down to gather another old suit.

Edmund laughed. "The answer is so foolish, I shouldn't even tell you."

"Aw, now! Colonel, you can't tease me like that!" Eleanor argued amicably.

"I thought you liked to be teased!" he countered mischievously as he gathered up an old cravat and let go of his grip on his open coat to focus on tying it.

Eleanor desperately wanted to hop across the mess and jump him, but as she contemplated the lack of pragmatism in her plan, she settled on watching him lustfully from afar. He finished up tying the ridiculous, fluffy old tie and offered her the same elaborate bow that he had done once before in her presence on the night of their fateful first meeting.

"That is the bow I was required to present to Queen Victoria, by the way," he said as he gathered up an old top-hat to add to his outfit. "And I kept the clothing in case it came back into fashion. It was, perhaps, one of the most foolish notions I've ever entertained."

Eleanor giggled as he hopped back across the mess to pull her into his arms.

"I dunno, I think you're pretty stylish," she teased as she fluffed the old cravat.

"Well then, I know what I'm going to wear this evening to dinner in the village. Do you think they'll notice I've forgotten my trousers?"

"They'll be too distracted that I've forgotten my dress!" Eleanor declared as she licked his lips teasingly and then invited him into another embrace.

They reveled in their silly game until another burst of arousal bombarded them, and they looked around the unappealing spot and pushed forward together.

"We came down here on a mission," Edmund declared.

He hopped across the mess into the shadows on the other side of the room.

"It's rather convenient that this house has a secret lair. You didn't make it yourself, did you?" Eleanor asked curiously.

"The brilliant idea would never have occurred to me," Edmund replied as he carefully wiggled a loose stone block out of its position in the wall and placed it on the floor beside him. "This house belonged to a prominent Catholic family at one point. I looked up the records shortly after I bought it. I believe they probably put in this secret cellar to hide from Protestant attacks. This room may have even been used for illegal Catholic worship; it was common practice after the Reformation for them to worship in secret. That would at least explain the vast size of the room and the ceilings that are much taller than the staircase down. They make it feel rather religious, don't you think?"

"Yes, I suppose they do," Eleanor agreed as she squinted to observe the stone ceiling in the dim light of the paraffin lamp.

"There are also a number of removable stones in the wall, behind which I've been able to hide my most incriminating objects. The whole thing is really useful, actually. I discovered the passage by accident after I'd already lived here for twenty years. You can imagine my thrill when I made my way down the staircase into this massive medieval cellar."

"You must have been floored!" Eleanor exclaimed. "Who wouldn't be!"

"Ah ha!" he exclaimed triumphantly as he reached his hand deep into the dark crevice and pulled out a thick stack of old photographs.

As he hopped back over the mess with the photographs in hand, Eleanor could hardly contain her curiosity. She lifted up the paraffin lantern that had been resting on the bottom stair and held it up to the top photograph.

"Good lord!" she squealed. "You look just like Ebineezer Scrooge! I suppose everyone starts to look like that at some age, and the spectacles clipped to your nose don't help."

She hoped that her reaction wouldn't send her gentle soldier right back into his shell.

"Yes… er… I suppose I did look a bit Scrooge-like. That was me in my oldest physical state, and the styles of the era were not particularly flattering… That was shortly before I re-set myself. Now you can see why." He shuffled through the stack. "This one is perhaps more interesting to you…"

He presented her the first daguerrotype he'd ever had taken, back during the Great Exposition of 1850.

"What a dashing young man you were! Not so different from now, really."

"Yes, I think I looked about thirty there." He squinted in the dim light to take in the image himself.

"How old were you really at that point?" Eleanor held it up to compare it to his current state.

"I don't know… perhaps about forty."

"You're not sure?"

Edmund shrugged. "I don't know exactly what year I was born. The orphanage didn't know, and so neither do I. I don't remember my early childhood in the orphanage, which I'm sure is a blessing. What I do remember of it was extremely unpleasant. I assume I was born sometime around 1810, but exactly when is one of the many great mysteries of my life."

"How sad…" Eleanor murmured.

"It doesn't really matter. It was all a very long time ago," Edmund said with a burst of cheer. "Now, shall we return to the light of day to review my most incriminating booty? I took a photograph every year starting in 1860 so that I could study how I changed physically. You might find those interesting."

"I'm sure I will, darling."

42

As he made his move towards the stairs, she grinned and let her coat fall open one last time, using her free hand to entice him into a passionate kiss.

"You never thought you'd be kissing your wife down here, did you, Colonel?" she asked mischievously as she used the distraction to steal his hat and place it on her own head.

He pulled her into his arms, kissing her deeper and deeper, until she almost dropped the lantern in their frenzy.

"Never in my wildest dreams, Eleanor. Now let's get some water boiling so we can review the incriminating evidence in each other's warm, naked arms. Shall we?"

"I can't think of anything I'd rather do."

They skipped up the ancient stone staircase of Edmund's secret lair, back to the light of day, but as they re-entered the kitchen, the sound of someone approaching on the front steps threw them both into a panic.

"Hello, Colonel? Miss MacLeod?"

"It's the chauffeur!" Eleanor hissed, unable to control her guilty giggles at their precarious position. She hastily buttoned her coat and tied the belt, but as she turned to Edmund, she could see that he was not finding the intrusion nearly as entertaining as she was.

"Just one minute, Mr. Quince! Please wait outside the front door!" Eleanor called.

She buttoned up Edmund's coat and returned his top-hat to him, creating a silly combination of anachronistic fashions. Edmund squeezed the stack of incriminating photographs.

"Ah, I see why you're nervous." Eleanor worked to free them from his unusually tight grip. As soon as they were free, she placed them face down on a small wooden cutting board. "How about you wait here, and I will go see what Mr. Quince wants?"

"What if he'd come in while we were playing down there in my secret lair! There isn't even a front door to keep intruders out!" he exclaimed. "How could I have been so foolish?!"

"Darling, we are miles from the village, and it is not a British custom to enter a home uninvited, even if the home is missing a door," Eleanor said calmly, hoping against hope that the fear he was feeling at the situation would not undo the tremendous progress he'd just made in returning to his pre-war self.

"How are we going to explain the door?! I kicked it in with superhuman strength! It was a solid door, Eleanor! Very solid!"

"It's an old house, darling. I'm sure he will believe that the wood rotted. Now wait right here, and I will go see what he wants."

Edmund nodded his agreement and began frenetically tapping his foot as he tried to keep his burgeoning nerves under control.

Eleanor dashed to the door, hoping that Mr. Quince would not notice her scandalous lack of undergarments.

"Yes?" she asked with annoyance as she reached the foyer. "We would prefer privacy as we celebrate our engagement, Mr. Quince..." She trailed off as she spotted an enormous basket of picnic food in Mr. Quince's arms.

"I thought that without a staff to help you out, perhaps you two might need some food for the rest of the weekend," Mr. Quince said excitedly.

"How very kind of you!" Eleanor exclaimed. "I was wondering what we'd manage to scrounge up ourselves in this old house. Thank you!"

Mr. Quince looked like he might burst.

"Oh, Eleanor, I'm so excited for you! We are so, so, *so* happy that you and Edmund found each other!"

Eleanor paused as she fully processed the implications of his statement, but before she could say a word, he pulled her into an exceptionally awkward motherly hug.

"You are not Mélusine," she said astutely.

"Oh, no, Lady Mélusine is far more discreet than I am," Mr. Quince admitted unapologetically. "I simply couldn't stop myself from saying hello. Now, you scamper off and enjoy your time with Master Edmund, and if you'd like it, I can pop over here again tomorrow with another picnic basket. I'd offer to fix the door, but my dear boy is observant enough to recognize that level of intrusion. But this, Eleanor, this basket of morsels you can easily explain. Tell him that my wife runs a bakery in town, and that I am hoping for more business as your chauffeur."

"Alright..." Eleanor said as she worked to hide her bewilderment. "Kuveni?"

Now Mr. Quince *really* looked like he might explode.

"Oh, Mistress Eleanor, you truly are one of the cleverest humans I've ever had the pleasure of meeting! How perfect that your cleverness is paired with such virtue. Oh, if only such a combination were more common!"

He pulled her into another motherly hug, and then seemed startled as he pulled away and closed his eyes, whispering a quiet mantra.

"You'd best get back to Master Edmund. He's at his wit's end worrying about what's transpiring between us at this very moment. But, if you don't mind, I might pop over to visit you in Scotland next week. We have a wedding to plan, my dear girl! Oh, I have so many ideas! It's been positively *ages* since we've had a good wedding amongst us!"

Without waiting for Eleanor's response, Mr. Quince dissolved.

She looked down at the beautiful picnic basket, and for the first time, she had an accurate inkling of what she was signing up for.

"And I thought I'd escaped having a mother-in-law..." she muttered.

She took a deep, calming breath and pushed her anxiety at the difficult prospect aside.

"Darling," she called. "No need to worry! Mr. Quince has brought us a picnic basket!"

She gathered up the small banquet and headed back to her naked fiancé in the kitchen, ready to perpetuate the new batch of lies that her future mother-in-law had just initiated.

CHAPTER 3 – FOREIGN RELATIONS

It was 2am on a Thursday. Eleanor had just finished up her fifth twelve-hour shift of the week, and the exhaustion was starting to catch up with her. She had sustained her long working hours for years by making up for her lost sleep on her lazy days off, but now, *now* she had much better things to do with that time. She sighed as she thought back lovingly to her passionate, naked weekend in Edmund's country home.

They'd been apart for two weeks already, and her whole body burned with desire every time her mind wandered back to her many arousing memories of their recent intimacy. *More, you want more!* Her whole body sang in unison.

But it wasn't simply that Edmund was such a shockingly good lover (by far the best she'd ever had, so much so that there really was not even a worthy comparison). The painful longing she felt now was far more than a physical sensation. She felt as if a piece of her soul was suddenly lost in his absence, and the sensation annoyed her. She had vowed for the vast majority of her life, ever since her father's selfishness had destroyed the lives of everyone in her family, that she would not, under any circumstance, allow herself to care so much about a man that his betrayal would ruin her. And yet, here she was. She couldn't bear the feeling of being away from him.

As she wandered up the winding, medieval stone alleyway to her small flat in the old town of Edinburgh, she let her mind wander as she mulled through the memories of lounging about with Edmund in his full, honesty-inspired glory. Watching her gentle, half-human soldier go about his business in his old house had been far more entertaining than she'd anticipated. His comfort with the old-fashioned techniques required to do basic tasks with the Victorian tools he had available in his manor was thoroughly fascinating. He approached every chore with an earnest excitement that she had never seen before in another human being, and she wondered in passing if he enjoyed the mundanity of the processes more because of his unusual upbringing, almost as if the effort itself was a novelty.

She clomped up the dark stairs to her flat, politely foregoing the electric hallway lights for the sake of her grumpy neighbors, as she always did. She smiled secretly to herself. They had gossiped for years about the wanton morals of Robby MacLeod's spinster daughter, and on Edmund's first visit after their fateful meeting in October, she'd finally given them something real to talk about. She was not going to be sad to leave the dank rot of the old building or the prying eyes of her nosy neighbors; although, she did worry that she would miss the freedom of her single life. She was still not used to justifying her various whims to anyone. She'd spent decades of her life extolling the virtues of her unmarried modernity, for god's sake! Alas, her feelings on the issue of marriage remained intensely ambivalent. If it weren't for Edmund, she was quite sure that she would have lived and died very happily without it.

48

Her stomach rumbled as she switched on the electric lights and threw her keys down on the small entry table of her sitting room. It had been fourteen hours since she'd eaten, and she was not the least bit interested in frying something up. She would be happy, she had to admit, when Mrs. Murray would join her marital household with Edmund. In an excessively kind gesture that she did not find surprising in the slightest, her thoughtful fiancé had already paid Mrs. Murray a handsome sum to retain her chefly services, and had subsequently offered her a six-month sabbatical to visit her sister in Yorkshire until it was time for all of them to come together in Basingstoke after what was sure to be an epic whirlwind, globe-trotting honeymoon.

She got goosebumps as she anticipated the exciting prospect of accompanying Edmund to India, back to the land of his childhood and of his most favorite adventures. Back to the land where he felt most like himself, and where, she was quite sure, his great destiny awaited. He had said many times that Basingstoke felt most like his home, but she already knew him better than he knew himself. Every time he mentioned India, she couldn't ignore a certain twinkle in his eye. It was the same twinkle she spied every time he referred to her. It was his subtle manifestation of the divine, soulful love that stirred deep within his passionate being. But India was not even going to be their only exploit. She'd mentioned in passing while they'd lounged in the bath until the water turned cold that she had always wanted to see Paris, and before they'd even managed to rip themselves from the water, Edmund had already concocted an elaborate honeymoon itinerary from Paris to Constantinople on the Simplon Orient Express and thence by steamer all the way to Bombay.

"We have to go through Europe to get to India anyway!" He'd declared triumphantly. "We might as well do it in style!"

"But, darling, can you take that much time off? And won't that passage be excessively expensive? The Orient Express is world-famous for its luxury!"

"Eleanor, the generals have already offered me however much leave I want, and we don't have to worry about money. My tens of thousands of ordinary paintings fetched enough over the years to keep us quite comfortable," Edmund had argued.

"Quantity over quality?" Eleanor had teased.

"Exactly!" She'd found the childlike excitement in his expression to be utterly contagious. "And I've never in my life ever had an occasion to *want* to spend that money! What would've been the point?! But now, *now*, Eleanor, we can spend it together! We will go first class all the way!"

She'd pushed back a rumble of similar anxiety to what he had already expressed. It was too good. All of it. Far too good for her. She was just one of Robby MacLeod's many fiery little bastards. Some part of her feared that it was all just a cruel joke, a prank put forth by the wicked universe to tease her with something that she didn't deserve. She'd pushed the fear aside and agreed enthusiastically to his plan. Now it was happening. He'd already bought the tickets. It was all really happening...

She let out an involuntary, overwhelmed sigh.

She only had one more week of work at the veteran's hospital in Edinburgh, and then she would really be headed full-steam-ahead into the great unknown. Her stomach churned with anxiety at the prospect. Edmund had already made several inquiries through his chain of command in an effort to procure her a position at the veteran's hospital just outside of Basingstoke, and so far, he had received exactly the response she'd anticipated: No work for married women. She sighed sadly at the memory. He'd looked more devastated than she was when he'd received his first rejection on her behalf. He'd escalated the matter a level higher by the end of the day, and now they were playing the waiting game. She was sure it was only a matter of time until that rejection would come too, and then it would be up to her to figure out her next move.

She'd already uncovered two open offices in the old village of Basingstoke, both of which could serve as reasonable private counseling centers for veterans. The work wouldn't have the variety of frenzied action that she had come to love, but it would be something. She would not let herself succumb to the societal travesty of wasted women's talent, as Edmund despairingly described her plight. She sighed lovingly. God, how she loved that man.

She walked slowly to her small kitchen and opened the barren cupboard. She'd stopped refilling her foodstocks as soon as she'd returned to tie up her affairs after their engagement, but she had been finding the last few days to be especially disappointing when she got home starving from work. She sighed with hungry annoyance.

She'd been sighing a lot these days, for good and bad and neutral reasons. Her emotions were in a wild state of upheaval… just like her life was. Love was so dastardly inconvenient! She hoped that her patients hadn't noticed her symptoms of stress.

As she collected a mostly-empty box of shortbreads to take to bed with her (one of many unadvisable single habits she hoped wouldn't annoy her future husband), her heart skipped a beat as she glanced over to her small dining table to observe a fresh, steaming-hot shepherd's pie.

"Mélusine?" she called into the seemingly empty room.

"Sshhh!" a disembodied voice hissed. "There's no need to invite Lady Mélusine to join us!"

As the voice echoed strangely through the small space, creating a distinctly ghostly effect, a jolly, red-faced, plump older woman, clad in a regency-era, empire-waisted servant's dress with a messy, stained apron, materialized before her. She looked very familiar, as if she were Mr. Quince's buxom twin sister.

"Kuveni?" Eleanor asked questioningly.

"Oh, my clever girl has done it again!" Kuveni exclaimed as she forcefully gathered Eleanor into a motherly hug. "You really are the cleverest human I've ever had the pleasure of meeting!"

"Thanks," Eleanor said as she worked to hide her bewilderment.

"Oh, please don't let me stop you! Eat! You must be starving! I couldn't believe you flitted about for hours and hours on a roaring empty stomach! No wonder you're just skin and bones!"

Before Eleanor could comment on the unpleasant revelation that Kuveni had apparently been following her invisibly all day, Kuveni escorted her to the small wooden dining table and sat her down in the chair before the steaming pie.

"Try it! It has been my specialty for two thousand years! Even the Rakshasas will eat it, and they don't go around eating anything willy-nilly, mind you. Master Edmund is a true exception with his healthy appetite for solid human food."

"Does that mean that you are not a Rakshasa then?" Eleanor asked astutely as she picked up on Kuveni's reference to 'Rakshasas' in the third person.

"Not one drop," Kuveni confirmed. "I am a Yakshini, through and through. I am the same ancient race as Lady Mélusine's father. Yakshinis are the sacred keepers of Earth, and our talents and our vices are a bit different than our Rakshasa cousins'. We can both change our forms, though, which is why we seem so similar to the untrained observer. In reality, we are really quite different from each other, but I'd best not get into the details."

As a flood of follow-up questions rushed through her mind, her stomach growled. She looked covetously at the steaming pie, which Kuveni had provided without any utensils, and then glanced over to her silverware drawer. She considered her options, and then wiggled out of the chair, worked her way around the barrier Kuveni had created with her fleshy form, and collected a fork.

"Aw, now, carpenter's pie was not intended to be stabbed, my dear girl! It's already dead!" Kuveni protested.

Eleanor could not tell if she was joking, and Kuveni gave her no indication with her dead-pan delivery of the statement.

"I'm supposed to eat it with my hands?" Eleanor asked with puzzlement. "But it has steaming hot gravy inside!"

"That is how the Romans would have done it," Kuveni advised her.

"Well, that explains it. I'm a Scot." Eleanor shrugged melodramatically. "I'm a barbarian through and through, fork and all."

Kuveni burst into laughter. "I know exactly why Mélusine loves you, my dear girl! Eat! Use the barbarian fork, if you insist!"

Kuveni watched her intently while she took her first bite.

"It's delicious," Eleanor said as she let herself give into her hunger. "Thank you. It is much better than the stale shortbread would've been."

"Oh, Mistress Eleanor, I'm so glad you approve!" Kuveni exclaimed. She did not give Eleanor a moment to recover before she jumped straight into the real motive for her appearance. "Now, I've come because we have many important things to discuss! My dear boy is getting married, and we must get moving on the plans! Now, I was thinking that June would be the loveliest time for the Druidic linden grove, and that way I can grow out the morning-glories in May, and Master Edmund won't notice anything unusual... Don't you just love purple? I was thinking that you might want to carry morning glories in your bouquet to match the surroundings, but perhaps they will need to be mixed with another color... I've always loved yellow... Perhaps yellow roses and morning glories, yes, those would be lovely together..."

Kuveni took Eleanor's overwhelmed silence as an invitation to continue.

"By the way, I had a roasted goose sent over to the Hampshire Registrar General's office as you suggested, so our pagan chapel will now be referred to as a 'non-denominational Christian church' when the registrar is lingering about." Kuveni winked. "And then we will need to make sure that only the right people are around for the Rakshasa portion of the rituals, which I'm thinking you can tell Edmund are a Scottish tradition so that we don't arouse his suspicions there… yes, yes, we'll have to be very careful not to give ourselves away, but the Rakshasa rituals would really only be proper… By the way, do you think two thousand guests will be too many? We wouldn't want the local villagers to get too suspicious; they're always so dastardly quick to pull out the pitchforks, if you know what I mean… Perhaps we can cut down the list to one thousand, although that will certainly snub the Peruvians… Now, tell me this: Who will be giving you away? Will it be your father? Has he met Edmund? Mélusine insisted that I desist with my eavesdropping, so I must rely on you to fill me in on all the pertinent details."

"I wasn't planning on having anyone give me away…" Eleanor murmured.

"No one! Oh, but my dear girl, you must have someone! Every culture on Earth has the bride given away by someone! Surely your father would want to be involved… Good lord, he approves of Edmund, doesn't he? How could he not? I might need to go have a word with him…"

"My father shot himself!" Eleanor blurted.

Kuveni looked as if the news had attacked her.

"My sisters and I were his second family. Unbeknownst to us, he was a scoundrel of a polygamist, and when the world found out, he put a gun in his mouth and shot himself. Ever since then, as you can imagine, my mother has not been particularly cheerful at weddings (nor is she thrilled that I'm marrying a sassanack), and I'm not particularly keen on having her there at all, but some sacrifices must be made for the greater good… Now, I've been avoiding the idea of who will give me away for almost thirty years, and I had hoped to avoid it a little bit longer. In any event, I shouldn't really be having this conversation with you at all, I should be having it with Edmund. Now I have the pleasure of having it twice, which is two times more than I ever hoped I would."

"Alright then…" Kuveni said quietly.

"And we've already set the date." Eleanor reined in her sharp tone. "We're getting married on March 15. Edmund thought it would be a little irreverent joke to get married on the Ides of March, and I couldn't think of any objection. It is a Saturday, and he thought the daffodils would be out by then, and we didn't really want to wait until summer to get things going…" Eleanor gathered her courage. "And I was thinking more like fifty people for the guest list… all of my relatives, a few of my friends from the VAD, and Edmund's friends and colleagues from the barracks… I didn't realize there were so many… er… non-human guests to accommodate… Mélusine said there weren't so many Rakshasas left."

A strange look shadowed Kuveni's expression. "Oh… Alright then… I'll just make a note of that."

Eleanor cringed as Kuveni let out a loud sigh of concession.

"Well, Lady Mélusine will have to speed up her updates to the property, then. She can't make them too fast, or else he'll become suspicious—as it is, he was asking a few too many questions when she informed him that she was Lord Blakeney's personal property engineer—and it will be absolutely absurd by human standards to fully update the plumbing and run electricity in such a short period of time… But, never you mind, we have done it before and we will do it again. I will leave the lies up to Mélusine this time…"

"I'm sorry?" Eleanor asked as she couldn't control her curiosity. "You've done what before?"

"Where do you think his cellar came from?" Kuveni laughed. "He'd become desperate for a hiding place for his most treasured possessions, and so I just popped that secret lair down there one night while he was sleeping soundly upstairs. Oh, he was so wonderfully excited when he stumbled upon it the following week!

It was like Christmas morning for my beautiful boy! Mind you, I had to really call his attention to the brick wall entrance, since Master Edmund does not normally spend very much time in the kitchen, but it was really the only location where I could believably put a room of that size without him noticing. He came up with that story about the secret Catholic church all on his own! His lively imagination makes our meddling so easy!"

A burst of anxiety rushed through Eleanor as the phrase reminded her of the dire warnings Mélusine had offered upon their initial meeting.

"What is it, my dear child? What's wrong?" Kuveni asked with concern.

"Kuveni, I appreciate all you've done to help us already, I really do, but meddling is bad, isn't it? Mélusine told me that your meddling always leads to tragedy for Edmund. She told me that your leader has strictly forbidden it."

A look of genuine fear crossed Kuveni's expression. "You must not tell Lady Mélusine or Lord Vibhishana about my meddling. Neither of them will approve in the slightest!"

Now Eleanor was really in a bind. The painful lies she'd already been forced to tell Edmund on behalf of Kuveni's unsanctioned meddling rushed into her mind, and suddenly, her emotional turmoil burrowed its way to the surface, and she couldn't control the bursting dam.

"What have you done?!" Eleanor exclaimed. "Kuveni, think about what you've done! Edmund doesn't have any idea how hard things are for normal people, does he? I thought his childlike innocence was due to his unusual upbringing, but it isn't just that, is it? You've been secretly helping him, making even the most mundane problems disappear for him for a century!"

"Well, I wouldn't put it like that..." Kuveni argued guiltily.

"The station!" Eleanor exclaimed. "You were secretly watching us, and the moment we ran into a minor mishap, you rushed to the rescue! You used your identity as Mr. Valov to make the excuse for your meddling!"

"I'm not Mr. Valov, dear girl!"

Eleanor assessed her skeptically, deciding whether or not she believed her. "Then who is he? Is he another guardian I haven't met? He does seem rather stoic compared to you and Mélusine, I suppose."

"My dear girl, Mr. Valov is simply a good human butler! All exceptional humans are not Yakshas in disguise, you know. There really aren't very many of us left."

Eleanor contemplated the obvious question of who Kuveni's two thousand desired wedding guests were if there were only a few Yakshas left. She wondered if the misunderstanding was simply due to a difference in perception, just as her misunderstanding of Edmund's 'young' age had been, or if Kuveni had an army of human helpers waiting somewhere in the shadows… She decided to press on with the more important question.

"You're saying that Mr. Valov has served Edmund all this time, anticipating his every need, and he has nothing to do with any of you?"

Kuveni closed her eyes for what appeared to be a moment of meditation. "Mr. Valov is not one of us. Lady Mélusine just confirmed it."

"Huh…" Eleanor said as she thought back to her many interactions with him. "So at the station, you lied to Edmund, assuming that he would never ask Mr. Valov whether or not he had called for a chauffeur? That seems like a lot of risk to help Edmund with such a minor difficulty, don't you think?"

"I don't see what's wrong with helping…" Kuveni said defensively. "Poor Edmund has been working for four long years to get over the trauma of that wretched war. That was what happened when I wasn't allowed to be involved at all. He is still tormented every single day!"

"Mélusine seemed very convinced about the necessity of Edmund understanding the darkness of war."

Kuveni humphed.

"And daily life in postwar England is not the same as life in the trenches. He doesn't need constant coddling anymore." Eleanor regretted her harsh tone, but she couldn't regret the words.

"I helped you both avoid an annoying inconvenience!" Kuveni argued haughtily. "Someday, when Master Edmund ascends to his rightful position, he will have the help of many powerful Yakshas at his beck and call. Why must he suffer now? My beautiful boy isn't spoiled, you know. He values work more than any Rakshasa I've ever encountered. More than most humans, mind you! And more than any other prince on Earth!"

"Prince?" Eleanor murmured. "Yes, sure, why not... Of course, he's a prince..."

"Lady Mélusine did not tell you that Edmund is the heir-apparent to the Rakshasa throne?"

"Lady Mélusine failed to mention that detail..." Eleanor replied quietly. "Wait a second... He's not promised to some Rakshasa princess somewhere, is he? Because that isn't going to work for me. I am far too much of a modern woman to allow myself to be the third wheel in some fairy tale love triangle."

"Ha!" Kuveni laughed awkwardly. "No, my dear girl, there is no princess waiting in the wings for Young Edmund..." Eleanor did not like Kuveni's contemplative pause, but Kuveni pushed forward. "I suppose it's best Mélusine waited to reveal that particular detail to you. Now we know you weren't after him for his position." A hint of self-consciousness entered Kuveni's voice, as if she was contemplating the wisdom of her visit seriously for the first time.

Eleanor worked hard to rein in her emotions in the wake of another round of shocking revelations. She knew that she was in dangerous territory, straddling the unpleasant precipice of insulting her future mother-in-law's parental choices, but she simply couldn't contain herself.

"Kuveni, it hadn't even *occurred* to Edmund to order a car for our arrival at the station in Basingstoke. The next time around, it might not occur to him again, because it didn't cause us any problems! He hasn't been given the opportunity to learn from his mistakes. No wonder he's so strangely unaware of the difficulties most humans face on a daily basis."

Kuveni looked distinctly disturbed by the assertion, and she sat herself down in the chair opposite Eleanor.

"What makes you think he's unaware of human hardship?"

"He had no idea that most women had to become housewives upon marriage, for one. You know what he asked me within a few hours of us meeting? He asked why people would dismiss their house staffs upon marriage! He couldn't fathom the idea that not *everyone* would have a house staff."

"Oh dear…" Kuveni whispered.

"And there was no boiler at his house, Kuveni. Nothing to warm it, except for the fireplaces, which hadn't been tended to in almost thirty years. And did he notice that there was nothing keeping the house warm when 'Lord Blakeney's' staff was tending to us on a snowy day in October? No! I assumed that there was a boiler, but there wasn't! He confirmed it when we were there two weeks back, but I don't think he even thought about how his house was warm! I really don't think the idea even crossed his mind that it should have been freezing in there! Speaking of which, did we run into any problems showing up there on a whim on a crisp, January day? Not in the slightest! We rolled around naked for hours in his warm parlor before it occurred to either of us that we might need a heating source for the evening. Now, you wouldn't have any idea how the parlor of his unheated house was so warm on a winter's day that we didn't need any clothing, would you? Is this a scenario that an average human, or even a privileged one, would ever encounter? And don't even get me started on the chamber pots... as nice as it was for them to magically refresh, he thought that the phenomenon was a result of innovative Victorian technology! No wonder he didn't feel a need to update his house! You'd already made the old-fashioned inconveniences magically convenient! He'd have quite a rude awakening without your constant help, don't you think? Is that, perhaps, one of the many reasons that the war was so traumatic for him?"

Kuveni paused to think about Eleanor's point for an uncomfortably long moment.

"This is bad. This is very, very bad..." Kuveni murmured.

Eleanor's heart raced at Kuveni's fresh showing of reticence.

"I'm sorry, Kuveni. I didn't mean to offend you... I really didn't want to get off on the wrong foot with my future mother-in-law, but I have never been very good at hiding my feelings. I guess it's the barbarian in me."

"What did you say?" Kuveni asked with a shrill tone.

Eleanor's heart beat even faster. "I have never been very good at hiding my feelings..."

"You called me your mother-in-law!" Kuveni exclaimed. "Oh, my dear girl, we must have confused you dreadfully! I am not Edmund's mother! Didn't Mélusine tell you? I was his nanny!"

"Any woman who raises a child and loves him as her own is a mother in my book," Eleanor shrugged.

Kuveni looked like she might explode, and then she burst out of her chair, ripped Eleanor up, and engulfed her into a dangerously tight hug.

"Oh, how I love you, Mistress Eleanor. I have never loved a human like I love you right now. Never," she whispered as tears streamed down her face.

Eleanor stood in position as she waited for Kuveni to release her.

"Well, now, you are as wise as you are loving, my dear girl," Kuveni said as she wiped the tears from her eyes. "Lord Vibhishana will not be pleased at all if he notices what you have noticed in your months with my beautiful boy. We were ordered not to meddle to prevent the exact problem you are bravely describing to me now. Master Edmund *must* understand the hardships facing most humans. It is an absolute necessity, and I have unwittingly stepped in the way of destiny. This is very, very bad. Destiny becomes very violent when she feels thwarted… very violent indeed…"

"That is what I was afraid of," Eleanor muttered.

"Well, the meddling stops this instant!" Kuveni declared. "Well, I suppose not *this* instant…" she corrected herself. "Mélusine must finish the updates to the house in time for the wedding. There is no possible way humans will be able to do it, and my beautiful boy has decided that he will be married on the Ides of March, and that is what he will do. It is curious, though…"

"Why? It's not bad luck, is it? I thought it was just a Shakespearean reference."

"No… no it's not bad luck…" Kuveni murmured. She looked at Eleanor's questioning face, and then guiltily lowered her voice. "Certainly, I should not be telling you this…"

"Alright…" Eleanor hedged.

"The Ides of March were an important day for us, for the Avatars of Light. They were the first time in a thousand years that a human leader (and an ambitious one, that Julius Caesar was!) realized that Edmund's father was manipulating him, and stood up to his machinations. Edmund's father had him assassinated anyway, but it was a great triumph of light. It showed us all that human leaders had regained the capacity to reason. It is perhaps just a coincidence that Young Edmund chose the date—he was always very interested in the classics, and Shakespeare, that scoundrel, was always one of his favorites—but it will be symbolic for us, Eleanor. All of us. We all remember that joyous day, and it is really quite fitting that Edmund chose it for his celebration of light, for his marriage to you, my lovely girl."

Kuveni reached forward to stroke Eleanor's cheek affectionately.

"I could not be happier that he found you. You are a perfect match. I'm sorry that I made you uncomfortable with my tasteful suggestions…" Kuveni looked like she was battling with a thought, and then she smiled and let it pass. "Now, tell me, Eleanor dearest, what can I do to help you with *your* wedding?"

Eleanor was at a total loss. The pile of revelations that Kuveni had thrust upon her were bombarding her tired mind.

"Come on, my dear girl, don't be shy now!" Kuveni urged.

"Kuveni… If you don't mind, I'd rather not know what you're doing. At all. Ever. After you dropped off the picnic basket, I was horribly distracted by having to lie to Edmund for the rest of the weekend about where it had come from. I was ever so grateful that he didn't seem to notice, but it hurt me. It took away from the beautiful experience of being with him. Do what you feel you must, but please, do not require me to lie on your behalf any more than I already have to. I want to revel in the unique honesty of our relationship just as much as he does, and your revelations, however well-intentioned, have taken that from me. Please do not add to my burden."

A look of immense sadness crossed Kuveni's expression, and she pulled Eleanor into a gentler hug.

"I will do my best, my dear girl," Kuveni promised. "Do not think of it again."

"I'm sorry."

"I am the one who is sorry, Mistress Eleanor," Kuveni corrected her. "Now, I will leave you in peace to eat your carpenter's pie like a barbarian Scot," she winked amicably, "and I will do whatever I need to do to make sure that you and Edmund will have your special day on the Ides of March. If you ever need anything, anything at all, just whisper my name. You do not need a talisman like the one Mélusine gave you to reach me."

"Thank you." Eleanor offered Kuveni a parting hug.

"Thank you, my dear girl, for so many things I have already lost count," Kuveni said with a wistful sigh.

"Oh… I do have one request… A request on Edmund's behalf, actually…" Eleanor hedged.

"Please, tell me!" Kuveni exclaimed. "Tell me what my beautiful boy needs!"

"Edmund misses the mysterious Mr. Johnson terribly, and I think it would mean a lot to him if Mr. Johnson came to the wedding. I assume you can pass along the invitation?"

Kuveni nodded her solemn agreement. "As sure as I'm standing here now, he will be there."

"Thank you," Eleanor reiterated.

"It is my pleasure, Mistress Eleanor. It is my pleasure, indeed."

And without another word, Eleanor's future mother-in-law dissolved. Eleanor looked down at the unusually delicious pie, and with a loud sigh of many emotions, she ate the rest of Kuveni's loving Yakshini offering in peace.

PART TWO
THE WEDDING

The Ides of March, 1923 – Basingstoke

"Eleanor Mary MacLeod, what's this yer sister's tellin' me? Ye aren't even goin' to have a minister at yer wedding?! Ye thought ye'd wait until the last minute to reveal yer sinful plan, did ye? Is this how they do things down here in the godless land of sassanacks? Well, ye can't get anything past yer shrewd mother, ye hear?! I've half a mind to get on the next train back to Elphinstone!"

"Mam, leave her be! It's her wedding day! It's a miracle that any man was willing to marry Ellie at her age!"

Eleanor cringed as the shrill voices of her charming relatives echoed through the sunny second-floor hallway of Edmund's country home.

"Ruthy, don't touch that! What will the colonel say if he realizes you were fingering his precious antiques? That vase is probably worth more than our house!"

"But, Mammy, I didn't touch it. I swear!"

"Martha, ye'd best lick that lyin' child if ye want her to mind you. Spare the rod, spoil the child, the wise men say!"

"Thank you for your advice, Mother."

"Debbie, hold yer sister's hand. Don't let her touch anything else!"

A loud crash and the wild cries of a guilty child indicated that young Debbie had not successfully prevented her sister from breaking one of Edmund's many antique porcelain vases, all of which had been filled to the brim with fragrant asiatic lilies and spread cheerfully throughout the house in preparation for the wedding festivities.

"I don't see why it matters. He has hundreds of vases! It's like he's the bloody Emperor of China!"

"*India*! He's the Emperor of India! Mammy said so!"

"Sshhh… I was only joking, Debbie. Colonel Marriner is English. He just *lived* in India because he was in the British Army. King George is the Emperor of India."

"Why is King George the Emperor of India, Mammy?"

"Because the sassanacks like to take over other countries and tell them what to do."

"Sshhh… What if Colonel Marriner hears ye say something like that? He's a good, tidy man to take on a spinster bride like Ellie. I thought she'd given up her last chance when she dumped that scrawny Teddy chap."

"Teddy? That lad was as queer as a nine-bob note!"

"Mam! Don't say such things in front of the bairns!"

"Why not? Moira MacLeod calls 'em like she sees 'em, and one should ne'er regret the truth."

"Well, the colonel is an *old* man to marry Ellie, don't ye think? Too old, really. He must be at least ten years older than her! And a *soldier*, I mean *really*. They're all mad as hatters these days."

"Sshhh! Ellie'll hear ye!"

"Ellie? Which room are ye hidin' away in? We're lost out here in the hallway with so many doors!"

Eleanor sighed as she prepared herself for her polite response. She had been lounging in her favorite silk kimono, enjoying the silence for many hours as she'd sequestered herself away in her so-called bridal chamber—one of the many spare rooms on the opposite side of the house from Edmund's master bedroom, which they had vacated two weeks earlier upon the arrival of Lord Blakeney's staff who insisted on cordoning it off to prepare it for their wedding night as an extension of their extensive modernization project. She'd been sitting at the ostentatious Louis XIV vanity for hours wrestling her hair into various elaborate up-dos and watching the flustered staff rush about like ants while Mélusine (under the guise of Lord Blakeney) guided them in the final tasks required to set up the property for the large reception which they planned to hold outside under the unseasonably warm sun upon a carpet of sweet-scented violets punctuated by patches of yellow daffodils that stretched all the way from the house to the early-blooming woods beyond.

It may not have been Kuveni's two thousand guests who would be descending upon them any minute, but Edmund's many friends and colleagues from his decades of military service had crawled out of the woodwork in droves from every corner of the Empire to attend their supposedly low-key affair. She couldn't blame him for not anticipating that almost every person he invited would reply with an enthusiastic yes (and a plus one!), but she did have to blame herself for not anticipating that her gentle soldier was far more popular than he would ever let himself believe. She should have realized that his modest view of himself did not match the world's view of him in the slightest. She loved him so dearly for his lack of egotism, but she vowed not to let it take her by surprise on such an epic scale again. Five *hundred* guests! Her heart raced as she contemplated what such a crowd would even look like, and then she smiled to herself as she thought back upon the moment they made the final count…

"Quantity over quality?" Edmund had said sheepishly.

"I didn't realize we even knew five hundred people!" she'd exclaimed.

"Neither did I…"

"I'm sure it will be lovely," Eleanor had reassured him as he'd sighed with stress. "Lord Blakeney has already offered us his entire staff to help everything run smoothly. It was the least he could do, given that his engineers almost didn't finish updating the house in time."

"Yes… yes, I suppose…"

Now, the first of the hordes of guests had arrived, and Eleanor wasn't sure she was ready to face them… especially the illustrious MacLeods…

"Just grin and bear it like you always do," she muttered to herself. "Just a few more hours, and they'll be out of your hair."

Eleanor took a deep, calming breath and stood up from her vanity to greet her new guests.

"Oh, Ellie, you look beautiful!" her sisters swooned as she swung open the door.

"Auntie Ellie!!!"

Eleanor gathered Debbie and Ruthy into a tight hug.

"How on earth did you get so many flowers?!" Martha exclaimed as she looked around the room with wonder, observing the thousands of purple, white, and yellow flowers of every imaginable variety that had appeared without a word of warning sometime in the dead of the night. "You must have raided all the hothouses in England!"

"Auntie Ellie, are you going to be the Empress of India?!" Ruthy asked excitedly.

Eleanor laughed. "No, darling. I'm only going to be the modest wife of a kind English soldier."

"Modest indeed," her mother muttered.

"Mam!" Mary hissed disapprovingly. "Leave Ellie alone!"

Eleanor's mother did not heed her daughter's request. "It's unsavory, that bright red lipstick of yours…" she complained instead. "But I suppose ye don't need to make a good impression on a man of God, since there won't be one anywhere in sight."

"Yes, Mother, Edmund and I agreed that the registrar would be perfectly sufficient for our needs."

"Do you want yer children to be bastards like you are in the eyes of God?" her mother asked with genuine concern.

"I think that God should have much better things to judge me by than the sins of my father. Don't you? I don't see why it would be any different for my children."

"We're having very fine weather!" Mary interrupted aggressively as Ruthy moved to ask a question about her Auntie Eleanor's intriguing statement. "It's hard to believe it's only March! It's still so dreary back home."

"Yes, we've been having unseasonably warm weather here for weeks. It has brought the spring blossoms out early. The cherry blossoms along the drive are magical, aren't they?"

"They're lovely, Ellie. Perfect for a wedding," Mary replied with a supportive smile.

Eleanor pulled her sister into a grateful hug for her assistance in wrangling their mother out of one of her typical puritanical tirades.

"This is a very fine house," Martha chimed in. "And the gardens are so vast! It feels like your colonel owns half the village! I thought when you said you'd decided to have your wedding in the garden, that you'd decided not to incur the cost of a public celebration. Clearly soldiers are compensated better than I thought!"

Mary threw Martha a look of strict disapproval, while Eleanor ignored the brazen financial fishing that the question represented and gestured for them to take a seat on an elaborately embroidered French divan. Ruthy and Debbie pushed and shoved into the final spot, and as Eleanor noticed the challenge to their sisterly peace, she wisely tossed her stray clothing from the old-fashioned velvet chaise by her vanity onto the floor, and gestured for her two little nieces to sit by her.

With all of her relatives wrangled, Eleanor took a deep, calming breath and responded to Martha's uncouth observation.

"Edmund's grandfather was a very successful painter," Eleanor explained as she sat herself back down at her vanity chair and returned to her efforts with her hair. "He presented at the Royal Academy twice, and he even met Queen Victoria."

"Really?!" Debbie and Ruthy exclaimed in unison.

Eleanor smiled. "Really."

"Queen Victoria indeed…" her mother scoffed.

"He attended the first birthday party of Prince Leopold in 1854 at Windsor Castle, to be precise." Eleanor addressed her statement directly to her mother. "The royal family was interested in commissioning some landscape paintings of the various royal gardens, and landscapes were Edmund's grandfather's specialty."

"Are these his paintings then?" Martha asked with piqued interest as she glanced around the room to observe the walls covered from top to bottom in Edmund's landscapes.

"Oh yes. Edmund still has many hundreds of them. If you ask him nicely, he might even give you one. They aren't worth gobs of money now, but his grandfather made quite a trade in them back in the nineteenth century."

"He's just giving them away?" Martha asked with some combination of disbelief and personal interest.

"He cares more about giving them a good home than about making any more money." Eleanor glanced into the mirror to observe her sisters' reactions. Her mother rolled her eyes, while Mary and Martha threw each other a look of intrigue.

"That's very sentimental of your English soldier!" Mary exclaimed as she noticed that Eleanor had caught their exchange.

"Edmund takes after his grandfather in many respects… It was his grandfather who purchased this estate, and Edmund has kept it all intact to remember him by. We're moving here after the honeymoon. Edmund has been longing to make it his home since he headed off to join the British Army in India almost thirty years ago."

"You're going to *live* here in this castle?!" Debbie exclaimed. "You *will* be like an empress!"

Eleanor laughed awkwardly. "It feels very homey, actually. Perhaps Edmund's love of it has rubbed off on me. It feels much more comfortable than his townhouse in London, although he has decided to keep that as well, at least for the time being, so that we can use it when we want to enjoy various activities in the city."

"He *owns* his townhouse in London? And this house?" Martha asked with wonder (and a hint of jealousy). "How many houses does one colonel need to own?!"

"Two, as far as I am aware," Eleanor replied simply. "Although, I wouldn't be surprised if we showed up in India and discovered that he had a palace somewhere. You know, since he's the emperor." She winked teasingly at Martha. "I hear the Taj Mahal is vacant at the moment. Perhaps it's waiting for our arrival."

"I knew he was the emperor!" Debbie exclaimed triumphantly.

"I canne believe ye're goin' to *India*." Eleanor's mother took the opportunity to needle her on yet another issue. "They're all savages, the lot of 'em! I read in the *Evening Herald* that two thousand missionaries from the Kirk went all across that godforsaken country given 'em loaves 'n fishes left 'n right and some of 'em pagans dunne even take 'em!"

"Perhaps they should have checked their dietary preferences beforehand," Eleanor replied half-jokingly. "Many Hindus don't eat meat, you know."

"What're they doin' instead? Chompin' on the grass like sheep? Savages, I tell ye. They dunne even wanna know how the civilized folk live. They just wanna stay outside, beatin' their chests like cavemen, worshipping a pile of tidy rocks like it's the bloody pope."

"I believe that the Catholic church said exactly the same thing about the Scots at one point, Mother," Eleanor shot back.

Her sisters both shifted uncomfortably, as Ruthy and Debbie nestled in excitedly for the show.

"Those Catholics aren't Christians," Eleanor's mother scoffed.

"Whatever you say, Mother. I'd rather not discuss religious philosophy on my wedding day. There is a reason we're having the registrar officiate our ceremony in a Druidic linden grove." Eleanor cringed as soon as the words came out of her mouth.

"Eleanor Mary MacLeod, I've half a mind to lick ye for blasphemy right now! You said you were gettin' married in the ruins of an ancient Christian kirk!" her mother exclaimed.

"I am," Eleanor corrected herself. "The ancient Christians took the pagan site and made it Christian. It's a celebration of pagans seeing the light of Christ, don't you think?" She took in a deep breath of relief at her indisputable argument.

"Eleanor Mary MacLeod, yer off yer heid. Ye'll be the death of me, ye know that?" Eleanor's mother muttered.

"I saved your life, Mother, if you'll remember, in more ways than one," Eleanor said sharply.

"So, ye're taking the Orient Express on your honeymoon?!" Mary interrupted.

Eleanor threw her another grateful look. "Yes. We're catching it in Paris and taking it to Constantinople, where we'll stop for a few days to explore, and then catch a steamer to Bombay. I'm not sure what we're going to do once we get to India. Edmund wants it to be a surprise. I suspect he has many old friends and colleagues he'd like to meet up with, although many are coming today. We have thirty guests making the journey from India just to attend the wedding."

"With only six weeks' notice?" Mary asked with surprise.

"I know!" Eleanor exclaimed as she finally relaxed. "We were shocked by it too! We have about three times the number of guests we anticipated. But, some very dear friends have been helping us prepare for the wedding, so luckily it all hasn't fallen on us."

"That Lord Blakeney is a strange bird," Martha pointed out. "He isn't like any lord I've ever seen."

"Have you seen many lords?" Eleanor asked cheekily.

Martha's face turned red with embarrassment. "You know, how lords should be," she corrected herself.

"Well, today you can see if real lords are how you think they should be. There will be at least seven that I know of attending the wedding."

Martha's eyes bulged at the intel. "Seven lords…"

"Several of Edmund's colleagues from the military are lords," Eleanor clarified. "He is not just hopping about the aristocratic circuit for the fun of it. In fact, he and I both find the formality of aristocratic company to be a bit tiresome."

"What a problem to have…" Martha murmured.

Eleanor sighed with annoyance as she took in her most recent attempt at her hair. It was too tight. It made her sharp features even sharper. The wedding styles of the day were designed for cute bobs, not for long, flowing, curly, red tendrils. The Juliet-cap veil she'd procured from a shop in London (by herself, mind you, as she had not wanted to deal with shepherding her sisters through the hustle and bustle of the London wedding circuit, nor had any of her friends from the VAD been able to join her) was meant to cover her head completely, almost like a hat, but her thick, wild hair wasn't having any of it.

She began hurriedly (and a bit violently) undoing the tight braids.

"Here, Ellie, let me help you," Mary suggested as she hopped up from her position and took over the job of unraveling Eleanor's hours of work. "Perhaps a more natural style would suit you better. Your hair is lovely on its own, you know."

"I suppose." Eleanor sighed with stress.

"Debbie, can you name any of these flowers?" Martha asked as the two little girls began wiggling with boredom.

"Rose!" Debbie exclaimed excitedly as she pointed to one of the hundreds of yellow roses on Eleanor's vanity.

"Daffodil!" Ruthy joined in.

"Tulip!" Debbie countered.

"Lily!" Ruthy squealed.

Eleanor took a deep, calming breath, grateful that her nieces' game had taken the burden of the conversation off of her. When Mary had finally finished, Eleanor looked at her haphazard mop of wild hair and sighed again, this time with annoyance.

"It doesn't look very bridal. I'm not sure what I can do at this point. The guests are already arriving."

She looked out the window to spy a gathering of colorfully-dressed visitors. Many men in military uniforms were standing about with their pastel-clad wives (who sported enormous spring hats, just as if they were attending the races), while several women in saris accompanied their husbands, who were decked out in their full traditional Sikh soldier regalia. Even a few women in niqabs accompanied their husbands who sported rather exotic-looking fezes. Her two fiery-haired nephews (who had been left in the charge of their father) were chasing each other across the lawn, while Lord Blakeney's staff was flitting about tidying up various disturbed place-settings and serving champagne. Eleanor was ever so grateful that she didn't have to worry about any minor detail of the party's management—she was certain that her magical allies would have every potential contingency accommodated to the nth degree.

A tap at the door distracted her from her observations.

"Come in?" she called questioningly.

A tall, middle-aged woman with short black hair, fair skin, and rosy cheeks, clad in an elaborate, beaded, violet silk flapper dress, who looked strangely similar to a female version of Edmund,

76

entered the room with a silver tray of champagne in one hand and a heaping basket of pastries in the other.

"Pardon the intrusion, my dear girl..." Eleanor's eyes bulged with surprise as the woman, speaking with a contralto voice and a posh accent very similar to Edmund's, offered her a knowing wink. "But, I thought that perhaps you'd need some food and drink to tide you over before the ceremony."

She put the basket down on the low coffee table before Eleanor's sisters, and then swooped gracefully across the room and placed the silver tray of champagne glasses next to Eleanor.

"We haven't been introduced yet." She turned right around to face Eleanor's sisters. "I'm Kuveni." Eleanor snorted her surprise at Kuveni's audacity in using her own name. "I'm Edmund's cousin from Somerset."

"Sounds foreign," Eleanor's mother muttered.

"Kuveni?" Martha asked. "It really is an odd name."

A subtle recognition of her error crossed Kuveni's expression, and then she melted it into a calm smile. "It is Lankan, darling. My cousin is the Emperor of India, you see, and I am therefore the Empress of Ceylon. Never fear, though, the colonel and I are old allies." Kuveni winked teasingly as she reached out her hand in an affected aristocratic manner to shake the hands of Eleanor's enamored relatives. "I'm just teasing you, of course. You can call me Kate. Kate Marriner."

While Eleanor's sisters were distracted by Kuveni's many unusual qualities, Debbie and Ruthy wiggled their way off the chaise to explore the pastry basket.

"Tss tss!" Martha hissed disapprovingly as she smacked Debbie's roving fingers.

"Oh, my dear girl, you must be famished!" Kuveni exclaimed melodramatically as she addressed the little girl. "Now, which would you like? We have French pain au chocolat, shortbread biscuits (although I'm sure you get enough of those back home), canelé de Bordeaux (I highly recommend those if you haven't tried one before), Kouign-Amann from Bretagne, Belgian waffles, and, of course, miniature pasties if you need something a bit savory. There is beef and chicken."

Eleanor's stomach growled at Kuveni's descriptions.

"My dearest Eleanor, you must be famished too!" Kuveni exclaimed. "Which of these can I use to tempt you? Perhaps one of each?"

Eleanor laughed. "I don't think one of each will be necessary. Perhaps a beef pasty, and that canelé you recommended."

Kuveni clapped excitedly as she picked through the basket to present Eleanor with her requested items. Then, without a word, while Eleanor set about devouring the offering, Kuveni poured five glasses of champagne and presented them to each of the adults.

"Alcohol is the Devil's drink," Eleanor's mother refused with an emphatic hand-gesture.

"Oh dear, is it? Then why did Jesus turn water into wine?" Kuveni asked without a hint of sarcasm. "Someone should have warned him!"

Kuveni smiled at her triumph as Eleanor's mother struggled for a proper response. Kuveni drank down the entire glass in one Yakshini gulp, and then threw a mischievous glance to Eleanor as she placed the empty glass back on the tray.

"It would seem the Devil and I are well-acquainted," Kuveni declared with a teasing wink. "Now, my dear girl, would you like some help with your hair? I have quite a bit of experience with these matters. Tell me, what would you like? Up or down? Modern or classic?"

"I don't know," Eleanor admitted. "I thought I wanted it up so that I could wear the veil, but it isn't looking very good. What do you think I should do, Kuveni?"

Kuveni ran her warm fingers through Eleanor's long, wild tendrils, and Eleanor shivered at the surprisingly relaxing sensation.

"Relax, my dear girl, you are in good hands today," Kuveni said soothingly. "Everything will go smoothly with Lord Blakeney's staff here to help out. Now, I think that your hair is too lovely to hide away under a veil. It is quite rare to have such natural fiery locks… it makes you look quite spritely, I think. So, if I were you, I would leave it loose, tied back with white ribbons and white wildflowers sprinkled throughout, perhaps with a bit of a Roman look to it. Then, if you still want the veil, which I don't think you need, perhaps we can remove the fabric from the bulky cap and attach it directly to your hair with a comb. But, I will leave it up to you. I am at your liberty, my dearest girl. Your wish is my command."

Eleanor smiled and reached up to squeeze Kuveni's hand gratefully. "I will take your suggestion. I am not particularly attached to the idea of the veil, either. I only got it because they are all the rage in the bridal fashion houses. I was actually worried that it would get in the way. I don't want to feel constrained, you know? Perhaps we can see how my hair looks without it, and then we can make the final decision."

"Very wise, Eleanor, very wise," Kuveni said approvingly.

Eleanor's relatives watched with silent interest as Kuveni set about expertly smoothing out the frizz of Eleanor's wild hair (seemingly with only the skill of her touch) until it all calmed down into silky tendrils. Eleanor finally took in a deep, calming breath and began sipping her champagne, as Kuveni continued on with her skilled movements for a very long while until finally she was finished, and Eleanor's hair looked every bit as lovely as she'd hoped it would.

"Thank you, Kuveni." Eleanor fought back surprising tears while Kuveni fit a few final white blossoms from one of the many flower arrangements into her hair.

"It is my pleasure, dearest Eleanor. It is my pleasure, indeed."

Kuveni squeezed her shoulders reassuringly, and then looked around the room and observed the mostly empty pastry basket.

"My dearest young ladies, you must be thirsty! How shameful that I overlooked your needs completely!" she exclaimed as she observed Debbie and Ruthy politely sitting on the chaise with sticky fingers and chocolate-covered chins.

She clapped her hands, and within a few seconds, a knock at the door responded to her command.

"How on earth did you do that?!" Martha exclaimed. "The servants are just waiting outside the door fer yer beck and call?!"

"Nothing but the best for our lovely Eleanor on her wedding day," Kuveni replied evasively as she rushed to open the door.

A young servant girl stood bearing a silver tray with a large carafe of water, five empty glasses, and two tall glasses of milk.

"Thank you, Illa dearest, very well done. You may wait in the hallway for my next command." Kuveni took the tray, and the girl bowed and scampered away.

Kuveni offered the milk to Debbie and Ruthy, who drank down their servings gratefully, and then she politely placed the water in front of Eleanor's mother.

"I don't think Jesus has touched that carafe yet, so it should be safe to drink," she said nonchalantly. "Now, my dear girl, I have something else to discuss with you."

Eleanor looked nervously to her enamored relatives as Kuveni reached into a secret pocket in her dress. She positioned herself to block Eleanor's relatives' view of what she was presenting, and she lowered her voice.

"My dearest Eleanor, I have debated what to do about this since our last chat up in Scotland." A burst of anxiety rushed through Eleanor as Kuveni presented an unassuming wooden jewelry box to her. "I know that you and my darling Edmund have already purchased your wedding rings, but I have something for you. I discussed the matter with Lady Mélusine, and she agreed that you were the rightful recipient."

Eleanor took the box into her hands and opened it.

"Good lord…" Eleanor gasped.

Inside the simple wooden box was the largest blue gem she had ever seen, mounted on a shining silver ring setting covered in tiny, sparkling diamonds.

"It is a blue sapphire," Kuveni explained. "It was Edmund's mother's. She asked me to keep it, so that Edmund could give it to his bride on his wedding day. You may tell him what you must about where it came from, and you may use it as you wish. If you'd like to avoid an uncomfortable conversation, I can keep it for you, my darling girl, but it's yours now."

Eleanor stared at it, trying to decide what to do.

"You may tell him what feels right to you about where it came from," Kuveni reiterated.

"Might I keep it here for a bit while I think about it?" Eleanor asked as she glanced around Kuveni to take in the intrigued expressions of her sisters.

"It is yours, Eleanor. You may do with it whatever you'd like, as long as you keep it safe."

Eleanor nodded her solemn agreement and closed the box.

"Thank you," she whispered into Kuveni's ear as she pulled her into a hug. "For everything."

"It is my pleasure, Mistress Eleanor," Kuveni whispered back.

"Now, shall we take a look at my wedding dress?" Eleanor said cheerfully to her sisters as she let go of Kuveni and walked over to the wardrobe on the other side of the room, leaving the misleadingly simple jewelry box on the vanity.

She carefully removed the dust-bag and stepped back to observe the flowing silk of the stylish, art-deco dress.

"How lovely!" Mary swooned.

"It looks like a nightgown!" Eleanor's mother exclaimed indignantly. "I've never seen any wedding dress that looked like that!"

"It's all the rage in London right now… at least according to the fashion magazines," Martha said with an air of authority as she joined Eleanor to inspect it. "Low waist, flowing silk, delicate lace… It could be worse, Mam. You know many women these days are wearing short wedding dresses. At least Ellie's goes all the way to the floor. Are you sure it will be alright out in the muddy garden?"

"Oh, there is no mud in the garden today," Kuveni interjected.

"I had it custom-made, so the length should work," Eleanor said as she observed the fine stitching at the bottom, grateful to be returning to a mundane conversation.

"Are those pearls sewn into the fabric?" Martha asked as she fingered one of the sleeves.

"I suppose they probably are. I told the seamstress my general ideas, and she concocted this design on my behalf. It is quite comfortable, more comfortable than I imagined a wedding dress ever being, which is nice…"

Kuveni startled as another light knock at the door interrupted them.

"Come in!" Eleanor called.

Edmund peeked his head in, and Eleanor's sisters gasped with disapproving surprise.

"Yer off yer heid!" Eleanor's mother exclaimed. "Men aren't supposed to come anywhere near here! And *you*, Colonel, oughtta know better! Ye'll invite the Devil right on in wit the breeze!"

"I don't believe that my luck could falter on the perfect day that Eleanor MacLeod becomes my wife," Edmund replied in perfect Gaelic.

Eleanor couldn't help but grin at his excellent wielding of the unique linguistic talent that he hadn't yet revealed to her family.

"*You* speak Gaelic?" Eleanor's mother asked with shock. "I thought ye were a sassanack!"

Eleanor blushed with embarrassment at her mother's loud demonstration of several of the characteristics she'd warned Edmund he would have to deal with in his future mother-in-law.

"I am a great many things, Mrs. MacLeod," Edmund said with a charming smile. As she struggled for words, he switched the conversation back into English and addressed the rest of Eleanor's entourage. "My deepest apologies." He couldn't hide a beaming excitement in his expression. He glanced at Kuveni questioningly, and then ignored her strangely familiar appearance to address Eleanor. "I really am sorry for the intrusion, Eleanor, but I wanted to introduce you to someone very special before the ceremony. Might we come in?"

Eleanor nodded her tentative agreement as she noticed Kuveni's growing anxiety.

Edmund, clad handsomely in his military dress uniform, entered the room and gestured for his companion to join him.

A relatively young, strikingly beautiful man with jet-black hair and sparkling blue eyes, clad in the simple clothes of a vicar, followed Edmund into the room. He made eye contact with every single person, offering each one a kind smile, until he landed his attention on Eleanor. She looked at him, and then at Edmund with utter puzzlement.

"Thank the Lord Almighty!" Eleanor's mother exclaimed. "The colonel's come to his senses on behalf of ye both!"

"Eleanor, *this* is Mr. Johnson," Edmund declared.

"Remember, Eleanor? I've told you all about him?" Edmund prompted as if she could have possibly forgotten the false name of the man Edmund believed to be his father.

Eleanor observed the seemingly young man again with intense curiosity. A certain type of silent power seemed to emanate off of him, a silent power not dissimilar to Edmund's, although much more acute.

"Mr. Johnson has offered to officiate our ceremony!" Edmund could not temper the giddiness in his voice.

"That's *Father* Johnson!" Eleanor's mother corrected him.

"It is a pleasure to meet you, Father Johnson," Eleanor said as she glanced over to her mother with embarrassment. Mr. Johnson only smiled reassuringly.

She worked hard to hide her many conflicting thoughts as she reached her hand out to greet him. His soft flesh pulsated with warmth, just as Edmund's did after he'd consumed an excessive amount of hot liquid.

"I cannot properly express what a pleasure it is to finally make your acquaintance, Miss MacLeod," Mr. Johnson said with a wide, happy smile.

He glanced around the room again, landing his gaze on Kuveni. Eleanor caught a hint of disapproval in his expression.

"I think, my dearest MacLeods, that the vicar would like a premarital word with our happy couple. Perhaps we can leave them alone for a bit." Kuveni made her way to the door.

"Eleanor Mary MacLeod, now is yer last chance to repent fer yer sins before ye bind the knot. Ye'd best be a right braw God-fearin' lass fer once in yer life," Eleanor's mother said sternly as Martha helped her up.

Eleanor and Edmund both blushed with embarrassment.

"I assure you with the highest authority, Mrs. MacLeod, that your daughter's repentance is not necessary," Father Johnson said too politely.

Kuveni assertively rallied the illustrious MacLeods into the hallway. "The ceremony is scheduled to start in less than an hour. I will make sure that our guests are ready when you are, Father Johnson."

With a nod of subservience to Mr. Johnson, Kuveni shut the door.

"Well, it looks like we're going to have a church wedding after all," Eleanor quipped. "Are you really a vicar, Father Johnson? I would have expected a more interesting profession for you based on what Edmund has told me."

Edmund's eyes bulged at her irreverence, while Mr. Johnson only smiled indulgently. "My authority on religious matters extends far beyond the petty squabbling of individual institutions, including the Church of England. But, for our large audience today, some semblance of institutional compliance seemed like it would be easiest. It is important, Miss MacLeod, not to let the facts take away from the greater transcendent truths, and the most beautiful truth of the day is that you two will be wed. Please, sit!"

He gestured for them both to sit on the chaise. Edmund took Eleanor's hand tightly into his as Mr. Johnson took a seat on the divan across from them.

"You look so beautiful, Eleanor," Edmund whispered into her ear.

"And you look very dashing, Edmund." Eleanor touched the heavy collection of medals he was wearing for the first time since they'd met. She was surprised he'd brought them to Basingstoke at all, as the last time they'd discussed it several weeks earlier, he'd left them behind in his library in London to avoid the guilty memories that they invoked. "I thought that you'd decided not to wear your uniform today."

"Yes… well, I felt more comfortable in it than in the tuxedo… and Mr. Johnson suggested that perhaps wearing it for such a happy occasion might balance out the painful memories that I associate with it… and with the medals."

"But do *you* feel that way? It's your wedding, darling. You should wear what *you* want to wear." Eleanor couldn't temper a feeling of defensiveness on behalf of her gentle groom. She had already come to recognize that any peep that came out of Mr. Johnson's mouth was pure gospel to Edmund. The fact that he'd been too afraid for over a hundred years to ask the man the simple question of whether or not they were father and son annoyed her. It reminded her of the helplessness she'd felt against her mother's aggressive judgments before she'd found the courage to run away to her spinster aunt in Perth to start a better life for herself, and, as it turned out, for her ungrateful mother.

"Eleanor is right," Mr. Johnson said seriously. Eleanor sighed with relief that her statement had not offended him. "Edmund, it is your decision what to wear on your wedding day. I only made the suggestion because you seemed uncomfortable in the tuxedo. Please, look into yourself and decide what *you* want."

Edmund thought about it for an extended moment while Mr. Johnson waited patiently.

"I suppose this uniform is as good as anything. I'd rather wear something comfortable, or perhaps not anything at all..." He blushed intensely as the words slipped out of his mouth. Eleanor squeezed his hand supportively while Mr. Johnson smiled. "I mean... I mean that... I just meant that none of my options are particularly comfortable..."

"I will leave it up to you," Mr. Johnson reiterated. "I should not have voiced my opinion at all. I have a bit of a problem with people taking my advice too seriously. I must always remind myself that my words have more sway than I realize. After too many centuries to learn the lesson, still I must be reminded. Thank you for doing so, Eleanor. You are a venerable ally."

Edmund perked up at Mr. Johnson's revelation, and as Eleanor let off a burst of anxiety that she knew both of her companions smelled, worrying that Mr. Johnson may have just given away her secret connection to his troop of magical guardians, Edmund took her fear to mean something else entirely.

"Many centuries?" he asked. "How many centuries, exactly?" Eleanor smiled at her gentle groom's proactive approach to questioning, which she had proudly watched him develop over their months together.

Mr. Johnson also noticed the change, and a look of ambivalence crossed his face, some combination of pride and stress.

"I have been around for many centuries. Many millennia, in fact." Edmund stared him down expectantly, and he shifted uncomfortably. "Five thousand years, give or take... I lost track many centuries ago when the calendars changed again."

"Five *thousand* years..." Edmund murmured. "Will I live that long?" Eleanor felt him tense as he prepared for the question he'd been waiting a lifetime to ask. "Are you... are you my father?"

A look of great sadness crossed Mr. Johnson's face. "I am not your father, Edmund. We are related in many ways, but not like that. And I cannot tell you how long you will live because I don't know the answer. I am unique. Nothing about me is a particularly good indication of how others like us will be, and you are far more human than I am. Your humanity makes your resilience harder to predict. But I have already said too much for now."

"Surely you must be able to tell me something?" Edmund pressed, emboldened by the calm confidence of Eleanor's supportive presence.

Mr. Johnson looked even more pained. "It is a profound act of love to withhold important information until the appropriate time, Edmund."

"Eleanor said almost exactly the same thing..." Edmund murmured. "Didn't you, dearest? Just a few weeks ago, after I revealed my secret to you!"

"I did," Eleanor admitted as she worked her hardest not to give off another puff of spicy fear. Mr. Johnson looked similarly concerned by the awkward turn of the conversation. Eleanor's mind rushed through her limited options. Her deep desire to be honest with Edmund worked its way to the surface, and as she contemplated the mess she was about to make, she simply couldn't help herself. She would not, she decided in that moment, lie openly to her groom on her wedding day. "Edmund, darling, I have a confession to make."

Mr. Johnson's concern morphed into a distinct look of fearful desperation, which he quickly transitioned into resignation.

"What is it, Eleanor?" Edmund asked nervously as he glanced over to Mr. Johnson, who now looked entirely calm.

Eleanor reached over and gathered the small wooden jewelry box from her vanity.

"Edmund, darling, a woman came to me and said she was your cousin. She gave me this box, and told me that it had been entrusted into her care by your mother. It was your mother's wish that you have this token to give to your bride on your wedding day, but she didn't feel like she could give it to you directly. She too believed that truths have their proper timing, and for whatever reason, it was not time for you to know her." She looked straight at Mr. Johnson. "I found her logic to be rather cruel, but I didn't think it was my place to argue. She insisted on my confidence, which I have now broken, but it is not acceptable in my book to lie to my husband on my wedding day. Perhaps you can shed some light on her logic, Mr. Johnson?"

Eleanor handed the box to Edmund, and he gasped as he opened it up and observed the enormous sparkling blue sapphire. He looked straight at Mr. Johnson.

Mr. Johnson paused for an extended moment as he considered his response. "There are powers far beyond my control that dictate how these things must be. It is not my place, nor is it hers, to tell you truths that you are not ready to know, Edmund. The misery brought on by thwarting these powers is greater than anything you have ever known—greater even than what you suffered during the wretched war. I only know them myself because I have lived for a very long time, and I have suffered mightily many times when I have made the mistake of giving into my base instincts. For your sake and mine, Edmund, I must suffer the agony of withholding the truths that you so desperately think you want to know until it is time for you to know them, and now is not that time."

Eleanor could feel Edmund's heart racing, and her heart almost broke as she watched the grimace of utter devastation work its way onto his face.

"I knew I shouldn't have asked…" Edmund muttered. "Please, Mr. Johnson, don't leave! Please stay for the wedding!"

Mr. Johnson threw Eleanor a distinct look of despair as he struggled for words.

"Edmund, darling, Mr. Johnson isn't going to leave just because you asked him a perfectly valid question. Is he?" She threw Mr. Johnson a commanding look. "In fact, I'd wager that Mr. Johnson agrees that you should ask every question that enters your head, no matter how fanciful. It is not healthy to avoid asking perfectly valid questions out of fear, is it, Mr. Johnson?"

"Edmund, my dearest boy, I am not going to leave," Mr. Johnson reiterated as he stood up and took a seat beside them on the chaise. He took Edmund's left hand into his. "I promise you that my required silence hurts me just as much as it hurts you, but it doesn't mean that I love you any less. I told you how much I loved you when I collected you from the orphanage, didn't I? And when I collected you from Abdul Barr and brought you back to England? And when I saw you off to London after your unfortunate incident with the soldiers in Bath? And when I came to you a few years ago after the war? I mean it as much now as I did all of those other times. I love you, Edmund, as if you were my own son, and I couldn't be prouder of the man you've become."

Edmund looked frustrated with himself as he fought back tears, and Eleanor held his other hand silently in hers, fighting back her own empathetic tears and stroking his palm gently while Mr. Johnson maintained his strong grip.

"I simply cannot be here all the time, Edmund, no matter how much I want to. It is not my place to stand by your side, otherwise, you will not develop on your own. My influence is too strong. But it is one of the greatest privileges of my life to be able to join you on a happy occasion such as this one, and I would not miss it for anything in the world. *Anything*, Edmund, do you understand?" Edmund nodded his unconvinced agreement. "And your lovely bride could not be more correct: You, Edmund, should never again be afraid of asking questions. Please, my dearest boy, ask everything that comes into your mind. You must forgive *me* for not being able to offer you sufficient answers. It is my burden, not yours."

The three of them sat for many minutes of silent catharsis, until Edmund finally gathered his wits. "Is it true, then? What this woman told Eleanor? That ring was my mother's?"

Mr. Johnson took the box into his hand and inspected the ring. He closed his eyes for an extended moment, as if he were meditating on the question, and then reopened them. "Yes. It is true. I was not there when your mother gave this ring to the woman in question, because I was not in the room when you were born. It was a place only for women. But your mother gave this ring to her, and she gave it to Eleanor, fulfilling your mother's wishes. It is yours to do with as you please."

"I have a cousin then?" Edmund asked astutely.

Mr. Johnson smiled and nodded encouragingly. "That woman is not really your cousin. That was a lie she told Eleanor to make things easier. You will know who she is someday, and she will be most delighted when that day comes. It is not here yet."

"But she is not my mother," Edmund pushed.

"No, she is not your mother. Your mother is dead, Edmund." He glanced to Eleanor and then paused to re-think whatever he was going to say. "She was human, and you were born a long time ago."

"Yes... yes, I suppose I was..." Edmund murmured.

Mr. Johnson reluctantly let go of Edmund's hand and stood up. "Now, your vicar is dreadfully late for the ceremony, and as lovely as that fashionable kimono is, I believe Miss MacLeod still needs to put on her wedding dress. Since we have already disrupted one of many Scottish superstitions by allowing you two to see each other before the wedding, I will leave it to you how you want to proceed. I will be down at the Druidic linden grove preparing. I hope you don't mind, Edmund, but I have incorporated a few of our people's traditions into the ceremony. There will be nothing that will tip off the generals as to your foreign background, of course, and nothing that will upset the puritanical tendencies of your mother, Miss MacLeod. Presenting myself as a man of the cloth, I've found, is highly effective in orchestrating these cultural coups without prompting too many inconvenient questions from our pious audiences." He winked, and Eleanor sighed with relief as she felt Edmund relax.

Mr. Johnson pulled them both up into a tight hug, and then kissed each of their foreheads.

"I am so happy for you both. It is a privilege I have only experienced a handful of times in five thousand years to join two such worthy souls in matrimony. I hope that I will do justice to the love that you feel for each other. It is a rare and beautiful gift that should not be underappreciated, nor should either of you ever feel the remotest guilt for reveling in its unique pleasures."

Mr. Johnson made his way to the door, and offered them a polite *namaste*. "I will see you both soon," he reiterated. "When you are ready."

Eleanor squeezed Edmund's hand as Mr. Johnson closed the door behind him, and they heard the click of the door's lock.

"Well, my beautiful, mostly-human fiancé," she said as she untied the loose belt of her kimono and let it fall onto the floor, "shall we make our final preparations? I believe that the vicar has given us his blessing."

Edmund pulled her into his arms and crushed her into a frenzied kiss. Her head spun as he let go and steadied her.

"God, how I love you, Eleanor," he whispered as he kissed her one last time before pulling down the lace curtains and then kneeling down before her.

She gave in completely to his skilled touch, and as she let her satisfied sighs echo through her bridal chamber, she finally, for the first time, reveled in the unburdened bliss that Edmund had already known for months. *Thank you*, she prayed to whomever was listening. And then, her prayers dissolved into a guttural moan.

"God, how I love you, Edmund," she whispered.

And so together, as their five hundred guests were slowly meandering into the early-blooming primeval woods, the two lovebirds enjoyed their last delightful moments of guilt-free, sinfully unmarried bliss.

CHAPTER 6 – AROUND THE FIRE

Edmund and Eleanor giggled guiltily as they dashed hand in hand across the violet lawn, straight over a pastoral stone bridge across a seasonal stream, to the mossy pathway through the early-blooming woods.

"It's so magical!" Eleanor exclaimed. The pathway was carpeted in pink blossoms, and sweetly scented petals fluttered in the air all around them like soft, fragrant snow.

"I think we're late to our own wedding… at our own house. It's a bit shameful, really," Edmund whispered as the gentle tunes of a string quartet echoed in the warm spring breeze.

Eleanor squeezed his hand. "We'll face the firing squad together, Colonel."

They slowed their pace and took deep, calming breaths.

Edmund straightened his posture and let the beauty of the moment wash over him as they reached the edge of the linden grove clearing. As Father Johnson noticed them and smiled welcomingly, his attention spread like a wave through the crowd, all of whom stood up from their white chairs to catch a glimpse of the happy couple.

Kuveni, who stood in the last row at the edge of the aisle, still in her preferred disguise as Edmund's aristocratic cousin, handed Eleanor a thick bouquet of thistles interspersed with babies' breath, and couldn't help herself as she reached forward to squeeze Eleanor's hand encouragingly.

Edmund paused to consider her presence with the new intel afforded by their conversation with Mr. Johnson, but the sea of eyes bearing down on them didn't allow him to contemplate how she might really be related to him for long.

"I'm so happy for you, old man!" Edward Rutherford whispered as he reached forward from the row in front of Kuveni to shake Edmund's hand. Edward's sour wife refused to even look at the happy couple as she stared distractedly into the distance.

"I am so glad you're here," Edmund whispered back as he shook Edward's hand. "We will talk more at the reception."

"I'm looking forward to it!" Edward declared with a jolly chuckle.

As Edward let go of Edmund's hand and Eleanor positioned her bouquet, the string quartet began Tchaikovsky's wedding march.

Edmund and Eleanor smiled graciously and offered polite nods to their supportive guests as they made their way slowly down the petal-blanketed aisle.

"The groom doesn't give away the bride!" Eleanor's mother hissed as they reached the front row. "What'll the vicar think?!"

"Quiet, Mam!" Mary hissed back.

Eleanor caught Father Johnson offering her mother a subtle nod of disapproval, and then glanced over to catch Debbie and Ruthy squealing with excitement (while their brothers naughtily poked each other), and Mary and Martha smiling happily beside their mildly bored husbands. Her mother's self-righteous posture deflated, and she finally held her tongue.

Eleanor and Edmund stood underneath an arbor that was covered from the ground up in fresh, open, wild purple morning glories, despite the sun's position low in the afternoon sky. Father Johnson stood slightly above them on a grassy pedestal surrounded by the mossy stone Druidic ruins. Behind him flickered hundreds of candles, placed precariously everywhere that a candle could stand up on the stone ruins, creating the distinct impression of a pagan altar.

Father Johnson gestured for the audience to sit, and he waited patiently for their creaky chairs and rustling beads to dissolve into silence.

Edmund and Eleanor kept their hands and their eyes locked on each other's as they took deep, calming breaths.

"We are gathered here today on this beautiful spring day to celebrate the joining of these two people—Edmund George Marriner and Eleanor Mary MacLeod—in holy matrimony."

Edmund's eyes bulged, and Eleanor squeezed his hands supportively as she realized that Father Johnson must have just given away Edmund's middle name to him for the very first time, as he had told her many times already that he did not have a middle name, nor did he know where his surname came from.

Father Johnson smiled and waited for them to compose themselves.

"I have officiated many weddings in my day, many more, I suspect, than anyone in this audience can imagine, but it is a rare and beautiful gift for me to stand before you today with two such virtuous souls to share with them this holiest of occasions. Many years ago, Edmund told me that he didn't understand how Shakespeare had been able to write such copious volumes of verse about love. He couldn't fathom that anyone, even a great master such as Shakespeare, could have so much to say on a topic that seemed so simple. I suspect that today, Edmund can fathom it a bit more."

Edmund smiled and nodded his agreement, and Father Johnson smiled and continued on with his sermon.

"Many a vicar has been known to use the occasion of a wedding to put forth a sermon of the ages. A sermon he is sure will bring the lost souls back into his chapel on Sunday morning, and that might stir the souls of those he believes to still be lost in godless ignorance into a spiritual quickening of sorts. I have always found this practice distasteful."

He paused for his audience to predictably mutter their surprise at his controversial statement.

"You see, this wedding today between these two worthy souls is not an occasion that requires a vicar to stand before you and preach about God, because God is here, celebrating with you." He glanced straight to the back row to Kuveni, and then over to Lord Blakeney who stood on the sidelines alongside a stern older man in a formal butler's uniform, monitoring the crowd. "God does not need a human vicar to spout his own opinions on earthly matters under the guise of the lord's decrees, nor does he need any mundane superstitions to distract from the beautiful transcendent truths of the day." He moved his gaze to Eleanor's mother.

"The vast volumes of religious scripture that have been written and edited by men over the ages cannot in the slightest capture the miracle of two virtuous souls who have found each other, who have recognized their connection, and who have chosen to commit themselves to each other for the rest of their earthly days. Such miracles speak for themselves, and I encourage you all to join me now in taking a moment to appreciate the miracle that you are witnessing before you today."

Father Johnson watched and waited patiently for the crowd to acknowledge his statement, while Edmund and Eleanor only smiled.

"Now, in honor of the ancient traditions of Eleanor's family, I will bind the hands of these two virtuous souls together, as a symbol of their commitment and a reminder that from this point forward they must move forward as one, as two perfect halves of a more perfect whole."

He presented a green silk ribbon embroidered with delicate thistles from his pocket and carefully tied their hands together in a loose knot.

"Now, in honor of the ancient traditions of Edmund's family, these two halves of a perfect whole will walk together around the altar seven times, offering their vows to each other before the sacred fire."

Father Johnson nodded encouragingly, and Edmund smiled at the inclusion of something, *anything*, that connected him to the traditions of his mysterious ancestry. Many of the Indian guests whispered curiously to each other as they recognized the familiar tradition, while Eleanor's mother muttered unhappily about the seemingly pagan turn of events.

Edmund and Eleanor carefully walked their first circle around the altar, while Father Johnson whispered quiet mantras under his breath. Edmund glanced up at him as he noticed the odd detail of the ritual and the extremely foreign tongue of the exercise, and Father Johnson stopped his mantras and smiled.

"Please, my children, whisper your first vows to each other. They are for your ears only," Father Johnson suggested.

Eleanor's mind raced at the unanticipated improvisation, so much so that after the fact, despite her deep love of her husband and her gratitude for the unusual ceremony, she could not, for her life, remember what either of them had vowed. She was certain it involved love, emotional and physical support, understanding, and... what else? *Seven* vows. There was something humorous in there, she was sure, and a reference to Ovid...

They walked hand in hand, whispering their silly loving statements to each other until they were finished, and they stood before Father Johnson and the altar, ready for the ceremony to continue on to its juiciest part.

"Now the couple will exchange their tokens," Father Johnson announced. "Repeat after me, Edmund…"

Edmund smiled as he reached into his pocket and pulled out the mysterious blue sapphire ring.

"Lord almighty!" Martha exclaimed.

Eleanor smiled at her sister's predictable reaction and held out her hand.

"With this ring, I thee wed…"

"With this ring, I thee wed…"

"I, Edmund George Marriner, take you, Eleanor Mary MacLeod, as my lawfully wedded wife. To love, honor, and cherish; to revel in the unique pleasures of true honesty; and to know one another as only two connected souls can. To help each other stay in the light, no matter how dark the world happens to be around us, and to make our own light when there is none to be found. To be your devoted husband, until death parts us."

Eleanor fought back tears as her gentle groom repeated the statement with an expression of pure, unabashed joy on his face.

When he was finished, she reached into the pocket she'd had designed into her dress for the express purpose of carrying the ring, and removed the small silver box with delicate thistles engraved into it that held the simple ring Edmund had chosen when they'd gone to the silversmith in Edinburgh several weeks earlier.

"Repeat after me, Eleanor," Father Johnson said as Eleanor took a deep breath.

"With this ring, I thee wed…"

"With this ring, I thee wed…"

"I, Eleanor Mary MacLeod, take you, Edmund George Marriner, as my lawfully wedded husband. To love, honor, and cherish; to revel in the unique pleasures of true honesty; and to know one another as only two connected souls can. To help each other stay in the light, no matter how dark the world happens to be around us, and to make our own light when there is none to be found. To be your wife, until death parts us."

Edmund could not hold back a tear in each eye as Eleanor gently placed the ring on his finger, and then she winked and smiled triumphantly.

"By all the power vested in me, I now pronounce you man and wife!" Father Johnson declared. "You may kiss the bride."

Edmund gathered Eleanor into his arms and dipped her into the most scandalous kiss that any of their human guests had seen performed in public, but the cheers and shocked whispers did not dissuade them from taking their time. And it was *their* time. Their first beautiful moment of enjoying the physical pleasures of marriage.

But, as the audience prepared to shower them in rice and flower petals, a loud clap of thunder and a flash of lightning brought everyone to attention as the sky turned an ominous dark gray.

Eleanor glanced over to Father Johnson, whose eyes momentarily flashed their demonic black as a look of pure fury entered his expression, and then he glanced over to Lord Blakeney, who took the crowd's sudden panic at the imminent rain shower as an opportunity to disappear unobserved. A few seconds later, his stern butler companion disappeared as well.

Eleanor glanced back to Edmund to see whether he'd noticed their supernatural exit, but Edmund was focused entirely on Kuveni, who was calmly shepherding the crowd back towards the house.

"Don't worry, my darlings, everything is under control," she reassured the passersby. "Lord Blakeney's staff has prepared the carriage house to accommodate the fine English weather. But, I reckon this storm will pass before we'll need to move inside."

She glanced back to Father Johnson, who offered her a grateful nod.

"My dearest children, please do not panic," he said with feigned calm to Edmund and Eleanor. "I will go check on the preparations for an indoor reception with Lord Blakeney. You should both make your way back to the house. And, Edmund, I am not going anywhere, so please don't worry that you won't see me again today. Alright?"

Edmund nodded his agreement and squeezed Eleanor's hand as Father Johnson jogged straight into the forest. But, as they took a moment to watch their guests disperse haphazardly, the clouds opened up, and the torrential downpour that the thunder had forewarned rained down upon them. A chorus of hisses echoed as the water put out the hundreds of ceremonial candles.

"Your dress! It will be ruined!" Edmund exclaimed as he crouched his tall body over her in a failed attempt to keep her dry.

"You said you would rather be naked today, didn't you? Perhaps this storm will hurry the process along," Eleanor laughed.

Edmund seemed unconvinced as he gathered up the wet silk of her skirt in an attempt to keep it out of the fresh mud.

"Please, Edmund, don't worry about my dress! I was only going to wear it once anyway. We have quite a wedding memory now, don't we? I think it's rather refreshing! Don't you? And very authentically Scottish. Besides, I thought you loved the rain!"

Edmund pulled her into another romantic dip.

"God, how I love you, Eleanor," he whispered as he pulled her back up into her standing position.

As another clap of thunder morphed the heavy rain into hail, Eleanor squealed, and Edmund rushed to shield her head from the painful pellets.

"Come!" A woman in a soaked niqab with only her eyes showing approached them. "Come with me. I will take you on a shortcut to the carriage house. Lord Blakeney had it made especially for you." She spoke with a scratchy voice and a lilting accent that Eleanor didn't recognize.

"Why would he do that?" Edmund asked as he assessed the woman skeptically.

"In case of an instance exactly like this one!" the woman argued with obvious annoyance. "Now, come!"

Edmund looked back to where Kuveni had been standing, but the hail storm had dispersed the last of the lingering guests with great haste, and Kuveni appeared to have followed them, leaving Edmund and Eleanor alone with the mysterious stranger.

"Come!" she hissed again. "Before it's too late!"

Assuming that the mysterious woman was one of Edmund's guardians, and that a sudden, unexpected rainstorm was not the only potential danger facing them at that very moment, Eleanor took his hand.

"Show us the path."

Eleanor gathered the soaked silk of her skirt into her hand, and Edmund took off his coat and attempted to hold it over her as they scampered through the wet forest, deeper and deeper into the woods.

"The carriage house is that way," he said as they reached a stray ancient linden. He pointed the opposite direction of where their mysterious guide was headed. "I have lived on this property for many years, and I know it intimately. Now, you will explain to me where you think you're taking us." He positioned himself protectively in front of Eleanor.

The woman glanced back and forth between Edmund and Eleanor, and Eleanor could have sworn that she saw a hint of pride in the woman's eyes.

"Very good, Colonel," she said with a shrill cackle. "Very good, indeed!"

Edmund's eyes turned black, and without another word, he grabbed Eleanor's hand and guided her at his top human speed straight into the forest in the opposite direction of where the woman had intended to guide them.

"Wait!" the woman screeched.

In a blur, the woman was standing before them again.

"Edmund, darling, calm yourself." Eleanor threw an enraged look at their mysterious adversary. "What game are you playing?"

The woman observed Edmund's vulnerable state and Eleanor's utter lack of fear at his demonic trait, and she took a step back to observe them again while Eleanor rubbed Edmund's back soothingly. The woman began muttering something incomprehensible to herself as she backed up several more feet until she hit a tree.

"Edmund, darling, take deep breaths, in and out," Eleanor whispered. "Yes, that's better. Close your eyes and count to three. Let the adrenaline pass."

He followed her instructions, and finally reopened his eyes, returning them to their natural human hazel.

"Darkness and light, darkness and light, all will be right when darkness meets light…" The woman sang the verse as if it was a nursery rhyme.

"How did you do that? How did you move so quickly? Are you like me? Like Mr. Johnson? Can I move that fast if I learn how?" Edmund asked her as he gathered his wits.

His curiosity morphed into fear as the woman's song became more frenetic, and she reached up to her face to scratch at the veil of her wet niqab. They noticed her monstrous, skeletal, clawed hands simultaneously, as she used them to rip gaping wounds into her own arms. Red metallic blood oozed out of the grotesque injuries.

"Darkness and light!" she screeched. "All will be right when darkness meets light!"

She ripped a heavy branch off of the blossoming tree and threw it onto the ground, creating a barrier between herself and them. She seemed momentarily surprised by her own strength, and then she began screaming nonsensical mantras as she stomped on the branch until it collapsed into smithereens. Eleanor noticed that the woman wasn't wearing any shoes. Her feet were just as ghoulish as her hands were.

As Edmund's eyes returned to their demonic black and he pushed Eleanor behind him protectively, Eleanor noticed the woman's eyes light up as she smelled his fresh burst of fear, but unlike Edmund's disgust at the aroma, Eleanor caught a distinct look of pleasure in the woman's expression.

"Edmund, we must leave here!" Eleanor hissed. "We must escape now! She's dangerous! Your cousin warned me that some of your people aren't good like you are! I think she's one of the bad ones! *Run!*"

"RUN!" the woman screeched as her voice dissolved into mad cackles. "Run, Young Edmund, Run!"

Eleanor grabbed Edmund's hand and pulled him along, out of his adrenaline-enhanced stupor. They took off running a second time, but this time the woman didn't follow, she only screeched her eerie song louder and louder while she ripped more branches from the tree until the distance spared their burning ears.

Eleanor held the skirt of her dress up as they ran and ran through the craggy, muddy forest, until they reached the far edge of the violet lawn.

As they burst into the manicured garden behind the house, the storm had already passed, and steam was rising peacefully from the lawn as the warm sun beat down upon them. The contrast between the two environments was hard for her overwhelmed mind to comprehend.

"Good lord, what just happened?" Edmund murmured as he struggled to catch his breath.

"Edmund... darling..." Eleanor struggled to catch her own. "Take... deep... breaths. Bring yourself back under control..."

Edmund crouched down as he tried his hardest to follow her advice, but she could still hear his racing heart. After a minute of attempting to ignore his plight, Edmund collapsed onto the ground and buried his face in his knees.

"I'm sorry, Eleanor," he whispered. "I'm so sorry. I don't even know how, but I'm sure this was my fault."

"This was *not* your fault, Edmund," Eleanor said sternly.

He did not accept her assertion. "Who knows what she could have done to us, Eleanor! Something wicked and violent! I don't know how, but I could feel her darkness. It was consuming her! And I couldn't have stopped her! I don't even know what she can do! You saw how fast she moved! And that branch! Even I can't rip a branch off a tree like that with my bare hands!"

"Colonel? Is everything alright?" Mr. Valov, Edmund's devoted Czech butler, noticed them from his position in the doorway of the carriage house and immediately set out across the violet lawn to intercept them.

"Edmund, darling, close your eyes and count to three!" Eleanor hissed as his demonic black eyes stubbornly remained intact.

"We're perfectly fine, Mr. Valov!" Eleanor called desperately. "There's no need to come to our rescue!"

"I'm sorry. I'm so, so sorry, Eleanor. You didn't agree to marry into *that*..." Edmund murmured.

"I love you, Edmund. I love *all* that you are, remember?"

"I'm sorry. I'm so, so sorry," he repeated.

"You have nothing to be sorry about, darling. Nothing at all." She kneeled down in the wet grass to rub Edmund's back. "There are plenty of lunatics in this world to go around, human and non-human alike, as it turns out. We have survived them before, and we will survive them again. We will help each other stay in the light from now on. Remember? We vowed it just a few minutes ago! Now, don't think anything of this startling incident. Don't think anything of it at all. Whoever she was, she means nothing to you. Nothing more than that madwoman who killed poor Ingrid Kauter. We evaded both of them, and if we face another mad adversary, we will triumph again."

"I'm so, so sorry," Edmund repeated despairingly.

"*Mon dieu!*" Mélusine exclaimed in the form of Lord Blakeney. She ran towards them from the carriage house, intercepting Mr. Valov. She engaged him in a heated debate, and then Mr. Valov shrugged unhappily and headed back towards the reception.

"What happened? Your guests are all waiting inside for you!" Mélusine exclaimed as she reached their position.

Kuveni ran at her top human speed to join them. "My darlings, what happened?! I thought you were right behind me when the hail started!"

Kuveni leaned down to observe Edmund's altered state, and then muttered something under her breath.

"I believe we just met a dangerous adversary," Eleanor said as she threw them both a desperate look. "A woman in a mohammedan shroud said that you had cleared a special path for us to the carriage house, but she attempted to lead us astray. My professional opinion is that she was certifiably mad."

Mélusine's eyes turned black with rage. "Stay here. *All* of you."

"Where does he think he's going?" Edmund asked as he watched her head determinedly into the forest.

"Lord Blakeney is going to investigate the scene of the crime, I suspect." Eleanor returned to rubbing Edmund's back. "But that isn't important now. You must focus on getting yourself back under control, darling. We can't move from here until you are back to your normal self. Now breathe in and out slowly, and think about the lovely truth that we are married now. Let that thought overwhelm your adrenaline."

"I'm sorry, Eleanor… just give me another minute," Edmund whispered. "You are so wonderfully patient with me."

Kuveni kept watch as Father Johnson appeared from around the back of the carriage house and ran at his fastest inconspicuous human speed to intercept them.

"Edmund?" he said concernedly as he reached them and took one good look at their tattered state.

Edmund looked up at Father Johnson with his black eyes, and Father Johnson could not hide his surprise at the development. Eleanor was not sure whether his surprise was because he had not anticipated that Edmund would demonstrate the physical malady at all, or that Edmund didn't seem to recognize that it was happening.

"I am perfectly alright," Edmund insisted unconvincingly as he struggled to stand up.

"Edmund, my dear boy, there is no need to lie to me," Father Johnson said calmly as he reached out his arm and pulled him up in one swift movement. "Come, I will help you practice some techniques for getting yourself back under control. I would have practiced these with you years ago if I'd realized you were struggling this much."

Kuveni helped Eleanor up. "Come, my dearest girl, I will help you get cleaned up. Mr. Johnson will stay with Edmund for now, and he will let us know when your gentle husband is ready to join you for the reception. Won't you, Father?"

"I will." Father Johnson agreed with new humility in his expression as Edmund's black gaze moved over to Kuveni. Eleanor wondered if perhaps Kuveni had been reporting Edmund's struggles to Father Johnson for quite some time, and he had not fully recognized the extent of Edmund's plight until that moment.

"You are her, then? The one who gave Eleanor my mother's ring?" Edmund asked as he looked her up and down.

She looked to Mr. Johnson. "I am."

"And you were there when I was born?"

"I was," she agreed. "I was the first person to have the privilege of welcoming you into this world, my dearest boy."

Edmund thought about her statement for many seconds of awkward silence as he decided what to ask her next. "But you are not my cousin? You look like me. We age similarly. We must be related somehow. You aren't... you aren't my sister, are you?"

Kuveni threw an apologetic glance to Mr. Johnson, and then cleared her throat, preparing herself to clean up the mess that her shapeshifting decision had created for their farce.

"No, Young Edmund, I am not your cousin or your sister. Despite our outward similarities, we are not related by blood at all. But it is not time for us to know each other yet. Mr. Johnson's wisdom in these matters is always correct. Now, we must all be patient until the beautiful day comes when we can be honest. That day is not here yet, but you can still revel in your honesty with Eleanor. It will have to be enough for now."

She nodded her subservience to Mr. Johnson, who offered her a nod of approval.

"Now, I will help Eleanor mend her wedding dress, and you two should spend a few minutes together, discussing things man-to-man."

She gathered Eleanor's hand into hers affectionately, and Eleanor offered Edmund a gentle kiss on the cheek.

"I'll see you in a few minutes, *husband*," she said with a wink.

Edmund watched with his demonic black eyes as Eleanor scampered alongside Kuveni back towards the house.

"You are a good girl, Eleanor. The best I've ever met," Kuveni whispered as they reached the front door. "Now, let us indulge in some Yakshini magic while the men discuss darker topics, shall we?" Kuveni giggled mischievously as she pulled Eleanor into the house.

Eleanor's strange new life as the wife of Edmund George Marriner had officially begun.

"What in the bloody hell was that?!" Eleanor exclaimed as soon as she and Kuveni were alone inside the house.

Kuveni moved to speak, and then dissolved completely instead.

"Kuveni?" Eleanor's voice echoed in the empty foyer.

Kuveni reappeared in her exact same position.

"I was making sure we were alone." She took Eleanor's hand and led her into the parlor. "The madwoman was Edmund's aunt, Surpanakha, and you were right, she is certifiably mad. If ever you encounter a person with a mangled face, or dressed in a way that can hide such an injury, you must escape, Eleanor. Do you understand? She can easily kill you and Edmund if she decides to do so. She is one of the most powerful Rakshasas on Earth, and she is evil, through and through."

"She let us escape…" Eleanor murmured.

"Yes, she did. If she had not decided to let you go, you would not be here now."

"Edmund's aunt..." Eleanor thought out loud. "His father isn't here, is he?!"

"Edmund's father is not here. Your distinguished guests would have learned all about our secret world if he'd decided to make an appearance. Subtlety has never been one of his strong suits. As far as we are all aware, Edmund's father remains unaware of his existence, which is a blessing for everyone, especially Edmund. Lord Vibhishana's wisdom has been most infallible in his efforts to keep Edmund protected."

"Lord Vibhishana... Is that Mr. Johnson's real name?"

Kuveni looked annoyed at herself for giving away the intel so casually. "Yes, Mr. Johnson is Lord Vibhishana." She paused for a long moment to consider how much to reveal, and then she lowered her voice. "He is Edmund's uncle, but his interest in Master Edmund, and his love for him, run far deeper than a familial sense of responsibility. Lord Vibhishana is the most virtuous soul who has ever walked the face of the earth, and his power and his wisdom go far beyond his age and his unusual race. He is..." she lowered her voice even more... "He is... holy. As holy as one can be, if you know what I mean." Eleanor's lack of response demonstrated that she did not, in fact, know what Kuveni meant. Kuveni muttered something to herself, and then dropped into a whisper. "He has been very busy throughout the millennia helping humans follow the path of righteousness, and he was especially busy... during the *Roman* era." Kuveni paused for dramatic effect. "His story that time around didn't end particularly well. Lord Vibhishana had quite a mess to clean up after his public crucifixion, and the strategy he chose had much more far-reaching consequences than any of us anticipated at the time."

Kuveni waited for Eleanor to fully comprehend her meaning.

"Are you serious?" Eleanor's mind began racing as Kuveni nodded. "That means the story had more truth to it than I thought it did. That means... that means that *He* officiated our wedding?!"

Eleanor ran through her memory of their earlier conversation with the new shocking context.

"Oh for Christ's sake!" Eleanor slammed her hand over her mouth as the curse tumbled out of her, but Kuveni only chuckled. Eleanor did not find the situation particularly funny. "Kuveni, I teased him like I was a wee cheeky lass! I told him that he should have a more interesting profession than being a vicar!"

"Now, now, Eleanor dearest, never you worry. Lord Vibhishana has a very good sense of humor. I would not worry for one second about offending him. He is an excellent judge of character, and your character, my dear girl, is very clear."

"Good lord…" Eleanor murmured.

"Is he how you thought he would be? He is quite different from how religious conservatives like to think of him. It has been that way since very early on."

"Ha! You can say that again! My mother would go absolutely mad if she knew how normal he was!"

Kuveni smiled. "I'm not sure how many humans would think of him as normal. Most people, I think, would be preoccupied with the fact that he isn't human."

"Everyone wants him to be whatever is convenient for them. I'm rather pleased that he has his own life to focus on, actually. It confirms that he has better things to do than to care about my father's poor judgment and my subsequent status as a bastard."

"Oh yes, he has many more important things to care about than that," Kuveni agreed. "Marriage didn't even exist in its modern form in Roman times, you know. But humans have always been very good at coming up with systems to judge and oppress each other. It makes him very sad that his messages of peace and acceptance are used to cause such suffering."

"It makes me sad too… I'm glad we have that in common."

"You have many things in common." Kuveni reached forward to stroke Eleanor's cheek affectionately. "Your capacity for unconditional love is a rare and beautiful gift, my dear girl. A gift that you should feel great pride in sharing with Edmund. You two are perfectly matched in that way."

"I hope so." Eleanor fought back a wave of bewilderment.

"I know so," Kuveni said reassuringly, but then she became more serious. "It is important that Edmund does not know any of this, of course. Do you understand, Eleanor? None of it. We have kept Lord Vibhishana's name from him for all these years because my beautiful boy can be rather tenacious in his research when he has a bee in his bonnet, and it would not take very long for him to uncover Lord Vibhishana's more ancient past; it is well-documented and rather famous, especially in India. He is referenced by name in both of the most canonical ancient Sanskrit epics. We do not want Master Edmund reading them yet, and we do not think it is a coincidence that his distaste for religious philosophy has allowed him to avoid stumbling upon them on his own. It is rather remarkable, actually, given how many thousands of books he's read, that he has never come across it, and Lord Vibhishana intends to keep it that way."

"I knew his life was complicated, but I had no idea, did I? We are not operating on a human scale of complexity here."

"I'm sorry, Mistress Eleanor. I hope we will not prove to be too much for you. If it is any consolation, you are the strongest human Lady Mélusine and I have ever encountered. If anyone can master the ins and outs of our world's madness, it is you."

She reached forward and placed her hand gently on Eleanor's stained, ripped wedding dress. She closed her eyes, whispered a quiet mantra, and in just a few seconds, the fabric healed itself and the stains disappeared.

Eleanor looked down with wonder to inspect Kuveni's handiwork.

"As good as new!" Kuveni declared triumphantly.

"Remarkable." Eleanor felt the freshly mended fabric. No trace of the mud remained in the silk.

"So, can Edmund's aunt control the weather, then?" Eleanor asked as her mind returned to the strange encounter. "She led us into the woods as soon as the storm began."

"No, only Yakshas can control the weather. The thunderstorm was caused by some ancient Yakshas who were unhappy to have been snubbed."

Eleanor was taken aback by the idea. "Blimey, Kuveni, you could have warned me about the stakes when we were making the guest list. We could have invited them if it really mattered so much."

"They wouldn't have been on the list. I would have snubbed them myself. They did not deserve to attend Master Edmund's happy occasion," Kuveni scoffed. "Lady Mélusine dealt with them quickly and cleanly, but their interruption left you and Edmund open to Surpanakha. She took advantage of our distraction to ensnare you. We never would have left you alone in the linden grove if we'd had any inkling that she was there. I will offer my gratitude to the gods every night for the rest of my life that she chose to let you go."

Eleanor closed her eyes as she thought back to the terrifying moments, which were even more terrifying in retrospect now that she was fully aware of the mortal danger they'd narrowly escaped.

"She was planning to kill us, I think… but then she stopped herself. Edmund's eyes turned black, and I didn't fully understand what was happening yet. I still thought that somehow she was one of his guardians, which is intensely foolish now that I think about it, since she was brimming with madness. But I was worried that someone would come upon us, that one of the *guests* would come upon us and catch him with his black eyes, so I focused on helping him out of his state, when I should have focused on our escape. But then something changed. She saw that I knew what he was and that I wasn't scared of him, and then she really lost it. She ripped at her own flesh and then tore a branch off a tree and demolished it right there in front of us… as if she was putting her destructive energy into those things instead of into killing us. I've seen various lunatics use similar primitive self-control techniques over the years. It was almost, now that I think about it, as if she was protecting us from herself."

Kuveni paused to think about Eleanor's astute assessment. "You are very wise, Eleanor. Very wise." Kuveni glanced out the window. Eleanor followed her gaze to observe Lord Blakeney emerging from the woods unscathed and muttering to himself. "If ever you encounter her again... if ever you even *think* you might be encountering her, you must do whatever you can to hide your fear and summon Lady Mélusine. She has an uncanny ability to tame Surpanakha's madness, and she will protect you."

"That will be easy to explain to Edmund... 'Oh, darling, I have no idea how Lord Blakeney happened to find us in this remote outpost in India...'"

Kuveni's joviality dissolved as she grabbed Eleanor's shoulders like a coach giving a lecture to her star player. "Do not worry in the slightest about keeping our farce in this scenario. Do you understand, Eleanor? If ever you are facing real danger, do not worry about keeping any of our secrets. You must protect yourself and Edmund. That is all that should be in your mind."

"I suppose that's something..." Eleanor murmured.

"I'm sorry, Mistress Eleanor. I debated heatedly with Lady Mélusine about how much to tell you about the darker characters amongst our crowd. We agreed that it wasn't fair to scare you away when Edmund has lived quite happily for a century without encountering them. But it would seem that they have found him now. This will probably not be your last encounter. I am sure, though, that Lord Vibhishana is warning Edmund of these dangers as we speak. He will not be as honest as I am being with you about the details, but he knows as well as I do that Edmund must be prepared to protect himself and you from now on. You must protect each other."

116

Kuveni took in a deep whiff, and looked Eleanor up and down questioningly. "Oh, my dear girl… you are so, so strong… Did you notice that your legs were still bleeding from your run through the forest?"

"I suppose I noticed a bit of discomfort," Eleanor said as she lifted up her skirt to observe her wounds.

"I wish I could do more for your injuries. All I can do is clean and bandage them." Kuveni reached forward and placed her hand gently on Eleanor's scratched, bleeding legs. "But, I promise you, my dearest Eleanor, being with Edmund in holy matrimony will be worth these inconveniences. His capacity for love in all of its forms is unmatched in this world."

She closed her eyes and whispered something under her breath as she held her hands over the scratches, and Eleanor watched with wonder as clean bandages appeared on top of her wounds. A few seconds later, Eleanor startled as the front door of the house burst open, but she relaxed as Lord Blakeney joined them. As soon as he reached them, he morphed into Mélusine's preferred feminine form in her typical white medieval dress.

"All of our uninvited guests have been dealt with," Mélusine reported. "I'm sorry that so many of our foreign enemies ruined your wedding, Eleanor. We do have a bit of a bad track record with weddings, but Mr. Johnson and I contained all of the intrusions, along with the help of another Yaksha friend."

"Your stern butler companion?" Eleanor asked astutely.

Mélusine smiled. "Indeed. I told him he looked too conspicuous, but Monty does what Monty wants, unless Lord Vibhishana tells him otherwise."

"Is Oberon alright?" Kuveni asked nervously. "He wasn't injured, was he?"

"Oberon!" Eleanor exclaimed.

"I already told you that Shakespeare was a scoundrel," Kuveni reminded her. "His comic lies will define us for millennia, it seems, even though almost nothing he said in that wretched play was remotely true."

"Some of us were forced to change our names after that debacle, although I managed to avoid that fate myself when Young Billy decided to use the name Titania instead of Mélusine." Eleanor's eyes bulged with surprise, but Mélusine only sighed with annoyance at Eleanor's predictable reaction and then returned to the more important matters at hand. "Oberon is perfectly fine. He's overseeing the reception now, and Edmund is ready for you to join him, Eleanor. Vibhi had a little talk with him. He knows now that he must be on the lookout for Surpanakha. He does not know her name, nor that she is his aunt. I assume Kuveni explained the need for the utmost discretion in this matter?"

"Aye."

"Summon me if you run into her again," Mélusine reiterated Kuveni's suggestion. "And don't hesitate. Every second counts."

Mélusine kneeled down and placed her hand on Eleanor's freshly bandaged wounds, and a euphoric sense of well-being rushed through her. "That will allow you to ignore the discomfort until tomorrow," Mélusine explained. "Unfortunately, I can't heal you, so you will have to do whatever human medicinal magic you do to keep them from becoming infected. I trust that you can see to that yourself."

"Thank you," Eleanor said as she shivered with pleasure at the unusual sensation of Mélusine's warmth traveling through her limbs.

Mélusine pulled Eleanor into a tight hug.

"Thank you, ma chérie, for being such a venerable ally. I'm sorry that we've ensnared you into our web of lies so thoroughly. If it is any consolation, Lord Vibhishana could not have been more impressed by your balance between honesty and discretion. It is a skill that many of us…" she threw an accusatory look at Kuveni, "still struggle with after many thousands of years on Earth."

"I'm glad that one so holy approves of my lying skills," Eleanor quipped.

Mélusine threw an infuriated look of disapproval at Kuveni. "*Sacre bleu*, Kuveni, can't you keep anything to yourself these days?!"

Kuveni shrugged. "Mistress Eleanor deserved to know. Lord Vibhishana will come to appreciate the wisdom of including her in our most inner circle someday. He already understands that giving her the ring and informing her of its real source was the right decision. Sometimes he needs a bit of time to come around."

"You are playing a dangerous game, Kuveni," Mélusine muttered.

"Life is a dangerous game," Kuveni countered. "And I have five thousand years of experience correctly deciding when to follow Lord Vibhishana's advice and when to ignore it, *my lady*."

Kuveni threw Mélusine a look of some sort of shared secret knowledge, and Mélusine shrugged her concession.

"Come, ma chérie, your husband awaits you." Mélusine put her arm over Eleanor's shoulders and guided her back into the foyer. "Lovely dress, by the way. I've waited a thousand years for the human race to return to such comfortable cuts for women. I never thought that my favorite dress would come back into fashion, but it isn't so dissimilar to yours, is it? Your waistline is a bit lower, and the beading is more intricate. This silk is quite similar, though."

Mélusine closed her eyes and returned herself to the form of Lord Blakeney.

"I will go ahead of you so we don't raise any eyebrows about my male presence within the bridal party. You two wait two minutes and then meet Edmund and Vibhi at the door of the carriage house. Relax, ma chérie, all of our enemies have been vanquished for the day, and now it is time for you and Edmund to revel in the beauty of your union. You know now what someone so holy thinks of these mundane religiosities, by the way. Keep that in mind the next time your mother is preaching on and on about her puritanical ideas."

Eleanor took a deep breath, reveling in the otherworldly euphoria of Mélusine's healing touch, and she pushed back all of the raging fears in her mind as she began her trek across the violet lawn, towards her gentle husband who was still chatting with his holy uncle as he waited for her to join him.

"Let the lies continue," Eleanor muttered.

"Transcendent truths, not facts, my dearest girl," Kuveni reminded her as she escorted her towards the waiting men.

"If you say so," Eleanor shrugged.

"The lord says so," Kuveni winked.

Eleanor laughed at the absurdity of the idea. "Come on, Kuveni. Let's go greet your dashing cousin before the vicar converts him."

"Oh, Mistress Eleanor, how I love you."

Eleanor picked up her speed as they approached the carriage house.

"You're looking better, my darling husband," Eleanor said cheerfully as she observed Edmund's hazel eyes and his freshly sun-dried coat.

"And you're looking radiant, my dearest wife," Edmund countered with beaming love in his expression.

She squealed with excitement as he pulled her into a romantic dip and kissed her passionately.

A few of their guests noticed their exchange from inside the carriage house. Eleanor's mother muttered unhappily, while several of Edmund's army mates and their wives cheered.

"I believe we have a wedding to attend to, Colonel," Eleanor declared.

Edmund offered her his arm with the archaic Victorian gesture that always made her laugh.

"I love you, Eleanor," Edmund whispered as he escorted her inside. "I hope you don't regret anything?"

"I regret nothing, Edmund," she said as she squeezed his arm reassuringly.

She thought for a moment about the truth of her statement, and then she took in a deep breath of relief. She meant every word of it.

CHAPTER 8 – THE RECEPTION

"May I present to you Colonel and Mrs. Marriner!" Vibhishana declared happily as Edmund and Eleanor entered the vast carriage house hand in hand.

The crowd burst into applause while Edmund blushed despite his wide, happy grin, and Eleanor guided him into a silly bow.

He grinned mischievously, and presented an even more flamboyant version of the bow he'd presented to Queen Victoria for the crowd, who laughed and cheered at the sight.

"That bow will be reserved only for my wife from now on," Edmund winked. "Preferably while naked."

"I can't wait!"

He took her hand and led her towards a small platform at the front of the room that featured a table for two people to sit side by side, so that they could look out over their audience together.

"It really is magical in here, isn't it?" Eleanor whispered as she took in the wondrous sights. "Although, I've never seen a carriage house that was anywhere close to this size. I think you could house the entire cavalry in here!"

"Maybe I'll suggest it. It would make my commute much better," Edmund said jovially. "I agree it's rather absurd. It was like this when I bought the place. Perhaps the former owners collected carriages?"

"Yes, perhaps."

She had a sneaking suspicion that Kuveni's meddling had something to do with the building's outrageous size, and she made a mental note to ask her about it sometime in the future. She took a moment to appreciate all that the Yakshinis had done at the very last minute (literally) to accommodate the unexpected rainstorm. She was certain that they had not predicted an uninvited visit from anyone whose control over the weather would put their outdoor reception plans at risk.

The large space, illuminated by thousands of twinkling candles mounted in elaborate crystal chandeliers, gave off absolutely no hint that it was a carriage house. Richly embroidered silks in green, purple, and blue hung from the walls, disguising the wooden structure and offering a vivid color contrast to the sleek white table settings.

"Can you believe Lord Blakeney's staff was able to pull this together in so little time?" Edmund asked with wonder. "And this was only a backup!"

"He is uniquely talented." Eleanor looked across the vast audience, spread out around at least fifty large circular tables

"He is, isn't he..." Edmund trailed off in momentary contemplation.

"Come!" Vibhishana interrupted Edmund's thought-stream to escort the happy couple to their honored position at the elevated bridal table. "Enjoy yourselves. It is your day. I will be close by. Whisper if you need me."

Eleanor couldn't help but analyze every mannerism that Vibhishana presented with the new context offered by Kuveni, and she annoyed herself as she felt the first wave of religious deference she had felt since her father's tragedy many decades earlier. But, as she watched Vibhishana work his way into the crowd to mingle amicably with various guests, her mother's sharp voice reminded her of the disdain that she still felt for the close-minded, judgmental tendencies of the Kirk. She smiled secretly to herself at her new knowledge that one so holy shared her opinion.

"That wasn't like any Christian wedding I've been to," Eleanor's mother muttered from her position at the closest neighboring table. The annoyed expression on Mary's face as she threw a look of commiseration to Martha indicated that it was not the first time their mother had made the complaint in the recent past.

"I agree," Margaret Rutherford said haughtily. "I found it to be distinctly pagan. Sinful, even!"

You see, Mélusine had thoughtfully reflected Edward Rutherford's status as Edmund's dearest friend by seating him and his sour wife at the table of Eleanor's closest relatives. It turned out, though, that Margaret and Eleanor's mother had a bit too much in common, thus creating a miserable situation for Eleanor's sisters, who found themselves escaping with their husbands to 'watch the children play on the lawn' while Edward managed to make his way to an improvised seat by Edmund at the two-person bridal table.

"Tell me, lovebirds, how are you faring on this most beautiful of days? I see a little rain couldn't dampen your spirits! Although, I'd expect nothing less from two people as special as you are," Edward said cheerfully as his sour wife muttered angrily about his uselessness to Eleanor's mother.

(I must point out, Ellie, lest you forget, that Margaret Rutherford is, embarrassingly enough, my great-grandmother...)

Lord Blakeney's staff didn't blink an eye at the variable seating arrangement, and served them each a generous pour of red wine and a beautiful plate of Edmund's favorite creamy northern curry complemented by a spicy chicken biryani and fresh, perfectly blackened naan.

"Can you believe Lord Blakeney's staff managed to get all of these spices in England? It tastes just like the biriyanis I ate when I was a child in Hyderabad! I haven't tasted a biryani like this in decades..." Edmund leaned in confidingly as he dropped his voice to a whisper to share his incriminating intel. "Nine decades, to be precise."

Edmund set about demolishing his first serving, and Edward and Eleanor only watched him with bemusement while Edward positioned his chair to block the many guests from observing Edmund's unusually ravenous appetite. As soon as he was finished consuming his first portion (before Edward or Eleanor had taken their first bites), Mr. Valov swooped in to replace his plate with a fresh one.

"Eat all you want, Colonel," Mr. Valov offered. "There is a seemingly endless supply."

"You'd better be careful what you say today, Mr. Valov," Edmund laughed. "I very well might take you up on that offer."

He drank down his wine in one Rakshasa gulp, and Mr. Valov dutifully filled his glass right up to the brim again.

"Eleanor, don't you want to try it?" Edmund asked as he suddenly noticed that she hadn't taken her first bite. "I hope it's not too foreign for you! You wouldn't have preferred something else, would you? I suppose we should have tasted the food before agreeing to Lord Blakeney's suggested menu..."

"It smells delicious," Eleanor reassured him. "But, Edmund, darling, perhaps you want to... er... localize your manners just a bit." Edmund looked down sheepishly as he realized that he was using the table manners of his youth in Hyderabad, using the bread to scoop up the curry without touching the silverware.

"Yes, yes, of course," Edmund agreed. "I got swept up in the spirit of the wonderful meal. I hope I didn't embarrass you."

He glanced around Edward to eye whether or not the crowd had noticed his indiscretion, but their attention, luckily, seemed focused on the cheerful company of their fellow diners.

Mr. Valov swooped in and handed Edmund a finger bowl, followed by a napkin, and as soon as Edmund was finished cleaning his hands, he began more politely eating his food in the typical British style.

Finally, Edward and Eleanor joined him in tasting their first bites.

"It's well tidy scran!" Eleanor exclaimed. "The flavor is so powerful! Do people eat this every day in India?"

"For every meal!" Edward confirmed. "More or less. Certainly they eat a similar amount of spice at every meal. The exact composition varies a bit."

"Oh Eleanor, we will eat so much flavorful food in India! This is only the beginning!" Edmund swooned as he finished off his second plate, and Mr. Valov seamlessly replaced it with his third. "Only a couple weeks in transit, and then we'll be there! Edward, can you imagine? I'm going to show Eleanor all of our old haunts! You don't suppose they've changed much, do you? It hasn't been so long since we were there... It just feels like a long time because of the war..."

"Old man, you will have a wonderful time!" Edward rescued Edmund from a dark thought. "And Eleanor, oh Eleanor, how beautiful you are. I am so happy that Edmund had the courage to pick a wild Scottish thistle." He winked. "You two will make the most beautiful children!"

Edmund paused as he contemplated the idea, seemingly for the first time. "Yes, I suppose we will, won't we, Eleanor!"

Eleanor worked hard to hide a burst of anxiety at the idea, as the personal topic caught her off-guard. "Yes, I'm sure we will, darling."

The loud return of Eleanor's relatives from their games outside on the lawn combined with the grating conversation between her mother and Margaret Rutherford to mercifully take her attention off of the even more unpleasant prospect of discussing the dangers of childbirth with Edmund.

"What in god's name is this?! Oriental food?! At a *wedding*?! Who do they think we are, heathens?" Eleanor's mother's sharp voice carried across the vast space. "Even in India, the civilized folk don't eat *native* food, do they?"

"I know exactly what you mean," Margaret Rutherford hissed. "It is as if they are punishing us for attending this reception. I have half a mind to leave right now."

Debbie took a big bite of biriyani and then exploded into a coughing fit. "Mummy, why does my mouth hurt?!"

"Of all the indignities!" Margaret exclaimed.

"Spices are the work of the Devil, ye know," Eleanor's mother declared as Martha rubbed Debbie's back soothingly and fed her a glass of milk. "That's why they burn yer mouth. That's the Devil dancing on yer tongue! He's warnin' ye not to eat like a godless savage!" She directed her last advice directly to Debbie, who burst into tears at the terrifying thought.

"Mother!" Martha hissed. "That is enough talk of the Devil! Darling, it is just foreign food that Uncle Edmund likes from his time living in India. Look up there, he and Auntie Ellie are enjoying it!"

"This is why I left my girls at home," Margaret continued her tirade with Eleanor's mother as they both eyed the wedding table judgmentally. "I have never liked that Colonel Marriner. Not one bit. He always struck me as off... dodgy, you know? Not right in the head."

"He has to be mincey to marry an auld working spinster like Eleanor. She's a bastard, ye know, and he dunne even care."

It did not apparently occur to Eleanor's mother until after she spoke the words that accusing her own daughter of being a bastard did not reflect particularly well on her. Margaret Rutherford's expression changed as Eleanor's mother realized her mistake.

"I was married to Eleanor's father," she rushed to clarify. "It wunne my fault that the marriage was null. The wicked registrars recorded his pagan hand-binding with some trollop from the isles as his legal marriage, and they dunne bloody care that the Holy Father had nothing to do with it. They were wicked, the lot of 'em!"

"Well, I'm not sure what a Christian woman like myself has to say about that..." Margaret Rutherford said haughtily as she suddenly began looking around the room for an escape.

(Remember, Ellie, that the charming Margaret Rutherford had become pregnant with her first daughter out of wedlock, and then her supposed fiancé died in the war. Her daughter (my grandma Sabrina) was, in all puritanical senses of the word, also a bastard, and Margaret Rutherford knew that perfectly well, the hypocrite).

"Oh, for the love of god..." Eleanor murmured as Margaret Rutherford stood up.

"Edward!" she screeched. "Edward Rutherford, what are you doing? Are you eating that satanic food?!"

"I'm dancing with the Devil as we speak, Maggie dearest," Edward replied cheerfully as if nothing Margaret said was remotely offensive.

As Margaret huffed and puffed and then noticed the disapproving looks of the many elegant people in her midst, who all seemed to be enjoying the food very much, she stormed out of the carriage house, leaving Eleanor's mother to another period of merciful silence.

Eleanor ate her meal, watching the vast crowd while Edmund and Edward caught up jovially, until Kuveni swooped in to distract her.

"Eleanor, dearest, how do you like the curry?" she asked as she pulled up a chair. "It is an old family recipe, you know."

She looked straight at Edmund as she said it. Eleanor had to smile as she observed Kuveni's exceptional skill at channeling Edmund's attention.

Edward took a moment to observe Kuveni's familiar form.

"Lovely to meet you, dear Edward." Kuveni held out her hand to him for an affected handshake. "I am Edmund's cousin... Kate. Kate Marriner."

"Your cousin?" Edward asked with genuine surprise. "Why... why I'd just always assumed that you were wandering about the world alone, old man!"

"I've been told that Kate here is not really my cousin. In fact, we have never even been formally introduced," Edmund said with a hint of intrigue. "But she is like me in many surprising ways. Aren't you, Kate?"

He reached forward to shake her warm hand, and looked even more puzzled as he pulled away. Eleanor had noticed several times already, as Edmund surely just had as well, that a Yakshini's natural warmth did not feel the same as a Rakshasa's after consuming hot liquid, nor did it feel the same as human warmth. It felt distinctly like something else. Something even more alive. Something that Edmund too had just noticed for the first time.

"We are more different than we are similar, my dear boy," Kuveni replied. "Now, I believe that you have many guests who have traveled far and wide to celebrate your happy day. Perhaps you and Eleanor should greet each of them and thank them for their attendance? It is a custom amongst our people to talk to everyone personally at a wedding, no matter how large the audience. Sometimes it takes days!"

"You know, that is a custom at Indian weddings as well!" Edward pointed out.

"Indeed, it is," Kuveni agreed with a knowing smile.

"I'd love to meet all of your old friends, Edmund!" Eleanor said as she stood up. "And I see a few tables of my friends from the VAD that I want you to meet. There's an entire table of women who hopped all the way over from France for the wedding! That is, if you've had enough to eat for now?"

Edmund blushed with embarrassment as he counted up the servings he'd just consumed.

"Seven?" he asked Edward.

"Eight!" Edward countered jovially. "An all-time record!"

"Yes, dearest, I think I've had enough for now," Edmund agreed as he took Eleanor's hand into his.

As they stood up together, Kuveni clapped her hands, and a young woman from Lord Blakeney's staff approached them with a bulky camera.

"Smile, my dearest lovebirds!" Kuveni exclaimed. "It's time for your wedding picture!"

Edmund squeezed Eleanor's hand as the young woman positioned the camera.

"Stand still!" the camerawoman declared.

The happy couple giggled while they attempted to obey. As soon as the smoke from a bright flash exploded into the air, Edmund gathered Eleanor into a romantic dip and kissed her for all to see.

"I probably could have held this position long enough," he whispered.

"Me too!" Eleanor giggled as she locked her lips on his, holding her position in their dip as their audience cheered.

With another puff of smoke, Kuveni was in hysterics along with Edmund, Eleanor, and Edward Rutherford, and the camerawoman was intensely pleased with her success.

"Very good, your highness!" she declared.

Edmund threw a puzzled look to Eleanor, who threw a desperate look to Kuveni, while Edward Rutherford dutifully pretended that he hadn't heard a thing.

"That is enough, Illa. Go ask Lord Blakeney where you should take your camera next," Kuveni said sternly. Her helper looked confused, and then dejected as she scampered away.

As Edmund turned his attention on Kuveni, unwilling to let the comment slide, she shifted uncomfortably. "Many of Lord Blakeney's staff are under the impression that you are the Emperor of India, Edmund. I didn't have the heart to ruin their fun." She laughed awkwardly.

"I told you he was the Emperor of India!" Debbie's voice exclaimed from Eleanor's family's neighboring table. "Didn't you hear? His cousin just said so!"

"I always thought that Auntie Eleanor should be a princess," Ruthy replied nonchalantly as she took in another happy bite of the creamy northern curry. "But an empress is better, isn't it, Mummy?"

"Yes, darlings, an empress is more important than a princess," Martha confirmed.

Edmund's stance relaxed as he accepted Kuveni's unlikely explanation.

"Come on, darling. We have gobs of people to greet," Eleanor whispered into his ear.

They started their rounds at the table opposite Eleanor's relatives, strategically leaving that to the end in the unspoken hope that perhaps Eleanor's mother might tire out and leave before they made it back to the vicinity.

For hours, Eleanor and Edmund worked their way from table to table, meeting and greeting, laughing and conversing with such a wide variety of people that Eleanor could hardly believe that the wedding was hers. Edmund's old army mates from India were so entertaining, so light-hearted, that she could hardly believe they were in the army at all, and the stories they told—oh, the stories gave her the full picture of the virtuous, diplomatic man she had married, including his humorous prankster side that she had only seen small hints of. It stirred great hope deep within her that someday, as the memories of the war that continued to torment him day and night finally calmed down, he might return to the man who had elicited such intense loyalty from the many men he'd worked with over the years.

By the time they reached the table of Eleanor's French VAD friends, Eleanor was secretly swooning over Edmund's utterly unexpected (and delightful) social prowess. She had not realized that once he was comfortable, he would become the life of the party, as she had only ever been with him when he was working intensely hard to control himself. But, as he joked lightheartedly in perfect French, and her friends threw her impressed looks at the amazing catch she'd managed to reel in, she began to see how the silly trickster who'd teased her in his underground lair really was an integral part of the man she'd just married.

As Edmund's excitement grew over the hours, with their many conversations rehashing the good ol' days before the war, at some point an orchestra began to play, and Edmund could not contain his excitement.

"Eleanor, dearest, shall we dance?!" he asked giddily.

"I'm not very good at dancing, actually," Eleanor demurred as she looked around at the large audience watching them.

Edmund coaxed her into his arms. "Don't worry, I'll lead. This too I learned in my tutorials. They were exceedingly useful, don't you think?" He winked, and Eleanor gave in.

As the orchestra began a waltz, Edmund guided Eleanor into the pattern and quietly whispered instructions and praise into her ear until she was comfortable. Her heart raced at the calm strength that his relaxed, happy countenance exuded, and as she felt his strong hand on her back and looked up into his kind, joyful eyes looking down at her, she pushed back a burst of arousal.

Not yet! She had to remind herself. She wanted to guide him right off the dancefloor and out of the crowds… perhaps to the soft, fragrant lawn of violets… yes, that would be nice…

She refocused on the present and pushed her arousing daydreams from her mind. With every step, she was falling even more in love with the man she thought she knew. Suddenly, as if by magic, her gentle, damaged soldier was being replaced by a confident, exuberant, quietly strong man, but the gentleness was still there, underlying and defining the transformation.

When they were finished with their dance, Edmund dropped Eleanor into a deep romantic dip, and the audience cheered.

"Thank you for indulging me, Eleanor," he whispered into her ear. "I have fantasized about dancing with the woman I love since I was a child. After a century of waiting, I can still hardly believe that it's finally happening."

He pulled her up and steadied her in his arms in the center of the dancefloor, and Eleanor stroked his cheek affectionately. "I love you, Edmund."

Edmund smiled and kissed her, and together they felt the overwhelming urge to give into their passions, but with the greatest strength they could muster, they managed to contain themselves.

"Well, shall we continue on with our greetings?" Edmund asked cheerfully.

"Only thirty tables to go. I think we might be done by morning," Eleanor laughed.

"We'd better hurry it up! We have a wedding night ahead of us!" Edmund exclaimed.

Eleanor laughed, and he blushed, looking around sheepishly as he realized that his private declaration had been far louder than he'd intended.

"Come on," he whispered as he took her hand and led her to the next table.

They continued on for another couple of hours until the energy of the audience began to wane, and Mélusine (still in the form of Lord Blakeney) used their slipping attention as a cue to bring out the wedding cake. With a number of helpers, Mélusine guided the trolley bearing a six-tiered white frosted cake covered in morning glories (just as the wedding arbor had been) into the center of the dancefloor.

"Good lord!" Edmund exclaimed. "We can feed an army with that cake!"

"That is indeed the plan, Colonel," Lord Blakeney winked. "Would you like to do the honors?"

Edmund looked around and spotted Vibhishana and Kuveni who both offered him supportive nods and smiles. Lord Blakeney handed Edmund the knife, and he gathered Eleanor's hand into his so that they could cut the first slice together.

The audience cheered as they finished up their task, but Eleanor caught a mischievous twinkle in Edmund's eye as he used his fingers to gather the slice of cake onto his hand.

"I think it has lemon curd in the center! What a treat!" A thick layer of lemon curd oozed onto his hand. "Would you like to try it, dearest?" He held up the frosted slice.

Eleanor grinned. "Only if you will try it with me." She reached her hand into the slice and gathered half the piece onto her fingers.

With their cake drawn, they paused for an extended moment of dramatic silence, plotting their strategies, until Edmund made the first move, and they both squealed and giggled as they stuffed the cake into each other's mouths with only their fingers.

The good-natured audience laughed, while Edmund stole a teasing suckle of Eleanor's frosting-covered fingers. She squealed with surprise, ignoring the disapproving utterances she was sure were bursting out of her mother at that very moment.

As Lord Blakeney's helpers offered them both napkins, they politely returned to their civilized manners.

"It was really quite delicious!" Edmund exclaimed.

"There will be a whole tier waiting for you in your marital bedchambers," Lord Blakeney whispered. "I recommend you continue on your game later without the constraints of clothing or an audience."

Edmund blushed at the suggestion, and Eleanor threw Mélusine a wink.

"Edmund, darling, let's get through the rest of our greetings. I'm starting to feel the pull of all that lies before us," Eleanor suggested.

Edmund took her hand, and with more haste than they had felt all day (except, perhaps when they were running for their lives from Surpanakha), they worked their way through the last of the tables, finally landing on Eleanor's family and the Rutherfords.

Eleanor's eyes bulged as she spotted Vibhishana sitting next to her mother, engaging her and Edward Rutherford in a heated debate. A burst of anxiety bombarded her at the thought.

"What's wrong?" Edmund asked nervously.

"My mother is going to say something horrible to Mr. Johnson. I'm sure of it!" Eleanor whispered. "Who knows what ignorance she's spouting right now with her head held high!"

"I think Mr. Johnson is well aware of your mother's limitations, and he does not hold you responsible, dearest. He told me that he is impressed that after growing up in her puritanical household, you still managed to develop your own moral center without limiting yourself to her stern, self-righteous judgments. He said that such a feat is quite rare in his experience, and that it is one of many examples that demonstrate your exceptional character."

"Did he?"

"He likes you, Eleanor. I knew he'd approve! How could he not? You're so... so perfect!"

"You'd better be careful lifting me up onto that pedestal, Colonel. I'm bound to fall off the higher I go."

"I'm rather tall, if you haven't noticed. I'll be quite happy to catch you," Edmund winked.

Eleanor squeezed his hand as they approached the table.

"So, you are telling me, Mrs. MacLeod, that you do not believe that Jesus meant everyone, when he said to 'do unto others as you would have them do to you'? That he only meant that you should treat your fellow church-goers, of your specific denomination that way?" Vibhishana asked curiously. "He didn't include Romans, or Jews, or Hindus, or Atheists, or any of the other thousands of sects that existed at the time in his statement? Only a few select followers of the Church of Scotland that was created fifteen hundred years after his crucifixion? That was rather limiting of him, don't you think? Wouldn't he have said so, if that was really what he meant?"

"Well, I wouldn't put it like that..." Eleanor's mother hedged.

"What do you make of the fact that Jesus himself was a Jew living within the auspices of the Roman Empire then, Mrs. MacLeod? That at the time the story took place, Scotland was a land of war-enthused, nature-worshipping pagans so frightening to the Romans that they had to build Hadrian's wall to keep them out of the empire? Do you think Jesus would have thought of you as unworthy of his love purely because of the culture to which you were born?"

"Well, I... I... I..." Eleanor's mother stuttered for a response.

"How do you see that as different from your judgment of people who are different from you in the modern world?" Vibhishana pushed.

"Ah! The lovers have returned triumphant from their quest!" Edward exclaimed, offering Eleanor's mother a merciful reprieve that she didn't deserve in the slightest. Eleanor rather wished that her mother would be forced to answer Vibhishana's questions every day for the rest of her life to make up for the many unpleasant lectures she'd suffered through as a child...

"It sounds like you're having a lively debate," Edmund said cheerfully.

"Indeed, we are," Vibhishana agreed with a wink. "We were just discussing the nature of Jesus's intent with his most famous sermons. Mrs. MacLeod was recounting the most fascinating interpretations of the Lord's word."

"I'm sure!" Eleanor laughed with a bit too much awkward enthusiasm.

"Never fear, Eleanor. I enjoy these debates very much," Vibhishana reassured her with a knowing smile. "Quite a bit more than your mother does, I reckon."

Eleanor's mother refused to acknowledge his statement.

Eleanor followed Vibhishana's gaze as Kuveni approached from behind the happy couple.

"You two are champions!" she exclaimed. "I didn't think you'd make it through the gauntlet! And with so much energy left!"

"Thank you for your suggestion, Kate. It was a wonderful idea to talk to everyone. It brought back many happy memories that Eleanor and I were able to share together." Edmund squeezed Eleanor's hand affectionately as he spoke.

"Oh, Edmund, my dear boy, how I love you," Kuveni sighed as she worked hard not to pull him into a motherly hug. "Now, you two had best save the rest of your energy for more enjoyable activities. Eleanor dear, your sisters have already returned to the village inn for the evening, but they have agreed to join us here for breakfast on the morrow, and we will all see you off on your honeymoon together. Lord Blakeney will see to the rest of your guests for the remainder of the evening."

Edmund suddenly looked torn as he glanced at Vibhishana.

"I will be here tomorrow," Vibhishana reassured him. "I will stay until you head off on your flight."

"Our flight?!" Eleanor exclaimed.

Edmund grinned. "Mum's the word, dearest. I have a little surprise planned for you. But until then, I think we have the surprise of our bridal chamber to discover together? Lord Blakeney's staff has been working on it for weeks. Given how glorious this reception is, I can't wait to see what awaits us."

Vibhishana and Edward Rutherford stood up.

"Have fun, old man," Edward whispered as he pulled Edmund into a brotherly hug. "It was wonderful catching up."

"Enjoy your discoveries tonight, Eleanor," Kuveni whispered excitedly as she pulled Eleanor into a parting hug.

"I cannot remember the last time I was this happy, Edmund. It is a greater privilege than I can express to see you in love with such a worthy partner," Vibhishana said as he pulled Edmund into a tight hug. "Congratulations to you both. You have made me so, so proud."

He glanced at Eleanor's mother and then offered his hand to Eleanor in a polite, appropriate vicar's handshake.

"Revel in your joy," he reminded them with a wink.

"The happy couple is ready to retire!" Kuveni announced to the remnants of the crowd.

A chorus of cheers interrupted the tipsy revelry of the remaining guests as Edmund lifted Eleanor into his arms to carry her straight out of the carriage house, across the violet lawn, and right up the stairs of their home to officially cross the threshold.

They both chuckled as they reached the front door to observe that it was already waiting for them wide open.

"Lord Blakeney's staff doesn't miss a beat, do they?" Edmund laughed.

"Take me over the threshold, Colonel," Eleanor declared.

And with one final step into the wide-open door, Edmund and Eleanor's epic wedding night officially commenced.

CHAPTER 9 – THE WEDDING NIGHT

"Good lord!" Edmund and Eleanor exclaimed in unison as they reached the open double french doors of their newly remodeled honeymoon chambers.

Edmund carefully helped Eleanor out of his arms as they both gazed around the completely transformed space. What had been Edmund's dark, old master bedroom with a simple, extra-long double bed that had always looked depressingly small compared to the rest of the large, drafty stone room was now a stately royal bedchamber complete with an enormous double-wide, extra-long canopied bed with intricately carved wooden posts and hanging emerald green silk curtains that matched the delicately embroidered green and gold pillows and duvet. The entire set-up looked as if Mélusine had stolen it right out of a maharaja's palace... or perhaps a Roman emperor's.

Where the attached sitting room used to be through another set of open french doors, an enormous mosaic bath, more akin to a small spa or pool (which you, Ellie, would certainly recognize now as a classic Rakshasa bed) took up half of the room by the window, while a new room had been carved out of the corner by the inner hallway to house a new, fully-plumbed, nicely private water closet (an improvement that Eleanor particularly appreciated). A double vanity with two mosaicked sinks and large, antique mirrors filled in the space between the spa and the new WC.

The room was lit by hundreds of flickering candles, and two silver trays—one of dusty cognac bottles and one of steaming hot teapots—both with adorable pairs of matching cups, awaited the happy couple's use on the new side tables beside the bed, while a large selection of red wine bottles and two large glasses beckoned them from a new, purpose-built shelf in the corner next to the Roman bath. And most importantly for their immediate escapades, the extra tier of their wedding cake awaited them right in the middle of the bed on a silver platter without a hint of silverware in sight.

Edmund walked slowly around the room, inspecting the many intricate details of the updates. He stopped at the modern sinks and crouched down underneath to inspect the modern plumbing. "Fascinating… it just pulls the water in from the well and sends it back out again to some mysterious place where it won't bother us…" He spoke as if he had never observed the workings of modern plumbing up close before. "How could Lord Blakeney have possibly completed all this work in a few weeks?" Edmund asked, mostly rhetorically, as he approached the Rakshasa bed and ran his hand along the elaborate Roman mosaics.

"It is a very valid question, darling." Eleanor hoped that Edmund might finally recognize the unusual nature of the Yakshini magic that was continuing to subtly define his life.

"How lovely…" He squinted to inspect the setting of the tiles. "This craftsmanship is utterly superb. If I were going to guess how long this took, I would say many months at the least. I attempted mosaic-work once, when I was an apprentice in Hyderabad. It took far longer than I expected to get the placement of the tiles just right, and that did not accommodate the unusual angles of this bath. Lord Blakeney must have some exceptionally skilled artisans at his beck and call."

He shivered with pleasure as he dipped his hand in the steaming-hot, rose-scented water.

"It's nice and warm." He finally returned his attention to Eleanor. "Perhaps a perfect start to our night of marital pleasures?"

"Shall we try it out together?" She joined him by the pool and reached her arms around his neck.

He leaned down to lick her lips enticingly, and then he pulled her into a more frenzied embrace.

"I've been waiting to do this all day," he whispered as he set about unbuttoning the back of her dress.

Eleanor followed suit, unbuttoning the many gold buttons of his dress uniform.

"I could barely control myself on the dancefloor, you know," she confided. "I wanted to take you outside, rip your clothes off, and pummel you on the violet lawn."

"You should have!" Edmund exclaimed giddily. "It would have made the day even more memorable!"

"Ha! Especially to my sisters and their innocent children. Think of the stories they'd be able to tell for years to come!"

She triumphantly pulled off his coat and flung it across the room, causing a louder clomp than she'd intended as his heavy cache of medals hit the mosaicked floor of the new bath area.

They both giggled, and continued on with their game.

"They were rather adorable, your sisters' children," Edmund said more seriously as he reached the top buttons on the back of her dress and kissed her neck as he undid the final clasp. "They made me rather enthusiastic about producing some of our own."

Eleanor froze, as the unpleasant topic knocked the wind right out of her. Edmund, of course, noticed her immediate change in tenor.

"What is it? It's not… it's not me, is it? It's not frightening to you that I'm different? That our children might be different too?"

A heated debate erupted in Eleanor's mind as she struggled to decide how much to reveal. Edmund had made such incredible strides just that day in escaping from the crippling anxieties that had been holding him back since the war, and she couldn't bring herself to risk bringing them back.

Eleanor caressed his cheek. "Edmund, darling, I love you. I love *all* that you are. I would be ever so elated to have a child like you. Think of how convenient it would be if we didn't have to worry about her ever getting hurt! But, to be totally honest, darling, my life has been turned upside down in these last few months of our engagement. I haven't been able to catch my breath, and I don't even know what I'm going to be doing with myself once we get back from our honeymoon. I just need some time… some time to get used to being married before jumping into the great unknown of rearing children. I hope you aren't too disappointed?"

It wasn't the whole truth, but it wasn't false either. Eleanor knew exactly why he was feeling the pull, because she was feeling it herself, but she simply couldn't let herself discuss the ugly truths of the world on her wedding night. Mélusine had given her the knowledge of the unique dangers facing her in childbirth, and it was her choice how or if to share it. She chose, for one beautiful night, to ignore the raging demands of destiny and revel in the simple beauty of their union, just as Vibhishana had so wisely suggested.

Edmund pulled her into his arms and kissed her. "We have all the time in the world now, Eleanor. I will wait for you to be ready."

Eleanor took in a deep sigh of relief. "I love you, Edmund."

He kissed her again, and their frenzy to rip each other's clothes off recommenced, this time with far more vigor than their first romantic go-around.

But, as she removed Edmund's shirt revealing his attractive chest, his excitement was brought to a grinding halt as he unclasped the back of the belt sewn into the low waistline of her silk dress, revealing her bandaged legs.

"Eleanor, what happened?! You're injured!"

"Oh, it's nothing really." She looked down to observe a trace of brown dried blood peeking through the bandages. "Kate helped bandage me up after our run through the forest. It's just a few scratches. Nothing that won't heal quickly and cleanly. I'd forgotten about them, actually. They don't hurt at all."

With a whoosh and a draft, Edmund was backed up against the vanity with wide, black eyes.

"Oh dear…" Eleanor whispered as Edmund's new talent and the unpleasant fact that her minor amount of blood had just aroused him competed equally for her attention.

Edmund squeezed his eyes closed as he took in several deep, calming breaths in a row, whispering a quiet mantra to himself. As he reopened them with their human hazel, she smiled encouragingly.

"Are you alright, darling? You look like you've gotten yourself back under control. Does that mean that Mr. Johnson managed to teach you some useful techniques earlier?"

He was too distracted to answer her. "Did you see that? Did you see me hop across the room in the blink of an eye?"

"I did, darling." Eleanor debated whether or not to come any closer. She had, in fact, seen him display this talent once before, at the Baron of Heathfield's estate during their encounter with the murdered girl's outraged father. In that instance, the room had been dark and Edmund had been thoroughly preoccupied, but Eleanor had noticed his unusual speed, as had Mr. Kauter. Whether or not she should mention that this was not a new talent entered her raging internal debate, and she decided to take one step closer. But, as Edmund flinched, she held her position. "Did you not mean to do it?"

"I don't know…" His hands were shaking. "I don't know if I meant to do it or not… it happened too quickly…"

"Well, it seems like quite a useful talent, doesn't it?" Eleanor spoke with her typical feigned cheer in the face of Edmund's unusual challenges. "It will help you outrun any adversaries who can do the same. Don't you think?"

"I suppose..." Edmund was more frightened of the development than she was. "But, Eleanor, this is very, very bad! I didn't consciously do anything! I don't even know what I did! What if I do it again in front of other people?!"

"Why don't you try doing it again now? Try hopping over to me as fast as you can."

Edmund hesitated as he eyed her bandaged legs.

"Darling, I hate to break it to you, but if you can't handle the scent of even a hint of my blood, then we are going to have some serious problems at least once a month. I hope that your tutorials covered that much about human female anatomy?" Eleanor used the gentlest tone she could muster.

She thought back to the lucky (or unlucky) timing of their various premarital meetings that had allowed them both to avoid the unpleasant topic of how Edmund would handle the normal symptoms of her feminine cycle. She berated herself silently for not anticipating that something so mundane might create problems for his unusual brand of blood sensitivity.

"Yes, Eleanor, I am aware of many aspects of female anatomy, including that one," Edmund said with annoyance, whether at her or himself, she wasn't entirely certain. "You are not the first woman I've been with, you know. I was even... never mind."

"You were even what?"

"I was even married once..." Edmund cringed as he completed his unintentional confession. "It was a very long time ago, and it didn't end well. I would rather not talk about it. I should have told you sooner, but I didn't want to..." He trailed off as he thought the better of his statement.

"You didn't want to what?" Eleanor wouldn't let him back-peddle.

146

Edmund contemplated his answer for an uncomfortably long pause. "I didn't want to make you feel like you weren't my first true love, Eleanor. I didn't even know what love was when I married her, and our time together didn't teach me. Only you have taught me that. I wish rather intensely sometimes that I'd never met her, so that you, dearest, could be my first of everything that matters."

Eleanor was somewhat taken aback by the painful honesty of his confession, and her momentarily stern attitude towards his current struggle melted away.

"I'm glad that you had the chance to hone your approach, darling. Having mediocre experiences with other partners is good for us. They teach us to appreciate what we have when it is truly special, physically and emotionally. If I hadn't had many bad experiences myself, I wouldn't have been able to appreciate what a unique catch you were when we met." She winked, hoping to bring back some humor to their situation. "My judgment is impeccable. I'm still being proven right day after day, and today was no different. My friends from the VAD were quite taken with you, you know. They couldn't figure out how an old fiery spinster like me had managed to seduce a charming colonel like you so thoroughly, and that was without any of them knowing how exceptional you are at tickling my fancy."

Edmund finally gave into a smile and took a deep, calming breath.

"Now, darling, I have complete confidence that my minor wounds will not upset you further. You have too much self-control for that. So, let's see if you can hop over to me in the blink of an eye, and then we can experiment with other ways in which your unusual speed can be made useful."

He rolled his shoulders, and then made one big human leap into the center of the room.

"Blimey," he whispered disappointedly.

"I suppose if you've gone a hundred years not knowing how to do this, it should be no surprise that you can't just do it on a whim," Eleanor said as he assessed his unsuccessful position.

She approached him slowly and wrapped her arms around his neck. "I'm proud of you for trying, Edmund. I'm sure when the time is right, it will come quite naturally to you."

She kissed him, but despite her enticingly naked presence in his arms, he was too distracted to appreciate her charms.

"I've been hearing that a lot today. I'm normally quite patient, I think. Perhaps too patient. But the sheer number of mysteries that were revealed today by Mr. Johnson and this mysterious Kate character have reiterated for me how little I know about myself, and how much I am at their liberty in learning the most pertinent details. I mean, what if that mad creature had really hurt us? Mr. Johnson told me that she might return, and that she might try to hurt us again! How could he not warn me before now?"

"Clearly, he thought that he was protecting you by not telling you, darling."

"Protecting me?!" Edmund exclaimed indignantly. "I should be able to decide when to bloody be protected! I'm a colonel in the British Army for god's sake!"

Eleanor was surprised by his burgeoning passion on the topic, especially given his earlier deference to Mr. Johnson. "Many women, including me, feel the same way, darling. It is one of our many plights that men feel the need to protect us without giving us a say in the matter. I believe you are feeling a similar frustration to that now, as if they don't trust you enough to tell you the truth. I know why you are finding it difficult. I would feel the same way myself if I were in your shoes."

Edmund paused to contemplate her assertion. "I didn't even know what my middle name was until today. Why would they possibly keep that from me?"

"Yes, I saw how surprised you were during the ceremony."

"I'd understand if it was an unusual name… Something that I could use to learn more about myself, to learn something that they didn't want me to know. But half the bloody men in England are named George! It's hardly an inspiring revelation!"

"It is a rather generic name," Eleanor agreed.

"And that ritual, Eleanor! That ritual around the fire in the traditions of *my* family—it was an Indian ritual! I've been to my fair share of Hindu weddings over the years, and what we did today was exactly the same! How in the hell does that bloody fit into the picture?" He held out his fair hands before him. "Do you think it's possible that I'm really half Indian? That that's why I was put into that Indian orphanage as a boy? But Mr. Johnson is so fair! He's just as fair as I am! I suppose he could be a very fair Parsi… but then, the ritual was a Hindu one, not a Zoroastrian one, I'm sure of it! And if he really is a Hindu, why would he have put me in a Christian mission orphanage run by nuns, and then sent me along to apprentice for a Muslim painter, all the while, never mentioning a peep about his own beliefs? For god's sake, Eleanor, none of it makes any bloody sense! I know even less than I thought I knew about myself when I woke up this morning!"

Eleanor was at a loss at his pile-up of astute observations. "Perhaps you should ask him about it, darling. It is very reasonable for you to want to know."

"It *is* rather frustrating, if I'm going to be honest. I feel, in some ways, like I am still a child being kept in the dark. But I'm really bloody old, Eleanor! Too old to be so ignorant about myself!"

Eleanor led him over to the Roman bath and began slowly unbuttoning his trousers.

"You should keep pressing them, darling. I believe that is what they want. Kate told me as much when she came to visit me with your mother's ring."

"Thank you for telling me the truth about that, dearest. Your honesty gave me more of a connection to my mother than I've ever had in my life." Edmund gathered Eleanor's hand into his to inspect the ring. "It is rather ostentatious, isn't it? She must have had quite a bit of money to own a ring like that. I wish I knew more about her. Perhaps I should corner Kate *Marriner* at breakfast to ask her." Edmund rolled his eyes as he said her false name.

"I believe that Mr. Johnson is already unhappy with the amount of information Kate has shared with you. I'm not sure what I think about the whole thing. Mr. Johnson seems to have his reasons for withholding certain details. Whether or not they are valid is a different question. I suppose his wisdom on the topic will have to stand the test of time." Eleanor felt herself tottering on a precipice between truth and lies. She didn't like it one bit.

"I don't believe that Mr. Johnson intended to tell me anything at all when he arrived today. He almost got away with it too. I was so excited to see him that I didn't question anything about his visit. *Anything*, Eleanor. Like how did he even know to come? We didn't even have an address to send him an invitation! And yet, every time something monumental happens in my life, he is there, and today was no exception. It's as if he's watching over me all the time… except when I was in the trenches. I kept waiting for him to come, to rescue me from the nightmare, and it never happened. I felt incredibly foolish afterwards for expecting his intervention…" He trailed off in silent contemplation.

Eleanor squeezed his hand supportively. "I'm sorry, darling. I'm sure that his absence was as difficult for him as it was for you. It is very painful to watch people you love suffer without being able to do anything about it."

"I'm sure that he could have done something about it if he'd wanted to," Edmund said with an unusual sharpness in his tone. He took a moment to contain himself. "I suppose that isn't fair. I could have told my men to desert, too. I could have saved so many of them in so many different ways, but I didn't. I just followed my orders, maintained the status quo, convinced myself that it wasn't my place to intervene. I'm just as guilty as he was… although, I suppose he is probably judging himself similarly harshly. He told me something to that effect earlier today while you were inside the house with Kate."

"I'm glad you two had a chance to really talk." Eleanor returned to nonchalantly unbuttoning his trousers.

"Yes, I am too." Edmund began running his cold fingers gently along her arms while she continued undressing him. "I've been treating his role in my life as others treat God, I think. Our expectations are too high, the lot of us. Perhaps that is why poor Mr. Johnson feels like he has to stay away from me. Because I'm still too much of a foolish child, worshipping him as if he's some combination of Santa Claus and the bloody pope... or I suppose as many people think of Jesus."

Eleanor was so surprised by Edmund's insight that she had no idea what to say. She realized that Edmund's horrific circumstances in the war were only the beginning of the trauma he'd suffered. He had suffered something far harsher, the same thing that so many soldiers had—he'd realized that the very foundations of the world around him that he thought were immovable, were, in fact, self-delusional. He had not been rescued by Vibhishana any more than the millions of other soldiers had been saved from their grim fates by Jesus, and all of them had been forced to recognize that the divine intervention they'd always believed would be theirs was never coming. The irony of Vibhishana's true identity in the context was so great that she could hardly wrap her head around it, and she dissolved into an internal debate about what she should do next. Should she derail Edmund's strikingly intuitive thought-stream and send him in a false direction, or help nudge him towards the truth? She wished dearly in that moment that she didn't know the truth herself. She chose a hedging option.

"Let's say for a moment, darling, that Mr. Johnson were divine. What if he really were some sort of heavenly creature?

Would that change how you think of him? Of how you think about yourself, or your odd circumstances?"

Edmund thought for a long time before answering. "I have trouble entertaining the very idea. I don't believe in divine things, and I never have. The idea that Mr. Johnson is in some way holy is utterly absurd to me. I only meant that I was treating him *as if* I were worshipping him, not that he was indeed worthy of being worshipped. No one is, in my opinion, including him. It is a rather controversial thing to say, I know, but I've never been particularly fond of religious philosophy. I find that it gives people a chance to avoid thinking for themselves, especially when they want excuses to do horrible things to each other. I have worked very hard not to allow myself to fall prey to the same mindset, and I am rather unhappy with myself for doing so with Mr. Johnson. I suppose that means that I'm no better than the religious zealots that I'm harshly judging."

"Really, darling? Do you not sense anything unusually powerful about him? Anything that strikes you as strangely similar to yourself?" Eleanor wondered if somehow Edmund's own underlying power kept him from noticing the similar power that emanated from Vibhishana. "You, more than anyone, know that there are amazing things in this world that humans know nothing about. I should think that would make you more apt to believe in divinity, not less."

"You don't think I'm divine, do you, dearest?" Edmund asked with a burst of anxiety. "I know Edward Rutherford thinks that I'm some sort of angel, and I haven't done enough to discourage his foolishness on that front, but *you*, Eleanor. I don't think I could handle that... It is almost as bad as being thought of as..." He trailed off with a look of utter misery in his expression.

"Being thought of as?" Eleanor stroked his face encouragingly.

"Being thought of as a demon..." Edmund whispered. "Angels and demons are the same brand of nonsense. For one to exist, so must the other, and I'd much rather live in a world free of both. I'm really very ordinary, Eleanor. I have a few quirks, I will admit, but if some religious zealot were to observe my unique talents, certainly he would assume some sort of false religious explanation. You have helped me remind myself that everything about me must be explainable within the rational context of the world we live in. No gods. No demons. No fairies or magic or monsters. Only unexplained science. If I were to start looking for magic or divinity all around me, I'm quite sure I would go certifiably mad, just as I did during the war when I believed so deeply that someone or something would step in to rescue me. Only now do I realize what a blessing it was that I learned the harsh lesson that the world is still, after everything, extraordinarily ordinary. It means that I am ordinary too, and I *need* to be ordinary, Eleanor, to keep myself sane."

That was the moment when Eleanor realized that Edmund's lack of tenacity in questioning his circumstances throughout his century on Earth had not been due to the ideas never crossing his clever mind, but rather, it had been an exercise in allowing him to keep himself anchored solidly and sanely in the human world. With his guardians meddling constantly, he had needed to protect his humanity, and avoiding the hard questions that he knew deep down would have outrageous answers had been his primary mechanism for self-protection. Vibhishana, she realized, had recognized this phenomenon as well, in a way that Kuveni, and even Mélusine hadn't. It suddenly occurred to her that encouraging Edmund's incessant questioning of his circumstances was not necessarily the perfect plan she'd assumed it was. There was some part of him, a large part, that really wasn't ready for the full truth. Her head began spinning at the complexity of it all, and so she did what she did best—she plowed forward full steam ahead anyway.

She reached past him and gathered up one of the many bottles of red wine that was awaiting their consumption by the Roman bath. She drank down a long swig and then handed the bottle to him.

"I think, darling, that you are extraordinarily ordinary for the unique life that you've lived. I hope you can take that as a compliment."

"It is the nicest thing anyone has ever said to me." Edmund smiled as he finally relaxed, finishing the rest of the bottle in one long Rakshasa gulp.

Eleanor took the opportunity to rip off the remainder of his undergarments.

"Now, I think that we have some extraordinarily ordinary pleasures to enjoy in this warm bath. I've never been with someone under water before."

"Me neither." Edmund guided her up the mosaic steps into the steaming pool. "It will be a night of beautiful firsts, Eleanor. Of the only firsts that matter."

Edmund sighed as he submerged himself entirely in the water, and then Eleanor watched curiously as he returned to the surface and all of the water absorbed right into his thirsty skin, leaving his hair completely dry. He pulled her into a gentle straddle, and she shivered with excitement.

"I'm not too cold still, am I?" he asked concernedly. "I thought the bath would take care of that."

"You're perfect."

She reached her arms around his neck and positioned herself on top of him, and then she sighed with satisfaction as they became one for the first time as married partners.

"I love you, Edmund. I can't wait to spend the rest of my life with you," she whispered as she relished the sensation of their bodies intertwining.

"You taught me how to love, Eleanor."

And together, as their satisfied sighs dissolved into guttural moans, the two married lovebirds indulged in the first of many exceptional pleasures of their intensely unordinary wedding night.

CHAPTER 10 – MORNING GLORY

Eleanor awoke as the early morning light tickled her sleeping face through the uncovered window. She took a moment to gauge her surroundings. Royal canopied bed. Cake frosting and lemon curd all over the sheets. Her gentle, sleeping husband... in the bath.

She smiled. She'd noticed him eyeing it as she was falling asleep, but after their hours of pleasurable games, she hadn't had the energy to return for a second go in the water that had mysteriously remained ever so steamy all night. She had let herself give into a very human sleep, and she couldn't blame him for choosing not to spend the few remaining hours of the dark night on the sticky silk sheets.

Despite her minimal sleep, she felt an invigorating energy as she tiptoed out of bed to join him in the bath before he stirred. But, as she approached, what she observed, even with everything she had come to expect, thoroughly surprised her. If she was going to be honest about it, she found it rather disturbing.

Floating peacefully on the top of the steaming hot water all around her sleeping soldier was a thin layer of violet metallic liquid, and as she approached the scene and noticed the vibrations of her movement reflected on the surface of the water, the alien substance scurried with unquestionably intelligent movement back into every crevice of Edmund's body. It took all of her mental acuity to hold in the squeal that was itching to burst forth at the bizarre sight.

That was the moment when Eleanor realized that the substance that was responsible for Edmund's unique self-healing ability was not simply an alien color of human blood. No, it was an integral part of who he was. It was, in some way, *him*. The idea was so puzzling that she couldn't even form a coherent judgment about it.

As the final drop of his Rakshasa plasma scurried grotesquely up his chest and into his mouth and disappeared, Edmund took in a deep, awakening Rakshasa breath, and his eyes popped open.

"I'm sorry!" he exclaimed. "I planned to rejoin you in the bed after a quick dip! I must have fallen asleep!"

"Don't worry, darling. I wasn't offended…"

"What is it? What's wrong?"

Eleanor struggled mightily with what to tell him. She'd kept his black eyes from him since the day they'd met—why, she wasn't entirely certain. Mélusine hadn't even asked her to. Perhaps she was trying to keep his nerves under control, as he was already worried enough about being discovered without realizing that he was displaying a thoroughly alien trait for the world to see with every provocation of his adrenaline. Now she'd dug herself so deep with that one that it would be extremely uncomfortable to confess that she'd known about it all along. But this? Should she keep this from him? What even was it?

"Eleanor?" Edmund pushed.

"Darling, have you ever slept in the bath before?" She dipped her hand in the silky hot water.

"From time to time," Edmund admitted. "To be honest, I find it more relaxing than a bed. I often dream of being weightless when I sleep in the bath. Sometimes I even dream of flying, and they are rather pleasant dreams. I hadn't had one since the war until just now."

"I'm glad you were having an enjoyable dream, darling…"

"What has you distracted, dearest? I'm sorry I left you last night. I really did intend to just warm myself up and hop back over to join you. I wanted us to wake up from our wedding night together."

"Really, Edmund, I'm not offended."

She contemplated joining him in the water, but the image of his violet metallic substance was stuck solidly in her mind. Some childish part of her worried secretly if it might try to work its way into her. After all, the sight of it scurrying back into him had been rather grotesque.

"You don't regret anything, do you?" Edmund asked more anxiously.

"No, darling, I don't regret anything."

Eleanor sucked up her ambivalent emotions and hopped into the bath to join him. She was not going to make herself any more of a liar than she already was. She had told him many times that she loved all of him, and apparently, that included his bizarre, intelligent liquid side. She sighed her concession. It really could have been worse. Plenty of women discovered horrific secrets about their husbands within a few hours of marrying them, and really she knew she shouldn't be surprised. She'd seen the substance before. She just hadn't been prepared to see it sleeping on its own, right out in the open like that. Her heart raced as she decided to just tell him the full truth for once.

"Darling, it's just… you know the violet metallic substance that heals you?"

"Yes?" Edmund's heart began racing at the uncomfortable reference.

"Well, you see… it was just, I suppose, sleeping in the water with you, here, floating on the top of the bath," Eleanor said with her gentlest tone. "When I approached, it… er… scurried back into you. Into your nose, your eyes, your ears, your mouth, and I think even your fingernails…"

"Good lord… How grotesque!"

Eleanor smiled and relaxed. "I will admit it was an odd thing to watch."

"I'm sorry, Eleanor. I don't know what to say…" Edmund blushed with embarrassment. "I've never slept in the bath with anyone else around. I didn't know that such a thing could happen."

"Well, I suppose from now on, you shouldn't be sleeping naked in the bath in public," Eleanor winked.

"I hope that it didn't frighten you?" Edmund asked self-consciously.

"Frighten isn't the right word… I will admit it took me by surprise." Eleanor worked her way into a straddle, and kissed him softly on the lips. "I told you never to stop surprising me. I can't blame you for fulfilling your solemn vow."

Edmund kissed her back, but then pulled away. "Those were not the kind of surprises you meant. And neither was being chased through the forest on our wedding day by a raving mad monster."

Eleanor suddenly wondered if Edmund's unusual form of rest had reduced his focus on keeping the world around him sane and scientific.

"One cannot pick and choose their surprises, darling. Otherwise they wouldn't be surprises."

Eleanor leaned forward to kiss his neck.

"I suppose… but it makes me worried about what else I might unwittingly have in store for you, dearest."

"We will have to face it together, Colonel." Eleanor worked her way up to nibble his ear. "I don't see any evidence of your violet substance here, but I will have to make a more thorough inspection to be sure."

Edmund sighed and relaxed as her tongue tickled his soft flesh, until a fresh burst of arousal bombarded them both, and they gave into another delightful round of wedding night bliss.

"I think wine for breakfast shouldn't be taboo for someone who isn't affected by alcohol," Eleanor said an hour later as she reached over to the edge of the bath to the one remaining bottle of red wine.

She took a long swig and then handed the bottle to Edmund.

"I hate to think how expensive these wines were. They're so old, the labels have fallen off." Edmund drank down half the bottle in one gulp. "Lord Blakeney really has been exceedingly generous, hasn't he? Although, I suppose I haven't seen the bill for the property improvements yet. I told him to spend whatever it would take to get it done in time for the wedding. We might end up impoverished by the end of our honeymoon."

"I can still get my one-room flat back in Edinburgh," Eleanor teased. "I've found it quite cozy for many years. I don't think I need all this grand space."

"Yes, I would be quite happy to live in a one-room cottage with you, dearest. Although, I'm not sure where Mrs. Murray would stay. And Mr. Valov. And I have it on good authority that you will not be taking over our home maintenance as a housewife."

"You've got that right, Colonel!" Eleanor giggled as she stole the bottle and took another swig. "Besides, I think you'd tire of my Scottish cooking within the first meal. All I know how to do is fry things, mostly tough, flavorless meats, to be precise."

"Perhaps you can teach Mrs. Murray a thing or two."

"We don't want to insult her, darling. My cooking is rather atrocious."

Edmund's stomach growled at the reference, and Eleanor handed him the wine bottle.

"It sounds like it's time for us to face the world as a married couple, Colonel."

Eleanor stood up and hopped out of the bath. She took a moment to appreciate that the air in the room and the tiles on the floor were unusually warm for an English country house.

She grabbed the lone towel hanging by the bath and began to dry off while Edmund finished off the last of the wine in one Rakshasa gulp.

"All of this wine was utterly superb. Some of the best I've ever tasted." Edmund hopped cheerfully up out of the water and joined Eleanor on the warm floor.

She watched with the same fascination she'd had the many other times they'd gotten out of the bath together and Edmund's body absorbed every drop of water right before her eyes, and she ran her fingers through his perfectly dry hair and then along his lovely chest.

"That is a rather useful talent, isn't it?" She said as he shivered with pleasure at her touch. "I wish I could be dry so quickly. Especially my hair. It takes hours to dry after I wash it. The annoyance of my wet hair was almost enough to convince me to cut it short, but I still didn't have the guts."

Edmund ran his fingers through her long, curly red tendrils. "Your hair really is the most beautiful hair I've ever seen, Eleanor."

"I'm glad you like it, darling. Now, shall we find our clothing? I'm not sure where Lord Blakeney would have put it, actually…"

At her declaration, they both heard a timid knock at the door.

Eleanor slipped on her favorite silk kimono that someone had thoughtfully moved from her bridal chamber and hung on a hook by the bath, while Edmund slipped on a new violet silk robe that hung next to it.

As he held out his arms to inspect the flamboyant garment, they both burst into laughter.

"Certainly Lord Blakeney chose this for me. He does have a rather outrageous sense of fashion." Edmund tied the belt as another knock at the door interrupted them. "To be honest, I'm rather embarrassed for anyone to see me like this."

160

"Oh, come, come." Eleanor took his hand and guided him to the door. "You're the master of the house, Edmund! You can wear whatever you want!"

She swung open the door, and Edmund hopped behind her with a deep red blush as Illa, whom Eleanor had now seen twice (first, during her bridal preparations with Kuveni, and second, when Illa served as their wedding photographer) bowed deferentially.

"Please pardon my intrusion, my lord," Illa said as she returned to a standing position and presented a neatly folded stack of fresh clothing. "Lord Blakeney wishes me to inform you that the breakfast banquet is ready, and that the wardrobe is down the hallway on the right. He designed this wing of the house to be just for you, and so in the future, you should be able to go to the wardrobe yourselves in privacy. In the meantime, he suggested I bring you your clothes."

"Thank you, Illa." Eleanor took the clothes, noticing the ever so subtle pulsating Yakshini warmth in Illa's hands as they brushed against hers.

"Illa…" Edmund hedged. "Why have you been addressing me as 'my lord'? Surely you are old enough to realize that I am not the Emperor of India."

Illa looked pained as she closed her eyes for a moment of meditation, and then she took a deep breath. "I'm sorry, Colonel. It is a habit. I work for Lord Blakeney, and that is how I address him."

"Well, there is no need for honorifics with me," Edmund said jovially as he relaxed at the believable (and untrue) mundane explanation. "Thank you for your help. Will you tell our guests that we will join them soon?"

"Yes, my lord," Illa agreed with another deferential bow. As she looked up at Edmund one last time, she cringed with annoyance at her mistake. "I mean *Colonel.*"

Edmund smiled approvingly, and Illa scampered away, slamming the door to their private hallway as she went.

Eleanor handed Edmund the suit folded on the top of the stack and then held out a pair of wintery wool trousers and a thick cashmere sweater for herself.

"It looks like Lord Blakeney is expecting a change in the weather today! I hope he realizes what that will do to the trees that have been blooming early… Maybe I should warn him…" Eleanor trailed off as she contemplated the many side-effects that the Yakshinis' weather shenanigans must have been having on the entire county for the many unseasonably warm weeks leading up to the wedding.

"Does Lord Blakeney have orchards? He doesn't strike me as the farming type—not even the gentleman farming type. In fact, I'm still not entirely certain where exactly he lives. Somewhere in Shropshire, I think you said? It seems odd that a Secret Service agent lives in Shropshire, don't you think?"

"I'm not sure…" Eleanor's mind raced. "I think that perhaps it is his ancestral home in Shropshire. I get the sense that he travels a lot for his work."

"Now that you mention it, I have thought from time to time that his enthusiasm for helping us has been rather odd. Surely in the Secret Service he has far better things to do than to plan the wedding of an ordinary colonel and an extraordinary nurse… unless…" Edmund trailed off as an unhappy thought darkened his expression.

Eleanor's heart skipped a beat. This was it. She was ready for the relief to wash over her. She was ready for him to finally recognize the extent of the madness around him.

"Unless, darling?"

"Unless the Secret Service knows something… Dearest, you don't think that they noticed something about me during the war, do you? Maybe *I'm* his secret assignment! You said he told you the details of his assignment! Please, dearest, you must tell me! It will

162

be very dangerous for both of us if the government knows something! Who knows what they'll do to me!"

Eleanor was utterly perplexed. She didn't want to dig herself deeper into her abyss, but she couldn't let him panic over the reasonable, if incorrect, scenario he'd just stumbled upon.

"Darling, please don't panic. It isn't nearly as dire as you think..."

Edmund began pacing back and forth across the bathroom, hissing to himself in an especially foreign tongue that Eleanor didn't recognize.

"Darling... Lord Blakeney isn't in the Secret Service. He's part of a different, more secret organization. I swore to him I wouldn't reveal his mission, and I'm quite sure that if I don't keep my word, the consequences will be devastating. I promise you that his mission does not put you in danger. I would never have kept my word to him if it had, nor would I have allowed him anywhere near us. You must trust me enough to believe that, Edmund."

He finally stopped his pacing, and then addressed her in the odd foreign tongue.

"I can't understand you, darling. I don't even recognize the language that you're speaking." Eleanor approached him and put her arms around his neck.

Edmund closed his eyes and concentrated. "Can you understand me now?"

"Loud and clear, Colonel." Eleanor smiled as she reached up to kiss him gently on the lips. "Trust me, Edmund. Please trust me on this. Lord Blakeney is not a threat to you, or us. He is here to help."

Edmund paused for a long moment to consider her statement. "He's here to help? To help us? To help me?" Edmund asked astutely. "Then I *am* part of his mission?"

Eleanor's mind raced even faster. "Darling, Lord Blakeney is under the impression that you are... er... royal. I believe that is why Illa is calling you 'my lord.' I thought it best not to discuss with him the validity of his assumptions, because I didn't want him to dig deeper into your past."

Edmund thought carefully about her assertion and then burst into laughter. "How absurd! Royal? *Me*? Who do they think I'd even be? King Edward VII's bastard son with an actress? Why would they even care about a royal bastard? There must be scores of royal bastards hopping about!"

"I don't know, darling. But they must have their reasons." Eleanor was rather pleased at the success of her half-truth. It was, after all, not entirely false. Edmund was the heir to a throne he didn't even know about, with a royal father he undoubtedly wouldn't appreciate being related to, based on all of the intel his guardians had whispered into her ear over the months. She was astute enough to notice their euphemisms, to read between the lines and recognize that Edmund's father was not the nicest of kings. She had wondered from time to time since Kuveni's revelations some months earlier, if perhaps their painful silence was rooted in protecting Edmund from that singular unpleasant fact.

"It explains a lot, actually... Lord Blakeney's staff has shown an odd deference to me, although he himself has acted rather authoritatively... In fact, he seems rather royal, don't you think? Perhaps he believes we're related! He'll certainly be proven wrong about that!"

"I hope he is not proven anything, darling," Eleanor said as she kissed Edmund again. "I think it's best that we let him think what he thinks, don't you? He obviously has some story about you in his mind that we do not want to challenge with the even more outrageous truth."

"Yes... yes, I suppose," Edmund conceded. "But I can't promise not to laugh now when they address me with a royal moniker."

"I would expect nothing less," Eleanor smiled. "Now, I suspect our guests are waiting for us to arrive late to yet another event hosted at our own home."

"Quite right." Edmund relaxed and began buttoning up his shirt. "I suppose our naked wedding night is over." He sighed with disappointment. "Now we'll have to wait hours before we can enjoy each other's naked bodies again."

Eleanor, still naked, approached him and wrapped her arms around his freshly clothed self.

"One last taste?" she offered as she stood on her tip-toes to entice him into a final naked embrace.

Edmund kissed her, and then as a burst of arousal bombarded them both, he guided her swiftly to the bed. She threw herself on top of the sticky sheets and spread her legs enticingly, while he hopped right onto the bed to straddle her.

Eleanor's guilty giggles at being late to their wedding breakfast dissolved into satisfied sighs and blissful moans as together, they celebrated one last naughty go-around of naked wedding-night bliss.

CHAPTER 11 – TAKING FLIGHT

"It's so warm! Why did Lord Blakeney think it would be cold?" Eleanor exclaimed as they scampered out of the house onto the violet lawn where a large white tent had been magically erected sometime in the night. Underneath the tent, an imposing banquet table held heaping silver platters of a classic Yaksha feast, which their familial guests were already enthusiastically enjoying.

Edmund grinned as he pointed to the far end of the carriage house, where the large doors had already been opened to reveal his honeymoon surprise.

"I think Lord Blakeney's clothing suggestions were aimed at helping us dress properly for our flight. It gets quite cold a few thousand feet up in the air."

He pointed to a bi -plane parked just inside.

"Blimey, Edmund! You didn't buy it, did you?"

Edmund laughed. "I thought about it, but I wasn't sure if you'd like it. I thought we'd try it out, and perhaps we might buy one when we return from our honeymoon. That one there I borrowed from one of the generals. Lord Grimby uses it for his personal sojourns. He has been most kind, actually. I asked him over to help assess whether the fields in the back of the carriage house were flat enough to use as a landing strip, and he insisted on loaning us his plane."

"And you know how to fly it?" Eleanor asked with wonder.

Edmund nodded the affirmative and smiled at being able to surprise Eleanor with something mundane. "I learned just after the war. I'd always wanted to fly, perhaps because of my pleasant dreams about it. The army was looking for volunteers to become pilots, so I signed up. I was rather good at it, but they wanted me to start training young officers for combat, and I couldn't stomach the idea of more combat of any kind, as they'd assured me many times that the wretched war was the war to end all wars, so I told them I was going to retire. That was when they offered me any commission I wanted if I stayed, so I chose the Household Cavalry. I was quite sure being assigned to coddle the king's horses would keep me away from more combat. It was a rather cowardly decision, I know. But I wasn't willing to put my pride ahead of the well-being of those I might have harmed in the wrong circumstances with my disgraceful symptoms of shell shock."

Eleanor squeezed his hand supportively. "You don't need to justify your choices to me, Edmund. I can't imagine how any man with a heart and a mind could sign up for more combat after the brutality of that worthless war. I'm glad that you had the wherewithal to create a situation for yourself that allowed you to recover."

Edmund reached over to sneak a kiss. "I love you, Eleanor."

As they approached the banquet, Eleanor's mother eyed them disapprovingly, while Martha and Mary waved, and Edward Rutherford rushed to greet them. Vibhishana, still dressed in the simple clothing of a vicar, stood up from his position in the center of the table more slowly. As Edward engulfed Edmund into a brotherly hug, Eleanor noticed that Kuveni was not in the crowd, while Edmund noticed another conspicuous absence.

"Where is Margaret?" he asked Edward with more curiosity than care.

"She wanted to return to the girls. She left on the first train out this morning," Edward shrugged. "Amy is still a baby. Margaret's sister was taking care of the girls while we made this little voyage alone. I think she was worried that Amy might be too much for poor Beatrice."

"Yes, yes, of course. How thoughtful of her," Edmund said supportively, as everyone, even Eleanor's mother, was overjoyed by her absence.

Edward immediately engaged Edmund in a jovial conversation, and Eleanor squeezed his hand and let him go. She knew how much Edmund missed his best friend in all the world, and how rare his opportunities were to catch up with him without Margaret's hawk-eyed, judgmental oversight. Eleanor's sisters observed her wifely decision and jumped in to support her.

"Good morning, sleepy head," Mary said as she pulled Eleanor into a hug. "Ye'd better get some breakfast into you before yer flight! I can't believe the colonel knows how to fly one of those things, but I suppose that's one benefit of marrying a soldier."

"You can call him Edmund now. He is your brother-in-law, after all," Eleanor corrected her.

"Aye, I suppose he is! I'm so happy for ye, Ellie. This is all I've ever wanted for you."

"I'm glad I didn't disappoint you."

Eleanor, of course, had known for too many years that all her sisters wanted for her was for her to join their club as a married woman. After fighting them tooth and nail, she decided to finally give into one minor convenience of marriage—to never have to explain her choice to stay a spinster again. She hoped secretly that perhaps her fantastic match with Edmund might demonstrate to her young nieces that marrying the first man who proposed upon their eighteenth birthdays was not necessarily their best option— that they could, in fact, have fulfilling careers and find their value in positions beyond just being a wife. She most sincerely hoped that she'd be able to prove to them that she could maintain her position as a nurse while enjoying the many benefits of being married to the man she loved. She sighed with stress at her lack of options on that front, and pushed forward to avoid a moment of impending melancholy.

"I'm starving. What do we have to eat?" she asked as she guided Mary back to the banquet table.

"It's a real Scottish breakfast, just like Christmas!" Debbie exclaimed as she popped a bite of sausage into her mouth.

"A full Scottish breakfast?" Eleanor asked excitedly. "Even with black pudding?"

"It's well tidy scran," Martha confirmed as she gestured for Eleanor to sit between her and Ruthy.

"I like the beans!" Ruthy exclaimed.

"The mushrooms are also scrummy," Mary added. "Like you and Da used to forage in autumn in the glen. How anyone found them in spring in England is beyond me."

"How thoughtful," Eleanor murmured. "I haven't had a full Scottish breakfast in years." She glanced over to Vibhishana who offered her a kind smile.

"Eat!" a familiar voice urged. Eleanor looked behind her to spot Mrs. Murray enthusiastically approaching Edmund.

"Mrs. Murray!" he exclaimed as he broke off his conversation with Edward to address her as if she was an old family friend. "I thought you were in Yorkshire with your sister! What a treat to see you here on this fine spring morning!"

He shook her hand jovially, and she blushed at his personable enthusiasm.

"Lord Blakeney called me down for this special occasion, Colonel. He said that my spiced sausages would be the perfect addition to your wedding breakfast!"

"He was right!" Edmund exclaimed as he took a seat at the table next to Vibhishana, and Edward plopped down next to him. "I cannot think of anything I'd rather eat!"

"Well, I thank you kindly, Colonel!" Mrs. Murray said as she lifted up one of the silver covers to reveal a heaping pile of spiced sausages.

"Did you cook *all* of this yourself?" Edmund asked with impressed surprise.

"Oh no, sir. Lord Blakeney's staff was ever so helpful. I made a small batch to teach them the recipe, and then they made the rest."

Mrs. Murray looked quite pleased as Edmund collected eight sausages onto his plate and began popping them into his mouth with only his fingers.

Eleanor smiled with bemusement and hoped that her sisters wouldn't comment on Edmund's unusual appetite (and manners), while Edward settled in to begin his standard tallying of Edmund's mealtime consumption. Vibhishana watched the phenomenon with fascination while drinking down an unusually large cup of coffee at an admirable approximation of human speed.

"Thank you for staying over last night," Edmund whispered to Vibhishana as soon as he'd finished up his first serving. "I hope your accommodations were adequate? I've heard that the village inn isn't the most comfortable place, but there aren't so many options here. I would have invited you to stay here in the house if I'd had my wits about me yesterday; there was just too much going on."

"Please do not worry for one moment about me, Edmund. I was perfectly comfortable," Vibhishana reassured him.

Vibhishana refilled his large coffee cup and drank down an entire extra serving in one go. As soon as he was finished, Mrs. Murray noticed his minor plight and rushed to collect his empty coffee pot.

"I will be right back, father!" She grabbed the coffee pot and headed across the violet lawn back towards the house.

"I have observed, Edmund, that you have an unusual talent for evoking an exceptional form of loyalty from the virtuous souls you encounter. How long have you known Mrs. Murray?"

"Just a few months." Edmund smiled as Mrs. Murray engaged Mr. Valov in a lively conversation, pulling him into the house along with her. "I rescued her from a wretched situation, although her talents in the kitchen are truly exceptional. I did not take her on as a charity case. I simply offered her a new avenue for her undervalued skills."

Vibhishana smiled at Edmund's modest response. "It is an incredibly valuable talent, and one that does not come naturally to most. I am very proud of you for it… and, of course, for many other things."

Edmund blushed with embarrassment at the compliment, and then his expression darkened. "I have done many things that you would not be proud of."

"As have I." Vibhishana lowered his voice into a whisper. "Nothing you have ever done will make me love you any less, Edmund. *Nothing.* Not even your darkest moments in the trenches. Do you understand?"

Edmund stared before him pensively without answering, and Vibhishana took his hand under the table.

"Someday, my dearest boy, we will confess our sins to each other, and it will be a painful and glorious day. In the meantime, you must believe that you are worthy of forgiveness, and I do not say that to everyone. Forgiveness must be earned, but, you, Edmund, have earned every ounce of it." Vibhishana's gaze moved to Edward Rutherford, who was politely focusing on another plate of Scottish breakfast while pretending not to hear their conversation. "That goes for you too, Edward. You are forgiven for every moment of darkness you suffered in the war."

Edward glanced at Edmund and Vibhishana with a distinct look of enflamed piety that immediately drove Edmund to grimace.

"Thank you, father," Edward said as he averted his eyes.

"I have not done enough to combat this false religious pretext," Edmund blurted. Vibhishana looked vaguely surprised by his outburst, while Edward looked more startled by it. Edmund eyed Eleanor's sisters who were focused on their children and lowered his voice. "Edward, I am really very ordinary. We both did horrific things in the trenches, as the circumstances required. But they were very human things. *Everything* I did was human. I am hardly any different from you, and it worries me that you think otherwise."

"Whatever you say, old man," Edward agreed disingenuously. He reached forward and served Edmund up an inhuman portion of Scottish breakfast, but Eleanor caught a knowing glance from him.

Edmund threw Eleanor his own glance as he sighed with stress, but with one covetous whiff of the delicious steaming plate, he shrugged his concession and allowed himself to focus on enjoying his second course.

"Lasses, why don't ye go join yer cousins on the lawn," Martha suggested as Debbie and Ruthy began to squirm.

"Aye!!!" they exclaimed in unison as they hopped out of their chairs and raced each other across the sweetly scented violets with roaring giggles.

"I'll leave ye to it," Martha whispered into Eleanor's ear. "I'm sure ye have a lot on yer mind with all these changes."

Eleanor was embarrassed that her eavesdropping on Edmund had resulted in a thoroughly anti-social impression on her sisters, but as Martha and Mary's laughs echoed from the lawn, and her mother stood up and headed towards the house without a word to anyone, Eleanor's attention returned to Edmund as he finished off his serving and popped two more sausages into his mouth directly from the serving platter. He then spotted a steaming coffee pot across the table and drank down its entire contents in one Rakshasa gulp.

As he wiped his mouth politely with his napkin, Edmund looked around the table to assess their privacy, and then lowered his voice and addressed Vibhishana in Gaelic. Eleanor leaned in, as she realized immediately that his choice to use the obscure language that she spoke fluently was intended to include her in their otherwise private conversation.

"I wanted to ask you, Mr. Johnson, about something unusual that happened last night."

Vibhishana shifted uncomfortably. "Yes? Please do not be shy, Edmund." He did not appear to entirely mean it.

Edmund glanced over to Eleanor, and she nodded encouragingly. "I... er... hopped across the room in the blink of an eye. I didn't mean to do it, not consciously, and I couldn't reproduce it afterwards when I tried. But the madwoman yesterday... she had done the same thing. Is this something that I can control with more practice? I'm worried, you see, that I might do it unintentionally in front of the wrong people."

Eleanor smiled with pride at his proactive approach to convincing Vibhishana to give him a useful answer to his question.

Vibhishana relaxed and smiled with relief. "Come with me, both of you." He stood up and gestured for Edmund and Eleanor to join him. "Let's go somewhere more private where we can discuss this. The simple answer to your question is yes. You can control your rapid speed with more practice. It is a good talent for you to hone, given your encounter yesterday. Let's practice together and see if you can make some progress before you need to head off on your flight."

A look of utter elation crossed Edmund's face, but as he looked down at Edward who was politely pretending that they weren't having a sensitive conversation in Gaelic right next to him, Edward shooed them away.

174

"I'll stay here, old man. Do what you need to do. Shall I distract Eleanor's relatives on your behalf?"

"You are a venerable ally," Edmund said jovially as he slapped Edward on the back.

He gathered Eleanor's hand into his and squeezed it lovingly as they followed Vibhishana out of the tent, across the violet lawn and around the back of the carriage house to the empty fields that would shortly become their runway. Eleanor noticed Vibhishana whispering something under his breath, and as they arrived at the far end of the carriage house, near the bi-plane's parked position, Vibhishana smiled, whispered his thanks, and jogged forward to collect a cricket bat and ball that were awaiting him neatly on the ground.

"Do you like cricket, Edmund?" Vibhishana asked casually as he threw the ball to him. Edmund, of course, caught it effortlessly.

Edmund's grin could not have been wider. "It is my favorite sport."

"Mine too," Vibhishana smiled. "Now, perhaps Edmund should start as our batsman, Eleanor can be our non-striker, and I will be our bowler and our fieldsman."

Eleanor nodded excitedly (ignoring the utter absurdity that she was about to play cricket with *Him*), rolled up her sleeves and her trouser legs, and removed her high-heeled shoes to skip barefoot onto the soft spring grass. Edmund could not temper his giddiness at the beautiful reality that his life-long fantasy of playing cricket (or doing anything fun, for that matter) with the mysterious Mr. Johnson was finally coming true.

"We're missing the wickets!" Eleanor pointed out.

"We won't need them. I expect our batsman to be caught out every bowl," Vibhishana winked. "Now, Edmund, don't hold yourself back. You should hit the ball as far as you can, and I will catch it. I am going to focus my attention on you as you swing, then I'm going to follow the ball with my eyes and command my entire body to catch up with it."

Edmund took a deep, calming breath, readying himself to impress his idol and his wife with his sporting prowess, while Eleanor positioned herself dutifully beside Vibhishana and readied herself to run, despite the fact that she knew full well that Edmund would make the first hit perfectly and his uniquely talented uncle would catch it.

Without any more warning, Vibhishana bowled the ball faster than any professional player, and a booming crack echoed as Edmund hit it many hundreds of meters into the air, all the way to the hedge between the forest and the fields.

In a blur that was barely visible except for a streak of black from his vicar's habit, Vibhishana reached the ball's position and waited for it to land right in his hands.

"Good lord," Edmund murmured.

In another blur, Vibhishana was back where he'd started with the ball in hand.

"Not bad!" Vibhishana exclaimed. "Eleanor, would you like to bat now? Edmund, why don't you bowl this time."

Edmund handed the bat to Eleanor, and she ensnared him in a quick kiss.

Edmund took his position next to Vibhishana, who lowered his voice. "Now, Edmund, once someone like us knows that he can do something, he is much more likely to do it. Your encounter yesterday with the madwoman in the forest is probably what prompted your unexpected use of the talent later in the evening. Now you've seen me use it. Try to emulate what you saw me do to catch the ball when Eleanor hits it."

"I'm not sure I'm going to hit it far enough for it to matter," Eleanor warned them.

"We shall see," Vibhishana winked.

Eleanor stood in position, like she had as a girl when she'd played with her father and her sisters in the garden, and she pushed back the melancholy memory that she had refused to think about since his tragic demise.

Edmund smiled and bowled the ball to her.

With the first swing she'd taken in almost thirty years, Eleanor hit the ball and watched it soar high into the sunny sky.

"Not bad!" Eleanor declared triumphantly.

"Eleanor dearest, you're a natural!" Edmund exclaimed with a swoon.

"Go!" Vibhishana urged Edmund jovially. "Catch it, my boy!"

Edmund took a deep breath, rolled his shoulders, looked up into the sky, locking his eyes on Eleanor's impressive hit, and in a blur (only slightly more visible than Vibhishana's had been), he appeared halfway into the field, right underneath the ball, and caught it.

He paused for a moment to observe with wonder his position and the ball in his hand.

"Come on back!" Vibhishana called.

Edmund leapt towards them with a wide human leap, and then stopped to observe his failure. With an annoyed sigh, he jogged back to them at human speed.

"It would seem that I am not successful when I'm thinking too deeply about it," he said as he handed the ball back to Vibhishana.

"Don't worry, that is not surprising," Vibhishana reassured him. "Try to relax and focus on the fun of the game. The talent will begin to come more naturally to you. I will be the batsman next, Eleanor can be our bowler, and you, Edmund, will be our fieldsman. Start here, where I'm standing, and catch my hit wherever it happens to go. It will be quite far, though, so prepare yourself."

Vibhishana handed the ball to Eleanor in exchange for the bat, and they each positioned themselves for the next round of fun. After a moment of hesitation, Eleanor bowled, and Vibhishana hit the ball even higher into the air than Edmund had.

"Run, my boy!" Vibhishana urged. "Follow the ball!"

Edmund disappeared in a blur, this time as fleeting as Vibhishana's had been, and reappeared farther down the hill where a seasonal stream ran along the edge of the forest.

"Yes!" Vibhishana and Eleanor exclaimed in unison as he caught the ball.

In another blur, Edmund was standing before them with a wide, triumphant grin.

"Not bad, if I do say so myself!" he said as he tossed the ball to Eleanor.

"Not bad, indeed!" Vibhishana slapped him on the back. "How did that feel?"

"Exhilarating. And much more natural that time."

"I'm glad. Now, I believe we're back to your turn to bat, Edmund. Remember, there is no need to hold back. Hit it has high and as hard as you can."

Edmund took the bat, but as he jogged at human speed to position himself, Vibhishana suddenly stopped in place and cocked his head. He motioned for them to both be silent, and then with a momentary look of panic which he quickly relegated, he jogged at human speed into the open doors of the carriage house.

"There is no need to be frightened," he said calmly. "We aren't going to hurt you. Come, my children, let's talk to Auntie Eleanor and Uncle Edmund together, shall we?"

The blood drained from Edmund's face, and a burst of anxiety exploded inside of Eleanor as Vibhishana led Debbie alongside Mary's boys, Charlie and Howie, into the open.

"You have been watching us play for some time?" Vibhishana asked.

All three children stared up at him with wide eyes.

"We were playing hide and seek in the barn by the airplane, and then we heard you playing..." Debbie whispered. "We couldn't help but watch..."

"But you were not frightened until you were caught," Vibhishana observed as he squatted down to address them face to

178

face. "It is natural for you to be frightened when you are caught doing something you know you shouldn't. But tell me, my children, when you saw us playing with our unusual talents, why were you not frightened then?"

"Be not forgetful to entertain strangers…" Charlie whispered. Vibhishana smiled and nodded for him to continue. "For thereby some have entertained angels unawares."

"That has always been one of my favorite passages," Vibhishana winked. "And were the two of you also thinking of scripture as you watched us flit about the field faster than the eye can see?"

"You were having fun," Debbie squeaked. "And Auntie Ellie wasn't frightened."

"I see. And so you trust Auntie Ellie's judgment, then?" Vibhishana asked.

"Auntie Ellie is always right," Howie agreed. "And she's always so much nicer than Gramma. She's the nicest grown-up in the world."

"I see," Vibhishana nodded approvingly. "I think you are right about that, my young friend. Your Auntie Eleanor is one of the nicest grown-ups in the world. She knows that just because people are different, it doesn't mean they're bad, and sometimes it even means that they can do special things that make their lives more beautiful than normal people will ever know. But many grown-ups don't understand that. It is important that you do not tell anyone what you've just seen. Do you understand? All three of us could be in danger if you tell anyone that Uncle Edmund and I are different."

"Like Jesus," Debbie whispered.

Eleanor startled, but Vibhishana only looked intrigued.

"Tell me, my child, what do you mean by that?" he asked. Despite all she knew about him, Eleanor was thoroughly impressed by Vibhishana's ability to hide the great depths of his true identity.

"Jesus was different, and Judas betrayed him, and then he got crucified," Debbie explained shyly.

"Yes, you are right, my young friend," Vibhishana agreed. "He suffered great pain because he was different. Unnecessary pain because of the fearful ignorance of those around him."

"We do too," Charlie admitted. "Because of what our grandfather did. Everyone is mean to us because we're different."

Vibhishana looked upon their earnest faces with an expression of simultaneous love and pity. "As painful as your struggle is now, my children, you are all better people because of it. You are wise beyond your years. Each of you understands how painful it is to be ostracized, don't you?"

"Aye," they agreed in unison.

"To understand such pain and not let it ruin you is a rare and beautiful gift. It is a gift that your Auntie Eleanor shares. And so, I believe that we can trust you to keep our secret?"

All three children nodded.

"You mustn't tell another soul what you've seen, or we too might be crucified," Vibhishana reiterated. "Now, what shall we do now..." He looked to Edmund and Eleanor.

"Can we..." Charlie hedged.

"Can you?" Vibhishana coaxed.

"Can we play cricket with you?" he asked shyly.

"Where are the others now?" Eleanor asked as she glanced through the empty carriage house.

"Captain Rutherford is telling them stories about being in India with Uncle Edmund," Debbie replied.

"Ha! Well, that will keep them occupied all day!" Edmund exclaimed giddily as a wave of relief washed over him.

"I think that we have some time for a game before the happy couple has to head off on their honeymoon flight," Vibhishana agreed as he stood up cheerfully. "Perhaps, Edmund, you and I should be the fieldsmen, while Eleanor bowls, and Debbie, Charlie, and Howie take turns batting. Do you think, my children, that we will be able to catch you out every time?"

"Let's see if they can!" Eleanor rallied them as she ran to the bowler's position with the ball. Edmund handed the bat to Debbie, while Charlie and Howie formed a polite line to bat next.

"Edmund, I'd like you to take three lessons from our experience just now," Vibhishana said in Gaelic as they reached Eleanor's position.

Edmund leaned in expectantly, like a child waiting to hear an important declaration from his father.

"Firstly, as you have noticed, this new talent of yours is one of the most noticeable. It gives away our unique nature quite readily to anyone who observes it. You must be extra careful from now on to make sure that you are not being observed, even secretly, when you are using it. It was irresponsible of me to not check the carriage house before we began our tutorial, so as you can see, even after quite a long time on Earth, I too need to remind myself of this lesson."

"I should have checked it myself," Edmund replied.

"We will both remember next time," Vibhishana reassured him. "But our error has opened the door for our next two lessons. Our second lesson is that religious philosophy does not always have to be oppressive. The children's understanding of the lesson of Jesus's crucifixion is helping them accept truths that otherwise can be difficult for humans to fully comprehend. In beautiful moments like this one, we can see the way that religious stories can help them empathize with us even though our foreign nature is frightening to their human sensibilities."

"I suppose," Edmund conceded.

"That was it for the vicar's lesson," Vibhishana winked. "Our third lesson is the most important. It is the one I want you to hold closest to your heart: Not every human who stumbles upon our secrets will despise us. While Eleanor is an exceptional example of acceptance, there are many humans who will not fear us. You have just met three more. Humans are capable of immense kindness, and when they learn more about us, we often give them the opportunity to embrace their exceptional virtue. I hope, my boy, that as you continue to make your way through the world, you will notice and appreciate the virtuous humans around you, and let them transform the burden of your secrets into a blessing. Sharing your secrets with a worthy audience is a beautiful gift, and it is a privilege that is yours, Edmund. You may use your judgment, just as you did with Eleanor, to decide when to accept worthy friends into your inner circle."

"But don't you think..." Edmund trailed off.

"Don't I think?" Vibhishana coaxed.

"Don't you think it's too risky? Malice and fear aside, if these children accidentally said something..."

"Darling, think about how it will sound to Mary or Martha if their children tell them that Uncle Edmund and the vicar have magical powers at cricket," Eleanor interjected. "They'd no sooner believe that you are the Emperor of India."

"What makes you think that he's not?" Vibhishana asked. Edmund and Eleanor threw each other a startled glance at the suggestion until Vibhishana's serious expression melted into a mischievous grin that reminded her distinctly of Edmund's. "I'm sorry, I shouldn't tease you like that. Even I can't help it sometimes. Let's get playing, shall we? You'll need to leave soon to make it to Bretagne before dark. I will take the left field, you take the right field, my boy."

Eleanor positioned herself to bowl, and as Debbie entered her stance, Eleanor made a perfect pitch. A triumphant crack rang out as Debbie's bat made contact with the ball, but as it went straight up into the air above her, she and her brothers all squealed and ran out of the way. In a blur, Vibhishana was standing between them with the ball in his hand, and they were looking up at him with wide eyes.

"One for us," he winked. "Charlie, I believe you're next."

He tossed the ball to Eleanor, and then blurred back to his position in the field behind her.

The children were ignited by the wonder of seeing Vibhishana's unusual talent up close, and their excitement was contagious as Edmund and Eleanor settled in for the next round.

As Eleanor bowled, Charlie swung too early, but as the ball flew past him, once again, in a blur, Vibhishana was in position, catching it before it landed.

"Two," he winked as he tossed it back to Eleanor. "Let's see if we can get one into Edmund's territory."

Eleanor bowled again, and this time Charlie hit the ball high into the air, over Edmund's head, and in a blur, he was halfway into the field, ready to catch it. As it landed in his hand, the children squealed with delight, and in another blur, he returned to his position and tossed the ball to Eleanor.

"Biordinair," Charlie whispered excitedly.

He handed the bat distractedly to Howie as his eyes were now solidly glued on Edmund's next move.

"Three," Vibhishana declared.

Their fun continued with increasing laughter and cheer until the sun reached its apex in the sky, and Vibhishana reluctantly brought their game to a close.

"Forty!" he announced as he caught the ball and blurred to Eleanor's position one last time. "I think, my young friends, that we must help Auntie Eleanor and Uncle Edmund prepare for their flight now."

"Aww!" the children complained in unison.

"You were all thoroughly challenging opponents!" Edmund exclaimed.

"You were wicked, Uncle Edmund," Charlie praised shyly.

"Thank you, Charlie," Edmund replied with a hint of remnant timidity. "It was a thoroughly enjoyable game."

"You got the most hits, Debbie," Eleanor said as she put her arm over her shoulders. "You remind me of me!"

"Thanks, Auntie Eleanor." Debbie put her arm around Eleanor's waist. "I hope I can be a nurse someday like you."

"Me too." Eleanor squeezed her affectionately. "And just remember, you can do whatever you set your mind to."

Eleanor collected her high heels and rolled down her sleeves and trouser legs, and then the group followed Vibhishana past the bi-plane, through the carriage house, and across the violet lawn.

"I believe that Lord Blakeney has already loaded your luggage into the plane, so now you just need to say your goodbyes. You'd best hurry. You'll need to land in Bretagne by sight, and you only have about six hours of light to make the journey now," Vibhishana suggested.

Edmund handed the bat to Charlie. "Why don't you go run ahead and tell Captain Rutherford that we're ready to head off."

"Aye, Uncle Edmund!" Charlie exclaimed.

Vibhishana handed the ball to Howie, who took off running after his brother, and Eleanor urged Debbie to follow. She laughed as she watched the three of them race across the violet lawn, but then a pang of sadness went off somewhere deep inside of her at the dismal prospects of having some adorable fiery children of her own. She pushed it away.

"Thank you," she said to Vibhishana. "It was a thoroughly enjoyable morning that I'm certain none of us will ever forget."

Vibhishana stopped to address them before they reached the earshot of the crowd. He reached forward and kissed Edmund on the forehead and then repeated his gesture for Eleanor. She shivered as he pulled away.

"It was such a privilege to be here with you for your wedding. Please know that I will be missing you dearly as I reinitiate my necessary absence. This time is yours now to be together, but I will be thinking about you and wishing you well with all of my heart." For once, even Vibhishana could not hide the emotion in his voice, and Eleanor and Edmund both fought back tears. "I love you both so much."

184

Edmund pulled Vibhishana into one final hug and whispered into his ear. "I hope I will not have to wait decades to see you again."

Vibhishana tightened his grip. "So do I, my dear boy. So do I."

As Edmund pulled away, they both looked self-consciously to Eleanor and wiped their tears back into their skin, hiding the evidence of their emotions as the group approached.

Edmund addressed the crowd with forced joviality. "I hear you've been making me into a legend, Captain. I daresay whatever young Edward has told you, you'd best take as a grain of salt."

"Did ye really steal a camel from Lord Curzon's valet?" Martha asked.

"Did *I* steal that camel?" Edmund's jovial tone became genuine. "The captain has thrust his own crimes upon me! I demand a jury! Did he tell you what prompted this serious crime?" He looked upon his enraptured audience with satisfaction. "Young Edward mistook the camel for his own! I told him he ought to start decorating his camel with brightly colored ribbons, and Lord Curzon agreed. Young Edward here was the only lieutenant in India with a dandied-up ride!"

His audience, along with Edward, burst into laughter.

"Guilty as charged, old man. Guilty as charged." Edward pulled Edmund into a brotherly hug. "Say *namaste* to the maharajas for me."

"Take care of yourself, Captain, and of those two beautiful girls. We'll pay you a visit when we're back from our honeymoon." Edmund worked hard to control a rush of emotion.

"I'm looking forward to it," Edward agreed cheerfully.

Eleanor hugged Mary and Martha. "Where's Mam?" she asked as she noticed her conspicuous absence.

"Don't worry, I just checked on her as I put Ruthy down for a nap in the house. She was sleeping peacefully on a divan in the parlor," Mary said as she hugged Eleanor again.

"Bye, Auntie Eleanor!" Debbie exclaimed.

"Bye, Uncle Edmund!" Howie and Charlie exclaimed in unison as they pummeled him into a hug.

"I see that the way to a lad's heart is through some cricket!" Martha laughed. "I hear ye're quite the sportsman, Colonel! Perhaps this summer we should get a game together up in Scotland!"

"I'm looking forward to it," Edmund said as he threw a wink to the children. "Although, I think perhaps my talents have already been exaggerated into legend."

"Have they? The children said you and the vicar caught every hit!" Mary laughed.

"Well, I suppose they were telling the truth after all," Edmund conceded jovially. "I played for quite a few years with the British Army in India. Perhaps this summer I can teach them a few of my favorite tricks… although some of my secrets I will have to keep to myself."

He threw them a knowing look, and they nodded their agreement.

As he and Eleanor took one last look at their entourage, Kuveni, in the form of Kate, rushed across the lawn from the house, right past Vibhishana, and engulfed Eleanor into a hug.

"Happy honeymoon, my darlings!" she declared as she moved right along to pulling Edmund into the motherly hug she'd been coveting for two days. "May the adventures continue!"

She winked at Edmund as she pulled away from him, and then she plowed forward without giving him a moment to get a word in. "You must take off straightaway, my darlings! The winds are absolute perfection at this very moment!"

She skipped forward, and Eleanor took Edmund's hand tightly into hers. "Are you ready to fly, darling?"

Edmund grinned and let her enthusiasm pull him into a jog.

As they reached the plane, two leather bomber jackets and two sets of goggles were awaiting their use in the two seats.

"How perfect!" Eleanor exclaimed as she wiggled the jacket on. "You look so handsome, Edmund!" She giggled as he pulled down the funny-looking goggles over his eyes.

"And you look quite yellow, Eleanor," he laughed. "Perhaps soon they will make some more flattering colors for these things."

"Fly safely!" Mary exclaimed as Edmund helped Eleanor hop into the back seat and then took his place in the front.

"Bring us something back from India!" Martha exclaimed.

"We will bring you the emperor's treasure!" Eleanor joked.

"I knew it!" Debbie exclaimed.

Eleanor and Edmund both laughed, and Vibhishana guided the audience out of the way to make room as Edmund turned on the engine and drove the plane out onto the makeshift runway.

"Are you ready to feel the wind in your face, my dearest thistle?" he shouted over the loud clanking of the propellers.

"Let's fly, Colonel!" Eleanor exclaimed.

And with the perfect wind, the clunky plane sputtered across the mostly flat field, and Edmund and Eleanor took off into the warm, sunny sky towards their next marital adventure.

PART THREE
OVERLAND

CHAPTER 12 – BRETAGNE

"Did you like it, Eleanor?" Edmund asked giddily as he helped her out of the plane. She was shivering uncontrollably. "Good lord, are you alright, dearest? Was it too cold for you?"

"I'll be fine," Eleanor replied unconvincingly through chattering teeth. "It was lovely. We were very lucky to have our route so thoroughly clear of clouds." Eleanor knew that luck had very little to do with it. "The white cliffs of Dover were magical."

Her shivers overwhelmed her enthusiasm as Edmund gathered her into his freezing arms. She squealed and pulled away.

"I'm sorry, darling. You're like an ice man at the moment. Let's go somewhere where we can both warm up. I assume you landed here for a reason?"

With one swift movement, Edmund hopped up onto the body of the plane and gathered their small suitcases from the footholds.

"This is Lord Grimby's holiday home," he explained as he guided her across the green windswept field he'd used as their runway towards a large white-washed, thatched-roof traditional

191

Breton house overlooking the craggy shoreline. The warm yellow lights on inside the house beckoned them as dusk fell.

"Curious…" he said as they reached the front door. "I didn't think anyone would be here. I hope it's the right place. I navigated by sight based on his instructions, but I suppose I could have been off by a bit…"

Eleanor reached her shaking hand up to knock. "I must warm up, Edmund. Even if this is the wrong house, perhaps they will give us shelter."

"Yes, yes, of course…" Edmund said apologetically. He glanced at her hand and then remembered his own frigidity and dutifully kept his distance. "I hope the flight wasn't too unpleasant for you."

"I loved feeling the wind in my face. It was even more exhilarating than riding the thoroughbreds as a lass. Really, it was a wonderful experience. Next time I'll just have to dress more appropriately. Live and learn, the wise men say."

"Yes… yes, I suppose…" Edmund did not seem convinced enough to forgive himself for his oversight of her human needs.

"Colonel!" A merry, red-faced woman in a traditional Breton outfit answered the door and welcomed them with an odd accent in English that sounded vaguely like a mix of Welsh and French. "And you must be Madame Marriner! Come in, come in!"

She shook their hands and then grabbed their suitcases and escorted them inside, slamming the door behind them.

"I am Norwenn, Lord Grimby's housekeeper. He warned me that you were coming."

"Well, jolly good on Lord Grimby!" Edmund exclaimed.

"Yes, jolly good on him…" Eleanor murmured. She'd entirely expected Norwenn's hand to pulsate with Yakshini warmth, but her handshake felt entirely human. Based on Edmund's reaction, he hadn't appeared to plan the trip in enough detail to account for their basic needs beyond shelter and transport. The luck that Lord Grimby just happened to have a staff on-call at his rural holiday home to feed them and keep the house warm seemed a bit unlikely, but without the Yakshinis to take credit, Eleanor was quite puzzled by the phenomenon, and, of course, she was more puzzled by it than Edmund was.

Norwenn guided them through the hallway, past a parlor with a roaring fire that Eleanor found especially appealing, and then into a small dining room with its own roaring fire. Eleanor loved how old houses, including Edmund's in Basingstoke, had a fireplace in every room. They reminded her of the house she'd grown up in before her father's demise.

"You must be hungry," Norwenn said as Edmund's stomach growled loudly. She smiled as he blushed with embarrassment. "Don't worry, Colonel. I have prepared you a traditional Breton meal. Perhaps you'd like to take a seat by the fire, and I will bring you some tea to warm you up before your meal. You look like your flight froze you right through. The water closet and the powder room are just through there." She pointed down a dark hallway.

"I must say, your English is excellent," Edmund said affably.

Norwenn smiled. "My father was Irish, Colonel, so you'd best save your praise for the other Bretons who speak English. They are few and far between. Now, please relax, and I will be back shortly."

She disappeared with their suitcases in hand, and Edmund and Eleanor both stood directly in front of the fire, warming their hands.

"Darling, please don't take offense, but I must ask you… what exactly were you planning for us to eat tonight if Norwenn hadn't been here?"

Edmund thought for a moment about his answer. "I didn't think about it… I suppose I assumed that this house would be close enough to a village that we'd be able to walk to a restaurant."

"Did you ask Lord Grimby about it when he gave you his directions?"

"It didn't occur to me…" Eleanor could hear a burst of personal frustration in Edmund's voice as he contemplated his error for the first time.

"I see… and, darling, what would we have done if we'd arrived here at dusk as we did and the house was empty as you'd expected with no firewood to be found?"

"I suppose I didn't think about it…" Edmund admitted.

"I see… so, darling, we're really quite lucky that Norwenn was here, don't you think? Perhaps we'd best look at our itinerary and make some clearer plans for some of our stops. We will be in Paris tomorrow night, which should not produce these same problems, but I think we would both benefit from reviewing the itinerary with more scrutiny before we arrive cold and hungry somewhere else without a godsend like Norwenn to tend to us."

"Yes… of course, you're right," Edmund agreed. "I suppose I'm often quite lucky. My colleagues and Mr. Valov are always very thoughtful in anticipating my needs. Although, perhaps it isn't just luck this time…"

"What do you mean?" Eleanor asked with piqued interest.

Edmund looked pained as he thought about how to phrase his response. "I saved Lord Grimby's son in the trenches. He was one of many young men I carried out of the line of fire after the first mustard gas attack. He lost his arm in that battle, but he came back mostly intact, which made him far luckier than most of the others who were caught off guard."

Eleanor leaned forward and kissed Edmund gently on the lips. Now that she had the roaring fire to warm her, she enjoyed spending time in his arms, even though he still felt like an ice man.

"You're right, Edmund. There is probably more than luck playing into Lord Grimby's support of our little excursion. It is a great gift you gave him by saving his son's life. A gift that a few favors will hardly begin to repay."

"He owes me nothing. I did what every man in my position should have done. What I myself should have done far more than I did."

Eleanor knew that it was futile to argue with him on the point, as she had already tried it unsuccessfully many times, and so she ignored Edmund's frigidity and gathered him into her arms. "Let's not let the melancholy memories invade the happy present."

He gave in and kissed her, and they both enjoyed the unusual sensations of each other's cold touch until Norwenn re-entered the room bearing a large silver tea service with two large teapots and two porcelain cups.

"Please, let me help you!"

Edmund rushed to gather the heavy tray from her. He placed it on the table beside two place-settings that were already set for their dinner.

"Thank you, Colonel," Norwenn said amicably. "I trust you can serve yourselves? I will go finish preparing dinner."

Without waiting for a response, Norwenn left them alone.

Edmund poured Eleanor the first cup and carried it hastily to her position by the fire.

"Thank you, darling." She took her first sip. "It's really very hot. Perhaps you should drink an entire pot yourself. I will need some time to let it cool or it will burn my tongue."

Edmund glanced towards the dark hallway through which Norwenn had disappeared. He positioned himself with his back to the hallway so that she wouldn't be able to see him if she flitted back into their vicinity, and then he drank down the entire second teapot straight from the vessel in one long Rakshasa gulp.

In a blur, he was standing beside Eleanor, taking her free cold hand into his pulsating hot ones for a gentle massage as she took another small sip of her tea.

"Your speed seemed quite natural that time. It seems your practice today with Mr. Johnson was fruitful."

"It was, in some ways, the highlight of my life," Edmund admitted. "All of my childhood fantasies came together at once. With you there, dearest, and him, and the novelty of our honesty, and the fun of our game…" He helped her switch her tea into the opposite hand so he could continue his massage. "To play cricket with my wife and my father, without any requirement to hide my secrets… it was a desire my boyhood mind longed so dearly for, but I never believed in my wildest dreams it could really happen."

"Your father, darling?" Eleanor asked with surprise. "You still believe, after what Mr. Johnson told you, that he's really your father?"

"Why else would he act the way that he does? You saw the love in his eyes, the pride. I was ever so grateful to see it myself… more grateful than you could ever know, dearest. Obviously, there is some reason that he won't admit that it's true, but I can feel our connection. When he is close to me, I feel a quickening of sorts. It's quite hard to explain. It feels as if I'm home."

Eleanor looked into the earnest eyes of her husband as he massaged his own warmth into her hand, and her mind flitted to the unpleasant reality that Edmund's real father was not the virtuous, loving figure that Vibhishana was. She smiled and embarked upon one of her many profound acts of love. "I'm so happy for you, darling. I'm happy that Mr. Johnson was able to stay and spend some real time with us. He is quite a wonderful man, isn't he? I see many similarities between you."

"Do you really?" Edmund asked with childlike enthusiasm. "I do think that we look quite similar, don't you?"

"Yes, darling, I suppose you do." She had to admit the observation was true. Their fair skin, rosy cheeks, and jet-black hair did make them look related, although Edmund had a certain humanity to him that his uncle lacked, a certain type of subtle, natural imperfection that made him look and feel more real. She wondered if their similarities did, in fact, demonstrate a family resemblance or if they were just another skilled farce, as Kuveni's convincing impression of Edmund's cousin had been. "But that's not what I meant. You both have a delightfully tricky sense of humor, and there is a gentleness about you. You are both very expressive about your love. It makes you more beautiful than anyone else I've ever met."

Edmund took Eleanor's teacup and placed it on the mantle so that he could engulf her into a passionate embrace.

"I love you so much, Eleanor," he whispered into her ear.

Eleanor pulled away as she became lightheaded. The sensation was pleasant, as if she was swimming in light, but also a bit overwhelming.

"Are you alright?" Edmund asked concernedly as he steadied her.

"Yes, I'm fine," she said as she regained her balance. "I haven't eaten anything since breakfast. I think the hunger is catching up with me."

"I am rather famished myself. My unusual exercise this afternoon was especially draining." Edmund guided her to the tea service and poured her another cup. "I think I hear Norwenn coming now."

Eleanor listened carefully until she too heard the footsteps approaching.

"Dinner is served!" Norwenn declared as she returned bearing an enormous silver platter covered in the widest variety of shellfish either of them had ever seen—lobster, crab, shrimp, prawns, cockles, scallops, oysters, mussels, and several other local sea creatures that neither of them recognized.

"Brilliant!" Edmund moved the tea service out of her way.

"Now, these are best eaten with the hands," Norwenn advised. "Even Lord Grimby is willing to overlook his British table manners to appreciate the Breton sea fruits in their traditional fashion."

"That will be no problem for us!" Edmund said excitedly as he pulled out a chair for Eleanor and then seated himself.

"I will be right back with the chouchen. It is a mead that pairs nicely with the food."

Norwenn disappeared back into the dark hallway.

Edmund rubbed his hands together as he eyed the platter, deciding which offering to dig into first. As Eleanor made her first choice with a prawn, he grabbed the large steamed lobster, seamlessly cracked its shell with his strong fingers, and then gracefully set about removing the meat.

"Ha! Very good, Colonel! Not everyone has the skill to break open the shells without help!" Norwenn laughed as she returned with a bottle of mead, two glasses, and a metal device for cracking shells.

"I hope it wasn't rude that I did it this way?"

"Enjoy yourself, Colonel. Here you are free to eat as you please. I will be in the kitchen if you need anything."

Norwenn offered them both a polite nod and left them alone.

"Oh Eleanor, you must try this!" Edmund exclaimed giddily as he offered her a large chunk of lobster with his fingers.

"It's delicious! It's so naturally sweet! Try this!"

She fed him a chunk of prawn, and she giggled as he suckled her fingers.

They continued their game, feeding each other the crustaceans and drinking down the entire bottle of mead, until the sound of the phone ringing in the hallway interrupted their pleasant evening.

"Colonel, Mr. Valov is on the telephone for you," Norwenn said apologetically.

"How odd… I didn't even give him the number…" A subtle sense of alarm worked its way into his tone.

"You'd better go figure out what he needs," Eleanor suggested calmly. "I'm sure it's nothing, darling."

Edmund followed Norwenn out of the room, and Eleanor worked hard to relegate her concern. But, as she dug through the pile of crustaceans in an effort to distract herself, Mélusine materialized right beside her.

198

"Jesus Christ!" Eleanor covered her mouth sheepishly, and then lowered her voice into a whisper. "Edmund is just in the other room!"

"I know. I shouldn't be here," Mélusine whispered. "I have a few items to report, and then you will hopefully not see me again any time soon. I wanted to warn you about your mother, Eleanor. She was in the house earlier today snooping around your bedchamber. I followed her invisibly to see what she was up to, and as you can imagine, she wasn't pleased when she stumbled upon the sticky sheets and the cache of empty wine bottles."

"Blimey," Eleanor whispered.

"It gets worse. She spotted your game of cricket out the window. She saw Edmund and Vibhi using their Rakshasa talents. And so... I did something, Eleanor. Something I hope you will forgive..."

"You didn't kill her, did you?" Eleanor blurted.

"*Mon dieu*, of course not!" Mélusine exclaimed indignantly.

"Sshhh!" Eleanor hissed.

Mélusine looked guiltily down the dark hallway towards Edmund's position, and then, without any warning, she pummeled Eleanor. In the blink of an eye, they were both standing in the powder room with the door closed.

Eleanor leaned heavily on Mélusine as a moment of hot dizziness overwhelmed her. "Is that how it feels when Edmund does it?"

"No. That wasn't speed I just used. It was a Yakshini talent. I transported us from one place to another. But that is beside the point. Your mother is not the type of human who should know anything about us, ma chérie. I'm sure I don't have to explain to you why."

"No, you certainly don't."

"And so, I made her believe that the entire episode was a dream. I've done something similar to thousands of humans who have stumbled upon my secret lair in France over the centuries. I made the experience outrageous, and then I used the same talent that I have used on you—the infusion of euphoria—but I used it in a much higher dose. When I infuse humans with too much of it, it makes them a bit... shall we say... intoxicated. I used enough of it to make her lose consciousness, and then I placed her in the parlor to finish off her nap. I'm quite sure that it worked. I've been observing her all day since she woke up, and she hasn't mentioned anything about the experience to Martha or Mary yet, but I wanted to warn you in case she says something odd. You may need to help us cover our tracks to Martha and Mary."

Eleanor sighed with stress.

"I'm sorry to interrupt your fun like this with bad tidings." Mélusine squeezed Eleanor's hand affectionately. Eleanor felt lightheaded for a moment as Mélusine's warmth traveled up through her hand, thawing the remaining frigidity left over from her flight.

Eleanor squeezed her hands back with thanks. "Thank you, Mélusine. You have averted a disaster. As long as my mother doesn't have anything coherent to say about it, I'm quite sure that Martha and Mary will not believe her, even if she says something. She's gone on and on about demons and devils and such nonsense since we were lasses."

"I thought as much. Now, I also wanted to warn you so that you can have proper expectations that Vibhishana has reiterated his orders against our meddling. He has had quite a strict talk with Kuveni, and so you should not expect her to be popping in to rescue you from minor inconveniences anymore. I'm hoping that you can help Edmund navigate any human unpleasantries associated with this plan. I am also going to hold off on meddling unless you are in dire straits, so you are on your own from now on. We must hand him over to you, ma chérie, to teach him what we couldn't ourselves about ordinary human life."

"I think it is for the best," Eleanor agreed. "Edmund didn't even think about how our needs would be met tonight. It was exceptional luck that Lord Grimby's housekeeper was here to feed us. I don't think there's a village for miles."

"Edmund didn't plan it that way?" Mélusine asked with piqued interest.

"He didn't!" Eleanor exclaimed. "Apparently Lord Grimby called ahead and told her that we were coming! I thought she was one of you until I shook her hand, and it was entirely human!"

"How could you tell?"

"Yakshinis feel different. Your warmth feels more alive than human warmth. It's hard to describe, but I knew Illa was a Yakshini because she felt very similar to Kuveni... although her mannerisms gave her away much earlier than that, of course. She must not be very experienced at your farces."

"You are very perceptive, ma chérie. You are by far the cleverest human I've ever encountered." Mélusine closed her eyes. "Edmund's conversation with Mr. Valov is over. He's returning to the dining room now."

"How do you know?" Eleanor asked.

"Kuveni is spying on him invisibly, and Yakshinis can communicate telepathically with each other. Whenever you see us meditating, we're probably consulting our brethren on some topic or another. Poor Illa was impossibly lost when she accidentally called Edmund 'my lord.' Her lie was my suggestion."

"Huh..." Eleanor said as she thought back to the many moments she'd observed them make that gesture.

"But Kuveni and I will both be leaving you alone now. Good luck and safe travels, ma chérie." Mélusine pulled her into a quick hug and then kissed her on each cheek. "Welcome to the family."

With a pleasant breeze, Mélusine dissolved, leaving Eleanor alone in the powder room. She rinsed the crustacean juice off her hands, took a deep breath, and emerged.

"Is everything alright?" she asked as she joined Edmund at the dinner table. The piles of empty shells had been cleared, fresh settings had been set, ramekins of sugar and melted chocolate were neatly placed in the center of the table, and Edmund was pouring her another glass of mead from a fresh bottle.

"Perfectly fine," he said happily. "Mr. Valov had some suggestions for restaurants we might enjoy in Paris. He offered to make us some reservations for the next few evenings."

"How kind of him…" Eleanor murmured. She found it very hard to believe, even now, that Mr. Valov was not one of Edmund's Yakshini guardians.

"And Breton crepes for dessert!" Norwenn declared as she approached with a large pile of fresh crepes.

"How wonderful they smell!" Edmund exclaimed.

Norwenn smiled as she presented the platter and sprinkled a layer of sugar and melted chocolate from the ramekins.

"I placed your suitcases in the room at the top of the stairs. You are welcome to take your time and retire when you wish. I will be in the kitchen doing the dishes, and then I will head to bed myself. *Noz vad. Bonne nuit!*"

As soon as Norwenn flitted out of the room, Edmund gathered his first crepe up and popped it straight into his mouth with his right hand. Eleanor laughed and followed his lead.

"This is a good technique for you to practice," Edmund said as he devoured his second helping. "You'll use the same technique to eat most of the breads in India."

A blob of melted chocolate landed on her chin, and Edmund swooped in to lick it off.

"I think we can eat the rest of these in bed, don't you?" Eleanor suggested naughtily as she stood up and a burst of arousal bombarded her at the thought.

"Yes, I think we can!" Edmund enthusiastically gathered up the platter while she grabbed the mead, and with an explosion of mischievous giggles, they tore up the stairs into their new bedroom and slammed the door.

With the most carefree haste they'd felt since their wedding, they ripped each other's clothes off and tumbled onto the bed.

Eleanor wiped the melted chocolate all over her naked breasts, and Edmund set about licking it off of her.

"Our first adventure seems to be going well..." Eleanor sighed at the touch of Edmund's tongue on her flesh.

"Let's see if we can make it better," Edmund suggested as he straddled her.

"Yes," Eleanor moaned.

And together, the two lovebirds set about relishing the many tasty flavors of their second night of marital bliss.

CHAPTER 13 – GARDEN OF EARTHLY DELIGHTS

The next day, with the help of Norwenn's brother's carriage pulled by two beautiful Breton horses that Edmund and Eleanor found thoroughly enchanting, the happy couple made their way to the train station in Saint-Brieuc and thence to Paris through the rolling, grassy, rainy countryside of Northwestern France.

Eleanor found it difficult to keep her eyes open after her second delightfully sleepless night of marital pleasures, and so she leaned her head on her gentle husband's shoulder and slept most of the way. She could feel the subtle pulse of Edmund's calm, gentle power emanating from his contented being, and she sighed with sleepy satisfaction as he gathered her hand into his and held her for many hours while the heat from his three coffee pots at breakfast slowly dissipated.

When they arrived in the Gare de Lyon, Edmund gently nudged her awake.

"We're here, dearest. Welcome to Paris," he whispered as she groggily returned to the waking world. She could tell it was already dark outside, and a wet, musty scent indicated that it had been raining for quite some time.

Edmund gathered both of their small suitcases into his left hand and helped her up with his right. She glanced at the empty hooks beside their seats, only to be reminded that they hadn't packed anything remotely appropriate to wear in the cold, rainy weather. They'd left the bomber jackets with Norwenn to be returned to Lord Grimby upon his upcoming visit to collect his plane, and so all Eleanor had to wear was the cashmere sweater and winter wool trousers she'd played cricket in the day before. She hoped none of the fashionable Parisians would notice the grass stains.

Still feeling a bit disoriented, Eleanor let Edmund guide her off of the train, through the crowded station, out to the road, and straight into a line of queued up taxis.

With an air of calm authority, he gave his orders to the driver in perfect French, and they were off, speeding through the wet streets of Paris.

"It's quite adorable, isn't it?" she murmured as they passed a series of patisseries and flower shops. "There's something a bit more coherent about it than London. I can't really put my finger on what."

"It looks much better than it used to. I suppose London does too. Both cities have greatly benefitted from the technology marvels of the modern age. I'm ever so glad they didn't demolish historical swaths of the city to build a train line. The metro is such a brilliant project."

"I've never thought about the loss that modern roads might cause to the integrity of a city. Can you imagine them replacing these beautiful cobblestones with something to accommodate motorcars? How wretched! It wouldn't feel the same at all!"

"It will happen. It is only a matter of time, I think. The speed at which London has built up since I lived there the first time is still hard for me to fathom."

Edmund squeezed her hand and pointed to the Seine. A little girl ran after a grumpy clown carrying a handful of wet balloons while her angry mother chased after her. They both laughed at the absurdity of the sight.

"How strange for you to see so many changes with your own eyes. I wonder how that must feel for Mr. Johnson with his five thousand years of watching entire empires rise and fall."

"I cannot fathom it," Edmund reiterated.

They both sat in contemplative silence, observing the many amusing sights and sounds of the vibrant city until the taxi pulled up at a grand white façade, and two bellmen rushed to greet them.

While Edmund paid the driver, one of the bellmen whisked Eleanor inside under the protection of an umbrella, while the other gathered their small suitcases and followed.

"*Bienvenue*! Welcome! You must be Madame Marriner!" An enthusiastic man in an elaborate old-fashioned uniform that looked vaguely like it had been inspired by Edmund's military dress uniform greeted them in heavily accented English as he bowed regally before her. Eleanor smiled at the odd reality that she was, in fact, now Madame Marriner. The idea still seemed quite foreign to her. "Ah, and you must be Colonel Marriner! Your butler informed us of your exact itinerary. Please, come with me. I am Monsieur Renault, and I will be your personal valet during your stay here. I will show you to the royal suite at once, and we will do the paperwork tomorrow."

Eleanor and Edmund both threw each other a thrilled glance at the surprising quality of service.

"First class all the way," Edmund whispered into her ear with a wink.

They followed Monsieur Renault through a marble hallway, decorated with sweetly-scented flower arrangements bursting with Asiatic lilies just as Edmund's house had been for their wedding day, until they reached an enormous set of french doors, already open in anticipation of their arrival.

"Biordinar," Eleanor whispered as she took in the palatial suite.

A sitting room with furniture that looked like it had been stolen from Versailles gave way to a huge bedroom with an oversized canopied bed. Next to it, an entirely marble bathroom with a bath even larger than the Rakshasa bed in their room in Basingstoke was already filled with steaming hot water and white gardenia petals.

Monsieur Renault skipped ahead of them and pushed open two golden closet doors revealing a vast walk-in closet filled with a his-and-hers collection of perfectly tailored outfits, pressed and laid out for their perusal. In the center of the closet, two new matching trunks awaited their use for the rest of their journey.

"I told you not to worry about packing enough for our honeymoon," Edmund said with a happy grin.

"*You* planned this?" Eleanor asked with genuine surprise. She had to admit, she'd drastically underestimated his foresight. She wondered if perhaps she'd been far too harsh on him *and* Kuveni. For the first time since they'd met, he'd managed to anticipate their needs before she had.

"I knew we wouldn't be able to bring very much with us in the small plane. Certainly not entire trunks of the fashionable clothing that's required for us to enjoy our first class journey in style, so I asked Mr. Valov to call ahead and have these ordered. I hope you don't mind, dearest, but I secretly borrowed a few of your dresses so he could have them measured by a French tailor friend of his."

"Of course I don't mind!" Eleanor swooned. "Edmund this is glorious! I thought we were going to have to waste our first day in Paris shopping! I didn't even bring a proper coat!"

Monsieur Renault clapped excitedly as he disappeared behind one of the open doors to collect an enormous mink coat. Eleanor gasped. "Edmund, that must have cost a fortune! I don't need anything as grand as that!"

Edmund smiled. "Our honeymoon is not about need, my dearest thistle. It is about indulgence."

Eleanor desperately wanted to rip Edmund's clothes off, but as she glanced at Monsieur Renault, she worked hard to contain herself. "Thank you, Edmund. I never dreamed I'd have a coat like that."

"I never dreamed I'd have a life like this one, Eleanor, with a wife as perfect as you are."

Monsieur Renault noticed their honeymoon moment and re-hung the coat in the closet.

"I will leave you two for now. The kitchen is open twenty-four hours. Just ring if you'd like anything brought over."

"*Merci, Monsieur Renault…*" Edmund continued with several sentences of gratitude in French as he shook his hand amicably.

"Colonel, your French is perfect!" Monsieur Renault exclaimed as he made his way to the door.

"*Merci*," Edmund said simply as Monsieur Renault bowed and closed them into their room in privacy.

As soon as the doors were closed, Eleanor rushed into Edmund's arms, and they tore each other's clothes off with such haste that they could hear the seams ripping. They didn't pause for a second. Instead, they just laughed as Eleanor scampered across the room, straight into the steaming bath. Edmund grabbed a bottle of champagne that had been thoughtfully left for them in an ice bucket in the sitting room, and with a blur and a loud splash, he was sitting in the bath across from her.

"I love you, Edmund." Eleanor straddled him with more enthusiasm than she'd ever felt in her life. "I can hardly believe that you're my husband."

Edmund placed the champagne bottle on the floor and wrapped his arms around her.

"I am the luckiest man in the world, Eleanor. I promise you, I will never forget that."

Eleanor licked his lips and then his tongue, and together with loud moans of satisfaction, their first night in the city of love commenced.

For the next several days, the honeymooners wandered about the city hand in hand, popping into bistros and cafés every time the rain picked up, allowing Edmund to enjoy at least two lunches per day, followed by a series of intermittent afternoon snacks. Their romantic food fest was interspersed with walking along the Seine, touring the famous sights, and exploring the many museums while Edmund explained the various stylistic nuances and recounted colorful personal anecdotes about his artistic colleagues whose work remained on display.

On their fifth and last day in the city (and quite a rainy one it was), while Monsieur Renault packed their trunks in preparation for their departure on the Orient Express, they returned to the Louvre for a final look around. After quite a few hours of relaxed meandering, they happened to pop into the English landscape gallery, where Eleanor spied a very familiar piece displayed prominently right in the center.

"Edmund, darling, how could you not tell me that your work was on display at the Louvre?!" she exclaimed as she ran up to inspect it.

He shrugged. "They buy tons of paintings, dearest. I assumed they'd cached it away in the basement where it belongs."

"I think their curators have quite the eye, darling. Your painting wouldn't be on display for the world to see if they thought that it belonged in the basement. Huh… Look here: It says that you lived from 1818-1895. That seems like a reasonable assumption."

Edmund stared at the placard for almost a minute. "I have never seen the years of my life summarized in that way. 1818 is the birth year that I put on my application to the Royal Academy. I wonder what they thought happened to me in 1895."

210

"You didn't arbitrate a scheme with a badly burned cadaver or some other such nonsense?" Eleanor asked jokingly.

"I was far too preoccupied with not getting caught to attempt anything of the sort. I kept the house in a trust that Mr. Johnson's agent had set up for me years before, and hoped that anyone who noticed my absence would assume I'd skipped off somewhere for my retirement."

"Huh… I've never thought about what kind of complications you must face keeping your own property through your transitions."

"I wasn't very good at it myself, to be honest. I was keeping all of my money in my house until an agent from Mr. Johnson arrived at my door in 1850 and insisted that I do something more intelligent with it. He helped me set up various trusts in several different banks that I would be able to access regardless of my apparent age. He even helped set up a salary for me from a company set up by Mr. Johnson. That is yet one more reason why I think he is my father. The company was called 'Jack Johnson and Sons, Ltd.' I tried to look up the records, but he had done an exceptional job of hiding them."

"I suppose he must be quite experienced in those matters. I'm glad he got involved early enough that you were able to keep the profits from all of your hard work. This painting is really quite good. You seem to have a passion for the subject-matter that I think was lacking in the later ones. Was it done earlier in your career?" Eleanor skillfully changed the subject.

"You should be an art critic, dearest," Edmund winked. "I think that I painted this during my first spring in Basingstoke. I spent months exploring the nuances of how the seasonal waterfalls changed with the weather patterns. Do you recognize the setting?"

"Is that… is that the little stone bridge into the woods behind your house?" Eleanor asked with delight.

"*Our* house," he corrected her. "It is, in fact, the exact bridge that we scampered across on the way to the Druidic linden grove.

I still didn't capture the life of the water, I think. There was a vivacity to it that I could never get quite right."

Eleanor wrapped her arms around his neck and enticed him into a kiss. "Well, I think it's lovely, and so does the Louvre."

"Well, I think you're lovely, so we will have to leave it at a draw."

As Edmund kissed her again, a proctor walked past the door and barked something at them in French.

"Well, that's rather strict of them, given Parisian culture, don't you think?" Eleanor said with surprise. "People are kissing each other all over the city!"

Edmund smiled. "He was telling us that the museum is closing."

"Ah, I see. Did he have to sound so angry about it?"

"It is just the Parisian style. The people in the countryside are much nicer. I suppose that's true of England as well. I've had many unpleasant interactions with Londoners over the years."

"Yes… yes, I suppose that's true."

Edmund took her hand, and together they meandered towards the exit.

"Dearest, we're leaving Paris tomorrow morning. Is there anything here you'd like to do on our final night? I'm getting rather tired of the formal settings of Mr. Valov's suggested restaurants. As delicious as their food is, I'm rather sick of everyone watching us eat."

"Really? I was rather enjoying their shocked looks as you commandeered my uneaten food onto your plate," Eleanor winked.

"You were not privy to their snide comments."

"You should have been translating them for me!" Eleanor exclaimed. "We could have kept a tally!"

Edmund smiled. "Yes, that surely would have made it more enjoyable."

"I have been thinking…" Eleanor hedged.

"Yes?"

"What do you think of going over to the Moulin Rouge? I know the neighborhood has more than its fair share of opium addicts and prostitutes, but it is rather famous for its outrageous antics and artistic freedom. Perhaps we should see that side of Paris too."

"What a wonderful idea! I was wondering about it myself. There are supposed to still be many artists hopping about on Montmartre. I've wanted to explore it for decades, but I never seemed to have the time."

"Why didn't you suggest it, then?" Eleanor asked curiously as she noticed the familiar loving twinkle in his eye.

"Ovid would not have approved of suggesting a trip to a den of prostitution and drugs for our honeymoon."

"He was a Roman! He probably would have gone there first!" Eleanor laughed.

"Perhaps," Edmund conceded amicably. "I believe there are plenty of restaurants on Montmartre, and I suspect they don't need any reservations. Shall we go straight there?"

"I will follow you, Colonel."

Eleanor squealed, and Edmund dutifully held the umbrella for her as they ran through the large, slippery courtyard of the Louvre to the closest road and hailed a taxi.

As Edmund gave his instructions to the driver in French, the driver eyed them disapprovingly in the rearview mirror. He engaged Edmund in a minor argument that made Eleanor desperately wish that she spoke French, and then Edmund sat back and ran his hand along her wet mink coat, absorbing all of the droplets of water into his thirsty skin.

"That is a rather useful talent, isn't it?" Eleanor whispered in Gaelic. "Next time I get out of the bath, I'll have to forego the towel and just let you caress me dry."

"I like that plan a lot," he whispered as he invited her into a delicious, wet kiss.

"What was that argument about just now?" Eleanor asked as soon as he pulled away.

"The driver didn't think that upstanding citizens such as us should go to a neighborhood like that. I told him that we had nothing to worry about. He said that he will drop us off at the Moulin Rouge, but to get to Sacre Coeur and the restaurants at the top of Montmartre, we'll have to climb the hill by foot. Are you up for it? It is raining rather hard."

"A little rain has never been able to stop me. It's in my blood, you know. If Scots couldn't handle the rain, we'd never go outside."

Edmund guided her into a more passionate kiss and worked his hand naughtily into her coat and onto her thigh, tickling her skin through her thin silk dress. They ignored the driver's annoyed humphs for quite a long ride until they pulled up to the tell-tale red-lit windmill, and the driver interrupted them with what sounded like a sharp admonishment in French.

Edmund hastily wiped the last of Eleanor's red lipstick off of his lips and paid the driver, and then with guilty giggles, he helped Eleanor out of the car, and they scampered hand in hand through the pouring rain, right into the lobby.

A short, bald, red-faced man who reminded Eleanor of a bookie she once knew (and disdained) at the Musselburgh racetrack with her father, hissed something dismissively at them in French, and Edmund smiled amicably and engaged him. Edmund's voice exuded calm authority as he reached into his pocket and handed the man an astonishingly thick wad of bills. The man's eyes bulged with surprise, and then he gestured for them to wait as he rushed through a private door.

"He said that we were too late and that it was sold out. I told him I was sure that he could find a way to accommodate us. He agreed," Edmund reported with subtle pride.

The man returned with two can-can girls clad in scandalous feathered costumes, one on each arm, and Eleanor burst into laughter. "Darling, I think you've bought us quite the entertaining evening!"

"Good lord," Edmund murmured.

His face turned the deepest red blush she'd ever seen, and he re-engaged the man to sheepishly explain the misunderstanding. But, as the conversation progressed and the man refused to accept Edmund's protestations, one of the can-can girls wrapped her arm around Edmund while the other ensnared Eleanor, and before they could protest any further, they were swept through a pair of imposing double doors, straight into a dark theater auditorium with a politely seated audience gazing upon a brightly lit stage filled to the brim with shimmying, kicking can-can dancers in glittery feathered outfits.

"This isn't so bad, I suppose," Edmund whispered. "It seems just like a normal theater."

"Imagine how popular the ballet would be with those costumes," Eleanor whispered back.

They both laughed as they relaxed at the seeming normalcy of the situation, while the can-can dancers led them around the back row of the theater, up the far aisle, and through another door. They followed their escorts dutifully up the stairs, until the can-can dancers pushed open a padded leather door, and a puff of sickly-sweet scented smoke engulfed them.

"Good lord," Edmund murmured again.

Inside the room, scores of guests were engaged in an array of bizarre sexual activities that I'm quite sure even Eleanor would be too shy to describe to anyone, especially her daughter.

"Good lord," Eleanor seconded.

The can-can dancers urged them into the room, but with one glance towards the far corner where glassy-eyed opium smokers lay naked and deranged, Eleanor grabbed Edmund's arm, and with just as much Rakshasa force as he felt he needed to extricate them from their escorts' custody, he pushed his way past them, guiding

Eleanor into the hallway and slamming the door to the den of sin behind them.

"Well, I think that's enough of that for one night, don't you, darling? I'm glad my mother's not here. She might have had a heart attack," Eleanor quipped cheerfully, hoping that keeping her tone light might keep Edmund's adrenaline from calling forth his most obvious demonic trait.

"Indeed. I think I understand Bosch's *Garden of Earthly Delights* now. I'd never thought of it as a work of realism. He was a man ahead of his time…" He squeezed her hand and led her down the stairs at his fastest human speed.

As soon as they reached the ground level, he pushed open an exit door, and they tumbled out into a dark, wet alleyway.

"We wanted an adventure, and I'd say we got it!" Eleanor exclaimed.

"I wish I hadn't given that man so much money… Perhaps less money would have gotten us tickets to the tame little theater show."

They looked at each other and then burst into laughter.

"I think I'm ready for dinner in an adorable little bistro, how about you, darling?"

"I can't think of anything I'd rather do."

Edmund took her hand, and together, they headed up the mountain.

CHAPTER 14 – MONTMARTRE

The rain dissolved into a delicious mist, and Eleanor was grateful for the reprieve as they hiked up a hill so steep that she felt like she was back in the highlands of Scotland until they reached the steps of the imposing white domes of the Sacre Coeur basilica.

Edmund sighed. "It is such a beautiful work of architecture. It's too bad it was erected solely to please an angry god who doesn't exist."

Eleanor couldn't begin to decide what to say in response, and so she kissed him, until a burst of arousal reminded them both that they had a warm, rose-scented bath awaiting them back at their hotel room, just as Monsieur Renault had arranged for them (upon Mr. Valov's suggestion), every other evening.

"Let's get some dinner and then head back for our last night of romance in Paris," Eleanor suggested.

Edmund squeezed her hand, and together they hastily made their way around the side of the cathedral, into the winding streets of the artistic center of Montmartre.

"These all look so cute!" Eleanor exclaimed as they reached a central plaza lined with restaurants. "How can this possibly be so close to the Moulin Rouge? It's like we're in a different country!"

"This must be it. This must be where Renoir painted his delightful depictions," Edmund said excitedly. "I'm glad we came here, even if we narrowly escaped a depraved, drug-enhanced orgy."

"It's all about the story, isn't it? What a colorful story tonight is. More colorful than any other night, to be honest. I like the wild adventure of it. It makes it all feel more real."

"So do I." Edmund pulled her into a passionate embrace and dipped her. "Now, which of these adorable little bistros should we add to our story?"

"That one there looks especially cute." Eleanor pointed across the plaza.

"Let's try it!" Edmund declared as he guided her through the tree-lined little park to a restaurant with ceilings so low that he had to duck to get through the door and remain crouching as they waited for the slow maître to welcome them.

"Is this alright?" Eleanor asked as Edmund smiled self-consciously at his hunched posture.

"This is not the first nor the last time that I will be too tall for my surroundings. It is a reality of my life that I have accepted," Edmund reassured her.

He exchanged some jovial words and a few good-natured laughs with the maître, and then they were escorted to a private table in the back. Eleanor took off her warm mink coat and placed it on the hook beside the table. She was grateful that for the first time since they'd arrived in Paris, she could see where it was while they were eating, as she wasn't accustomed to the standard coat check at the intensely formal restaurants of the prior evenings, and she had already become quite attached to the thoughtful gift from her generous husband.

With great concentration, Edmund translated the menu for her, as he had done on the prior evenings, and with a sense of relaxation they hadn't enjoyed since their evening in Bretagne, they ordered the food that fit their fancy, and drank down a seemingly endless supply of house wine provided in carafes that the maître himself began refilling upon their fifth liter.

As the clock rounded nine, the door burst open, and a painter dressed in exactly the outfit anyone would expect from a French artist—red and white striped shirt, white sailor trousers, curled mustache, and beret—entered the room and began offering his services to the diners.

Edmund finished off his sixth course while Eleanor finished off her third, and a wide grin spread across his face as the painter approached their table.

"Edmund, darling, I'd much rather have a painting by you than this random peddler," Eleanor said with a slightly intoxicated level of honesty.

Edmund only grinned wider. He handed the painter a few heavy coins (clearly having learned from his first faux-pas what too much money would buy him), and then he got up and switched seats with the peddler, sitting himself down on the simple painter's stool, while the man sat down in Edmund's seat at their small two-person table to watch the odd tourist begin his foolish plan.

Edmund began swiftly using the painter's palette and portable easel to paint a portrait of Eleanor.

"Edmund, darling, what are you doing?" she asked as a smile crept onto her face. She knew exactly what he was doing. "I thought you didn't paint portraits!"

"I've only ever painted two. One of myself, and one of the Nizam of Hyderabad… yours shall be the third, my dearest thistle."

The painter watched with increasing interest as Edmund's skilled strokes became more frenetic, reaching an almost inhuman speed as he gazed intently at Eleanor and worked his way through the copious details required to represent her timeless beauty on a canvas. The rest of the diners noticed his spectacle, and even the maître made his way over to their table, refilling their wine as he stole glances of Edmund's unusually fast progress.

"Done!" he declared as he turned the canvas around to show Eleanor.

Before her was a painting unlike any she'd ever seen. It looked like her, yes, but the style was impossible to pinpoint. There was absolutely an eastern aesthetic to it, perhaps from his apprenticeship in Hyderabad, but there was also an unusual glowing softness to it informed by his decades of landscapes. The combination of his precise lines and the dreamy impressionistic overtones created a style that looked entirely unique and unquestionably modern.

"My god, Edmund. It's wonderful!" Eleanor exclaimed.

"*Mon dieu! C'est magnifique!*" the painter exclaimed as he leaned forward to take a closer look.

"I suppose we can't carry it home in the rain," Edmund said nonchalantly as he took another look at it. "Perhaps I can ask the maître to ship it back to Basingstoke. We don't need to carry it all the way to India with us, but it is quite a nice reminder of this adventurous night."

Eleanor leaned forward and pulled him into a kiss. "It's a wonderful momento, darling. I honestly had no idea how talented you really were until now. I think you should not limit yourself to landscapes. You've created something entirely modern and utterly superb."

"I am rather pleased with it," Edmund admitted.

He summoned the maître with only a glance, and after a jovial conversation in French with the maître and the peddling painter, the maître enthusiastically gathered up the masterpiece, and the painter shook Edmund's hand, offering him profuse praise that needed no translation. The painter handed Edmund back his coins, and then bowed respectfully as he gathered his easel and palette and made his way out the front door of the restaurant.

"What just happened?" Eleanor asked excitedly.

"The maître will mail the painting back to Basingstoke for us. The painter said that he should have paid *me* for the privilege of watching a masterpiece be made. I told him he was pulling my leg, and he disagreed. I think we parted on good terms, though, despite our disagreement."

"I think you're right," Eleanor winked.

As they both drank down another glass of delicious red wine, the maître returned with an île flotante in one hand and a crème brulée in the other. He declared something effusively as he placed them in the middle of the table, and then he flitted away with an especially cheerful air about him.

"The desserts are on the house," Edmund explained. "He apparently enjoyed my little spectacle, as did the other diners."

"I enjoyed it very much myself," Eleanor said as she cracked into the crème brulée.

They fed each other bites of their desserts while they each finished off a hearty pouring of a very rich Sauternes, followed by Edmund drinking down three coffees to warm himself for the trek back to the hotel (a detail that the maître noticed, and interpreted with a wink to Eleanor and a supportive slap on Edmund's back).

As the final table of other diners nodded their respect to Edmund from afar and skipped out of the restaurant, Edmund wrote down their address in Basingstoke in his lovely archaic cursive and handed it to the maître with a few more amicable words. Eleanor yawned and entertained a moment of fleeting gratitude that they were not still held up in the Moulin Rouge, and then Edmund helped her into her mink coat, paid the bill, waved goodbye to the enthusiastic maître, and escorted her into the night.

The light of the yellow streetlamps flickered, reflecting beautifully from the puddles and the shimmering cobblestone, and Eleanor looked straight up into the misty sky.

"I love the mist. It reminds me of my childhood summers," she said as she took in a deep breath.

"I love it too. It is so satiating."

He gathered her into another romantic dip and kissed her, but as they both perked up with arousal, they looked around the empty courtyard, and Edmund shrugged his concession. "We've got quite a trek down this mountain before we'll be able to hail a taxi."

"The sooner started the sooner done," Eleanor sighed.

They walked hand in hand around the plaza, and when they reached the far corner (on the opposite side from which they'd come), Edmund skipped down an alleyway and made an assessment of a dark wooded hillside park.

"I think if we go straight down through the park it will be faster than if we go back the way we came. It might be safer too, avoiding the Moulin Rouge crowd."

Eleanor walked at the top speed that her feet would allow in her wet high heels to join him.

"Let's do it, Colonel. I'm ready to be back in the warm bath."

"Me too."

They headed down a steep stone staircase, through increasingly deep woods, with moments of openness through which they could see the twinkling lights of the city.

"I can't believe there is a mountain this steep in the center of Paris!" Eleanor exclaimed as she worked to keep up with Edmund's quick pace. "Blimey!"

One of the heels of her shoes broke right off, and she leaned on Edmund as she took it off to inspect it.

"Well, I'm not making it down the rest of these stairs in these." She took off the other. "The question is, to keep them to be fixed or just give up."

"We will buy new ones, dearest. I'd rather get back to the hotel straightaway."

Edmund looked around the dark forest, and Eleanor could sense his nerves picking up.

"Aye, Colonel. I'll just leave them then."

She tossed them into the woods, and then took his hand and continued hastily down the hill.

As they reached a fork in the road, and the stairs disappeared into a horizontal path, they had to stop to assess their location.

"Which do you think, Eleanor? Left will take us towards the Moulin Rouge. Right... I'm not sure."

"Let's go left. We know there are people and taxis there," Eleanor suggested.

Suddenly, a crackling of footsteps on the forest floor aroused both of their attentions. Edmund's posture straightened, and Eleanor darted her eyes around in the dark, trying to spy their unwanted company.

"Let's go," Edmund whispered as he squeezed her hand.

As they headed onto the left path, a young, dirty, stinking man in tattered clothing stepped out from behind a tree with a knife poised. A second man, in similarly impoverished apparel, stepped out from the tree next to Edmund, wielding a second knife.

They hissed something in French to Edmund, and he hissed something back, pulling Eleanor closer into his arms. She was too overwhelmed with her own pumping adrenaline to worry about his demonic eyes or his chivalrous pose.

But, before the situation could escalate with more words, the vagrant closest to Eleanor lunged at her, and she gave into her instincts and kneed him in the groin. As he collapsed onto the ground with a surprised whimper, Edmund punched his aggressor in the stomach.

A burst of triumphant pride rushed through her as the man hit the ground.

"Edmund, let's go!" she exclaimed.

Boom.

Eleanor ducked as the loud crack of a gunshot rang out, but as she looked around frantically trying to identify the source or the target, Edmund collapsed onto the muddy ground beside her. Her heart almost exploded.

"Edmund!" she screamed.

A fourth attacker rushed at her from the darkness, and as she momentarily struggled with what to do—to fight or tend to her injured husband—he punched her solidly in the eye.

A flash of hot pain rushed through her, and she became lightheaded. As she regained control of her faculties, the attacker ripped the mink coat right off of her and slammed her onto the ground.

She fought back at him with all of her might, channeling her fiery outrage at everything that had ever been wrong with her world into her hands and her feet, but as she kicked at him and scratched at him with her fingernails, the gunman rushed towards her.

She screamed as he bent back her ring finger, ripping Edmund's mother's ring right off.

"*On y va!*" he hissed to the other able-bodied attacker.

They took one final look at their downed comrades, and then their victims, and took off running together into the dark night.

Eleanor struggled to stand up, contemplating momentarily the foolish idea of chasing after them, but as she looked down at her bare feet and her bandaged legs, she begrudgingly admitted her defeat.

A whimper of pain from her ailing husband brought her attention back to the most important matter at hand.

"Edmund!" She kneeled over him to assess his wounds. "Darling, you've been shot!"

"Are you alright, Eleanor?" he asked, barely conscious, as a combination of red human blood and violet metallic plasma oozed onto the ground underneath him.

"I'm fine, darling. They got the coat and your mother's ring, but I'm perfectly fine. We must focus on you. What do you need?"

But as Edmund got a whiff of the fresh blood oozing from Eleanor's injury, his eyes turned black, and a look of terrifying demonic fury darkened his expression. In a blur, he stood up, and the remnants of the violet metallic plasma wriggled up his leg, back into the gruesome wound in his lower back.

"Darling, I'm fine. Please, you've been shot. We must get you somewhere safe and private where you can heal."

Edmund took in a deep whiff, eyeing the path on which their attackers had escaped, and with a whoosh and a draft, he disappeared into the darkness.

"Bloody hell," Eleanor hissed as she looked at the two downed attackers at her feet. "You chose the wrong couple to mess with tonight, you bloody hooligans. And I swear to god that if my husband comes back from this ruined, I will kill you both myself."

As one of the two men attempted to get up, Eleanor channeled all of her burning rage into her foot and kicked him in the stomach again. He returned to his fetal position, while the other watched her with glassy, fearful eyes.

She waited and watched, keeping her eye on her charges for an excruciatingly long time, until finally, as the rain began to pick up, in a blur, Edmund returned carrying her mink coat in his right hand. Eleanor spotted red human blood that wasn't his on his left as he gazed at the two other attackers with a covetous look in his black demonic eyes.

"Edmund, are you alright?" she asked nervously.

He coaxed her back into the coat and then kneeled down on one knee as he placed his mother's ring back on her finger.

"Edmund?" Eleanor asked with more fear.

Without a word, Edmund reached forward and pulled both of the downed attackers up. He screamed something at them in French, and then, as they looked into the face of a vengeful demon, they both ran at their fastest speed away into the dark night.

"Did you kill the others?" Eleanor asked with feigned calm.

Edmund looked down at the blood on his hand, and then he turned to look at his lower back, observing the large bullet wound that his Rakshasa plasma was still working hard to heal. She grimaced as he dug his hand into the wound and ripped the bullet right out. With one look at his gruesome triumph, he dropped the bullet and collapsed onto the ground. Eleanor rushed to gather him into her arms.

He wailed like a wounded animal as he gave into the pain.

"Edmund, what is happening? What can I do?" Eleanor asked as she worked her hardest to stay calm. "Is it a mortal wound? Are you changing back into a young man?"

"I don't know!" he cried. "I really don't know! It hurts so much, Eleanor! More than it ever has! It's burning and seething and eating me from the inside out!"

"Sshhh… Everything will be alright, darling. I'm here. You're not alone. We will both get through this."

She coaxed his head into her lap and ran her fingers soothingly through his dry hair. She debated heatedly with herself whether she should summon Kuveni or Mélusine, but he wasn't dying, she was quite sure. He was suffering something that their meddling could not remedy. He was suffering as *destiny* had intended him to.

She watched helplessly, whispering assurances into his ear as he writhed and moaned, until finally, he calmed down as the agony subsided, and he looked up at her with his black demonic eyes.

"Am I young again?" he asked as he brought his hands up to observe them and then felt the soft wrinkles by the corners of his eyes.

"You look the same as you did before, my darling," Eleanor said as she continued to stroke him soothingly.

Edmund took in a deep breath, and then burst into tears.

"Sshhh…" she whispered. "Everything is alright, Edmund. We're both safe now."

"What would have happened if I'd re-set just now?!" Edmund exclaimed. "Our lives would have been ruined! We'd never be able to see anyone that we loved ever again! You'd have to leave me, Eleanor! You'd have to choose between me and your family!"

"We would have figured it out, my darling," Eleanor reassured him calmly. "You would have been alive. I will take my gentle husband alive and young over dead any day. I think we talked about a homestead in New Zealand once? That would be a lovely option, don't you think? And they'll think that I must be the greatest lover in the world to have seduced such a handsome young man into marrying an old crow like me."

Edmund gathered her hand into his and kissed it while his violet tears flowed freely.

"Did you kill them?" Eleanor asked again.

Edmund's tears morphed into loud sobs. "I wanted to! I wanted to *so badly*, Eleanor. I was so close. Closer than I've been since the war. Their fear tasted so good! I just wanted more and more of it! I wanted to make them pay for what they'd done to you! To us!"

"But you didn't?" Eleanor pushed gently. "You wanted to, but you didn't?"

"I broke their arms. I broke the arm that held the coat, and the arm that held the ring. I snapped them as if they were nothing, and the *sound*, Eleanor... I loved the sound of their pain. It rang in my ears like music. It was only the thought of explaining to you what I'd done that allowed me to break out of my stupor. But, Eleanor... I *loved* it! I loved it and hated it at the same bloody time!"

"Sshhh," Eleanor whispered. "You didn't kill them, darling. Even in this desperate state, you had the self-control to stop before it was too late. How you felt about it doesn't matter. I wanted to kill them myself. But you did the right thing, and so did I."

Eleanor let her tears flow, and together as the rain picked up, they cried.

"I love you so much, Eleanor," Edmund sobbed. "I have always been so bloody alone when this happens. So bloody alone..."

"You're not alone now," Eleanor whispered. "For the first time, neither of us are alone."

They cried in each other's arms until the gentle rain subsided.

"Edmund, darling, I think we have a warm bath awaiting us, and you have a bullet hole in your suit. Let's go back to the hotel. We can sneak into our room through the terrace so no one in the lobby will see, and then we can both clean up."

Eleanor helped him up and pulled him into a gentle embrace. She worked her hardest not to shiver at his intense frigidity. "Edmund, darling, close your eyes and do whatever Mr. Johnson told you to do to get your emotions under control. I can see that you aren't entirely recovered yet."

Edmund closed his eyes and whispered a quiet mantra. When he reopened them, despite the blood on her facial wound and on his hands, his eyes had returned to their human hazel.

"Very good, darling. I'm so proud of you. Really, Edmund. It is a wonder to me that you have so much self-control."

Edmund moved to argue and then held his tongue. Instead, he gathered her tightly into his arms, and in a whirlwind of speed far faster than their airplane flight had been, they emerged down at a busy road, only a few hundred meters from the Moulin Rouge.

"So that's how it feels," she murmured as she balanced her woozy body against his.

Edmund moved to hail a taxi, but she gently took his bloody hand into hers and hailed it for them. He helped her into the back seat, and with a few short words, he communicated his commands to the driver, and they were free to stare silently, holding each other tighter than they ever had before, as they looked out the window at the bustling midnight city.

When they arrived back at the hotel, Edmund said nothing as he threw a few bills at the driver. Eleanor steadied him as they limped around the side of the building. He lifted her effortlessly up over the wall to their private terrace, and then hopped over himself.

As they re-entered the suite through the double french doors, a fresh bottle of champagne sweated in its ice bucket and the rose-scented bath awaited them, as if nothing had happened. The tranquility of the scene seemed almost as if it was mocking them.

Eleanor silently slipped off her coat and helped Edmund remove his ruined clothes. Without a word, she took his suit to the crackling fireplace and dropped it on top of the logs. She removed her clothes and guided him into the bathroom where she washed the strangers' blood off of his hands and then washed her own blood off of her face. She used a cloth to clean every inch of their bodies, removing the blood and sending it down the drain with every gentle dab. When she was finally finished, she guided Edmund to the human bed.

"Let's sleep in each other's arms tonight, darling. I think we should embrace our humanity."

"You're too forgiving, Eleanor," he said as he fought back a ball in his throat.

She pulled down the covers and slipped inside, and he followed her in a daze. She gave into one final shiver at his incredible frigidity, and then she curled herself up in the nook of his cold arm and laid her head on his chest.

"I love you, Edmund. I love all that you are," Eleanor whispered.

"I love you, my dearest Eleanor," he whispered.

And together, in each other's loving arms, they slept.

CHAPTER 15 – TRAIN RIDE

Eleanor awoke groggily to a knock at the door.

"Colonel? Madame Marriner? Your train departs in an hour!" Monsieur Renault called.

Eleanor nudged her gentle sleeping husband awake.

"Edmund, darling? Edmund, we have to get up. We're going to miss our train."

With an awakening Rakshasa breath, Edmund's eyes popped open. He took a panicked moment to remember where they were, and as the memories from the prior night rushed back to him, a look of horror crossed his face.

"Eleanor, your eye!" He reached forward to gently stroke her black bruise, and she flinched with pain. "Dearest, what can I do?"

"Really, it feels fine, Edmund. I've always had a high pain tolerance," Eleanor reassured him half-truthfully. A throbbing pain picked up as she felt the area with her fingers.

"It looks like I abused you!" he exclaimed.

"Blimey. That should be fun to explain for the rest of our honeymoon…" she muttered.

Another set of knocks reiterated Monsieur Renault's message.

"We'll be ready in a few minutes!" Edmund called.

"Very good, sir. I'm leaving a tray with fresh coffee and pastries out here in the hallway. Your car is waiting out front, and as soon as you're ready, I will have the porters gather your trunks. You must move quickly. The Simplon Orient Express always leaves on time."

"Darling, you're quite frigid. Why don't you hop into the bath, and I'll gather our breakfast and join you in a moment," Eleanor suggested as she threw on a robe hanging on a hook by the bed.

Edmund agreed and blurred into the bathroom, while Eleanor sighed with stress at the annoying prospect of every stranger questioning Edmund's husbandly virtue until her black eye healed. But, as she gathered up the tray and carried it hastily to the coffee table in the sitting room, a pleasant breeze indicated that she wasn't the only one who was worrying about their plight.

Mélusine pulled Eleanor into the closet and shut the door. "*Mon dieu*! It's just as bad as Kuveni said it was!"

"I thought your meddling was over!" Eleanor whispered as Mélusine gently inspected her wound.

"You and me both." She rolled her eyes. "And what happened the moment we stepped away? Our beautiful boy was shot by some worthless thieves! I had half a mind to kill them myself! Oh Eleanor, you were so perfect last night. So, so perfect. So worthy of being included in our inner circle. I wish so dearly that I could heal you with my hands, but *I* am not the one with that talent. I do, however, have two thousand years of experience with human medicine, and I have brought you an ancient remedy. I will take away your pain with my talents, and then you must rub this paste on the wound so that it will heal as fast as possible. Hopefully, you and Edmund won't have to put up with judgmental looks from strangers for too long."

232

"You read my mind."

"Not exactly. None of us can read human minds." Mélusine took her statement literally. "I am just a skilled observer of humanity, and I know how annoying your next few days will be with this injury in the company of the so-called high society people with whom you'll be socializing."

Mélusine snapped her fingers, and a small leather pouch appeared in her hand. She opened it right up, gathering a white paste onto her fingers and began spreading it across Eleanor's wound. Eleanor shivered with pleasure as Mélusine's warm touch pushed a dose of euphoria straight into her, dissolving the throbbing pain.

"Luckily, the paste isn't very noticeable once it's on. It's mostly translucent, and it will hide a bit of the bruise. It is a remedy from ancient India, but the Romans coveted it when news traveled through the empire of its unique effectiveness. Do you need some for the scratches on your legs?"

"I'd forgotten about those," Eleanor admitted.

Mélusine kneeled down and rubbed more of the paste on Eleanor's scabs, and then stood up and closed the leather pouch into her hand.

"Take this, and use it whenever you think about the wound. It will refill itself automatically, so you won't run out. Now, you really will miss your train if you don't get moving. I hope I don't see you again soon, but somehow I suspect you're in for quite the dangerous adventure. I am going to try my hardest not to meddle. À bientôt, ma chérie."

"Eleanor! Come look!" Edmund called. "Eleanor, dearest? Are you alright?" His voice got closer as he came into the sitting room to look for her. "Eleanor?"

"I'm in the closet!" Eleanor called guiltily.

Mélusine snapped her fingers, producing a perfectly-pressed outfit laid out for their use on each trunk, and then with a wink, she disappeared.

Eleanor pushed open the closet doors. "Sorry, darling. I was trying to get our clothes out of these well-packed trunks. Monsieur Renault didn't leave anything for us to wear when he packed them up…" She trailed off as she observed a large black and blue bruise on his eye. "Good lord, what happened?"

"I don't know!" he exclaimed. "I was thinking about your injury while I was looking in the mirror, and it started itching as if there were fire ants under my skin. I felt like I might rip my eye out for a moment! But as soon as I was done scratching it, this bruise was there!"

"Does it hurt?" she asked as she examined his wound. She poked it gently, and he produced no reaction, and then she pushed harder. Still nothing. "It doesn't seem to be bothering you."

"It doesn't feel like anything, but it looks rather atrocious, doesn't it?"

"It does…" Eleanor murmured as she thought through the odd circumstances. "But, darling, have you ever bruised in your life?"

"Not that I can remember." Edmund stared into the distance, working through his memories in his mind. "No, I'm quite sure I haven't. I assume it's supposed to hurt, right?"

"Yes, darling. Normally bruises hurt, especially when you press on them."

She pressed down with more force, and Edmund remained unmoved by any pain. As she let go, she noticed a hint of violet metallic plasma in the corner of his eye that quickly dissolved out of sight. Her official medical conclusion was that Edmund had just stumbled upon his first instance of shapeshifting. She did not share her prognosis.

"Well, we'll be quite the invalid pair then, won't we?" Eleanor declared instead.

"This is wonderful, dearest! We can tell everyone the truth about what happened. Or, at least, mostly the truth. They'll believe us if I have a bruise too!"

"Yes, darling, I think you're right. It's actually rather convenient."

Edmund approached her to examine her wound, and as he noticed the paste, she held up the pouch to show him.

"I was also in the closet digging this out of my suitcase. It's an ancient Scottish remedy. I'm hoping it will help me heal faster. Do you want some? I'm rather fascinated to observe what will happen naturally to your new injury, but you are welcome to as much of it as you'd like."

Edmund's cheer dissolved. "I'm so sorry, Eleanor. Neither of us should have to think about healing bruises on our honeymoon. I should have kept us safe."

"Don't you even start with that," Eleanor admonished as she began hastily dressing herself. "It was my suggestion to go to that seedy neighborhood in the first place. We are equally to blame for putting ourselves in danger, and I think we should both focus on learning a lesson. No more wandering about infamously dangerous neighborhoods in the dead of night. Agreed, Colonel?"

"Yes, sir," he agreed as he followed her lead and pulled on his trousers.

They hopped awkwardly about inside the closet in a rush to get out the door, and then Edmund guzzled down the entire pot of coffee that Monsieur Renault had brought to them, while Eleanor gathered several pastries into a napkin and stuffed them into her purse.

They rushed out the door, and Monsieur Renault was waiting at the end of their private hallway flanked by four porters, who, upon his command, rushed past them to gather their trunks.

"Colonel? Madame?! What happened?!" he asked as he spotted their matching black eyes.

"We were mugged," Eleanor explained. "Last night we went to dinner on Montmartre, and we were mugged in the park on the way back to the road."

"*Mon dieu! Quelle horreur!*" Monsieur Renault exclaimed. "Please, you must forgive my fine city! And on your last night here? It was very bad luck, indeed!"

"Please, think nothing of it. We were safe, and they didn't get away with anything of value," Eleanor reassured him.

"I am just glad you were safe! And on a horrible night like last night?! The Devil must have been wandering about!"

"I'm sorry?" Edmund asked with a burst of anxiety. "What do you mean?"

"Ah, you haven't heard the ugly news yet in your hurry. Never mind. Here come the porters. You must leave immediately or you will miss your train."

Monsieur Renault whisked them out the front door of the hotel's lobby, straight to a waiting Rolls Royce.

He barked sharp orders to the porters as they loaded the two heavy trunks into the back. He shouted instructions at the driver, and then offered them a smile and a wave, and with a screech of the tires, they were on their way back to the Gare de Lyon.

Edmund leaned forward and engaged the driver in a conversation. Eleanor watched as Edmund's expression became puzzled and then concerned as he asked a series of follow-up questions. The driver nodded his head solemnly as he answered.

"What is it? What happened?" Eleanor asked nervously.

"There was a massacre of sorts last night. Four bodies were found dismembered on the steps down to the Seine over by the Eiffel Tower. One had a confessional note apologizing for being a worthless murdering thief. The police have no suspects. It was painted to look like a murder suicide, but obviously that man did not dismember himself."

"How horrible," Eleanor whispered.

"It isn't just that… the bodies were naked, and their clothes were left with them. They were tattered vagrant clothes, and there was a revolver and three knives found at the scene. Don't they sound like the men we encountered?"

"There are scores of vagrants in Paris, darling. We can't assume they're the same ones," Eleanor reassured him with feigned confidence. He was, of course, right. How could it not be the same men? How many vagrants traveled in groups of four, carrying a revolver?

"Yes... yes, I suppose... but that language, Eleanor... the confessional note... it used *exactly* the language I'd used with them. I'd accused them of being worthless, murdering thieves when I broke their arms to get back the items they'd stolen." He suddenly shifted uncomfortably as an unpleasant thought occurred to him. "I swear to you, Eleanor, I didn't kill them." He sounded almost as if he was trying to convince himself.

"I believe you, darling." Eleanor took his hand into hers and squeezed it. "Besides, I was guarding two of the four, remember? And you and I were together the whole time after you returned. Even if I didn't believe you, you wouldn't have even had the opportunity to kill all four of them, nor would you have been able to carry them across the city to send some macabre message. Even you're not that fast."

Eleanor's mind wandered to Mélusine and Kuveni. She wondered if perhaps either of them might have been capable of the crime. They didn't seem to be, but they did have a knack for surprising her. Mélusine had mentioned that their people had a particular weakness for humans who imparted injustice on each other, and humans who had attacked their beloved divine child over a pittance surely would have been fair game... But then Mélusine had already said that she'd *thought* about killing them, implying that she hadn't...

"Dearest?" Edmund pushed. "What is on your mind?"

"Oh... nothing," Eleanor lied. Edmund did not believe her. "I was just thinking about whether or not... never mind." She didn't want to put ideas in his head.

"What, dearest? Please, what were you thinking?"

"I was thinking about whether or not someone might have been watching you when you chased them down."

The color drained from Edmund's face. "If they had, they would know many of my secrets."

"Yes, I know. That's why I didn't want to worry you. It is likely that this is just a coincidence. There are tens of thousands of vagrants in Paris. This crime sounds as if it would have taken hours to commit, and the language was rather generic, don't you think? They *were* worthless, murdering thieves. It's not like your words were poetic. I don't think we should panic."

"Yes… yes, I suppose you're right…" Edmund was not convinced, but Eleanor appreciated his attempt to calm his own raging nerves.

As the car pulled up to the station, Edmund paid the driver, and as he helped Eleanor out of the car, a familiar man rushed to greet them.

"Come, come! I convinced them to hold the train for you, but they've only given us five minutes!" Mr. Valov exclaimed with his thick Czech accent as he gestured to four porters who opened the boot and gathered their trunks with military precision.

"Mr. Valov?!" Edmund exclaimed.

"I will explain later, Colonel. Follow me. We have no time to waste."

Mr. Valov guided them swiftly into the station, straight through determined crowds that darted about like schools of fish, to the farthest platform where a completely modern steel train car with the famous Company Wagon-Lits logo in blue and gold awaited them.

"Go! Go!" Mr. Valov urged as he pushed them onto the train.

Eleanor watched as Mr. Valov ordered the porters onto a separate baggage car with their trunks and then hopped up behind them. A grumpy conductor eyed them suspiciously, and then blew his whistle. Without a second wasted, the train started moving.

"Just in the nick of time!" Eleanor exclaimed as she caught her breath.

"Jolly good on Monsieur Renault… and Mr. Valov, I suppose. What do you think he's doing here, Eleanor? I couldn't have been clearer that we wanted to have an adventure on our own."

"I think that is an excellent question to ask him, darling. And, what a coincidence, here he comes now."

"What happened, Colonel?!" Mr. Valov exclaimed as he rushed towards them and immediately landed his attention on their matching black eyes.

"Nothing of consequence," Edmund lied.

Mr. Valov stared at him with puzzlement, and then moved his attention to Eleanor.

"We were mugged on Montmartre last night," she explained. "They didn't get anything, in the end."

"I'm not surprised! They should have known better than to take on a war hero like you, Colonel! Or a Scottish warrior-maiden like you, Mrs. Marriner."

"Ha! I'll keep that title, thank you very much," Eleanor laughed.

Edmund shifted uncomfortably as he prepared himself for his unpleasant confrontation. "Mr. Valov, I appreciate your help. It has been indispensable. But you must explain to us why you are here. I thought I made it perfectly clear that we wanted to be alone together on our honeymoon."

"I'm sorry, Colonel. I simply couldn't resist. Lord Blakeney had everything under control back in Basingstoke, and I felt like you could use my help to make your journey more enjoyable. I promise you, you won't even know that I'm here. I booked myself passage in the farthest second class berth, and I will leave you to yourselves now. I am here solely to help however you want me."

"It does not feel very adventurous to have a butler at our beck and call…" Edmund muttered.

"He did get the train to wait for us," Eleanor whispered. "We wouldn't be having a very fun adventure if we'd missed it with our perpetual tardiness."

"Yes… yes, I suppose."

"I think we've managed to have quite a bit of adventure on our own already," Eleanor added. "Thank you, Mr. Valov. Your help has been most useful."

She reached forward and aggressively pulled Mr. Valov's hand into hers for a shake. She held on for an extended moment, feeling for any evidence of Yaksha warmth, but there was nothing. Only a typical sweaty human hand. Her puzzlement only grew more intense.

"Shall I procure some aspirin for you, Mrs. Marriner?" Mr. Valov asked as she let him go. "Your eye looks like it probably hurts quite a bit."

"It feels fine at the moment, actually. But aspirin is probably wise. I'm sure the pain will return later."

"I will have it sent straight to your berth. This one is yours, by the way." Mr. Valov pointed to the first door on the left. "And now, Colonel, I will leave you two to enjoy yourselves. I hope that you will forgive me for my intrusion, and I will endeavor to make my assistance valuable enough to warrant my disobedience."

With an apologetic bow, Mr. Valov left them alone. "Oh, and the dining car is this way, Colonel," he added as he made his way through the heavy door into the next car. "Lunch will be ready in about an hour, but it is open for tea and spirits all the time."

Edmund sighed with ambivalence. "I think perhaps I've lost my commanding touch."

"Well, we're on the train, it's moving, and in a few days we'll be in Constantinople. Now Mr. Valov will coordinate our luggage, and we won't have to think about it, which is, quite frankly, nice. I was wondering how we'd deal with hauling it all over creation."

At that moment, two little girls—twins, no doubt—with platinum blonde hair tied up in curly pig-tails and clad in pink frilly dresses, chased each other with loud squeals and giggles through the door from the next car into the hallway and began using Edmund and Eleanor as pawns in their game of tag. But as one brushed her hand up against Edmund's and shivered, she strained her neck to look up at him.

"Are you a giant?" she asked.

"No. I am an abominable snowman," he said matter-of-factly. After a long moment of taking in their curious expressions, Edmund growled at them, and they squealed and exploded into roaring laughter.

"Does this look like a children's playground to you?!" An angry middle-aged balding American man screeched as he popped his head out of the berth beside Edmund and Eleanor's to throw them all a furious look.

"Daisy, Lily, dearests, you must calm down!" Their overwhelmed mother, who looked only to be in her mid-20s, pushed her way through the door from the next car, followed by their unamused father.

"I'm so terribly sorry." She looked apologetically to Edmund, Eleanor, and then the angry American. "They've never been on a train before. Girls, you must remember your manners. This place is like school, not the park."

"But, Mummy, we found an abominable snowman!" Daisy protested.

Their mother looked around at the empty hallway, and then sighed with stress.

"She means me," Edmund explained as he reached out his hand for a friendly shake. "She asked if I was a giant, and so I indulged her imagination a bit." The woman threw an embarrassed look to her husband. "Out of the mouths of babes," Edmund winked. "Please don't fret. She was not the first person to notice my excessive height. I'm Colonel Edmund Marriner, and this is my wife, Eleanor."

Eleanor caught a giddy bent to his tone as he said the phrase, and she let the same feeling wash over her. It was nicer than she wanted to admit.

"Colonel," the woman's husband said reverentially as he looked up at him and shook his hand. His gaze landed on Edmund's black eye.

"We were mugged last night in Paris," Edmund explained. "Eleanor and I fought them off, but they left a bit of a mark."

"How horrid!" the woman exclaimed.

"They didn't know they'd taken on a colonel in the British Army, did they? I bet they didn't know what hit them!" Something about the man's patriotic tone rubbed Eleanor the wrong way.

"They most certainly didn't," Edmund agreed truthfully. "Are you a military man?"

"Oh no. I sure wish I had been, though. I was disappointed to miss out on the real action of the war—you know, being a hero for king and country and such. Why, how many Krauts did you kill, Colonel? Scores, I'm sure!"

Edmund shifted uncomfortably. "Being a war hero is not what you think it is, Mister...?"

"Oh, Mr. George Ridgeway! And this is my wife, Eloise." He shook Edmund's hand enthusiastically again. "I was a post-graduate researcher in Applied Chemistry at Oxford during the war. I did research on topics of great interest to the Crown, and they decided I would be better use to the cause continuing my research. I still wished I'd been able to get my hands on at least a few of those Krauts myself, though. You know, to show them what I thought of them personally."

Eleanor could see a darkness working its way into Edmund's expression. This man had undoubtedly been one of the infamous research scientists who had participated in inventing the horrific chemical weapons with which Edmund had far too much personal experience. He was certainly one of the many men who had absolutely no concept of the agonizing deaths his mind had inflicted on millions, and who still fantasized about the nonexistent glories of combat from which he had mercifully escaped. Edmund and Eleanor had already discussed several times that *these men* were the most dangerous. *These men* were the ones rearing for another war.

"Pleased to meet you," Edmund said curtly as he worked hard to push back his emotions.

"Oh my, you are cold," Mrs. Ridgeway said as she shook his hand.

"We were caught out in the rain, and we haven't had a chance to warm up yet," Eleanor explained on his behalf. "We almost missed the train completely. In fact, we haven't even had a chance to see our berth yet. If you'll excuse us…"

She pushed open the door to the berth and guided Edmund inside.

"Nice meeting you!" Eleanor said cheerfully as she slammed the door. She took off her enormous mink coat and hung it on a hook by the door, stopping for a moment to observe the absurdity that it took up more than half of the wall.

"Thank you for rescuing me, dearest," Edmund whispered as he gathered her into his arms for a gentle kiss.

Their gentle kiss escalated into a more passionate embrace, but as they looked down to assess their options, they both immediately recognized a number of challenges to their romantic escapades. As Edmund attempted to stand straight up, his head hit the ceiling, and as they eyed the small sitting area that would be converted into their sleeping bunks later in the evening, it was obvious that the length of the beds would not be even close to what Edmund would need to lie down, and certainly there was no chance that they would be able to squeeze onto one bunk together.

"The best laid plans…" Eleanor sighed as Edmund sat down on the sofa and stretched out his legs until they hit the washbasin on the opposite end of the berth. "I suppose that means there aren't any bath or shower facilities, either. I'm not sure what I thought the Orient Express would be like, but it wasn't this. I don't even want to know how much you paid for this, darling."

The muffled (but still quite loud) angry barks of their next-door neighbor yelling at the conductor penetrated through the wall. Eleanor squeezed into a tight spot next to Edmund and sighed with disappointment.

"Please don't worry about it, Eleanor. This part of the journey was a means to an end anyway. In a few days we'll be in Constantinople, and then we will be off to India. The passage to India always has a bit of discomfort. I find it rather reassuring, actually, that in this modern era there are still some small personal sacrifices required to hop across the globe. It makes hopping across the globe still feel special."

"What a funny way of thinking about it." Eleanor leaned over and kissed him. "I've never thought to appreciate hardships in that way. Once again, Colonel, you've delightfully surprised me."

They slowly and awkwardly began unbuttoning each other's clothing, but as they both struggled to lie down together on the small sofa, Edmund's head and Eleanor's elbow hit the wall, and the next-door neighbor banged angrily back.

Eleanor giggled guiltily for a moment, and then sighed with disappointment as they both gave up and sat side by side, re-buttoning their clothing.

"Soon enough we'll be in Constantinople," she reiterated.

"Well, shall we go to the dining car?" Edmund suggested. "I think perhaps we'll be there for the next three days. Perhaps I should have booked us into the baggage car."

They both smiled at his little joke.

"Aye, Colonel," Eleanor agreed. "Let's go claim some territory."

The doors to the other berths were all closed as they walked hand in hand through two more sleeping cars until they reached the dining car.

244

In the far corner, an old woman clad in a black, beaded chiffon dress in a style that Eleanor hadn't seen since before the war sat alone with a tiny, fluffy white pomeranian in her lap, feeding it biscuits from her plate. As a waiter entered the compartment from the kitchen, the pomeranian growled, and the woman whispered something into its ear and fed it another bite.

Across the aisle from her, an American girl who looked only slightly older than a teenager was chatting cheerfully at a silent, broad-shouldered brunette woman. Both of them were clad in very plain dresses, although the American girl had made quite an obvious effort to fancy hers up with poorly matched ribbons and bows. She scribbled notes on a small notebook while she talked, and despite the fact that her dining companion did not show any interest whatsoever in what she was saying, she continued her lively chatter undeterred.

At the next table, two priests, an elderly bald one with a few wisps of white hair and a younger one with freckles and ginger hair (only slightly less fiery than Eleanor's) sat quietly playing a game of chess and drinking tea. Next to them, a sour-looking older couple dressed in layers of Russian furs that seemed particularly out of place in the warm car sat silently scowling at the rest of the passengers.

At the farthest four-person table in the middle of the car, Daisy and Lily sat poking at each other and squealing at an ear-shatteringly shrill pitch. Mr. and Mrs. Ridgeway stood blocking the aisle many empty tables away, while Mr. Ridgeway engaged a seated couple in a blokish one-way conversation.

The broad-shouldered, muscular man seated at the table had an unusually straw-like color of blond hair and tan, leathery skin marked by many deep wrinkles that contrasted strangely with his otherwise youthful appearance. The woman had a much softer look about her, with a pink glow, delicate features, and striking blue eyes that complemented her short auburn hair beautifully. They were both dressed extremely fashionably, indicating that despite the man's rugged appearance, they were endowed with quite a bit of wealth. As Mr. Ridgway continued on and on with another uninformed patriotic rant, they began to look rather desperate.

"I've often wished that I could have been a medic in the field. You know, saving lives and such. Such a noble calling you had! How many lives did you save, Lieutenant Helmsworth?"

"Far fewer than I lost," the man replied quietly with a thick Australian accent.

Eleanor squeezed Edmund's hand, and then guided him to the table.

"You!" she exclaimed as she addressed the woman who sat silently beside the desperate Aussie. "I can't believe we're meeting again like this! Mr. Ridgeway, Mrs. Ridgeway, I hate to interrupt, but I can hardly believe that we ran into these old friends of ours! I think Daisy and Lily are ready for your attention at your table over there."

The seated couple eyed Eleanor and Edmund with confusion as Eleanor sat right down next to the woman, and Edmund followed her lead, sitting himself down next to Lieutenant Helmsworth.

"Have a lovely lunch, Mr. and Mrs. Ridgeway!" Eleanor added with a flourish.

"Yes, you too," Mrs. Ridgeway said politely as she and her husband begrudgingly went to join their daughters, who had taken to proudly making a ruckus by banging the empty plates with their spoons.

"I'm terribly sorry," Eleanor leaned in to whisper. "I thought you looked like you needed to be rescued. Mr. Ridgeway already cornered us in the sleeping car. He doesn't seem to understand that the war heroes he worships so much don't want to talk about it."

"You were in the war?" the Aussie asked.

"Colonel Edmund Marriner," Edmund subtly reached his hand over for a shake. "I was a commander in the trenches of Belgium for four hellish years."

"And I'm Eleanor MacLeod… Actually, I'm Eleanor Marriner now," Eleanor corrected herself. "It's our honeymoon. I was a nurse in the VAD in France for most of the war."

Finally, the Aussie's eyes lit up, and his companion smiled.

"Pleased to meet you. I'm Jack Helmsworth, but my friends call me Oz." He reached forward and shook their hands, politely avoiding comment on Edmund's frigidity. "This is my wife, Yvette, but those in the know call her Yvie. She was a nurse in France during the war. That's how we met. I was a medic near Reims for three long years."

"Pleased to meet you," Yvie said shyly with a thick French accent as she demurely shook their hands.

"Shall we call you Yvette or Yvie?" Edmund asked. "Or, I suppose, I should remember my manners and call you Mrs. Helmsworth."

"Colonel, you are more polite than any Aussie I've ever met." Oz gasped with feigned offense, but Yvie only smiled. "Including my husband. Please call me Yvie. I'm used to all the Aussie nicknames now, although my mother was not particularly pleased by the uncivilized change."

"Aw, Yvie, isn't that more reason to embrace it?" Oz asked teasingly.

Yvie looked around guiltily as if her mother could hear her. "*C'est vrai*, Ozzy. I prefer being uncivilized." She winked, and Oz squeezed her knee.

As she glanced at Edmund and Eleanor, Oz returned his attention to Edmund. "Thank you for the reprieve, Colonel. I can never find a polite way out of conversations like that."

"I know exactly how you feel," Edmund agreed. "Do you mind if we join you for lunch?"

"Please do!" Oz said cheerfully. "So, it's your honeymoon, eh? Good on ya!"

"Thanks," Eleanor smiled. "And what brings you here?"

"My sister was married last week in a village near Reims. We came from Australia to visit a month back, and now we are taking the scenic route home," Yvie replied.

"How lovely!" Eleanor exclaimed. "So you moved to Australia after the war? That must have been a change!"

"I was glad to get away. Reims was only a pile of rubble by the end. Even the cathedral was gone." Yvie looked pained as she answered the question honestly. "Most of the people I grew up with died in the war. It was nice to get away from it all. It let me pretend that it hadn't happened."

"I'm sorry," Eleanor said solemnly.

Yvie shrugged. "We are here for a happy visit this time, the first since I moved out with Oz to the edge of the world."

"You know, we have often talked about skipping off to New Zealand to start a homestead." Eleanor offered Yvie an escape from the sad topic.

"You should!" Yvie exclaimed, bringing them all back to cheer. "It is the greatest adventure in the world!"

"You'd sure have your work cut out for you," Oz laughed. "My family owns a few cattle ranches in Western Australia. As you can see, the sun takes its toll." He held out his wrinkled, tan hands. "I reckon I'll look like a fair dinkum oldie by the time I'm thirty-five."

"Fair dinkum?" Eleanor asked.

Oz laughed. "You'll have to forgive my Strine. It still slips in from time to time. I reckon I'll look like a bona fide old bloke in a few years."

"Huh… I suppose I've never thought about how strong the sun is down under," Eleanor said as she observed Oz's many wrinkles with fresh eyes. "Perhaps it isn't such a perfect idea. I found France to be insufferably hot in the summer, and in the scheme of things, it was really quite mild."

"Yes, compared to Western Australia, France has lovely weather," Yvie said wistfully.

"Poor Yvie didn't really know what she was signing up for marrying an Aussie digger like me," Oz admitted. "I hope it was worth it?"

Yvie smiled. "We all make sacrifices, Ozzie. Besides, the oceans down under are more beautiful than anything I ever imagined. They are a color of blue that we don't have in France. I stay in our house overlooking the sea most of the year, you see. In Perth."

"I grew up in Perth!" Eleanor exclaimed. "The original Perth, that is. In Scotland."

"I reckon you get a lot more rain than we do," Oz winked. "Although, the ranches are much drier than Perth is. Luckily, I only have to live out beyond the black stump a few months a year."

"Oz only has to tend to the ranches when his brothers have other business. They manage it together, taking turns breaking their backs," Yvie explained.

"What a brilliant idea!" Eleanor exclaimed. "I've never heard of such a thing."

"Well, I suppose it was one good side effect of the war," Oz said modestly. "It was supposed to go to me—I'm the oldest, you see—and my father was very traditional. But when I was off in France, my father died, and my brothers were both lucky enough to be too young for service, so they took it over. When I came back, they'd done such a bonza job of managing it, I decided to split it three ways."

"I'm envious of your familial situation, Oz," Edmund admitted amicably. "I'm an only child myself, so I've never had the pleasure of siblings."

"It is not always so good," Yvette confided. "My living brothers have always been quite... eh... unpleasant."

"Your living brothers?" Eleanor hated to ask.

Yvie shifted uncomfortably as she fought back her emotions. "I lost three in the war. I have two left." Oz squeezed her hand, and she smiled sadly. "We just spent four long days with Jean-

Pierre and Benoit teasing Ozzie about his Australian English. I feel guilty saying so, because I should be grateful they're alive, but I was glad to get away. Neither of them were ever particularly kind. My kindest brother died a month before the war was over..." She trailed off, giving into a moment of melancholy before catching herself. "I'm sorry. I don't know why I'm telling you this... I usually don't talk so much about myself for many reasons, my shameful English included."

"Your honesty is refreshing," Eleanor reassured her. "And your English is really quite good. I hope it's not uncouth to say so, but at my hospital during the war, very few of the French nurses spoke any English at all."

"My grandfather was English," Yvie explained. "I went to private schools that taught in English and French. My parents thought it would be good for all of us to learn with politics as they were, and I suppose they were right. I could never get the accent, though. It makes it sound like my English is worse than it is."

"Aw, Yvie, that's not true!" Oz argued. "Your English is perfect!"

"*Ce n'est pas vrai,*" she protested.

Edmund said something in French in response, and Yvie's eyes lit up.

"*Vous parlez français, Colonel?! C'est parfait!*"

Edmund closed his eyes and concentrated on returning to English. "I have a bit of a linguistic deficiency, actually. I speak many languages, and I often get confused. Please forgive me if I speak to you in some odd foreign tongue. If you remind me, I will return to English."

"Do you speak Strine, Colonel?" Oz asked jokingly.

Edmund grinned and then responded with an accent that mirrored Oz's. "I commanded my fair share of diggers, mate, so I gave it a burl every so often. I think I still sounded like a yobbo, though, and I didn't want them to think I was a whacka."

Oz burst into laughter. "Good on ya, Colonel! I oughta declare you an honorary true blue Aussie!"

Eleanor squeezed Edmund's leg secretly under the table. For the first beautiful moment of their marriage, together as a couple, they had just made some delightful new friends. It was an experience that was far more fulfilling than she'd ever let herself imagine during her decades of spinsterhood.

The raucous noise of the Ridgeway's undisciplined daughters calmed down as the waiters began serving lunch, and Edmund and Eleanor sat for many hours of jovial conversation with their new friends listening to tall tales about Oz's childhood on the ranch and telling tall tales of their own adventurous exploits, as lunch morphed into tea, which morphed into a cocktail hour followed by a four-course dinner, and then more tea, until late in the evening, when the four of them were the only passengers remaining in the dining car, and Oz stood up reluctantly.

"Well, mates, I think it's time for us to turn in. I can't believe the day's gone by so quickly." Oz rubbed his belly. "Colonel, I was glad to finally meet a bloke whose appetite could compete with my own."

"It was thoroughly enjoyable meeting you both," Edmund said amicably as he and Eleanor stood up to say their goodbyes. "We might end up staying here in the dining car all night. It turns out the sleeping berth is decidedly too small for me."

"Strewth!" Oz said as he looked up at Edmund, noticing for the first time exactly how tall he was.

He suddenly looked pensive as he stared at Edmund until Edmund shifted uncomfortably.

"We were mugged last night in Paris. That's where the bruises came from," Edmund explained proactively.

"Oh no!" Yvie exclaimed.

"We were perfectly fine," Eleanor reassured her.

"I was wondering, but I didn't want to ask about it," Oz admitted. "I'm sorry, Colonel. I didn't mean to stare. It's just, I've heard of you. I thought your name sounded familiar, and now seeing you a head taller than I am... *You* are the one who rescued all those men from the first round of mustard gas attacks... I just thought the legends were exaggerated. You really are very tall. It makes more sense now how you were able to carry so many."

Edmund's posture deflated. "I only did what every man in my position should have done."

Oz looked annoyed at himself. "I'm sorry, Colonel. I shouldn't have said anything. I'm sure you were enjoying your anonymity on your honeymoon. I know the feeling myself. Back in Australia, everyone knows me. My family's ranches provide half the dairy cows in the country. It's been wonderful being here in France where no one cares. I won't say another word about you to anyone."

"Thank you, Oz. I appreciate your discretion," Edmund said distractedly.

Oz took Yvie's hand. "Perhaps we can dine together again tomorrow? I still have the story of the king snake in the dunny to tell you, unless you've tired of my tales already."

"We're looking forward to it," Edmund agreed with a friendly wave as he finally released himself from the momentary melancholy of his war memories.

Oz and Yvie waved their goodnight, and then disappeared into the next sleeping car.

"Well, that was surprisingly pleasant," Edmund whispered.

"I will take as many pleasant surprises as I can get. Speaking of which, darling, I think we should go try to make our sleeping berth work. My back is starting to hurt from sitting in these uncomfortable chairs for so many hours. I think mixing our uncomfortable positions might be the best plan to make it through three days of this."

"I suppose you're right," Edmund agreed.

Edmund grabbed the half-empty teapot (the tenth of the day), and they tiptoed past the many compartments of sleeping passengers back to their berth, which happened to be in the farthest location from the dining car on the entire train.

Edmund pushed open the door, and Eleanor gasped as she took in the wondrous sight. Inside their room, rather than the bunkbeds that they were expecting, a custom-shaped mattress had been placed lengthwise across the room in front of the door, converting the entire berth except for the area immediately below the water basin into an admirable approximation of a bed. The room itself was still too narrow for Edmund's exceptional height, but it was much better than either of them had expected, and a fluffy down comforter and piles of pillows made the entire set-up surprisingly inviting.

Eleanor's mink coat had been replaced by her favorite red kimono, and Edmund laughed as he spied the absurd violet silk robe that Lord Blakeney had left for him on their wedding night back in Basingstoke hanging next to it. Inside the washbasin, there was a fresh cloth, and on top of the fresh cloth, the leather pouch of Mélusine's ancient Roman remedy awaited their use.

A fresh bottle of red wine and two glasses were secured on a small pull-down table in the corner, held steady by a brilliant contraption that strapped the items into their position.

"Jolly good on Mr. Valov!" Edmund exclaimed.

"Aye…" Eleanor was not convinced that Mr. Valov had anything to do with it.

As they heard their grumpy neighbor stir, Eleanor pulled off her shoes and hopped into the berth, and Edmund tumbled in behind her. He reached out with his long arms and placed their shoes neatly in front of the door, and then he pulled it closed.

"Do you want any more tea, dearest?" he asked thoughtfully.

"I'm not sure I'll ever want more tea," Eleanor laughed. "We've been drinking it all day."

Edmund drank down the entire pot and then cracked open the door to place it by their shoes. He re-closed the door, locking and bolting it, and then he stretched out as much as the small space would allow and invited Eleanor into his arms.

Suddenly, the train hit the brakes, and Eleanor was thrown on top of him, and they both waited for a moment of anxiety for the speed to normalize again.

"Ah, it's like traveling in the good ol' days." Edmund sighed with nostalgia as he coaxed her into the nook of his arm. "Are you alright, dearest?"

Eleanor wiggled herself up and pounced on him playfully. "You traveled like this in the good ol' days? Who was she, darling? Why haven't you told me about her?"

Edmund laughed. "Well, not exactly like this. I never had the pleasure of sharing a berth with any lady at all. You are far better company than the foul-mouthed soldiers I had to sleep with."

"I'm glad to hear it!" Eleanor giggled as she straddled him and began unbuttoning his trousers.

As their grumpy neighbor banged on the wall, Eleanor flinched guiltily, and then continued on her quest with silent laughter and a very mischievous grin.

"I think our night is going to be better than his," she whispered as she pulled off Edmund's trousers triumphantly and then pulled off her silk dress. She tossed them both into the far corner.

Edmund helped remove the rest of her clothing while she pulled off his undergarments, and as his body pulsed with warmth, Eleanor found herself uncontrollably aroused.

"I'm finding the movement of the train rather stimulating," she said as she leaned on top of him and let the vibrations of the movement travel through his body into hers.

"I know exactly what you mean, dearest…" Edmund trailed off into a sigh as they became one and felt the vibrations traveling through both of their bodies.

"Perhaps this journey isn't going to be as bad as I thought," Eleanor whispered as she worked hard to hold in a moan of pleasure.

And together, only a few feet from their angry neighbor, the two lovebirds discovered the unexpected pleasures of riding on the Orient Express.

CHAPTER 16 – THAT PESKY ORIENT EXPRESS

When they awoke the next day after a night of hushed pleasure, it was already well past noon.

"The lulling rumble of the train is so relaxing." Eleanor yawned as she stretched herself out across the bed and ran her fingers along Edmund's cold chest.

"I thought I'd finally tired you out with my superhuman stamina." Edmund ran his cold fingers along her naked breasts.

"Never!" Eleanor straddled him playfully. "Didn't you say that our honeymoon was about indulgence?"

"Indeed, I did," Edmund agreed happily as he reached up to lick her breasts.

Eleanor giggled as Edmund's stomach grumbled with hunger.

"Perhaps we should rouse ourselves for another form of indulgence? I think we might have already missed lunch!"

Eleanor crawled across the bed to gather their clothes from the corner.

"I could lie here all day and all night with you," Edmund sighed. "You know, we really aren't missing anything by staying in here naked all day. We can see the view out the window, and I'm quite sure we can call for food to be brought to us."

"Then why don't we?" Eleanor asked excitedly. "Here!"

She tossed him the outrageous purple silk robe and slipped on her kimono. "Let's call for some food to be brought!"

Edmund moved to protest, and then he grinned as he gave in to the fanciful notion. "Yes, let's!"

He picked up a telephone receiver built into the wall by the door.

"Yes, hello, this is Colonel Marriner in berth number one… Yes, thank you… You read my mind! Has he now? Tell him we are ready whenever he is… Oh, did he? He's there with you now, is he? Ha! Of course… much appreciated… Thank you very much." Edmund put down the phone. "Mr. Valov already had them prepare us a picnic feast that we can eat in our room!"

"Did he?" Eleanor wasn't surprised, although she was still intensely puzzled. Was it possible that he was simply the best human butler who'd ever lived?

"Mr. Valov also wanted to inform us that the entire carriage is empty at the moment with people gathered in the dining car, so we are free to scamper to the loo in our robes."

"Let's go!" Eleanor exclaimed. She had been thinking about it for hours, but the prospect of fully dressing herself and leaving their lair had been too daunting. Edmund pulled open the door, and together with guilty squeals, they leapt the two meters or so from their door to the two loos at the front of the car.

As soon as Eleanor was done with her business, she took a long moment to observe her black eye in the mirror. It was healing quite fast with the help of Mélusine's Roman remedy. She wondered if Edmund's feigned injury would somehow subconsciously match hers, or if, after his parallel time looking in the mirror in the other loo, it might just suddenly disappear.

258

How odd his life must be, she thought lovingly (as she often did). She was once again grateful that her body did not do bizarre things without her knowledge. She'd taken for granted the predictability of her humanity her whole life, and it was only by being with Edmund that she realized how frightening her life could be if she couldn't depend on such seemingly obvious truths. It was a wonder to her that Edmund did so well in his uncertain circumstances, and she took a moment to give him credit for coming across as normal as he did. After all, they'd just spent a solid fifteen hours in jovial conversation with new human friends, and Edmund could not have done a better job of skillfully padding his truthful stories in lies that made them plausible to his unknowing audience.

As she heard the clanking of someone in the hallway, she roused herself from her thoughts, washed the remnants of Mélusine's remedy off her eye in preparation for applying another dose back in their berth, and then she pushed open the door and darted back into their compartment, where Edmund was wearing a new pair of black silk pajamas, sitting cross-legged (a position that looked surprisingly natural for him that she'd never once seen him use before), inspecting a beautiful silver tray piled high with fragrant baguettes, French cheeses, a wooden board covered in heaps of charcuterie, two whole bunches of red grapes, six canelés, two pain au chocolat, four bottles of red wine, a sweating bottle of champagne, a large carafe of water, and six glasses—three pairs, each properly shaped for their three beverages.

"How lovely!" Eleanor exclaimed as she tiptoed carefully to the position across from Edmund.

He'd already compiled a bite with a soft, oozing cheese spread on a chunk of baguette, and he reached across their picnic and popped it into her mouth.

"Mr. Valov said just to call when we'd like some more. He said he already has some coffee brewing for us. Oh, and apparently,

259

it's already four o'clock in the afternoon local time. He suggested that we might as well just stay in. Oh, and he brought us the paper."

"Jolly good on Mr. Valov," Eleanor murmured.

"Oh, and he brought us these pajamas. You have a pair too. They're there in the corner. He also said to ring if we want our clothes, and he will bring us just what we need from our trunks in the baggage car, since there's no room for storage in here."

"He really is an immensely helpful man, isn't he?" Eleanor said as she slipped on the silk pajamas and attempted to emulate Edmund's position. "You look very comfortable like that, darling. I'm not sure how you're doing it. It makes my legs hurt immediately."

"This is how I learned to sit," Edmund explained as he ripped open another baguette and began spreading huge piles of French cheese onto it. "In India, all the children sit like this, as do the adults quite often. In Hyderabad when I was an apprentice, we always sat in this position to eat. It feels quite natural right now, actually, pretending to dine on the floor. It makes me feel nostalgic."

Eleanor wiggled out of the uncomfortable position and lounged on her side to begin eating the feast.

"This really does feel like a honeymoon." She poured two large glasses of champagne and offered him one.

"To our honeymoon!" He happily clinked her glass.

They ate and they drank until they were both entirely content (with Edmund finishing up whatever Eleanor didn't want, as he always did), and then Edmund called Mr. Valov, who arrived cheerfully to collect their dishes in exchange for a large coffee pot and two cups.

"We are just reaching Milan," Mr. Valov reported. "From here, there will be a number of longer stops as the various cars get shuffled. You will be perfectly fine remaining where you are. Oh, and I've taken the liberty of having your neighbor moved into an empty berth in another sleeping car. The compartment next door to yours is empty now. Enjoy yourselves."

Mr. Valov winked and shut the door.

Edmund blushed intensely, and then they both burst into giggles. "I suppose we must not have been as quiet as we thought we were last night," Edmund said guiltily.

"Oh please, these walls are made of paper. That man was complaining when we sat down on the sofa, remember? But jolly good on Mr. Valov, indeed." Eleanor took a sip of coffee. "Finish that pot off, Colonel, so we can get it out of the way."

Edmund guzzled down the entire pot of coffee, while Eleanor finished the few sips in her cup, and then he cracked open the door, leaving the empty pot in the hallway just outside, and then locked and bolted it again.

"This morning was quite enjoyable cold, but I'm craving hot now," Eleanor said naughtily as she undressed him. He hastily undressed her, and once again they were naked in each other's arms.

"Is this hot enough?" Edmund asked as he straddled her. His pulsating warmth aroused her deepest desires.

"Not yet," Eleanor teased as she spread her legs.

"How about now?" Edmund asked as he dipped inside.

"Not yet."

"And now?"

"Yes," Eleanor sighed with satisfaction.

And together, they set about thoroughly enjoying their louder evening in.

Eleanor awoke as the train came to a stop. She sat up groggily and peeked out the frosted window. It was snowing outside, and the muted light made it seem like it was probably morning or late afternoon. Eleanor didn't like not being able to tell. She shivered and sat back down next to Edmund, wrapping the fluffy blanket around her.

"Edmund, darling, I think we must be in Bulgaria already."

With an awakening Rakshasa breath, his eyes popped open.

"Good morning, dearest," Edmund said with a sleepy smile.

"I think perhaps you should say good afternoon."

"Did we sleep that long?" Edmund sat up and reached over to peek out the window. "Yes, I suppose we did. We're certainly not in Italy anymore. We must be quite far into the east for there to be snow like this at the end of March."

"I'm feeling rather disoriented, actually." Eleanor looked around their messy compartment. "I think perhaps I'm ready to return to the wider world."

Edmund leaned over with his long arm to pick up the phone. "Yes… oh, we are? Oh, he is? Wonderful. It is? Perfect! Thank you very much." Edmund hung up and gathered up his robe. "We're in Serbia, between Belgrade and Sofia. Mr. Valov will be here in a minute. He's been waiting for us to wake up. Apparently, we can make it to lunch if we hurry. It's almost twelve thirty."

"Huh… Serbia… How odd to be in Serbia. In some ways, this place is the reason the wretched war happened in the first place…" Eleanor trailed off as she realized that she shouldn't have put the idea in Edmund's head.

"There were many reasons for that war. Each one as worthless as the others…" Edmund trailed off pensively, but Mr. Valov's knock at the door distracted them both from their unpleasant thoughts.

Edmund unlocked the door and cracked it open.

"Thank you very much, Mr. Valov. Please tell them we will be there shortly. I think we could both use a hot meal."

"Very good, sir. I must warn you, though. All of the passengers are in the dining car at the moment, but I've managed to procure you a seat at a four-person table with Lieutenant and Mrs. Helmsworth."

"Jolly good!" Edmund exclaimed. "Thank you, Mr. Valov!"

"It is my pleasure, sir. Now, please, take these and dress quickly. They did not get the supplies they were expecting in Belgrade, so I think that they might run out of first class food, and I can tell you with great authority that the second-class food in the other dining car is not worth eating."

"Very good, Mr. Valov. Thank you for the warning," Edmund said as he gathered the clothes into the room and re-shut the door. "That man really is the best butler I've ever encountered."

"I wholeheartedly agree." Eleanor awkwardly maneuvered into a silk dress and relished a new marital convenience as Edmund buttoned her up in the back. She then helped him button up his trousers and his shirt, and then tied his tie, finishing off with a naughty lick of his lips.

"My hair is beyond helpless," she said as she looked down at the wild mats in her red curls. She gathered it into a loose ponytail and folded it under, tying it with a ribbon from her other outfit two days earlier that remained crumpled in the corner of the compartment. "I'll have to spend our first day in Constantinople bathing and brushing it out."

"It still looks lovely to me, dearest."

"That's how I know you're too in love with me," Eleanor winked.

Edmund finished putting on his well-fitted suit jacket and swooped in for a final kiss.

She pulled on a cashmere shawl and a beaded headband that matched the pale blue color of her low-waisted silk dress (one that she hadn't seen before that she assumed was from the closet in Paris), and then Edmund pushed open the door, and they both sat on the edge of their bed with their feet in the hallway putting on the fashionable shoes that Mr. Valov had left there for them.

As soon as they were finished, Eleanor made an unromantic beeline for the loo, and when she emerged, Edmund was waiting patiently for her in the hallway.

"Shall we?" he asked as he offered her his arm with the archaic Victorian gesture that always made her laugh.

"Aye," Eleanor agreed.

They skipped happily through the other sleeping cars to the first class dining car (they both felt a bit guilty that they hadn't realized there was more than one), and as they entered the crowded room full of fashionable people, most of whom they'd observed two days before during their food marathon with the Helmsworths, they spied their new friends and took a seat at their table in the closest corner of the room (the same table, coincidentally, at which they had spent their fifteen hours together before).

"G'day, mates!" Oz said jovially. "We were beginning to wonder if you'd fallen out the window!"

Edmund worked hard to control his embarrassed blush (that Eleanor, by the way, enjoyed very much every time it frequently surfaced. It seemed to her to be one of his most human traits).

"We decided to stay in yesterday to enjoy our honeymoon," Eleanor explained on their behalf.

"Ace!" Oz exclaimed. "Yvie, maybe we should try that!"

"*Mais oui*, Ozzie, maybe we should." She giggled.

A pair of waiters rushed to the table to pour Edmund and Eleanor some wine. They seemed concerned as one whispered something heatedly to the other, and then Edmund chimed in with their obscure Slavic language, to everyone but Eleanor's surprise. The two waiters were flustered as they rushed away, whispering to each other as they pushed their way back through the kitchen door.

"Strewth, mate. You weren't kidding about that linguistic deficiency, were you?" Oz exclaimed. "It's more like a linguistic power!"

"Did I do it again?" Edmund asked Eleanor with more than a hint of personal annoyance. "Bloody hell. Am I speaking English now?"

264

"Don't be shy about it! What did they say that they didn't want us to hear?" Oz asked excitedly.

"They speak very good English," Yvie chimed in. "They were only speaking Serbian or whatever it was to keep us from understanding them."

"They're running out of food. They are worried that our appetites are going to cause them problems, Oz," Edmund explained guiltily.

"Oh nonsense. These tickets were so exy, they wouldn't dare run out of food," Oz scoffed.

"Exy?" Eleanor asked.

"Expensive," Yvie translated. "I'm glad I'm not the only one who didn't know the word."

"Mr. Valov did say that they didn't get the expected supplies in Belgrade. If they weren't genuinely worried about it, why would they have only discussed their plight in Russian?" Edmund reasoned.

"Was it Russian?" Eleanor asked curiously.

Edmund closed his eyes with concentration. "It was Bulgarian, actually. They're both Bulgarian."

"Mr. Valov? Is that your man's name?" Oz asked. "Is he Russian?"

"Czech, actually. Although he's lived in Britain for quite a while," Edmund replied.

"I had half a mind to poach him," Oz admitted. "That man was hovering around the dining car all day yesterday just waiting for you to emerge from your slumber."

"Good luck," Edmund laughed. "I've never met a more loyal gentleman's gentleman than Mr. Valov."

As the waiters emerged from the kitchen door with silver trays on each arm, the rich scent of spiced meat wafted through the air, and Edmund's stomach growled with anticipation.

"Oh Eleanor, we are getting closer and closer to the Orient! The food is only going to get better from here. Do you smell those spices?"

Eleanor smiled with bemusement at Edmund's childlike enthusiasm for good food. "It smells delicious, darling."

The waiters rushed to their table to serve up hefty platefuls of a spiced rice and lamb dish, and Edmund dug in with reckless abandon, barely remembering before an embarrassing faux-pas to use a semblance of his proper British table manners.

"We've been keeping a close eye on our fellow passengers for you," Yvie said as she began eating her meal more slowly. "The pomeranian's mistress is a Hungarian countess, so you were right on that one. The two priests are Irish, and they're on their way to Baghdad to spread the gospel. The ginger one has never been out of Ireland before, and he's a bit overwhelmed. The Ridgeways are on their way to India, like you two, to visit Mrs. Ridgeway's brother who is a clerk in Bombay."

"Well, that should be a rude awakening!" Edmund laughed. "They can hardly control their children in a peaceful setting like this one! They'd better keep them closer in India. They can't just run about like wild beasts there. They'll be crushed by a carriage in an instant." He looked grim as he finished his thought. "Perhaps I should have a word with them so they know what to expect. A surprising number of British people arrive in India believing that it will be like Britain. They are thoroughly overwhelmed when it is proven to be quite distinctly foreign."

"That is quite kind of you, darling," Eleanor said encouragingly. "What else have you learned?" she addressed Yvie.

"Well, the chatty American is a journalist. She has been tasked with writing an article about the Orient Express for one of the big American newspapers, and she doesn't know her companion at all. They are just sharing a berth. The other woman is German, and I know nothing about her other than that. Then there are the creepy Russians. We know nothing about them either, except that they must be frozen to death all the time, because they've been wearing those ridiculous furs every time they enter the dining car. And that other group in black over there got on the train in Trieste. They speak some Slavic language, and have mostly kept to themselves."

Yvie pointed to a new group of men, dressed in somber dark wool suits. Their red faces and glassy eyes indicated that they had been enjoying the free-flowing spirits in the car for quite some time.

Oz leaned in and whispered as he pointed to the lone man at the table just across the aisle. "And your former neighbor is American. He's a businessman on his way to Syria to oversee some investments. He was grinning like a shot fox when your man helped him move to the other first class car. Brilliant idea, by the way. I wish we'd thought of it." Oz winked and then refocused on his meal as Edmund blushed.

They sat together enjoying the rich foreign flavors of the meal in jovial conversation, until the dessert course was supposed to be served. Instead, the waiters rushed into the dining room with panicked haste to collect all of the dishes, whether or not the passengers had finished eating. One of them dropped a handful of empty wine glasses on the floor, and when they shattered, he whimpered and collected the next set from the neighboring table, leaving the broken glass littering the aisle.

The Hungarian countess chastised him in a foreign tongue, while Mrs. Ridgeway whispered her disapproval of his conduct to her family. "What are we supposed to do now? Are we just supposed to walk across a field of shattered glass?"

"We aren't in Britain anymore," Mr. Ridgeway said haughtily. "This is exactly why the world needs the British Empire. Otherwise, they'd all just be walking on glass all the bloody time. It's a wonder this train is moving at all with a bolshie staff like this one."

"Something's wrong. Those waiters are terrified," Edmund leaned in and whispered as he watched the waiters scurry back into the kitchen.

"Do you think they ran out of food?" Eleanor asked.

"It's more than that. They're afraid for their lives," Edmund whispered. "I am very experienced in identifying that kind of fear."

He glanced at Oz and Yvie, and then threw Eleanor a look of warning. She knew that he meant that it *tasted* different.

"Do you think we should leave?" Yvie whispered. "Should we go back to our berths?"

"I don't know…" Edmund's fear was written across his face. "You should go. All three of you. I will stay here to see after the others."

"I'm not leaving you here alone, Edmund," Eleanor said with obvious annoyance.

"If something happens, we will need a medic," Oz added. "What do you think it could be, Colonel? What would make the waiters scared for their lives?"

"They must know something… something that we don't want to know." Edmund stared at the kitchen door and then made a subtle survey of the entire dining car and its passengers.

Suddenly, a loud commotion broke out in the next car.

A woman screamed. Then a man.

"That's the second class dining car," Oz said as he threw Edmund a nervous look.

Boom.

Boom.

Boom.

"Were those gunshots?" Eleanor hissed as she grabbed Edmund's hand under the table.

He looked around at the large crowd, and Eleanor could feel him tense with panic. He could not blur them out of there. He could not do anything unusual in front of these people.

The other passengers began to panic.

"What do you think that could be, George?" Mrs. Ridgeway asked with carefully controlled angst.

"Oh, I'm sure it's nothing," Mr. Ridgeway said unconvincingly. "Eloise, you take the girls back to our berth."

Boom.

Men began shouting.

"Come on girls," Mrs. Ridgeway urged.

"But, Mummy, the glass!" Daisy whined.

"Yes, the glass!" Lily echoed. "We can't cross the glass!"

Daisy squealed in shrill protest as Mrs. Ridgeway lifted her up into her arms, but as she attempted to carry her over the pile of glass, she tripped over a chair and dropped Daisy right onto the sharp shards.

Daisy began to scream, and Lily joined in.

Daisy tried to pull a piece of glass from the palm of her hand, and Lily only screamed louder at the grotesque sight as blood gushed from the fresh wound.

Boom.

Boom.

Boom.

A chorus of children screamed in the next car down, serving as an eerie harmony to the screaming children before them.

"Bloody hell," Edmund murmured as the scent of Daisy's blood and the acute panic of the escalating situation bombarded him with equal measure.

"Keep yourself under control, darling," Eleanor whispered into his ear. "Everything will be alright. Do what Mr. Johnson told you to do, and everything will be fine."

Edmund closed his eyes and whispered a quiet mantra, and when he reopened them, his eyes remained their human hazel.

"Excellent work, darling," Eleanor whispered. "Let's go back to our room right now. The others will follow our example, and we will all be out of harm's way with our doors locked and bolted."

She stood up, and Oz and Yvie followed her cue. But, as they made their move, Mr. Ridgeway noticed their plan, and did absolutely the most idiotic thing he could have possibly done.

"Where are you going, Colonel?" he yelled. "Something horrible is happening! It's a revolution! We've got to stop it!"

"This isn't a game, Mr. Ridgeway," Edmund countered angrily. "You must all evacuate immediately. There is nothing glorious about combat or innocent people meeting brutal ends."

"You're just going to run away? You're a coward!" Mr. Ridgeway exclaimed. "We can stop them!"

"You had best avoid flippant commentary on topics about which you know *nothing*, Mr. Ridgeway." Eleanor shivered as power emanated from Edmund's booming voice. She noticed that several other people shivered too.

"Oh, come on, Colonel! Be a bloody man!" Mr. Ridgeway egged him on.

As he spoke, the two old Russians in furs stood up from their table, as did the four mysterious men dressed in black. The old man reached into his oversized coat and pulled out a cache of guns, and then, without a moment of hesitation, he tossed a weapon to each of the men in black.

"You are right, you British bastards. This is a revolution. Stamboliyski has no spine, and he will not stop us! Macedonia is ours! Now stay where you are, or everyone dies!"

CHAPTER 17 – WHAT IT LOOKS LIKE

Yvie and Oz threw Eleanor ambivalent looks of hope and fear as Edmund engaged the man in Bulgarian with his greatest impression of calm authority. The revolutionary woman took a moment to get over her surprise at Edmund's fluency in Bulgarian, and then barked her disapproval at both of them. She pulled another gun from her coat, aiming it straight at Edmund, and then screeched something at the top of her lungs, seemingly into the air.

Four more burly men dressed in a more Bolshevik style than the dark-suited goons in the first class car burst through the door from the second class dining car with guns poised.

Daisy and Lily Ridgeway screamed, and the Hungarian Countess's pomeranian began to bark. The countess screamed as one of the men snapped its neck with a crunch.

The old revolutionary woman threw a wild look at Mrs. Ridgeway. "Silence those children or my men will do it for you."

Mrs. Ridgeway gathered her daughters into her arms. "You *must* be quiet, girls. Please, I beg you. Listen to Mummy just this once."

Lily moved to argue, and Mrs. Ridgeway slapped her and slammed her hand over her mouth. Lily and Daisy were both finally so shocked by their mother's punishment that they submitted to her request. Mrs. Ridgeway gathered them into her arms and sank down onto the floor between two tables.

"Silence, all of you! The next person who speaks is dead!" the woman commanded in English with a thick Slavic accent.

"*Baba Svaboda, ya...*" One of the revolutionaries from the second class car addressed the old woman in Bulgarian with what appeared to be a proud report of their carnage. Eleanor watched Edmund's face become more and more desperate as he listened to the man's bragging. His eyes wandered to assess his ten gun-wielding adversaries. Eleanor hoped desperately that Edmund would not attempt to take all of them at once. Even with his speed, she knew full well he would not be able to keep all of them from shooting into the crowd of innocent people.

As soon as the man was finished reporting to Baba Svaboda, the older of the two Irish priests stood up calmly from his position and attempted to address the revolutionaries. "Please, my children, there are women and children here. Surely you can let them go and keep just the men."

Boom.

Shocked gasps and screams rang out as the closest revolutionary fired his gun at point-blank range right at the priest's chest.

The priest collapsed dead onto the floor, and his blood gushed all over the garish carpet. The revolutionary who'd shot him hissed something snide in Bulgarian, while the young ginger priest cried silently, closed his eyes, and began whispering fearful prayers. Edmund closed his eyes and whispered his calming mantras more desperately.

Baba Svaboda barked more orders, and the revolutionaries began separating the men and the women, gathering both groups on opposite sides of the car and lining them up as if they were being readied for a firing squad. As the priest-murdering man grabbed Eleanor's arm, she threw Edmund a desperate look. What exactly she wanted him to do, she had no bloody clue. She knew that for the first time since the war, both of them were in an utterly hopeless situation. She annoyed herself with a momentary fantasy of Mélusine and Kuveni appearing to magically save the day. Certainly, destiny would consider *that* a dangerous form of meddling.

The American journalist began crying as one of the revolutionaries threw her against the wall, and Eleanor gathered her hand up and squeezed it.

"Sshhh…" she whispered. She didn't dare speak a word.

Baba Svaboda barked more orders, and then stepped over the body of the dead priest and the pile of broken glass to escort her male companion towards the second class dining car. She left her eight enforcers behind to guard the hostages.

"Oh, come on!" Mr. Ridgeway exclaimed. "Colonel, you're a war hero! We have to take them together *now!*"

Mr. Ridgeway didn't have time to take a single step towards the closest revolutionary when another gunshot rang out, and Mrs. Ridgeway, Daisy, and Lily all screamed.

"I've been shot!" Mr. Ridgeway exclaimed as he collapsed onto the ground, grabbing onto his shoulder as it gushed blood.

No one dared say a word or rush to his aid as all eight revolutionaries pointed their guns tauntingly around the car.

Mr. Ridgeway's surprise morphed into pain, and he whimpered from his helpless position.

As Eleanor's mind rushed to come up with any semblance of a reasonable plan that would rescue everyone and keep Edmund's secrets unrevealed, a commotion in the next car over caught everyone's attention. The two revolutionaries closest to the door barked something to their comrades, and then headed through the door into the next car to investigate. As another round of gunshots rang out, four more rushed to support them, leaving only two of the men in black to guard the group.

In the absence of the rest of their comrades, the remaining revolutionaries were less interested in corralling the hostaged men than they were in assessing the women. They walked back and forth in front of the women's line-up with their guns poised—one in the direction of the men, and the other in the direction of the women—licking their cracked lips salaciously as they anticipated their next ghoulish move.

Eleanor and Edmund threw each other desperate looks as the first revolutionary pulled Yvie into his bloody arms and ran his rough finger across her cheek. Silent tears poured from her eyes. The other rushed forward, grabbing Eleanor by the arm and forcing her into the aisle. After a moment of covetous inspection, he pulled the ribbon out of her hair so he could feel one of her fiery tendrils.

As a lascivious look of dark desire crossed his face, and Eleanor let out an involuntary whimper, Edmund's last ounce of self-control dissolved. What transpired next happened so fast that Eleanor could hardly process the order of events.

In a blur, Edmund was holding the man's neck in his right hand.

Women were screaming.

Maybe Mrs. Ridgeway. Maybe one or both of the children.

Edmund took in a deep, covetous whiff, spat something in Bulgarian, squeezed down on the murderous rapist's throat, and with an excruciating crunch, the man collapsed dead onto the floor with his head barely still connected.

Blood gushed onto the floor and soaked Edmund's hands.

Many more terrified screams rang out.

Edmund turned his black demonic eyes and his raging divine fury on the stunned revolutionary who was squeezing Yvie's arms, holding her up against his disgustingly aroused body.

Edmund reached forward and grabbed the man's wrists, ripping him away from Yvie. Eleanor rushed forward and pulled Yvie into her arms.

"Everything will be fine. We must let Edmund save us," she whispered into her ear as Yvie could not control her terrified sobs.

As the revolutionary begged for mercy, Edmund took in another covetous whiff of the man's fear mingling with the bouquet of fresh blood, lifted him up, and threw him across the car.

The man landed with a loud thud and a clank on the farthest table by the door to the second class carriage. Wine glasses and plates shattered with the weight of his impact, but the sounds were dampened by his heavy body.

Edmund blurred after him, and as the man screamed, Edmund whisked him up off the table and snapped his neck. He dropped the body onto the floor and took in another satisfied whiff.

Eleanor worked hard to ignore the obvious truth that Edmund was relishing the scent of fresh death.

He looked back at his horrified witnesses with his black eyes, and they only stared at him in stunned silence.

"Everyone, stay where you are!" Eleanor addressed the group. "Edmund, darling, there are at least eight more of them. You must stop them before they hurt anyone else."

Eleanor desperately hoped that addressing her husband as if he was a human hero would make him, and all the others witnessing his demonic fury, believe that he was just that. She knew the chances were slim all around.

Boom.

Another gunshot from the second class dining car resonated through the closed door.

More shouting.

Several loud thuds indicated some sort of hand-to-hand combat.

Edmund took in another whiff of collective fear mingling with fresh blood and prepared himself for his adversaries' return.

One of the revolutionaries pushed back into the car with his gun poised, and Edmund reached forward in a blur, snapping the man's neck with a flick of his wrist. As he picked up the body and tossed it into the corner with his last victim, two more revolutionaries rushed into the cabin.

As Edmund grabbed one by the shoulders and smashed his head into the wall, the other slashed a deep cut across Edmund's cheek.

Edmund grabbed the man's knife right out of his hand, slashed his throat, and threw both of the men's corpses onto the pile with the other two.

Baba Svaboda rushed into the carriage, looking back behind her in a panic, but as she made it only halfway through the door, she took one confused look at her five dead men and Edmund standing before her with blood-drenched hands and black demonic eyes, and she stopped in her tracks. She crossed herself and hissed something in Bulgarian (undoubtedly some epithet accusing Edmund of being a demon), and stepped backwards.

"Pray all you want, *Baba Svaboda*," Edmund spat as he leapt forward and grabbed her by the shoulders. He thrust her towards the body of the dead priest, forcing her to look at the terrified expression plastered on his face. "You will pay for your sins in this life."

But, before he had a chance to end her as he had the others, another gunshot rang out, and she collapsed dead in Edmund's arms. Mr. Valov stood behind her, holding a smoking revolver.

"I already got the others, Colonel. All the bolos are dead now."

Edmund dropped the body as he stared at Mr. Valov with a moment of confusion, and then glanced around, spying his carnage and the blood on his hands. He reached up to feel the deep cut on his face.

Eleanor rushed to Edmund's side and gathered his bloody hand into hers. "It's all over now, darling. You can relax and let the adrenaline pass. You saved us. You saved every innocent person who's alive right now." She voiced her praise loudly so the others would hear.

"You should all return to your compartments until we reach Sofia," Mr. Valov addressed the overwhelmed group. "The colonel and I will take it from here."

Mr. Valov glanced up at Edmund, and a look of fascination crossed his face as he watched Edmund's violet metallic plasma work hard to heal his wound. Edmund's eyes remained solidly black, but Mr. Valov did not show a hint of surprise. Eleanor realized that Mr. Valov knew far more about Edmund than he'd ever let on, and her puzzlement only grew. How could he not be a Yaksha?

"You heard him!" Edmund roared. "Go!"

The American journalist, her German companion, the angry American businessman, and the Hungarian countess all rushed to follow his orders, while Oz, Yvie, the young priest, and the Ridgeway ladies all rushed to Mr. Ridgeway's side. The priest conspicuously avoided Edmund's gaze and focused on his prayers, while Oz and Yvie set about stabilizing Mr. Ridgeway's condition.

"Sit up, Mr. Ridgeway," Oz whispered. "We need to stop the bleeding."

Yvie ripped off her headband and began tying it into a tourniquet.

"George, are you alright?" Mrs. Ridgeway asked in a panic as she kneeled down beside him.

"Daddy?!" Daisy cried. "Daddy, you're bleeding too! We're both bleeding!"

At the reminder, Lily burst into tears and collapsed into her sister's arms.

"I've been shot! Those bloody bolos shot me! On the goddamned Orient Express! Do they have any idea how much I paid for this?" Mr. Ridgeway whined with disbelief as Oz examined the wound. "It really bloody hurts, Eloise!"

"He really is an abominable snowman!" Lily broke out of her misery to voice her conclusion with a combination of wonder and fear as Edmund and Eleanor approached them to observe Mr. Ridgeway's condition from afar.

Mr. and Mrs. Ridgeway looked up at Edmund, but no words would come as he gazed at them with his black eyes while the violet plasma finished up its work on his face.

Edmund held out his bloody hands before him. "I cannot tell you how much I regret your children witnessing that depravity, Mr. Ridgeway. I hope we can now agree that there was nothing glorious about it, and I would thank you to remember the ugly details of this encounter the next time you go off calling anyone a coward for not crushing another man to death with his bare hands."

"You are not a man, though, are you, Colonel?" Mr. Ridgeway whispered fearfully.

Edmund looked to Eleanor and then shrugged. "I am a great many things, Mr. Ridgeway, and it was very lucky for you that a man with my talents was here today to save your lives."

Mr. Valov approached them from behind and whispered into their ears. "Colonel, you and Eleanor should return to your berth. You must clean yourselves up, and get rid of every trace of blood, so you can disembark silently in Sofia. The Bulgarian authorities are violent. They aren't going to do anything civilized about these revolutionaries, but I am sure they will be very interested in you. I will have the porters unload your trunks in Sofia, and I will help you book passage on the next train out of town. I will help you get to Constantinople within a day of your expected arrival, and no one will know you were involved."

278

"Mr. Valov…" Edmund said as he looked down at his bloody hands.

"Please, there is no time for explanations, Colonel. We must act now. You and Eleanor need to get ready to get off the train. It will be very cold. I will fetch your coats as soon as you're back in your berth."

Eleanor caught Oz and Yvie both looking up to watch them go, but she self-consciously avoided eye contact.

"Come on, darling. I'll help you wash off the blood," she whispered as she held Edmund's hand tightly in hers.

As soon as they reached their berth, Mr. Valov pushed them inside. "Be ready to disembark. We are scheduled for arrival in Sofia in twenty minutes. As soon as you're off the train, don't look back. Walk across the platform as if you know exactly where you're going, and get into the first taxi you see. Speak to the driver only in Bulgarian, and do not speak to each other. Have him take you to the Alexander Nevsky Cathedral. I will put some Bulgarian leva in the pockets of your coats to pay him. Use them sparingly. Wait for me at the cathedral. I will find you when it is safe for you to return to the station."

He closed the door, and Eleanor listened as his running footsteps dissolved.

"That man is not just a butler," Edmund declared as soon as he was sure Mr. Valov was out of earshot.

"You are certainly right about that. But, darling, he's not wrong. We must prepare. Everyone saw you use your talents, and you killed a number of people whom I'm sure *someone* will be very angry about losing."

Eleanor grabbed the clean cloth in the washbasin and began washing the blood off of Edmund's hands. As soon as she was finished, she helped him undress in the awkwardly cramped space, and then gathered his clothes from their first day on the train from their crumpled pile in the corner.

"Darling, close your eyes and whisper your mantras." She began smoothing out the wrinkles in his suit with her hands.

"Mantras?" Edmund asked.

"Whatever it is you've been whispering that Mr. Johnson told you to say."

"I suppose it is a mantra of sorts." Edmund smiled half-heartedly at the idea. "I am ordering myself to stay human. He told me that the dark part of me can be subverted with enough will, and that if I cling to my humanity, it will be easier to control."

"Well, his advice seems to be working." Eleanor reached forward to stroke his perfectly healed cheek. "I think you are close to getting your adrenaline back under control."

All of the evidence of his violet metallic plasma was gone, as was his feigned bruise on his eye, but his black eyes stubbornly remained.

He looked straight into her eyes as he gently took her hand into his and whispered his mantra. For the first time, she watched as the demonic black dissolved with his eyes still open, giving way to his human hazel. She smiled and leaned forward to kiss him.

"I love you, Edmund. You saved a lot of innocent people today."

"I enjoyed killing those men," he confessed. "By the end, I hoped there were more to kill."

"I enjoyed watching you kill them, Edmund. They deserved to die." Eleanor held his hands in hers as she looked up into his earnest eyes. "How we felt about it doesn't matter. They were evil, and you stopped them. Think of what they would have done to every innocent person on this train if they'd had the chance. They killed a priest in cold blood, and they were about to rape me and Yvie. They had us lined up to be executed. They deserved no mercy."

Eleanor could see that Edmund was battling with his ambivalent emotions just as much as she was, but before they could give into the distraction, they both heard footsteps approaching in the hallway.

Edmund scrambled to get into his clothes, and Eleanor gathered their bloody evidence into a ball, ready to pass off to Mr. Valov.

"Doesn't that sound like two people?" she asked as the footsteps reached the door, followed by a timid knock.

"Mr. Valov said he'd be back with our coats." Edmund took her hand into his, indicating that he too knew that it wasn't just Mr. Valov at the door.

Eleanor's heart skipped a beat as Edmund pushed open the door, and Oz and Yvie stood nervously before them.

"Mr. Ridgeway will be fine," Oz said as he looked up at Edmund with a combination of curiosity and reverence in his expression.

Edmund stared at them, but no words would come.

"Glad to hear it," Eleanor replied awkwardly on Edmund's behalf. She'd always hated small-talk in the face of an extraordinary elephant in the room. "Is there anything else?"

Oz shifted uncomfortably and then sucked up his nerves. "Colonel, you don't need to explain yourself. We've seen enough in the army hospitals to know when not to ask. We just came to thank you, and to tell you that we won't say anything to anyone about what happened in there. I'm just grateful that *all* of the legends about you were true."

Edmund remained speechless.

"We'd all be dead if it weren't for you," Oz reiterated. "If you hadn't used your legendary… er… talents… surely those bolshies would have killed everyone on the train, and it was obvious you didn't want to be doing any of that in front of an audience… or at all, for that matter."

"You are certainly right about that," Edmund said quietly. "I spent most of the war not using my talents as I should have because I was afraid of being discovered. Too many men died because of my cowardice."

"We are alive because of your courage, Colonel," Oz countered. "We owe you a big one."

"If you ever come to Perth, look us up," Yvie chimed in. "We have a lovely house by the sea, and we don't get many visitors. It might be a nice place for you two to escape to, if ever the need arises. It feels like we're at the very edge of the world down there."

"How kind!" Eleanor exclaimed.

"Yes, it is a very kind offer," Edmund seconded pensively. "Shockingly kind, after what you just witnessed."

"We already knew what war looked like, Colonel," Oz reminded him. "I hope none of us ever have to see it again."

"So do I," Edmund said as he reached forward and shook Oz's hand with both of his. Oz shivered slightly, but smiled and said nothing.

With a loud clank, the door to the carriage opened, and all four of them looked down the hallway with heightened awareness as Mr. Valov approached with the coats.

"It is time to move, Colonel. We are reaching the station now." Mr. Valov helped Eleanor into her mink coat. "Keep your hands in your pockets, Eleanor. Don't let anyone see the ring."

As the train came to a belabored stop, Mr. Valov pushed Edmund and Eleanor out the door onto the freezing platform. With feigned calm hiding the rapid beating of their anxious hearts, they made their way out of the station and into the first waiting taxi. Edmund commanded the driver in Bulgarian, and with a screech of the tires on the icy road, they were off towards the center of Sofia.

CHAPTER 18 – SOFIA

They rode silently through the snowy streets of Sofia, watching out the window as stoic people in dark fur coats went about their afternoon business. It looked exactly how Eleanor had pictured the cold, dark east, although, perhaps the people looked even more unhappy than she'd imagined. There was a pervasive depressive air floating about, and she didn't think that the grey skies and fluffy spring snow were the sole cause.

As the taxi pulled up into a wide-open square, the driver said a few words to Edmund, and he reached into his coat pocket and handed the man some coins. Edmund hopped out and rushed around the car to help Eleanor up, and then without another word, the taxi drove off, and he escorted her swiftly across the square towards an imposing structure that looked vaguely like a cluster of enormous mushrooms bursting forth from the floor of a snowy meadow. Sacre Coeur seemed miniscule in comparison, and the green and gold roofs of the bulbous orthodox domes reiterated that they had officially reached the edge of the Orient.

Edmund helped her walk up the icy steps, and then he pushed open a heavy, intricately carved door flanked by wide-eyed angels and scowling demons.

As they entered the vast space, Eleanor stared up at least twenty meters into the air, past a series of enormous golden chandeliers filled with burning candles, to observe the most ostentatious example of liturgical architecture she had ever seen, even after their days exploring in Paris. Larger-than-life mosaics of saints and winged angels filled the walls all the way up to the very top of the domed ceilings. On the ground towards the edges of the space, a series of pagoda-like white marble structures trimmed in gold and topped with eastern crosses made it look as if the outer structure of the building had engulfed an entire ancient city. Marble archways covered in thousands of symbolic carvings led into dark labyrinthine passages, while the center of the cathedral had no chairs or pews, leaving the space open as if it were a mosque. Elaborate checker-board designs covered the marble floors in the empty center of the room, and the only other people inside the cathedral appeared to be a few old women in thick furs lighting candles by various gilded golden altars.

Eleanor startled as the door closed behind them and the sound echoed across the cathedral, bouncing off the various marble and mosaic structures for a good fifteen seconds. Edmund squeezed her hand and led her across the open center, towards the largest white pagoda-shaped altar, through one of the many carved archways, and into one of the transepts, where several altars to various saints were lit up with flickering candles, and muted light shone through a small stained-glass window that was surprisingly simple compared to the mosaics all around.

They stood for many minutes while Eleanor's heart raced. She hoped that no one who knew anything about orthodoxy would approach them, for, despite Edmund's fluent Bulgarian, she was quite certain that neither of them would have the faintest idea what rituals to do if they were pressed. She wondered what was running through his mind as he guided her slowly to the edge of the room and began systematically inspecting the craftsmanship of the mosaics. She was glad he had something so mundane to occupy his mind after his massacre, and she was quite sure that the bloody images of the crucifixion peppered in various forms throughout the cathedral weren't helping.

She joined him in his self-distracting exercise for a very long time—at least an hour, maybe two or three—until a young priest approached them, and she felt Edmund panic. The man had large, soulful brown eyes and darker skin than any of the Bulgarians she'd seen on their silent taxi ride through the city. He looked almost Turkish, or even a bit like a gypsy, and he wore ivory robes with elaborate gold designs embroidered into them and an absurd golden hat that's shape reminded her of the bulbous domes of the cathedral. She wondered if every style in the Orient would involve bulbous shapes of one form or another—the Taj Mahal certainly did, and she didn't know very many other examples.

She tried to calm her racing heart as the man said something quietly to Edmund in Bulgarian. Edmund tried to brush him off, but the man wouldn't have any of it. He whispered something else in Bulgarian, and then placed his hands on their backs and escorted them assertively through another archway into a small chapel where the echoing of their footsteps was muted by a series of tapestries hanging on the walls. At the front of the chapel, there was yet another statue of Jesus suffering on the cross, but this statue looked different than any of the others. He had a distinctly middle-eastern look to him, and while there was no evidence of a bloody wound anywhere on him, the expression of divine sorrow in his eyes was palpable. As Eleanor stared at it for a long moment, she realized that he looked somehow familiar.

The priest closed the heavy wooden doors to the chapel behind them, and Edmund once again attempted to protest in Bulgarian, but the priest interrupted him.

"Please, Young Edmund, do not worry. You are not in any danger right now." He spoke with perfect British English with a posh accent exactly like Edmund's.

Edmund stumbled backwards with surprise, and Eleanor squeezed him tightly as she eyed the priest, trying to assess whether he was Kuveni or Mélusine.

Edmund took a moment to compose himself before he chose his first question. "How do you know my name?"

"I know a great many things, Young Edmund. Including many things that you, my child, are not ready to know. I am here now because Mr. Johnson asked for my assistance. He wanted me to check in on you after your trials of the last few days. He was worried about you."

"Mr. Johnson…" Edmund whispered. "Mr. Johnson knows everything that has happened? Even what happened earlier today? How in god's name could he know that?"

The priest smiled at his choice of words. "Mr. Johnson knows a great many things."

"You are making it sound as if he's God."

"Yes, I suppose I am." The priest glanced over to the crucifix. "You don't like that I make him sound like God?"

"I have never seen any compelling evidence that God exists at all, and I would thank you to keep Mr. Johnson out of it." Edmund followed the priest's attention over to the crucifix. "Just because someone is uniquely talented, it does not mean that he is divine. I know that perfectly well myself, and as an acquaintance of Mr. Johnson's, you should certainly know it too. He and I are both really quite ordinary."

"Are you really?" the priest asked curiously.

"What else would we be?" Edmund countered.

"You tell me," the priest shot back.

Edmund tensed as the priest's inquisitive style tipped off his suspicions. "I don't think I caught your name."

286

"It is not time for you to know it, Young Edmund, and I do not wish to tell you a lie," the priest demurred.

"Then I think I have already said enough." Edmund guided Eleanor swiftly to the door.

"Please, wait, Young Edmund." The priest rushed after them. "Please, talk to me a bit about what happened."

He took Edmund's hand into his right, and Eleanor's into his left. His Yaksha warmth pulsated with life, and he smiled as he noticed them recognize it.

"I see you have come to recognize how we feel. I know many who will be pleased by that development." He squeezed their hands and pushed his Yaksha warmth straight into them. Eleanor and Edmund both shivered at the sensation.

Eleanor wondered in passing if the Yaksha was actually a priest; after all, Vibhishana had seemed quite comfortable in the clothing of a vicar... Although, she supposed it was his right to wear any Christian regalia he fancied. She suspected he wasn't particularly keen on the ostentation of this particular priest's outfit, though. Her mind wandered to wondering who this Yaksha standing before them was, and why she hadn't met him yet. He had a certain confidence about him that the others lacked, and he seemed particularly comfortable in the sacred environment.

"You are like Kate?" Edmund asked, interrupting Eleanor's thought-stream.

The priest closed his eyes for a moment and then reopened them with a gentle smile. "Yes. I am like Kate. You can think of us as your cousins."

"Kate is not my cousin," Edmund informed him.

"I didn't mean the statement literally, my child," the priest replied calmly. "There are many truths all around you that can only be appreciated if you do not let yourself get too entrenched in literal facts."

"Truth is in the eye of the beholder," Edmund countered.

"The eye of the beholder can be easily fooled, Young Edmund," the priest rebuked. "Even an eye as clever as yours." The priest threw a glance at Eleanor that aroused Edmund's attention.

"Is there something that we can do for you, *father*?" Eleanor swiftly changed the subject. "We are in a bit of a hurry."

"I ask only that you stay here and talk to me for a bit while you wait for Mr. Valov. Mr. Johnson asked me to make sure that you were alright, and I do not have a sufficient report for him yet."

"Are you a spy of his? Have you been following us?" Edmund's expression darkened. "Did you kill those vagrants in Paris?"

"I did not," the priest said sharply. "I do not kill, and I never have."

Edmund let out an involuntary overwhelmed sigh. "That makes you far more virtuous than I."

"There are many kinds of virtue," the priest replied more softly. "It is a concept that has changed quite readily over the centuries, whenever it suits a human's fancy."

"Killing men in cold blood has always been wrong," Edmund countered.

"Has it?" the priest asked. "I believe the Catholic church declared it to be quite righteous during the Crusades, and many other times. The Reformation was rather bloody, and the Middle Ages... Oh, how quick those priests were to set fire to anyone who crossed them. Humans have inflicted so much pain on each other in the name of the Holy Redeemer that I've completely lost track."

"You were around back then? For all of those eras?" Edmund asked.

"I was," the priest replied simply.

"Then how, may I ask, do you still wear the robes of a priest? If you have seen the many gruesome things that were done in the name of religion?"

The priest laughed. "I have always been too much of an optimist."

"But…" Edmund trailed off. "Never mind. I suspect there is no point in debating the topic. I'm quite sure we won't agree."

"Oh, my child, there is every point in debating it! Please, make your argument!"

Edmund took a deep breath as he prepared to argue with the mysterious agent of the man he believed was his father. "How can you condone the hypocrisy that all of this represents?" He pointed to the mosaicked walls and then a gilded golden sepulcher underneath the statue of the crucifix. "There are beggars freezing to death on the streets outside while this building is gilded with enough gold to feed the country for a century. I hate to think of the slave labor that went into building this cathedral in the name of a man who, as far as I know, was a simple carpenter who preached about helping one's neighbors. I don't see how anyone could believe that a cathedral like this has anything to do with *God*," Edmund rolled his eyes as he said the word, "and the resources that went into building a monument like this that could have gone into easing the plight of humanity is utterly shameful… at least in my opinion."

The priest smiled. "You are not the only one who has that opinion, Young Edmund. It is an ugly truth that plagues many of us, even me. We have debated what to do about it from time to time, but every time our conclusion remains that there is nothing to be done. Humans will do what they want. In the end, meddling only makes things worse."

"Who is *we*?" Edmund asked astutely. "Is Mr. Johnson part of *we*? You two have been debating what to do about the atrocities committed by various institutions in the name of a kind-hearted carpenter?"

The priest laughed, but Eleanor could sense that he had not been prepared for Edmund to ask such a pointed question.

"He warned me that you had become more inquisitive. I understand now what he meant. I cannot tell you anything more than Mr. Johnson could about truths that you are not ready to know."

"Then I suppose we have nothing left to talk about," Edmund said with obvious annoyance. "You can send that back to Mr. Johnson in your report."

Eleanor smiled as Edmund gave into his first moment of adolescent rebellion in a hundred years.

The priest noticed the change in Edmund's tenor as much as Eleanor did. "I will most certainly send him your message. But, before I go, let me ask you this: Why do angels have wings?"

Edmund was taken aback by the seemingly irrelevant turn of the conversation. "I'm sorry? Is this exercise going to be followed by a debate about how many angels can dance on the head of a pin? Mr. Johnson knows how much I detested that exercise in my tutorials. I hated it so much, I told him so straight to his face."

"I remember him telling me all about it," the priest replied. "He couldn't have been prouder. Now, if I might beg your forgiveness while promising you that we will not delve into the absurdity of medieval philosophy, might you indulge me by answering the question?"

Edmund closed his eyes in thought, whether because he was strategizing a follow-up protest or his answer to the question, Eleanor wasn't sure. Then, as footsteps echoed in the distance and then dissolved, he opened his eyes and looked around the chapel at a number of mosaic angels hovering above otherwise mundane religious scenes alongside a few winged saintly statues fawning over the birth of the Christ-child. "Because they were necessary for the fictional plotlines in the religious stories. They probably needed to fly about informing various characters of important developments, just as Aries did in Greek mythology."

The priest burst into laughter. "You are right, their wings were very helpful for getting them around the Holy Land in a snap."

"Is that all then? It's a joke? I do not understand the punchline," Edmund said curtly, annoyed by the priest's flippant demeanor.

"No, I suppose you don't," the priest replied more seriously as he noticed Edmund's displeasure. "I have always found it fascinating that angels and demons both have wings. It makes them quite clearly different from humans, and yet similar to each other."

"They are similarly fictitious," Edmund said cheekily.

The priest was unfazed. "You are right that they both serve a useful purpose in religious symbolism. Angels remind humans that creatures who are different from them are not always evil. Did you notice how many angels are adorning the walls of this cathedral as you came in?"

"I didn't make a count."

The priest smiled. "Neither did I. But I think we can agree it is many. Perhaps twenty or thirty? Maybe more if we count the smaller ones like these." He pointed to the same mosaics Edmund had just assessed. "They look down upon the worshippers, demonstrating to them the beauty of the heavenly creatures who watch over them, and giving them an image that they can hold in their minds so that when they come across a strange creature like us, they will not only think of the demons that their fearful human minds cook up. They will think of the beautiful angels that bring them closer to God."

"They will be thoroughly disappointed if they believe in the fairy tale of guardian angels," Edmund muttered.

"Edward Rutherford doesn't think so," the priest countered.

Edmund was startled by the personal reference.

"Mr. Johnson sang his praises after his help with your wedding," the priest clarified. "It is useful for us to keep in mind examples of exceptional human virtue, my child, like your lovely Eleanor here and Edward Rutherford. They remind us what humans are capable of when they aren't demonstrating their many deficiencies."

"You speak as if we are quite separate from humans," Edmund pointed out.

The priest thought for an uncomfortably long moment before responding. "Some of us feel more separate than others. You are blessed with a stronger connection to them than most of us are."

"I am quite skilled at killing them."

Eleanor worked hard not to show her surprise at Edmund's dark turn.

"That is one connection," the priest conceded. "Love is another. Light cannot exist without darkness to balance it, Edmund."

"I have enough darkness inside of me to balance love for the entire human race," Edmund whispered.

"That, my child, is a profound gift. I am glad that you recognize it."

"I don't love the entire human race. Many of them are ignorant, destructive fiends," Edmund countered.

"I do not disagree with you," the priest continued, looking rather pleased with himself for coaxing Edmund into the confession he was there to procure. "But tell me, Young Edmund, what did you choose to do a few days ago in Paris when four human fiends ruthlessly attacked your wife, stole your mother's ring, and shot you in the back in cold blood?"

"I chased them down. I broke their arms and took back what they'd stolen. I relished their fear and their pain as they watched me impart my punishment."

"Why did you not kill them for their transgressions?"

"Because there was no point. I had what they'd stolen, and there was nothing to be gained by vengeance. There was only my soul to be lost."

The priest was startled by his answer. "That is very wise of you, Edmund. Wise beyond your years."

"I wasn't wise today," Edmund countered. "I gave into my basest desires."

"Today you killed five men, was it?" the priest asked casually. "What was different about today?"

"I lost control," Edmund whispered. "There was too much blood. They were going to rape Eleanor and Yvie. They threatened to kill the children. They killed a peaceful man as a violent showing of petty power, and who knows how many they'd already killed by the time they got to us. I had to make them stop."

"What would have happened if you hadn't acted today?"

"I don't know... Probably they would have killed everyone eventually... I wasn't willing to find out." Edmund looked pained as he contemplated the gory options. "I let too many men die by not using my talents when I had the chance. So many men... thousands and thousands of men. They haunt me."

"So you are haunted when you do kill, and you are haunted when you don't?" the priest asked.

Edmund thought about his statement. "It sounds like I'm damned, doesn't it?"

The priest smiled and pulled Edmund into a gentle hug. "You are not damned, my child. You are suffering from the divine conundrum that only people like us can truly comprehend. You are ascending, my dear boy, slowly but surely. Embrace your struggle. It makes you who you are."

"I am not divine," Edmund countered sharply. "I am really very ordinary. I am just as ordinary as you and Mr. Johnson are."

The priest made a sign of the cross and then offered a small bow.

"Indeed you are, Young Edmund, indeed, you are." He placed his hands on Edmund's head. "You are forgiven, my child. You are forgiven for everything that is haunting you. Now all that is left is for you to forgive yourself. *That* will be the most difficult task, I know, but you will achieve it all the same." He closed his eyes for a moment of meditation. "Your man is here. I will leave you two now. It was a pleasure checking up on you. I will let Mr. Johnson know that you are recovering nicely."

"Wait!" Edmund exclaimed desperately. He cleared his throat as he gathered his wits. "Tell me this before you go: What is it, exactly, that you do for Mr. Johnson, if you are not a spy?"

The priest smiled. "I am his spiritual advisor."

Edmund guffawed, and then brought himself under control. "He is five *thousand* years old, and he still needs a spiritual advisor? Who is your spiritual advisor?"

The priest's smile grew into a wide grin. "You are."

As footsteps echoed through the transept, the priest offered them a hasty *namaste*, and then exited the chapel through the far door, leaving them alone.

"I don't know what I have to say about that..." Edmund murmured.

As Edmund turned to watch Mr. Valov push open the heavy doors to the chapel and close himself inside with them, Eleanor was distracted as she noticed that the strangely familiar statue of the crucifix was gone. In its place, the golden sepulcher that had been at its feet was positioned prominently on display alongside a gaudy, jewel-encrusted bishop's hat.

"Here you are! I've been combing the whole cathedral looking for you! I know this place well, but I seem to have somehow gotten lost... Come, we don't have any time to waste. The next international train is leaving Sofia in half an hour. We will go down into Salonica in Greece and then switch to another train to Constantinople. Here. Take these passports. You will both be Scottish pilgrims on your way to the Holy Land if anyone asks."

"We will not go anywhere until you explain to us who you really are, Mr. Valov," Edmund countered with surprising authority.

Mr. Valov looked nervously around the empty chapel and lowered his voice.

"Do you remember, Colonel, four years ago when you took pity on me and kindly offered me a job? I told you that I was in Britain to escape a dark past, that I was a refugee, and I couldn't go home… Well, it was true… mostly. I was a refugee, because I had been a spy for the Czechoslovak Legions during the war. I was feeding information about the Central Powers to them and to the *British*, Colonel. I learned many useful things… things that I used earlier today to kill the other revolutionaries who held up the second class dining car."

"That does not explain why you are here against my orders, Mr. Valov. Nor does it explain how you procured those counterfeit passports in Bulgaria in just a few hours," Edmund pushed.

Mr. Valov looked more desperate than Eleanor had ever seen him. He leaned in and whispered: "We won the war, Colonel, but I made a lot of enemies. Enemies who are still around. Many of them are fighting for the Bolshevik cause now. I have kept in contact with my colleagues from the Czechoslovak Legions. We are wholeheartedly British allies. I sent out word to them from the train as soon as we neutralized the revolutionaries, and they sent a team to help us get out of harm's way. I didn't tell them anything about you, Colonel. Nothing of extraordinary interest. All they know is that you are an active colonel in the British Army, and you and I are responsible for killing those bolos. That's all they needed to know. Now they are helping us get out of here, and we *must* go now."

Edmund put his hand on the doors to stop Mr. Valov from opening them. "You were not surprised earlier when you saw my injury healing."

"Colonel, I have lived in your household for four years. I am a very perceptive man—it is a necessary skill for being a spy. You have demonstrated a number of unique talents over the years that it was impossible to ignore, but I haven't told a soul. I swear to you, Colonel, you have my loyalty, and you always will."

Edmund sighed his concession and pushed open the doors.

Mr. Valov whispered something in Czech, and Edmund squeezed Eleanor's hand and guided her swiftly through the cathedral, out a side door, and into a waiting car. Mr. Valov barked his orders at the driver, and with a screech, they were off.

When they arrived at the station, they followed Mr. Valov right onto a waiting train. The moment they were on, it started moving, and Mr. Valov guided them into an empty compartment.

"I'm sorry, but there are no sleeping berths on this train or the next. It will be a good four hours to Salonica, and then you will spend the night there. I have already made you a booking for an adequate hotel near the station. The train for Constantinople leaves early in the morning. It will take twelve hours, and you will arrive one day later than expected, leaving you with a day to relax before the steamer leaves for Bombay."

"Aren't you going to ride with us?" Edmund asked as Mr. Valov went to close the door to their compartment.

Mr. Valov smiled. "Thank you dearly for the offer, Colonel, but I have it on good authority that you'd like to spend your honeymoon alone together in peace. I will be in the next compartment over if you need anything."

He offered them a polite bow, and then left them alone.

"I don't know what I have to say about that..." Edmund murmured.

Eleanor squeezed his hand and kissed him gently. "Don't say anything, Edmund. Let's just focus on the beautiful truth that we're still alive. Mr. Valov and I have you to thank for that."

"I love you, Eleanor," Edmund whispered as he fought back tears.

"And so many people love you, Edmund. They will have to take their position behind me in line."

She smiled, and he let her pull him from his pensive melancholy as she licked his lips and then enticed him into a deeper kiss.

And so together, on an unnamed train on the edge of the Orient, Edmund and Eleanor pushed back the many complicated emotions of their inglorious triumph and celebrated their narrow escape from another dangerous adventure.

CHAPTER 19 – CONSTANTINOPLE

The train to Salonica and the uncomfortable night in the spartan hotel by the train station were mercifully uneventful, and Edmund and Eleanor finally began to breathe easier the next morning as they made their way through the Turkish countryside towards Constantinople.

When they arrived, Mr. Valov escorted them through the busy Haydarpaşa terminal (not the terminal at which their Orient Express had arrived the prior day), and straight into a sleek, black waiting car with a chauffeur dressed in formal British servants' attire.

"Colonel, I thought it best for you to not stay at the hotel where the other Orient Express passengers are staying. I have taken the liberty of arranging a stay for you at a private palace overlooking the Bosphorus instead. I will follow in another car with your luggage." Mr. Valov tapped the top of the car, and the driver sped away, onto the busy streets of Constantinople.

"We really are in the Orient now," Eleanor murmured as crowds of people scurried about, many of whom were dressed in colorful traditional Ottoman clothing. "I suppose I thought that with the British occupation and Atatürk's secular politics, the people would look more European."

"Culture takes quite a long time to catch up with politics," Edmund said as an elaborate Ottoman building caught his interest. "I rather hope that they never become so British that they lose what makes them uniquely beautiful. India has had to work quite hard to hold onto her culture under the Raj. Too hard, in my opinion."

"You'd best keep that opinion to yourself," Eleanor laughed.

"You are certainly right about that," Edmund agreed. "It is much better for someone in my position to say nothing at all about politics. It makes it easier to change the policies from within, especially in the colonies where the army has much more autonomy than it does back at home."

Eleanor was a bit taken aback by his surprisingly shrewd approach to spreading his own political agenda. She had heard so many of Edmund's colorful stories from his days in India, but she had never been able to wrap her head around why he had been willing to join the Colonial Army in the first place. Every colonial army man she'd ever met (other than Edward Rutherford, of course), had displayed an attitude of such condescension towards the "uncivilized natives" that she was sure they must have driven her gentle, open-minded soldier absolutely mad for decades. But now, with a fresh burst of new respect for him, she finally understood that Edmund had been playing a much more sophisticated game than she'd considered him capable of playing.

Eleanor sighed with satisfaction as the sun came out from behind a cloud and illuminated the water of the Bosphorus with a sparkling sheen, turning it from a dark gray into a bright, rich blue. After a week of cold rain and snow, she was ready to return to the warm weather she'd been too distracted to enjoy leading up to their wedding.

She and Edmund sat pensively hand in hand, looking out the window and soaking in the sun until the car eventually pulled up at a white marble palace (modest in size but decorated with exactly the elaborate façade anyone would expect from a sultan's palace), surrounded by a garden that extended all the way to the very edge of the Bosphorus.

Edmund moved to pay the driver, but the driver refused. Edmund asked him something in Turkish, and then accepted his response and helped Eleanor out of the car.

"He says Mr. Valov already paid him," Edmund explained.

"Well, jolly good on Mr. Valov," Eleanor murmured distractedly as she watched him pull up in the backseat of another black car. There was something about Mr. Valov's demeanor in the train station that was still bothering her, but she couldn't pinpoint exactly what.

"Welcome to Küçüksu Palace, Colonel!" Mr. Valov said cheerfully. Several porters rushed out to greet them, and Mr. Valov directed them to collect the heavy trunks from the boot of his car.

"How, may I ask, did you procure a palace this grand at the last minute for just us?" Edmund asked. "It isn't a hotel?"

Mr. Valov glanced at the driver of their car and laughed awkwardly. "Oh, a friend of a friend works for the Czech embassy, and he knew another friend who asked his cousin who knows a man who works for the British guard about palaces that were currently unoccupied and available for rental until the treaties are all worked out, and poof—here we are."

"I see." Edmund did not look entirely convinced by the story, but he too had picked up on Mr. Valov's unusually jumpy demeanor. "Thank you very much for your help, Mr. Valov. It looks more than adequate for our needs."

They followed him through an intricately carved white marble gate, into the garden that still showed no hint of spring growth, and up a series of grand marble stairs, through a slew of Roman columns, and finally into the building.

"Good lord," Eleanor murmured.

Before them, every inch of the palace was decorated with as much artistic embellishment as anyone on Earth could have possibly stuffed into a space that size. Two central curving staircases with gilded golden bannisters led up to another level, all illuminated by enormous crystal chandeliers that jutted forth from ceilings which were decorated with whimsical murals of animalistic fables and embossed with gold. It looked as if Versailles and the orthodox cathedral in Sofia where they'd encountered their mysterious "spiritual advisor" had mated and produced a child with enough flamboyance to trump either of its parents.

"Really, Mr. Valov, it's a bit absurd. Just the two of us will be staying here?" Edmund asked. "I do want to still have some money in the bank when we're finished with our honeymoon."

"Hahaha!" Mr. Valov laughed with a little too much force. "Don't worry about a thing, Colonel. With the sultan in exile and the Treaty of Sevres out the window, rents in Turkey are really quite reasonable. That's what losing a war can do! Now, follow me. I will show you to your bedchambers."

Edmund threw Eleanor a look of suspicion, but without an obvious alternative, they followed him up one of the absurd gilded staircases, through a series of similarly ostentatious galleries, up another staircase, and finally into a palatial room with a bed that looked as if it had been lifted straight out of the Arabian Nights. Several large windows looked out onto a dreamy view of the deep blue Bosphorus as the last streaks of twilight were dissolving into darkness.

"I will have your trunks brought up immediately." Mr. Valov glanced around the room, pausing for an extended moment on one of several ornately carved wardrobes along the far wall. "It is too dangerous for you to wander about the city on a dark night like tonight, so the staff is already preparing your dinner to be eaten in, but tomorrow you will be free to roam about as you please. I highly recommend the Blue Mosque and the Hagia Sophia, and you can get all of the honeymoon souvenirs you could ever want at the Grand Bazaar. Now, Mrs. Marriner, I know that you have been looking forward to dressing like the locals on this trip, so I'm sure that you will be happy to learn that there is a collection of Ottoman clothing just inside those wardrobes. You may wish to cover your fiery hair if you do not want to attract quite a bit of attention from the curious locals."

"Right, okay then." Eleanor hid her puzzlement, as she had never once mentioned any interest to Mr. Valov or Edmund in wearing Ottoman clothing.

"I'm just so happy for you both!" Mr. Valov exclaimed.

He rushed towards Edmund and engulfed him into the first hug Eleanor had ever seen them share. Mr. Valov whispered something into Edmund's ear, and then pulled away and engulfed Eleanor into a similarly awkward embrace.

"Trust me, Eleanor. Your lives depend on it," he whispered into her ear. "Oh, Eleanor! You are such a beautiful bride!" he declared loudly. "I will leave you two. Enjoy your honeymoon!!!"

He bowed and rushed out of the room.

"Dearest, perhaps we should look at your options for Ottoman clothing. I have been interested in inspecting the unusual fabrics for myself, and if you find something you like, you could wear it to dinner," Edmund suggested cheerfully as he squeezed her hand and guided her to the wardrobes.

He opened each one up, revealing a collection of rich brocades and silks worthy of the former royal residents. They looked like they hadn't been touched in several years, and as Edmund pulled one out to take a closer look, Eleanor fell into a sneezing fit at the puff of dust that encompassed her.

"This one is lovely, but I don't think it will fit you, dearest. Let me try to find you another one. Perhaps you should stand farther back to avoid the dust." Edmund put the outfit back and began shuffling roughly through the wardrobes, pushing his hand through the clothing and smacking it against the wooden backboards until he had made a thorough inspection. "I have a few choices for you, dearest." He began hanging several outfits on the outside of the wardrobes, latching the gilded golden hangers onto small gaps in the engraved patterns until all three of the wardrobes were completely covered in thick fabric.

"Oh Edmund, they're lovely!!!" Eleanor exclaimed. She threw her arms around his neck and kissed him with an especially loud smooching sound. "What did Mr. Valov say to you?" she said with her most swooning tone in Gaelic.

"The walls have eyes," Edmund replied in Gaelic with another loud kiss. "What did he say to you?"

"He said that our lives depend on trusting him." Eleanor guided him to the bed and sat down. She took his hand into hers and caressed it. "What do you think we should do?"

"Do you trust him?" Edmund asked as he leaned in for another gentle kiss.

"There is still something off. I can't put my finger on it. But I believe that he has our best interests in mind." Eleanor ran her fingers through his hair.

"So do I." Edmund returned her gesture.

Eleanor sighed lovingly. "He told us that we have to stay in tonight, and then he suggested we take a tour of the city tomorrow. Perhaps that was his suggested escape from whatever it is that has ensnared us."

"Do you think that if we try to escape now we'll be in more danger?" Edmund asked as he glanced around the room, pausing for an extra-long moment at the large windows that overlooked the dark sea.

"He said it was dangerous to go out tonight. I don't think he would have said so unless it was true. We must both be careful not to give anything away." Eleanor put her hand on his leg.

"I don't like the idea of being watched. I didn't find any sort of secret passage from the wardrobes, but they seemed like a good place for someone to spy, so I covered them anyway just in case."

"Good idea," Eleanor said as she squeezed his thigh.

Edmund looked towards the door, and Eleanor heard the footsteps a few seconds later. Four burly porters in elaborate Ottoman dress (who otherwise looked conspicuously English) carried their trunks into the room.

"Dinner is ready now," the largest one said with a thick ambiguously foreign accent. "The dining room is downstairs. You can follow us."

Eleanor returned to English. "Darling, I'm rather famished. I don't think that I need to wear any of these clothes tonight."

"Yes, I'm really quite tired," Edmund agreed. "I'd like to go to sleep early after all of our travel."

He offered her his arm, and they followed the porters down a gilded staircase into an enormous dining room with a table that could seat at least thirty people. At the far end of the room, the places at the head of the table and to its right were set for dinner.

"This looks lovely!" Eleanor exclaimed loudly. "Edmund, how romantic!"

As soon as they were seated, several servants in outfits similar to the porters' rushed to serve them a large platter of Turkish salads. Edmund's stomach grumbled with hunger, but he carefully served himself up a modest human portion.

"I hope the weather will be sunny tomorrow," Edmund said as he began to eat with the most impeccable rendition of British table manners Eleanor had ever seen him display.

"Oh yes, I do too. I could use some sun. I'm sure the sights will be more interesting with the right light," Eleanor replied.

They continued on for an hour politely eating modest portions of each dish that was served and washing them down with dainty sips of mint tea, while Edmund mercifully expanded their conversation from various descriptions of the weather to the history of the Byzantine Empire, until they each finished a sickly-sweet baklava soaked in honey, and Edmund stood up and yawned.

"Dearest, shall we retire?" Edmund suggested.

"Yes, I'm ever so tired… I'd like to stop in the loo on the way up. I suppose there must be one down here?"

Edmund took her cue, and together they started their search of the floor. They made it through three empty galleries, each one more ostentatious than the last, until the echo of footsteps on the marble floors brought them to attention.

"There you are!" Mr. Valov exclaimed.

"We were looking for the loo," Eleanor explained. "We got a bit turned around."

"I see. Yes, I can see how that would happen in a palace as grand as this one. I will show you to the closest one."

They followed Mr. Valov through several dark hallways, back to the grand entrance. He opened the door to a small water closet that was just as absurdly decorated as Eleanor expected it to be, and as she disappeared inside, hoping that Mr. Valov had guided her to a space that was not being spied upon by whomever their unseen enemies were, she heard him whisper something to Edmund in Czech.

As soon as she was finished, Mr. Valov guided them back to the bedchamber, bowed, and closed them into the room. On the bed, their matching pairs of black silk pajamas from the Orient Express were awaiting their use, and the Ottoman outfits remained hanging on the outside of the wardrobes.

"What did you two talk about?" Eleanor asked casually in Gaelic as she began switching into the pajamas without fully undressing, as she had done for many years in her shared dormitories while she was in the VAD.

"He said that we should continue speaking Gaelic, and that he was glad I got his message about the wardrobes. He said that we should be out of the house by seven o'clock tomorrow morning. If we are later than that, we will not have an excuse not to take the designated car, which is scheduled to arrive at eight. He said that he will find us while we are out, and we can discuss the situation then."

306

Edmund hastily undressed and hopped into the pajamas.

"I don't like the idea of spending the entire night in the midst of an unseen enemy," Eleanor said as she gazed at the bed, heaped high in richly embroidered pillows.

"Neither do I. I don't think that I will sleep. But Mr. Valov reiterated that our little honeymoon farce is necessary." Edmund pulled back the covers, slipped into the bed, and gestured for her to join him.

She crawled in next to him and took her place in his nook.

"Shall we sleep with the lights on, darling? You know how much I'm afraid of the dark," Eleanor suggested in English as she glanced around the room, assessing the various nooks and embellishments for clues of where someone might be hiding.

"Yes, dearest. That is a fine idea," Edmund agreed.

He took her hand into his and began gently massaging her fingers and then her arms. She sighed with a combination of stress and relief, and then together, in each other's loving arms, they spent nine long hours awake in the absurdly ornate bed of their unseen enemy.

As soon as the sky turned the hazy brown of predawn, they hopped out of bed, exhausted but jumpy with nerves.

"Darling, I have the most romantic idea!" Edmund declared loudly. "Shall we go watch the sunrise over the Hagia Sophia?"

"How lovely!" Eleanor swooned.

They rushed to dress themselves in the same clothing they'd worn the day before, and then without a glance at the many sleepy servants who watched them rush down the gilded staircase out the front door and into the chilly morning air, they left their palace prison. But, their momentary sense of triumph dissolved as they looked both ways along the dead-silent road. There was not a person or vehicle in sight.

"Perhaps we can hail a taxi on a bigger road," Eleanor suggested.

They scampered at their fastest reasonable pace towards a wide boulevard that they'd taken from the station the day before. Rows of bright pink blossoming judas trees on both sides of the road added a burst of color to the otherwise drab predawn scene.

Eleanor's feet were already hurting as they reached an intersection of the main thoroughfare, which was much farther than it had seemed the day before during their comfortable ride in the fancy car. The only sign of human activity was a lone donkey-drawn cart parked in front of a small bakery. The cart was already so loaded up with colorful goods—golden trinkets, tins of Turkish delight, wooden brooms, wool scarves—that Eleanor was certain it could only be headed for the Grand Bazaar.

She pointed and squeezed Edmund's hand, and he nodded his silent agreement, leading her straight across the road to approach the cart's driver who was supervising the final loading of a heaping basket of fresh bread.

Edmund engaged the driver in a jovial conversation, and after a few moments of skepticism at the surprising request from the rich foreigners who spoke fluent Turkish, the cart driver was inviting them whole-heartedly to join him on the small driver's bench, and Edmund was helping a young shop-boy finish up the bakery's load.

As they set off towards the Bosphorus, the sun rose with a warm, orange glow over the stirring city, and Edmund engaged the driver in friendly conversation, squeezing Eleanor's hand tightly in his for the duration of the slow ride. They were, at least for the moment, free from their mysterious captors.

When they arrived at the Grand Bazaar, Edmund helped the driver unload his cargo (to the driver's surprised delight), and then he said their goodbyes and handed the man a few shillings.

Eleanor stuck close to Edmund as they made their way silently through the bustling morning set-up of the market towards the Hagia Sophia, until Edmund was certain that the cart-driver was not following them.

"I suppose now we must follow the itinerary that Mr. Valov suggested until he finds us," Edmund whispered in Gaelic. "I don't like this situation one bit."

"Me neither," Eleanor agreed. "I had half a mind to sneak out of that absurd palace in the middle of the night. Who do you think this mysterious enemy is? Do you think they're related to the Bulgarian revolutionaries you killed?"

"I don't know..." Edmund became pensive. "I suppose the Bulgarians and the Turks were both our enemies during the war. Perhaps the revolutionaries in both countries are connected? I hate politics. So many millions are dead for nothing, and that cart driver and I just had a thoroughly amicable conversation. If this were five years ago, we would have been forced to kill each other. It was all such a bloody waste."

"I suppose we should go explore the sights that Mr. Valov suggested." Eleanor quickly changed the subject before Edmund fell into a distracting malaise. "I wish we could enjoy them without this spy game ensnaring us."

"So do I," Edmund commiserated.

"We're in this together, Colonel," Eleanor said more cheerfully.

"So we are." He squeezed her hand as he let her pull him away from his own disappointment.

They meandered through the Grand Bazaar, watching the many merchants set up their small stalls, and disguising their sense of purpose in casual honeymoon banter. They reached the imposing domes of the Hagia Sophia just in time to hear an exotic, distinctly Arabian song burst forth from one of the minarets. Within a few seconds, an eerie echo joined it from the direction of the Blue Mosque, and just like a Christmas carol sung in rounds, several more voices dissonantly joined the chorus from farther off in the distance.

"What is that? It seems a bit ghostly, doesn't it?" Eleanor whispered.

"They are the calls to prayer from the mosques." Edmund sighed with nostalgia. "They remind me of my childhood in Hyderabad. I still find them to be wonderfully relaxing. We will hear them in strict intervals throughout the day."

"I suppose we're really in the Orient now," Eleanor said with a burst of excitement.

"Indeed, we are," Edmund smiled. "Whenever traveled from England to India with the army, I felt like I was almost home when we reached the Muslim world. There are many similarities between this city and the old city of Hyderabad, in fact. Hyderabad is far less ostentatious, though. And much, much hotter."

"I can't wait to compare." Truthfully, Eleanor couldn't wait to watch Edmund revel in his homecoming.

"I have it in our schedule to visit Hyderabad together in a few weeks," he said excitedly.

As the calls to prayer dissolved one by one, Edmund took Eleanor's hand, and they continued along their purposeful journey.

For hours, they walked back and forth between the Hagia Sophia and the Blue Mosque, looking over their shoulders frequently for Mr. Valov or any mysterious adversary, until Edmund's stomach was growling so loudly that neither of them could ignore it, and they worked their way back towards the bazaar.

Edmund stopped at the first food stall of a long row of options in a crowded corner of the colorful bazaar, and as the rich scents of exotic spices mixing with roasting lamb filled the air, he temporarily forgot the dire situation that had ensnared them, and set about ordering a set of kebabs from each and every vendor. Eleanor looked around nervously as he devoured the offering from the first, then the second, then the third, working his way through the lines and offering her his favorites to try.

When they were finished, he guided her back into the labyrinth, straight to a little café where many old men were relaxedly playing backgammon. He ordered them each a pot of mint tea, and Eleanor ignored the disapproving glances from the old men as she sat across from Edmund on a small stool at a table in the corner. As he focused his attention on drinking down his tea at human speed, she let her tired body relax for a fleeting moment of respite.

"Why do you think he hasn't come?" Edmund whispered in Gaelic. "You don't think something happened to Mr. Valov, do you?"

Eleanor looked around the café suspiciously and then leaned in to whisper her response in Gaelic. "I don't understand anything about this situation. If the palace was under surveillance by Turkish revolutionaries, why wouldn't they have just killed us? And if it's not the Turks, who else would be spying on us, and how would Mr. Valov know about it?"

"Perhaps his contact in the Czech government informed him? They seemed helpful in getting us out of Sofia… You don't think it's them surveilling us, do you? Perhaps they want to know who he's consorting with?"

"Then why would he have whispered with you in Czech last night while you were waiting for me at the loo?"

"Yes… yes, you're right. He did. It doesn't make any sense. Do you think we should try to leave Constantinople altogether? We could certainly catch a steamer in Smyrna that would take us through the Suez Canal, and then we could change in Aden to get to Bombay."

"If something has happened to Mr. Valov, we will need to escape on our own," Eleanor agreed. "In any event, I don't think we should go back to that house. I think we should wait for Mr. Valov here until evening, and if he doesn't find us, we should take an evening train into the countryside. So much for our luggage… I will be sad to say goodbye to my kimono. I loved that thing."

"We will make up for it, dearest. We will dress you like a maharani as soon as we arrive in India," Edmund consoled her jokingly.

"If it's anything like the Ottoman clothing, I'll be so weighed down with gold I'll hardly be able to walk," Eleanor laughed.

She took in a deep sigh of relief at their moment of good cheer, and Edmund drank down the rest of his tea and reluctantly stood up. "I suppose we should go back to the bazaar. Perhaps Mr. Valov embedded another clue in our conversation last night. He suggested that we shop for souvenirs. Maybe he's waiting for us in one of the trinket stalls."

Eleanor followed him out of the café, back into the chaos of the afternoon bazaar. They walked for at least another hour through the labyrinth, meandering in and out of stalls and taking an extra careful look at any person who seemed to be lingering, in case Mr. Valov had disguised himself in local clothing.

"Things aren't looking good for Mr. Valov," Eleanor whispered as they reached the end of one branch of the labyrinth and cut through a colorful scarf shop to make their way into the next corridor.

"I suppose we could work our way back towards the Hagia Sophia to do another round…" As Edmund made his suggestion, he stopped and squeezed Eleanor's hand as a debate between two young Turkish men escalated into a shouting match. Three young women clustered together watching them as the shouting match burgeoned into a fist fight.

As one man punched the other in the cheek, Edmund rushed forward to separate them before any blood was drawn. But, as the women began shouting and egging on his adversary, a third man rushed out of a neighboring stall, past a display of large drums heaped high with colorful powdered spices, and joined in the fun.

"Edmund, darling, this altercation is between them. We should leave before anyone sees us here," Eleanor whispered, hoping he'd hear her.

But, as the third man joined the fight, a fourth rushed through the spice stall, yelling his enthusiastic support for one of the combatants. With one clumsy kick to the flimsy clap-board shelves holding up the display, the spice shelves collapsed, and a puff of multi-colored powder enveloped the scene. Their contents exploded into the air, raining down on them and covering everyone in a thick layer of fine red and yellow spice dust.

Each of the boys keeled over with wild sneezing and coughing, but as the air cleared, Edmund was unconscious on the ground, covered in a thick layer of the powders.

One of the boys began shouting and pointing. As the others joined him, Eleanor's heart jumped into her throat as she made the realization that they were shouting and pointing at Edmund.

As she ran to his side and observed his violet metallic plasma oozing slowly out of every open crevice in his body, Mr. Valov appeared, seemingly out of the shadows, to join her.

He ripped Edmund's unconscious body up from the ground, and Eleanor rushed to flank him. Together, they whisked Edmund away.

Eleanor said nothing as she let Mr. Valov guide them into a dark, vacant corner of the labyrinth, in a small alleyway behind a series of costume jewelry stalls. They dropped his unconscious body onto the ground as gently as they could manage, and Eleanor kneeled down to take a closer look at the grotesque malady. More of the substance than she'd ever seen at one time oozed out of his eyes, ears, nose, mouth, and fingernails. The intelligent movement of the substance was gone, replaced by a still, gelatinous state.

"Eleanor, you must call for help *now*," Mr. Valov whispered in perfect British English.

"Call for help?" she asked. Her tired mind was equally confused about what he meant and about his sudden lack of a thick Czech accent.

"Call his powerful allies!" Mr. Valov hissed. "You must call them *now* so they can get us all out of here before the others realize what just happened!"

Eleanor was dumbfounded.

"Please, Eleanor, I swear that you can trust me! Your lives depend on it! *My* life depends on it!" Mr. Valov implored.

Shouting and running footsteps echoed in the main artery of the bazaar just beyond the jewelry stalls.

Eleanor took one final assessing look at Mr. Valov, and then reached into her pocket and squeezed the sparkling green pendant that Mélusine had given her months before during their first fateful meeting.

"Mélusine," she whispered. "Mélusine, please help!"

With a pleasant breeze, Mélusine was standing before them in her preferred feminine form, clad in her typical white medieval dress.

"Good lord," Mr. Valov murmured at the blatant demonstration of Yakshini magic unfolding right before his eyes.

Mélusine glanced at Eleanor, then Mr. Valov, and then her eyes fell onto Edmund.

"*Mon dieu*, what happened?!" She reached down to gather Edmund into her arms, but as the spiced powder that still covered Edmund's body made contact with her form, she hissed and stepped back. Her arm was dissolving into violet metallic plasma. "*Sacre bleu! C'est un disastre incroyable!*"

She closed her eyes and whispered a quiet mantra, and with another pleasant breeze, Kuveni was standing beside them in the form of Kate, clad in a modern black silk dress much simpler than the one she'd worn to the wedding.

"Oh, my darling boy, what have you gotten yourself into now?" she whispered as she kneeled down beside Edmund and ran her hands across the powder, dissolving it with her touch.

Eleanor glanced over to observe Mr. Valov's fascinated expression as he watched Mélusine dissolve her limp plasma arm and replace it with a new one that appeared to form from thin air.

Kuveni closed her eyes for a moment of meditation, and then glanced down the empty corridor. "Come, we must leave here at once. My lady, you should bring our virtuous butler along."

Kuveni gathered Edmund into her arms, and the two of them disappeared.

Mélusine gathered Eleanor and Mr. Valov into a similar embrace, and with a flash of heat followed by a moment of dizziness, they were standing in a crystal cave with glistening black walls. At the far end of the vast space, an otherworldly soft white light emanated from an ancient well.

Kuveni snapped her fingers, producing a large, claw-foot bathtub full of steaming hot water right in the middle of the room, and then laid Edmund carefully inside it. The unhealthy plasma stirred and then released itself to float on the top of the water, just as Eleanor had seen it doing on the morning after their wedding. She found it thoroughly strange that she did not feel any of the ambivalent emotions she had felt the first time she'd witnessed her gentle husband's most alien trait. Instead, she was entirely relieved to see it recovering. She hoped that Edmund was enjoying his pleasant dreams of flying at that very moment.

As soon as Kuveni was satisfied with Edmund's convalescent position, she approached Mr. Valov. She looked at him straight in the eye until he looked away, and then she addressed him sharply. "Now, Mr. Cumberland, while Edmund recovers from his unfortunate bout of turmeric poisoning, you will explain to Eleanor and Mélusine who you really are and why you have attempted to infiltrate our world."

"You're a spy?!" Mélusine boomed as her eyes turned black with demonic rage.

In a blur, she held him by the neck up against the glistening black wall.

"I'm not your enemy!" Mr. Valov rasped. "Ask Lord Blakeney! He's one of you, isn't he? He must be! Ask him! He'll tell you I've only helped protect Edmund!"

Mélusine morphed straight into the form of Lord Blakeney. "I *am* Lord Blakeney, you swine! Now explain yourself!"

"Good lord." Mr. Valov was thoroughly floored by the shocking revelation. "We knew your people were shapeshifters, but no one had ever seen it happen… that was so fast, so natural!"

"Explain yourself!" Mélusine commanded.

Lord Blakeney's foppish caricature of an haute British accent had been replaced by a powerful booming baritone voice with the exact French intonation of Mélusine's standard female form. Her voice echoed off of the glistening walls, shaking the chamber, and Eleanor shivered as a wave of power emanated off of her.

"I'm an agent of His Majesty's Secret Service!" Mr. Valov whispered desperately. "My assignment for twelve years has been to observe Edmund Marriner. I make sure that he is not a risk to the Empire, and I cover up his supernatural qualities whenever they surface publicly. It is absolutely imperative that no one knows what he can do. Can you imagine what the damn Krauts would do if they got their hands on a soldier with his abilities?"

"Edmund Marriner will never be forced to do anything against his will," Mélusine countered.

"Edmund Marriner was forced to kill thousands of men for four bloody years. Was that not against his will?" Mr. Valov rebutted.

"Edmund stayed in those bloody trenches because we *let* him," Mélusine hissed. "We could have rescued him in an instant."

"Then why didn't you? It almost ruined him!" Mr. Valov exclaimed with surprising passion. Eleanor could see in that moment that he truly cared about Edmund, and as Mélusine loosened her grip on his neck, Eleanor realized that Mélusine had seen it too.

"Because pain is required for growth, mon chéri. He needed to suffer. If we'd rescued him from that grim fate, he would have been submitted to another. *That* is how destiny works."

Mélusine let Mr. Valov go. As he rubbed his neck, she subverted her black eyes and began pacing slowly, remaining in the form of Lord Blakeney, clad in the same flamboyant purple suit she'd sported during the days leading up to the wedding when she had worked quite closely with Mr. Valov, believing him to be simply a fantastic human butler.

"Tell us... Mr. Cumberland, is it?" Mélusine paused for Mr. Valov to nod in the affirmative. "If you have been spying on Edmund for twelve years, why did you come to him with your refugee sob story only four years ago?"

He eyed his audience and thought for a long moment before responding. As Mélusine stared him down, he gave in and lowered his voice. "We considered getting more involved as soon as his exceptional strength surfaced during the first mustard gas attack. The black eyes that began surfacing a few months later scared my superiors, and I must admit that I did not have the calm, rational reaction to the development that Miss MacLeod had when she stumbled across it. I noticed that the black eyes were a manifestation of some sort of bloodlust, and I worried that they were a sign he might be taking after his wicked father. My superiors and I agreed that I should get closer, into his household, to make sure he didn't become a danger to the Empire. It became clear soon enough that the malady tormented him, and that he did, thank god, have the self-control to keep himself from becoming a menace. I have used the excuse of my initial entry into his household to serve him ever since."

"I'm sorry. Unlike his wicked father?" Mélusine asked sharply. "What do you know of Edmund's father?"

Mr. Valov looked around the space, observing the complete lack of doors or windows, landing his gaze on the otherworldly glow of the Sacred Well.

"Where are we?" he asked. "Is this room secure?"

"This room is the most private location on Earth, mon chéri. Now answer my question."

Mr. Valov looked to Kuveni and then Eleanor, and then he sighed his concession. "We have been watching Edmund since one of you spirited his mother away from the Brighton Pavilion to the mysterious Brigadoon hidden in the foggy fields outside of Bath. The lords and chancellors were intent on ensuring that a child of *George IV*," he paused to emphasize some intrigue on the name as he looked to Mélusine and Kuveni, "would not be able to repeat what they had foolishly allowed him to do."

"George IV?" Eleanor interrupted. "Edmund's father was George IV of *Britain*?"

"George IV of Britain never existed," Kuveni explained. "His reign was a wretched folly, cooked up by Edmund's father and the selfish, conniving lords whom he had thoroughly wrapped around his finger."

Eleanor couldn't hide her confusion as she thought through the implications. Mr. Valov reached into his coat pocket and collected a cigarette holder. He offered one to each member of his audience, all of whom refused, and then he lit up and took a long, relishing swig before continuing.

Mélusine was annoyed by his bold gesture, but instead of chastising him, she snapped her fingers, materializing a small ceramic ashtray in his right hand. He looked down with a moment of confusion, shrugged with minor apology, and then took another long swig, this time revealing ever so subtly that he depended on the habit to calm his nerves.

"Edmund's father was the demon we allowed to impersonate the Prince Regent after the real Prince Regent was assassinated in a back alley of London in 1804," Mr. Valov clarified. "By the time George III died, we were stuck with him, and he ascended to the throne as George IV."

Eleanor looked to Mélusine the moment the word *demon* came out of his mouth. "Edmund is *not* a demon," she corrected him, ignoring the other shocking revelation.

Mélusine held her tongue.

"Yes, well, I suppose it depends on your definition of the term. Edmund is certainly a delightful contrast to his father. I'm sure that the Secret Service is not the only party with that opinion," Mr. Valov said diplomatically as he glanced to Mélusine and Kuveni.

Eleanor could see that they agreed, despite their lack of response.

Mr. Valov took their silence as a cue to continue. "We didn't realize at first how perverted Edmund's father really was. That creature, by all definitions, was evil incarnate, and we did not realize what we'd gotten ourselves into until it was too late. By then, all we could do was cover up our mistake until he chose to leave us in peace. The Secret Service kept what we knew of his monstrous exploits to ourselves, and by the grace of God, the monarchy passed along to William IV, who began the long process of cleaning up his messes."

Eleanor had not been entirely prepared for such a dark portrayal of Edmund's father, and Mélusine and Kuveni's silence on the matter only reiterated the accuracy of Mr. Valov's depiction. She didn't want to think about it.

"So, the Secret Service has been spying on Edmund for a hundred years?" she asked instead.

"One hundred and five to be exact," Mr. Valov confirmed. "He was born on April 26, 1818, if I'm not mistaken?" He looked to Kuveni and Mélusine, who nodded their agreement. "I am only one in a long line of agents assigned to ensure that he does not become a threat to Britain."

"1818?" Eleanor asked with surprise. "He thinks he was born in 1810! How is that possible?"

"Our children age quickly until they reach young adulthood. He was not particularly aware of the passage of time as a child," Kuveni explained.

"Huh…" Eleanor murmured.

Mr. Valov was suddenly nervous as he noticed Eleanor's contemplation on the secrets he had just nonchalantly revealed. "I shouldn't have told you any of this, Eleanor. I am sworn to secrecy under penalty of death, but I assumed you'd already learned these things from your knowledgeable allies. If anyone finds out I've told you, we will both be in grave danger."

"We have been evading humans for thousands of years, mon chéri. You needn't worry about anyone who is under our protection." Mélusine looked straight at Eleanor as she spoke.

"Yes… I will admit that you are far more powerful than I realized… than any of us realized… Edmund's father did not have anywhere close to the power that you have, did he?" Eleanor did not like the fishing tone of Mr. Valov's question.

"Edmund's father never understood the value of allies." Mélusine carefully deflected a direct answer to his question.

"You have been lying to the other spies about the extent of Edmund's talents for some time now, haven't you?" Kuveni changed the subject. "That is why you needed to warn Edmund and Eleanor when you were forced to lead them into the trap in Constantinople. The others wanted to check in on him for themselves."

"I can see I'm not the only spy here," Mr. Valov said as he raised his eyebrows with intrigue. "I suppose you won't reveal your methods. They are certainly more interesting than mine."

As Mr. Valov finished off his cigarette, he immediately lit up another.

"You already know too much about us," Kuveni refused. "But you didn't answer my question. Why have you been lying to your colleagues on Edmund's behalf?"

"It started quite a while back, since long before the current intelligence organizations that are publicly known came into existence…" Mr. Valov hedged.

"Mon chéri, we are thousands of years old. Whatever seems like a long time to you is a fleeting moment to us." Mr. Valov gave away a hint of surprise at Mélusine's revelation, and she sighed impatiently. "Answer the question, mon chéri."

Mr. Valov conceded. "We have always had a lot of support from the Crown for our efforts. Edmund ensured his protected status when he charmed Queen Victoria back in 1854."

"When he was invited to Prince Leopold's birthday party?" Eleanor asked curiously. "He didn't like it very much."

"Well, he must have done an excellent job of hiding any displeasure," Mr. Valov replied. "The queen had become aware of our expensive secret mission to support this mysterious royal bastard and demanded to know why he warranted such unusual treatment. When she learned the ugly details of the scandal, she demanded the opportunity to assess Edmund's virtue for herself, and so our agent arranged their meeting at the party. Whatever he did convinced her so thoroughly of his rectitude that we managed to operate unquestioned until just a few years ago."

"So what has changed, mon chéri? Why have you gone rogue to protect Edmund's secrets?"

"What else would it be? That wretched war!" Mr. Valov exclaimed with surprising passion. He reined himself in and lowered his voice. "But I'm not exactly going rogue. My division has been operating at the highest level of top secret military intelligence since long before the war. We have kept Edmund's talents secret from all of the other divisions, especially the new ones. I am not the only one who is working night and day to keep his secrets away from those who believe it is their right to exploit him."

"So there are other British spy organizations that know nothing about Edmund?" Eleanor asked.

"There *were*!" Mr. Valov exclaimed. "I am desperately trying to keep it that way! The departments that emerged during the World War are aggressive and foolhardy. They do not have the hundreds of years of experience that we have managing delicate relationships with powerful entities that can't be controlled with brute force."

He nodded respectfully to Mélusine and Kuveni before he continued.

"These new intelligence units do not understand nuance. They have not existed long enough to understand the dire consequences of failure, and yet, they are gaining power. Even now, while the Crown has officially cut the intelligence budget, they are secretly growing their ranks. If they find out that I have been keeping this kind of intelligence from them, there will be hell to pay for many, and the fallout will certainly ruin any possibility for you and Edmund to live a normal life, Eleanor. They will not see someone with Edmund's talents as a free citizen, and if they learn of his true origins and the glorious scandal associated with our demon king debacle, it could topple the very foundations of the Empire."

Mélusine snapped her fingers, and an elaborate Roman divan appeared beside Mr. Valov. She gestured for him to sit, and as he looked at his odd surroundings and his alternatives, he accepted her offer. She sat down next to him, to his surprise, and leaned back into a relaxed position that looked particularly natural to her in the male form of Lord Blakeney.

Kuveni continued her polite interrogation. "So you helped Edmund and Eleanor escape from your own government's spies, and now you've spent all day leading your colleagues astray. What prompted today's tiresome spy game?"

"Can you not guess?" Mr. Valov asked with genuine surprise. "Those damned revolutionaries on the Orient Express ruined years of hard work in a few minutes!"

"Yes... that ugly incident. It took all of my self-control not to get involved," Kuveni admitted. "My poor, gentle boy all covered in the blood of those villains..."

"Yes, well, your discretion was a blessing and a curse, *Kate*." Kuveni smiled as Mr. Valov cleverly used the name she'd used to introduce herself at the wedding. "Certainly you prevented me from having to explain even more of your fairy magic to those shrewd observers who noticed several oddities at the wedding."

"We are *not* fairies," Mélusine interrupted.

"Are you going to tell me what you actually are then?" Mr. Valov asked cheekily. "Don't tell me you're angels. After that strangely subversive sermon by the famous Mr. Johnson, I wouldn't believe it for one second." He looked to each of them hoping for a reaction and then shrugged at their excellent poker faces. "My point was that those bloody bolos on the train forced our hand. What was Edmund to do? Let them kill everyone? Of course he had to act! I don't blame him one bit. I killed six of them myself in the other car, but everyone in the first class car saw his talents on display right before their eyes! And lo and behold, even to my surprise, suddenly Edmund was moving so fast that all anyone could see was a blur! Since when could he do that?!"

"He's still learning to control it…" Eleanor said quietly. "It surfaced on our wedding day."

"Yes, well, he'd better get it under control ASAP." Mr. Valov gained confidence as the tone of their conversation felt less like an interrogation and more like a partnership. "That damned Ridgeway chap couldn't stop chattering about it to every bloody person he met. That car was littered with spies, by the way. The Orient Express always is. We have a little joke back at the home office that the route only exists for spies to check up on each other in luxury. The two Americans, the silent German, the Hungarian countess, and even that young ginger priest were all goddamned secret agents!"

"Really? Even the quivering priest?" Eleanor asked with surprise.

"Well, I suppose the term *secret agent* is a bit of an exaggeration in his case," Mr. Valov corrected himself. "He was an errand boy on his way to buy arms from the Turks for the Irish Nationalists. Didn't have any clue what he'd signed up for, I reckon. He tried to escape in Sofia, but my men caught up with him. He was bloody lucky that Edmund was on that train, or else my people wouldn't have bothered to intercept him. He'd have been left to MI-5's brutal interrogation techniques—techniques that I am desperately trying to keep away from you and Edmund, Eleanor."

"Oh dear…" Kuveni murmured. "This is bad. Very, very bad…"

"It is," Mr. Valov agreed frankly. "The good news is that the Americans took care of the two enemy agents for us. We found them both dead in their berths shortly after the train stopped in Sofia. But they are dangerous, my friends. Now the Americans know about our mysterious super soldier, and you can bet that their inquiries are what brought my colleagues from MI-5 down here to the edge of the western world to check up on our mysteriously talented colonel for themselves."

"Blimey," Eleanor whispered.

"This mess would have been jolly difficult to clean up even without our own government on our list of adversaries. But with a magnifying glass on all of us now, it was bloody impossible to fix. I told that Ridgeway chap and his family that they'd come across a highly sensitive classified mission, and I made them sign the standard non-disclosure agreements that I always use when people notice too much about Edmund, but there is nothing I can do about the Americans, or the Helmsworths, although, they at least seemed to be mercifully discreet about all of it. I thought momentarily about recruiting them."

"I am so glad you encountered them, Eleanor," Kuveni chimed in. "They are perfectly lovely people. So free of the dangerous ambitions that plague most humans."

"What do we do now?" Eleanor asked as she wandered over to her sleeping husband's wet resting position to examine his progress. "How long will this take to pass? It's from turmeric, you said?"

She placed her hand gently across his warm forehead, but he didn't stir.

"Edmund is allergic to turmeric," Mélusine said as she glanced at Mr. Valov.

"From what I saw, it seems like you are too," Mr. Valov baited her.

"You are an observant spy," Mélusine shrugged. "His reaction this time is particularly strong, *certainement* because he was absolutely covered in the filth. If he'd just eaten a bit of it, he might not have even had a reaction. I'm sure he will be back to himself in no time."

"It was dastardly good at revealing his foreign nature... and yours," Mr. Valov addressed Mélusine. "That is why I asked Eleanor to call for you. No one else knows of this weakness, and we must keep it that way. Now that he's piqued their interest, MI-5 will be actively looking for anything that will help them control him."

"You mean enslave him," Eleanor said sharply.

"Yes. That is exactly what I mean," Mr. Valov agreed. "But you must trust me, Eleanor. We are on the same side. For twelve years, I have watched Edmund Marriner lead men with a code of honor unmatched in this world. I will not let the small-minded greed of anyone, my fellow countrymen included, ruin his life."

Mélusine stood up and casually morphed back into her preferred feminine form. She leaned down, uncomfortably close, and gazed into his eyes until he looked away. "You are an honorable man, aren't you, Mr. Cumberland? I've never known an honorable spy before. I suppose there is a first time for everything."

"If I can live my life half as honorably as Edmund Marriner, I will die a happy man," Mr. Valov replied distractedly, eyeing her copious cleavage with appreciation. She noticed his attention wander and stood up.

"Being half as honorable as Edmund is a reasonable goal for you, mon chéri."

Mr. Valov looked annoyed at himself as she left him alone to kneel down beside Edmund's sleeping position. She placed her hand on Edmund's forehead and closed her eyes as she pushed a dose of euphoria straight into him.

Eleanor watched curiously as his Rakshasa plasma tensed and then relaxed again into sleep.

"He is making some progress," she reported.

"How are we going to get out of this mess?" Eleanor asked with a sudden burst of stress. "Where are we even going to go?"

Mr. Valov thought for a moment before he spoke. "I led you to the Secret Service's safe house in Constantinople because MI-5 demanded that I do so, and I couldn't admit to my real mission…"

"Wait a second…" Eleanor interrupted him. "If MI-5 has no bloody clue that Edmund is special, and they know that you are a Secret Service agent, what exactly do they think you're doing posing as his butler?"

"They think that I'm monitoring his politics, to make sure he doesn't become a subversive risk to the Empire. Edmund has been vocal enough in his support of Indian Independence that it was completely rational for him to be under constant surveillance. They're still very jumpy about maintaining loyalty within our military ranks after the Hindu-German Conspiracy, and an active colonel who has been open about supporting Indian cultural autonomy for decades is a ripe target for their paranoia."

"Huh..." Eleanor murmured.

"And so, Eleanor, you can imagine how aggressive they were when news traveled through the wires that the active colonel in the British Army who is already under surveillance for potential subversion of imperial causes demonstrated a plethora of superhuman talents in front of an audience of spies and fools."

"Blimey..." Eleanor whispered.

"It is not hopeless yet." Mr. Valov's tone softened. "There are many powerful men who owe a great deal to Edmund Marriner. Lord Grimby has been a very vocal supporter, as have many others... Even Lord Kitchener advocated on his behalf a number of times before the war, despite Edmund's vocal opposition to many of his policies. I believe that if we can go some time without another incident, MI-5 will decide that it is not worth the risk to pursue him. In the meantime, I have already been working on discrediting Mr. Ridgeway and the Americans so that their testimonies will not continue to hold the sway that they have had in the immediate aftermath of the incident."

"Well, I suppose that's something." Eleanor let out an involuntary sigh of stress.

"Now we must deal with the immediate situation. As far as you and Edmund are supposed to know, you are still enjoying your honeymoon..." Mr. Valov pushed forward, formulating his plan as he spoke. "You should go to Smyrna as soon as possible. If anyone asks, say that you simply couldn't resist visiting the ruins of Ephesus. You will need to book your own transport and accommodations. It must be clear to MI-5 that I had nothing to do with your escape from their surveillance. The steamer to Bombay will stop in Smyrna tomorrow evening as the first stop out of Constantinople, and you can catch it there. You will head off into the Orient without me, and I will catch up with you in India after I sort things out here."

"You are very good at this, aren't you?" Eleanor said pensively.

"Why else do you think I was assigned to the most sensitive mission in existence?" Mr. Valov asked with a hint of pride.

"Well, actually, you weren't entirely winning at your farce. I've known since I first met you that you weren't just an excellent human butler. I thought for quite some time that you were a Yaksha," Eleanor admitted.

"A Yaksha, you say?" Mr. Valov's eyes lit up with excitement, and butterflies exploded in Eleanor's stomach as she realized she'd just made a foolish revelation. "And what exactly is a Yaksha?" He addressed his question to Mélusine.

"Please swallow your fear, ma chérie," Mélusine reassured Eleanor. She turned her attention on Mr. Valov. "*Yaksha* is one of thousands of words used to describe powerful beings who live outside of the human world. You will find just as much truth in the literary depictions as you will in fairy stories and religious scripture. And for the record, Edmund is not a Yaksha."

"I will make a note of that." Mr. Valov could not hide his pleasure at procuring the unexpected tidbit.

"The note had better remain solely in your head, mon chéri," Mélusine said sharply.

"Yes… yes, of course," Mr. Valov agreed with fresh humility.

As Eleanor worked hard to quell her raging internal voice that was still loudly chastising her for her amateur faux-pas, a thought crossed her mind that she simply couldn't ignore. "Mr. Valov, your real name is Mr. Cumberland? But you have been speaking fluent Czech with Edmund for years, haven't you?"

Mr. Valov smiled. "My mother is Czech. My prior mission was as a spy for MI-2 in Bohemia. I used my contacts from that mission to procure your counterfeit passports in Sofia, but MI-5 still found out and tracked us down in Salonica. It was a dangerous sign of their growing sophistication."

"You probably aren't supposed to tell us that," Eleanor pointed out.

"I'm not supposed to tell you anything, Eleanor," Mr. Valov said seriously. "And you mustn't tell Edmund anything I've told you. He is exceptionally bad at keeping secrets for someone with so much to hide."

"I know all about it," Eleanor agreed. "I wondered how he'd been able to make it a hundred years without getting caught. I thought perhaps he'd lost some of his discretion with his shell shock"

"The war certainly didn't help, but he has never been particularly good at lying. We've helped him a lot over the years," Mr. Valov revealed. "But, Eleanor, if you give away any hint that you know who I really am, I will certainly be tried and secretly hanged… or more likely shot on the spot, and they will not replace me with someone who is a loyal supporter. I was not supposed to get emotionally involved at all, and they will see any revelation to you as a grave sign of weakness."

Eleanor sighed her concession. "I'll add it to my long list of lies."

"You are one of the most skilled liars I've ever encountered, Eleanor. If you didn't have far better things to do, I'd try to recruit you."

"Being an excellent liar to my unsuspecting husband is not a distinction I'm particularly proud of," Eleanor humphed.

"It is a most profound act of love…" Mélusine began.

"To withhold truths until the appropriate time… Yeah, yeah," Eleanor interrupted her. "I mentioned that to Edmund a few months back when he was apologizing for all of his lies to me. It led to quite an awkward situation when Mr. Johnson used the exact same phrase on our wedding day. It almost brought our house of cards tumbling down."

As Mélusine moved to respond, Edmund's Rakshasa plasma began to stir.

"Quick. We must get him out of here before he wakes up," Kuveni whispered. "Does Vibhi still own that palace overlooking the sea in Smyrna?"

"Yes, I think he does!" Mélusine exclaimed. "I'd forgotten about that one."

"Good lord," Mr. Valov murmured as she disappeared into thin air. "Can you all do that?"

"Can all humans run a marathon?" Kuveni asked him rhetorically.

Mr. Valov ruminated on her question for a moment of contemplation and then let it go. "But how exactly have you managed to keep an ancient palace secret in the middle of a bustling human city?"

"We have our methods," Kuveni said evasively. "But the palace in question is not in the center of the city. It is in a more rural area far outside the ancient city walls. We chose the location to be far enough away that it was unlikely to be swallowed by sprawling human development."

"In ancient times, you anticipated human cities sprawling as they do in the modern era?" Mr. Valov asked curiously.

Kuveni smiled. "You would not find the idea surprising at all if you'd seen how vast the ancient Roman cities were." Eleanor could see that the idea of Kuveni's firsthand account intrigued Mr. Valov. "The Romans had quite a bit in common with modern humans. It was a shame they destroyed themselves. We keep hoping you will learn from their mistakes, but humans tend to forget too easily with their short life spans."

Mr. Valov startled as Mélusine reappeared. "What a wonderful idea, Kuveni! Vibhi's old palace in Smyrna is the perfect place for this plan. I found it empty and well-preserved, just as we'd left it, and I've already aired it out."

As Edmund's Rakshasa plasma began sluggishly working its way back into his body, Eleanor began to panic.

"What's wrong?" Mélusine asked. "Have you not seen him sleep in water yet?"

"Oh, I have… It was an interesting sight to wake up to after our wedding night. I had to explain to him what I'd seen, because he wasn't aware of it himself. He thought the idea was grotesque."

Mélusine couldn't help but laugh. "I'm sorry. It isn't funny. You are so forgiving of our eccentricities, ma chérie." Mélusine pulled her into a hug.

"The violet liquid is him, isn't it? Just as much as anything I see on the surface?" Eleanor asked.

"You are as perceptive as you are kind, ma chérie," Mélusine agreed. "Now, tell me what prompted your anxiety."

"I panicked because I have no bloody clue what to tell him about how we managed to get ourselves all the way to Smyrna. I'm too exhausted to come up with believable lies after not sleeping at all last night," Eleanor admitted.

"Oh, ma chérie, don't worry! I am a master of lies! Tell him that after he collapsed, Mr. Valov found you. He helped you out of the bazaar, into a taxi, and then escorted you onto the train."

"You can tell him that I was late meeting you today because I was busy arranging the safe accommodation for you in Smyrna," Mr. Valov added.

"And you really think Edmund will believe that?" Eleanor asked skeptically. "That I got him all the way to Smyrna while he was unconscious?"

"Turmeric poisoning often causes memory loss, and Edmund has noticed it happen to him in the past," Kuveni reassured her. "You can tell him that he walked with you himself, but that he was in a bit of a daze."

Mélusine took Eleanor's hands into hers reassuringly. "Take a deep breath and let us help you this time, ma chérie. I will make sure that the palace remains safe so that you both can sleep soundly tonight."

As the last of Edmund's plasma slowly wriggled into his nostrils, Mélusine nodded to Kuveni, readying for action.

"Mr. Valov, we will leave you here for the moment," Mélusine said as an afterthought. "I will take you where you want to go after we've settled Edmund and Eleanor in. In the meantime, don't bother trying to escape, and stay away from the Sacred Well. If you get too close, it might entice you, and you are far too virtuous of a spying butler to die such a painful death."

Completely ignoring Mr. Valov's surprise at her nonchalant warning of dire danger, Mélusine hugged Eleanor, and with a dizzying breeze, they left their virtuous spy alone with the Sacred Well.

CHAPTER 21 – HIS FAVORITE HOLIDAY HOME

Eleanor leaned heavily on Mélusine as she combatted a moment of lightheadedness.

"Oh ma chérie, I'm sorry for the whirlwind ride. You will get used to it with more experience," Mélusine whispered.

"It feels stranger when you do it than when Edmund escorts me in his arms in a blur," Eleanor said woozily.

"That is no surprise. He doesn't dissolve your body and re-form it…" Eleanor couldn't hide a look of surprised disgust at the notion. "Sorry, ma chérie. It sounds worse than it is, I promise. We have transported worthy humans in this way for thousands of years, and no one has ever had a problem."

Eleanor stood up straight and took a more sober look around. They were standing on the ruins of a massive ancient stone city surrounded by tranquil hillsides dotted by bleating goats. At their feet, the broken marble bust of an ancient goddess was flanked by several collapsed Roman columns. Mélusine looked down at it and smiled wistfully with a thought she didn't share.

"Is this where we're going to stay tonight?" Eleanor asked confusedly.

Mélusine laughed. "No, ma chérie, you will be staying in luxury worthy of the greatest Roman emperor. I brought you on a little detour. These are the ruins of Ephesus. If your cover story is going to be that you and Edmund came here to see the sights, I thought you should see them for yourself."

"Will Edmund notice my absence?" Eleanor asked.

"Kuveni is with him now, and she will warn me if he awakens enough to notice much of anything. I thought I would give her a few minutes to mother him. She has been longing for decades to have the chance again, ever since the debacle of his first marriage led Vibhi to ban her from direct contact."

Eleanor was taken aback by the terrible thought. "How could he do something so horrid? Poor Kuveni! He seems so nice, so forgiving! Isn't he supposed to be the world champion of forgiveness?"

Mélusine smiled. "None of us are perfect, ma chérie, including him. And in that case, his reaction was not unfounded. Kuveni's meddling pushed Edmund far too fast into a relationship he was not ready for in the slightest, even after Vibhi and I had both warned her many times not to push him. I think Vibhi blamed her for the pain Edmund suffered at the hands of that wicked girl, and I don't think his blame was entirely out of place. That is why, ma chérie, I stepped in with you when I did. I didn't want Kuveni meddling too much."

"It seems you managed quite a bit of meddling yourself this time around," Eleanor winked.

"*C'est la vie…*" Mélusine shrugged. "You are right, of course. I have meddled far too much, but this time it is different. These tribulations you've faced these last few days are not normal for us. Edmund hasn't faced anything so complicated in his life. It makes me wonder…" Mélusine trailed off into contemplation.

"It makes you wonder?" Eleanor coaxed.

"*Rien*. I'm sorry, ma chérie. I mustn't say another word about it… Let's take a look at the ruins, shall we? Ephesus used to be quite a beautiful city." She looked around and sighed with disappointment at the sun-bleached rubble. "Everything turns to dust eventually… except for a select few of us, I suppose."

"That must be so sad for you," Eleanor murmured. "I don't think I'd like to live so long and watch everything I love dissolve."

"We have some power to preserve the things we care about most… except humans, I suppose. I've never loved a human enough for it to matter, but for others it is really quite painful. For Edmund, it will be utterly excruciating, just as it always is for Vibhi. Those two men love too deeply for their own good…" Mélusine looked startled, and Eleanor shifted uncomfortably at the extremely unpleasant idea that someday she would inevitably cause such excruciating pain for her gentle English soldier. "I'm sorry, I shouldn't have said anything so dreary, Eleanor. I suppose being here surrounded by a dead city that used to be so vibrant, I was thinking about how I will feel when your time comes. I think perhaps I will miss you more than any other human I've ever met."

"Well, we mustn't borrow trouble," Eleanor said with feigned cheer. "I have many more years to make you hate me so that when my time comes, you will not feel a thing."

Mélusine pulled Eleanor into a tight hug. "I don't think that's possible, ma chérie." As she pulled away, Mélusine wiped a violet tear into her skin. She looked around at the empty ruins and then a mischievous smile worked its way onto her face. "I think we are alone here. Let me confirm."

Mélusine dissolved, and Eleanor's heart began racing as her mind ran through what mischievous plan Mélusine might have in mind.

Mélusine reappeared with a fresh energy of excitement. "The unpleasant political situation must be keeping the tourists at bay. There are only a few groups wandering about at the amphitheater, which is many miles away from here. Would you like to know what Thomas meant when he asked Edmund why angels have wings?"

"Thomas?" Eleanor asked curiously. "The mysterious priest in the cathedral in Sofia?"

"Saint Thomas the Apostle, to be precise."

"Of course he's a saint…"

"Saints can be very helpful, you know. Saint Mélusine did all sorts of useful things," Mélusine winked.

"*You* were a saint?"

"Until they decided I was a witch," Mélusine shrugged. "Humans… I don't know what I thought would happen. Knowing them as well as I did, I shouldn't have been surprised… But, that's all beside the point. Vibhi asked Thomas to check up on both of you after Edmund's massacre. He was thoroughly impressed by what he found, including Edmund's surprising cheek. I'm sure we have you to thank for that. He's really making excellent progress."

"Glad to be of service…" Eleanor was feeling another bout of bewilderment taking hold.

"Don't fret, ma chérie, I have a surprise for you, if you are interested."

"Sure, why not." Eleanor buckled down, assuming (reasonably) that any surprise from Mélusine would be utterly shocking.

Mélusine took a few steps away from her, and with a momentary wriggle, enormous golden falcon wings sprouted from her back.

"Good lord!" Eleanor exclaimed.

"Do they look alright?" Mélusine asked as she looked over her shoulder. "My natural Rakshini wings are butterfly wings, but I thought I would show you what Vibhi's look like. Someday, I suspect, Edmund will have a pair like this too, but it will probably be decades until then."

Eleanor approached, and Mélusine flapped her wings gently as Eleanor inspected the perfect contours of the realistic golden feathers. "So the entire concept of angels is based on you? On Rakshasas?"

"Not entirely. Humans have had stories for millennia about heavenly creatures dropping out of the sky to save them. But the imagery of angels being depicted with Vibhi's wings was Thomas's idea, and a rather brilliant one, I think. In the early days of the church, we were all making quite an effort to remind humans to be accepting of those who were different."

"Be not forgetful to entertain strangers, for thereby some have entertained angels unawares..." Eleanor murmured, as she thought through the biblical quote that Charlie had quoted to Vibhishana at their cricket match in the new context of the Rakshasas' shapeshifting talents. "I didn't think anything in the Bible was so literal..."

"Vibhi wrote that line himself," Mélusine smiled. "And he was ever so insistent on keeping it when he attended King James' translation symposium back in 1604."

"Huh... You really have tried to keep the message focused on acceptance, haven't you? And yet, here we are with so many Christians like my mother judging other people so harshly."

"No matter what we try, humans always just do what they want, and often what they want is to make anyone different from them suffer..." Mélusine trailed off with a momentary lapse into melancholy, but then she wrested herself. "Shall we fly, Eleanor?"

Before Eleanor could answer, Mélusine swept her up into her arms, kneeled down, and shot them into the sky. Eleanor squealed and laughed with the thrill as Mélusine gained altitude.

"How wondrous!" Eleanor exclaimed as she spied the vast ruins of the ancient city sprawling from the sea to the mountains.

"I'm glad you approve, ma chérie. I'm sorry you won't be able to experience this pleasure in Edmund's arms. Look to your right. Every Roman city used to have an amphitheater just as grand as that one. During the gladiatorial games, we could hear the crowds roar from miles and miles away when a man was killed."

"Will those tourists see us?"

"From this height we look like a bird," Mélusine reassured her. "Rakshasas must learn very young how high we must go to avoid bringing attention to ourselves... Look there. That is where the great library of Celsus was. Vibhi and I went there for the grand opening to meet Celsus himself. He was a fascinating human, one of the few other than you whom I've liked over the centuries. He paid for the entire library himself to help educate the masses. Vibhi brought me there to prove to me that there was at least one human on Earth I could get along with. I hated to admit that he was right."

"He is often right, isn't he?" Eleanor asked pensively. "He is right about keeping Edmund in the dark about his evil father."

"Yes, ma chérie. He is almost always right, and he is certainly right about that. My father was just as evil as Edmund's, and I cannot tell you how much I wish I'd never, ever learned exactly how bad he was."

"I know what you mean."

"Yes, ma chérie, I'm sorry that you do. But if all my father had done was harbor a second family, I would have considered him a saint compared to the monster who enslaved me as a child."

"Enslaved you!" Eleanor gasped.

"It was a long time ago," Mélusine demurred. "Look there, that is where the great temple of Artemis was." Eleanor let Mélusine change the subject as she ruminated on the idea that her father's transgressions were not nearly as bad as they could have been.

They flew for a few more minutes until they had surveyed all of the ruins, and Mélusine had pointed out all of her favorite haunts, until Mélusine veered out over the sea and soared gracefully down towards the glistening water to an imposing marble palace propped precariously on a cliff at the edge of the Mediterranean.

Eleanor took a deep breath of fresh salty air as Mélusine released her and absorbed her wings into her back. They stood on the shaded terrace overlooking the bright blue water shimmering in rich mid-afternoon sun.

340

Mélusine morphed her white medieval dress into a well-fitted Roman one with intricate golden embroidery along the trim of a copious collection of silk bundled flatteringly around her form. Eleanor watched with wonder as Mélusine's hair tied itself up into a delicate up-do. When she was finished, Mélusine closed her eyes and snapped her fingers.

"Is that what you wore in ancient Rome?" Eleanor asked curiously.

"It is what I wore when I met Celsus," Mélusine smiled. "I have not tried to reproduce it in almost two thousand years."

"It's lovely," Eleanor said as she fingered the silk. "It feels so real."

"It is real, ma chérie. Everything we create is real. It is just as real as this palace around us. Our Yaksha talents have simply kept it intact so that it wouldn't dissolve into dust just as Ephesus did."

"It's lovely."

Eleanor looked around at the splendor of the surroundings with fresh eyes. There was something distinctly ancient about the details. Something wondrously untouched by the many disparate stylistic trends of the last many centuries.

"I agree, ma chérie. This was always one of my favorites." Mélusine looked around and closed her eyes for a momentary communication with some another Yaksha. Eleanor wondered if it was Kuveni, or someone else. When Mélusine reopened them, she sighed with disappointment. "I should leave you now, ma chérie. I have overly indulged both of us with that little flight. Now, Kuveni has already finished setting Edmund up in the Rakshasa bed upstairs. I'm not sure how sharp he'll be when he first wakes up, but he will certainly sleep quite soundly for many hours afterwards. Turmeric poisoning is wretched, and very debilitating. Edmund will be stiff and his movements pained for many days with the amount he was exposed to. I did not want to say so in front of our virtuous spy."

"I thought as much."

"Yes, well, hopefully I was more convincing to him than I was to your exceptionally clever self, ma chérie. Now, I have added a human bed for you in the bedroom upstairs. I hope that you will sleep well tonight, and dream of pleasant flights just as Edmund does."

Mélusine winked and then pulled Eleanor into a tight hug.

"Thank you," Eleanor whispered into her ear.

"It is I who must thank you once more, Eleanor. I don't know what we'd do without such a worthy ally. Now, I've left a small feast in the dining room for both of you to enjoy when you fancy it. Kuveni will come by with a car to take you to the port when it is time for you to go tomorrow. Please, ma chérie, try to enjoy yourself. After all, you are staying in a palace worthy of the greatest Roman emperor."

"Or our Lord and Savior himself." Eleanor meant the statement cheekily, but then she realized the gravity of the truth of it, and she became more solemn. "I will do my best."

Mélusine smiled and caressed her cheek affectionately. "*A bientôt.*"

Mélusine dissolved, and a warm, gentle breeze tickled Eleanor's face as she took another look around the ancient palace.

"Vibhi's favorite holiday home…" she murmured as she thought through the implications.

She meandered slowly across the smooth mosaicked floors into the living room dotted with intricately carved wooden chaises heaped high with silk pillows, quite distinctly different in shape than anything she had ever seen in the modern world, and then back out again onto the shaded terrace overlooking the sparkling Mediterranean. The weather was perfect. Just warm enough to be comfortable, but not so warm as to overwhelm her Scottish temperament. She wondered how it was still so light outside after their hours in Mélusine's crystal cave, and then she let the thought pass. She was too tired to wonder about such minor trivialities. As a wide yawn overtook her, she realized exactly how tired she was

342

after her stressful sleepless night followed by hours and hours wandering around Constantinople.

She took in a deep breath, appreciating the sweetly-scented sea air, and then walked into the dining room to inspect the feast Mélusine had mentioned. She gobbled down some grapes and a baguette sandwich, following them up with some sweet, fresh watermelon juice, and then she made her way up a mosaicked staircase.

"Good lord," she murmured as she entered the vast bedroom.

The high ceilings were entirely made up of elaborate mosaic murals, representing a story with monkeys and colorful humanoid creatures with monstrous faces and ghoulish spikes. The entire room was open to the sea, and beside a canopied bed heaped high with silk pillows, was a Rakshasa bed that looked quite similar to the one that had been added to their master bedroom in Basingstoke, except that this ancient wonder was at least twice the size, and a waterfall of fresh spring water refilled it constantly from a gilded spout in the wall. Underneath the spout, floating in the fresh water with the waterfall landing on his chest, Edmund slept peacefully.

He stirred and returned to sleep as Eleanor approached him. His violet metallic plasma floated on the surface of the water, and as her curiosity finally overwhelmed her distaste for the odd truth, she placed her hand right in the middle of the substance.

She shivered as the cold, silky plasma gathered around her hand in a weak embrace.

"How utterly bizarre," she murmured.

She opened and closed her hand gently, watching as the substance slowly interacted with her, slipping through her fingers and wriggling back onto her hand to encompass her warm flesh in an icy hold until it tired and dissolved its intelligent form back into a restful sheen on the top of the water.

"Keep sleeping, darling," she whispered as she kissed Edmund's forehead. "We still have a tiring journey ahead of us."

She wandered around the room, taking in the fine artistry of the various chaises and tables and then wandering out onto the shaded terrace to gaze out over the sparkling blue sea. But, as she contemplated how many long hours it seemed she'd need to wait until dark, she gave into the appeal of the bed and her own fatigue, stripped herself naked, and lay down in the silky sheets.

"Wake me if I sleep too long, Kuveni," she whispered as she stretched out and let her tense muscles finally relax.

To the gentle song of cawing birds and the waves crashing on the shore below, Eleanor slept.

When she finally awoke, the sun was high in the midday sky, and a feeling she had been dreading for weeks immediately took hold. Her entire pelvis felt like it was on fire, throbbing and pulsating with pain as she struggled to sit up.

"Blimey," she muttered as she wiggled out of the silk sheets and looked frantically around for a robe. "Kuveni?!" she hissed.

Kuveni appeared in her favorite old-fashioned chubby servant form. "Eleanor, my dear girl, what's wrong?" Kuveni asked with a burst of anxiety as she observed Eleanor's naked panicked state. As her eyes wandered to the stained silk sheets, her anxiety only grew.

"Kuveni, it's that time of the month! My cycle just started!" Eleanor couldn't hide her red blush. "What do I do?! How am I going to keep this from tormenting Edmund?"

"Oh dear..." Kuveni looked momentarily relieved, and then genuinely confounded, which only fed Eleanor's anxiety more. "Well, let us first get you what you need."

Kuveni snapped her fingers, and a red silk robe appeared in her hand. She wrapped Eleanor up, and then guided her down the stairs to the first floor of the palace. She snapped her fingers again, producing a fresh, steaming pot of coffee.

"Drink as much as you can, my dear. The caffeine will help reduce your pain."

344

"Will it, really?" Eleanor asked curiously. "I've never heard that!"

"Many tidbits of human wisdom have been lost over the millennia. Caffeine always helped Miryam. Now let me think about what else she did…"

"Miryam?" Eleanor asked.

"Lord Vibhishana's last human wife. What a dear, dear girl she was. Not dissimilar to you in many ways…" Kuveni trailed off in sudden thought. "My, that was a very long time ago, wasn't it? It was before Lady Mélusine even joined us in this world. Miryam loved this palace just as much as Vibhi did. They spent many winters here during their happy retirement together. Now come. Drink some coffee while I think."

Kuveni snapped her fingers, and a fresh basket of canelés and pain au chocolat appeared beside the copious remnants of Mélusine's feast from the day before.

"Sweets also help," Kuveni winked.

"I must admit, I am craving chocolate," Eleanor said as she poured herself a cup of coffee and devoured an entire pastry. She eyed an intricately carved chair, but she didn't dare sit down.

As Kuveni noticed her reticence, her eyes lit up, and she snapped her fingers. "Yes! That was what we did for her!" She handed Eleanor a pair of modern silk underwear that had just appeared in her hand. "Wear these, my dear girl. They will automatically refresh so that any lingering scent will be minimal."

"Someone wore *these* thousands of years ago?" Eleanor asked as she held them up.

"Well, I've updated the style just for you, my dear girl. Unless you'd like to see what the Romans wore? It wasn't particularly comfortable. Their innovative engineering skills weren't focused on women's comfort."

"So I can just wear these? Without a belt or a rag or anything?" Eleanor asked as the prospect of avoiding the uncomfortable modern options became intensely appealing. Kuveni nodded her agreement. "How wondrous!"

"Now, it is important, even with this little Yakshini offering, that you do not share Edmund's Rakshasa bed while you are bleeding, Eleanor. It is best not to tempt his darker urges..." Kuveni and Eleanor both shifted uncomfortably as she offered her advice. "But, I'm sure you'll use your impeccable judgment, and everything will be perfectly fine."

"Can I ask..." Eleanor trailed off as she thought the better of her question.

"My dear girl, you can ask anything your heart desires!" Kuveni urged.

"Can I ask how this worked with Edmund's first wife?"

Kuveni grimaced and then sighed loudly with annoyance at the memory. "She locked herself away in her own bedroom each month and refused to come out until it had passed. She prayed for God's forgiveness of Eve's sins the *entire* time." Kuveni rolled her eyes, and Eleanor joined her.

"Her own bedroom?" Eleanor picked up on the other interesting tidbit about Kuveni's revelation.

"It was not uncommon then for the master and mistress of a grand house to have separate rooms. We thought it best to give them each their space after it became clear that she wasn't nearly as good for Edmund as I thought she would be..." Kuveni stared pensively into the distance.

"When did it become clear?" Eleanor asked.

Kuveni sighed sadly. "About ten minutes after they were married. That's a bit of an exaggeration, of course, but it was clear what a mess I'd made by the next morning when she chastised his table manners with such reckless abandon that I hardly recognized the girl. She even threw a plate at him! We were both so shocked, neither of us knew what to do! I will never forgive myself for causing that debacle... Never... I have never been closer to causing a mysterious accident to get rid of a wicked human. The

346

only thing that stopped me was how sad my beautiful boy would have been about it."

Eleanor reached forward and squeezed Kuveni's hand, and Kuveni smiled and squeezed her back.

"You have restored all of the faith that I'd lost in humans, Eleanor. All of the faith that she stole. I will never be able to thank you enough."

"I don't think that I'm particularly unique. Surely there are plenty of humans like my mother, but there are also many people who are not judgmental wankers," Eleanor pointed out.

Kuveni only smiled wistfully. "Oh, how I love you, Mistress Eleanor."

As Eleanor shifted uncomfortably with a burst of cramping pain, Kuveni noticed her plight. "There is a Roman water closet just over there, and you will find its technology superior to anything in this modern world." Kuveni pointed to a non-descript door. "Go get yourself cleaned up, my dear, and I will wait out here."

Eleanor gratefully set about taking care of her mundane business. When she was finished, she washed her hands and her face, took a deep breath, and rejoined Kuveni.

"You are looking better already!" Kuveni declared cheerfully. "Oh, and I have thought of another remedy that helped Miryam greatly. I have added a dose of willow bark extract to the coffee."

"Excellent plan, Kuveni. Thank you." Eleanor smiled as she sat down and poured herself another cup.

"Do you know of that remedy?" Kuveni asked curiously. "I thought it was one of the many that was lost with the ages."

"We call it aspirin now. The ancient Scots held onto it too."

"Brilliant barbarians, you Scots always were," Kuveni winked.

Eleanor braced herself as she took a long sip of the fresh, aspirin-infused coffee, but it was so sweet that she couldn't taste the bitter extract.

"It is surprisingly delicious, Kuveni. Thank you," she reiterated as she drank down her entire cup and poured another.

"It is my pleasure as always, Mistress Eleanor." Kuveni squeezed Eleanor's hand affectionately.

"Why do you call me that? And why do you call Edmund 'Master Edmund'? The Yakshinis seem to be more powerful than the Rakshasas, from what I've witnessed. It seems somewhat strange to me that you relegate yourselves to servitude… I'm sorry, that sounded much worse than I intended as soon as it came out of my mouth…" Eleanor blushed with embarrassment, but Kuveni only smiled kindly.

"That question has a much more complicated answer than I can give you right now, dearest Eleanor. The truth is that we each have our own unique talents and our own weaknesses. We are strongest when we work together. But I do not call Edmund 'Master Edmund' because he is a Rakshasa, or because his father is their king. I call him that because…" She closed her eyes and shrugged. "I call him that because someday he will be our leader. And you, my darling girl, are an important part of him now, and so I have decided to show you the same respect."

"I will endeavor to be worthy of your respect."

"You already are, my dear girl. Now, I hate to be a bother, but if you are going to make your steamer, you must start moving. I will drive you two to the port in Smyrna, but it is a solid hour's drive, and the ship is scheduled to sail by six o'clock. It will take Edmund far longer than usual to get ready."

"Do you think we should go, Kuveni? With him in this state? And with my… er… feminine cycle to contend with?"

Kuveni thought for a long moment. "It is up to you, Eleanor. I will not tell you what I think you should do. I must control my meddling, which is already quite unhealthy, even by my lax standards."

Eleanor contemplated her choices as she devoured three canelés in a row. "These are really very delicious, Kuveni. I've never tasted anything like them. They are like custard and cake and a fine cognac all at once."

"I'm glad you like them," Kuveni said as she popped a few into her mouth. "They are one of my favorites too. Lady Mélusine procured the recipe off of a very interesting monk several hundred years ago." Kuveni silently refilled Eleanor's pot of coffee with a wave of her hand.

"I suppose we should go," Eleanor finally decided after many minutes of procrastination. "Edmund wants so dearly to visit India, and I have been looking forward to accompanying him. It will be a big pain, I suspect, making our way there if we miss the steamer. We won't have Mr. Valov's immediate help to reorganize all of our bookings."

"As you wish, Mistress Eleanor. I will wait outside in a Turkish form with a car. Mr. Valov already arranged to have your luggage loaded onto the steamer, so you will not need to worry about your wardrobe. But…" Kuveni grinned and snapped her fingers again. "You may wish to wear this. It is a Roman design, but I suspect you will be able to get away with it with modern fashions how they are."

Eleanor held out a delicate, slinky, lavender-colored chiffon silk dress with many layers of flowing fabric brought together with a low-waisted gold belt, not entirely dissimilar to her wedding gown's design, but with several unusual folds and cuts that made the dress excitingly unique.

"How lovely," Eleanor murmured.

Kuveni smiled and snapped her fingers again, producing a pair of flat golden Roman sandals with long laces to wrap up her legs. Then Kuveni reached forward and ran her hands along Eleanor's hopeless mat of knotted hair, smoothing it out and gathering the fiery tendrils into a Roman up-do very similar to the one she had produced on Eleanor's wedding day, in a fraction of the time she'd taken for the same task with Eleanor's sisters watching. Then she gathered Eleanor into a tight hug.

"Go awaken your sleeping husband, my dear girl. I have left a comfortable outfit of tropical linens for him upstairs in the bedroom. I daresay he will need your help getting into it. There is a cane in the corner behind the bed that he can use if he needs it."

"A cane! Blimey, maybe we shouldn't go…"

"It is up to you, Eleanor," Kuveni reiterated. "Perhaps you should ask him what he'd like to do."

"Aye." Eleanor began changing into the Roman outfit.

"I'll be outside." Kuveni kissed Eleanor on the forehead, and dissolved.

Eleanor walked up the stairs, stopping for a long moment to observe her Roman appearance in a large mirror. She smiled at the incredible novelty of it. After a moment of appreciating Kuveni's skilled improvement of her hair, she took a deep breath, rolled her shoulders, and skipped across the room to her sleeping husband's side.

She placed her hand gently on his cool forehead.

"Edmund, darling, it's time to wake up."

She watched as his plasma worked its way back into his body, slightly faster than it had moved the day before, but still much slower than it had the first time she'd seen it.

He took in a deep, awakening Rakshasa breath and opened his eyes.

"Eleanor?" he asked groggily. "Eleanor, dearest, you are a vision."

Eleanor smiled. "Thank you, darling. I'm wearing a local fashion at the moment."

"I had the most pleasant dreams." Edmund scrunched his nose, struggling to remember. "I was flying about the strangest places, and then… and then you joined me. I held you in my arms as we flew to… to India!"

"How were you flying about in your dreams?" Eleanor asked curiously.

Edmund thought carefully. "I think... I think perhaps I had wings. That's a bit silly, as dreams always are, I suppose... I think perhaps our conversation with Mr. Johnson's mysterious agent in Sofia influenced my sleeping mind..." He trailed off as he contemplated the idea.

"Do you remember what happened before you fell asleep?" Eleanor changed the subject and prepared herself to jump right into her web of lies.

Edmund looked around the beautiful space with an expression of disorientation. "I don't suppose I do. Where are we, dearest? I don't recognize this place."

"We are at a palace near Smyrna." She helped him slowly straighten his posture. "Mr. Valov arranged this safe accommodation for us. Our steamer is at the port now, and if we hurry, we can still make it in time."

"But... but how did we get here?"

Edmund held up his arms and observed his own stiff, belabored movements confusedly.

"Do you remember being in the Grand Bazaar in Constantinople? Waiting for Mr. Valov to meet us?"

"Yes... yes... and then... the fight..."

"A boy knocked over the barrels of spices, and you were absolutely covered in them, darling. I think you had an allergic reaction."

"Turmeric," he whispered. He inspected his fingernails and then felt the area around his eyes and his nose. "Good lord... What did you see, dearest? Was it grotesque? Was my violet blood oozing out for the world to see?"

Eleanor smiled and began massaging his shoulders. "It was not grotesque, darling. It was simply a bit foreign. Mr. Valov helped me get you out of there to a safe place where you could get yourself back under control, and now you have been resting for quite some time. Almost an entire day."

"Mr. Valov..." Edmund murmured.

"He knows everything, darling. I don't see much point in trying to hide anything from him now. He has been exceedingly helpful."

"Yes... yes, I suppose he has..." Edmund looked around the grand bedroom again, landing his gaze on the deep blue of the sea beyond. "This place is lovely."

"Yes, I have been enjoying it very much. Now, would you like to meet the steamer, or shall we change our plans? If we are going to make it, we must move now."

Edmund struggled to sluggishly get himself up out of the water, and as his feet hit the cool floor, Eleanor caught him as he almost collapsed.

"I'm sorry, dearest... I'm a bit of an invalid at the moment..." Edmund said as the odd sensation of his weakened state seemed to confuse him. "I've never felt this weak before. Not even when I was excessively old."

He took a wobbly step forward, and Eleanor held onto his arm as he worked his way towards the human bed. As he sat down to catch his breath beside the outfit Kuveni had laid out for him, Eleanor took the seat beside him and took his hand into hers.

"I don't like this one bit, Eleanor," Edmund muttered with frustration.

"You will heal in no time, darling. Now, would you like to convalesce here, or shall we try to catch our spot on the steamer?"

Edmund thought for a long moment about his response. "I have been longing to take you to India for months now." He sounded as if he was trying to convince himself.

"You will have plenty of time to rest on the steamer. We are scheduled to be on it for nine days," Eleanor reminded him.

"Yes... yes, you're right," Edmund agreed. "Let's try it then, dearest... except... except how are we going to get there?"

"Mr. Valov ordered us a car. It's waiting outside right now. Shall I help you dress?"

Edmund paused as an unpleasant thought occurred to him. "I have it on good authority that you have no interest in being a glorified nurse-wife, Eleanor. I do not want you to ever feel as if you are."

"Then it's a good thing I married a man who can heal himself in no time, isn't it?" Eleanor reassured him as she expertly helped him dress himself.

As she finished buttoning up his loose linen shirt, he pulled her into a weak embrace and kissed her gently on the lips.

"I love you, Eleanor," he whispered.

"I love you, Edmund," she whispered back.

"Hello... what's that?" Edmund asked curiously. Eleanor's heart jumped into her throat as he struggled to kneel down to collect Mélusine's green sparkling talisman necklace that Eleanor had foolishly left on top of her pile of clothes when she'd undressed the day before.

"Oh, that..." Eleanor's mind raced a mile a minute. "You don't remember it, darling? You bought it for me yesterday in the Grand Bazaar. Just before we came upon the fight. It's just paste, but I thought it was still very pretty."

Edmund stared at it blankly. "I don't remember. I'm sorry, Eleanor. Turmeric does quite a number on me."

"Don't worry at all, darling," Eleanor said guiltily.

He reached around her and clasped the necklace behind her neck. "It looks lovely with the dress. You almost look like a Roman nymph."

"That's what I was going for," Eleanor winked. "When in Rome, as they say, and this was part of the Roman Empire, wasn't it? Ephesus is not too far from here. If anyone asks, by the way, our story to keep ourselves out of trouble is that we skipped out of our itinerary in Constantinople to go to Ephesus. Mr. Valov went to great trouble to help us escape from the Turkish government's spies."

"Is that who had their eye on us in that gaudy palace?" Edmund asked.

"It was," Eleanor lied. "Mr. Valov's Czech contacts helped us escape."

"Well, jolly good on Mr. Valov," Edmund murmured.

"Now, are you hungry? There is some food left downstairs. We could take some with us." Eleanor hoped that Edmund couldn't sense her growing guilt at her lies.

He thought about her question for an extended moment. "No. No, I'm not hungry at all. It is... It is not uncommon for me to lose my appetite when something like this happens. I don't know how long it will be until it comes back. I'm sorry, Eleanor... I hope that my foolish accident doesn't ruin our time together."

"Nothing can ruin our time together, darling. Now, let's get going."

Eleanor helped him slowly and steadily up from his position, but as he leaned on her, she had to admit that she did not have the strength to bear the brunt of his tall body's weight. She glanced behind the bed, spotting the cane Kuveni had mentioned.

"Here, darling, perhaps this will help." She reached down and offered it to him.

He stared at it for a long moment and then begrudgingly took it and steadied himself with the skill of someone who had plenty of experience.

"I really am your old man now, aren't I?" he asked miserably. "I suppose you deserve a preview of the future."

"Oh, nonsense," Eleanor said sharply. "I won't have you ruining our time together with self-pity, Colonel."

"Yes, sir." He finally cracked a smile.

Eleanor watched with subtle interest as he walked with the cane to the edge of the stairs, straightening his posture as he went.

"You take to it quite naturally, don't you?" she said as she joined him at the top of the stairs.

"I have far too much experience. Now, I was never very good with stairs. I will need your help."

"Yes, sir," Eleanor winked.

She hoped her good humor would keep him from settling into his own malaise. She too didn't really want to think about what they'd do in twenty years when his arthritis kicked in. Would he stab himself again and make her an old wife coveting a young lover? She pushed the thought away.

She held his arm while he used the cane in his other hand to navigate the stairs, and he stopped as they reached the bottom to glance up at the elaborate mosaics.

"Mr. Valov sure has a knack for ostentation, doesn't he? This place is more tasteful than the last, though. The tilework is simply superb, and how lovely that the house is open along the terrace to catch the breeze. It feels… it feels almost ancient, doesn't it? I don't know why."

"It does," Eleanor agreed.

After he took a long moment to appreciate the artistry of Vibhi's ancient Roman palace, Eleanor guided him to the back door, and they emerged into a verdant garden, surrounded by a very tall stone wall covered in flowering nasturtiums and bright pink bougainvillea.

"How lovely," Edmund murmured.

An arched wooden door in the middle of the stone wall opened up from the outside, and Kuveni rushed to greet them, disguised in the form of a young Turkish man dressed in the flamboyant Ottoman clothing of a local.

"Come, we must go quickly to meet the ship," she said with a thick Turkish accent in English.

Edmund said something polite to her in Turkish as Eleanor helped him stiffly seat himself, and Kuveni threw Eleanor a supportive wink as Eleanor went around to the other side of the car to take her seat beside him.

"I hope this isn't a mistake, Eleanor," Edmund said as his eyes began closing with the lulling movement of the car. "I can't seem to stay awake."

"Sleep, darling. We have a long journey ahead of us." Eleanor took his weak hand into hers.

She threw Kuveni a nervous look, as they both knew the precarious situation her choice was getting them into, and then she sat back and looked out the window, hoping to distract herself from the painful cramps that had recently returned to plague her. As she glanced back towards Vibhi's Roman palace, it dissolved completely into the landscape, and as she caught Kuveni's eye in the rearview mirror, Kuveni winked.

"Never you worry, Mistress Eleanor. It is still there, waiting for our next command. Now, why don't you take your own advice and rest for a spell. We have a long drive ahead of us."

Eleanor took in a deep, calming breath as she worked hard to abide, but she couldn't ignore the nagging feeling that the next, even more dangerous phase of their honeymoon adventure was about to commence.

PART FOUR
BY SEA

CHAPTER 22 – ALL ABOARD

When they arrived at the port, Kuveni honked repeated warnings of her brazen plan to proceed at all costs while carefully dodging hordes of scurrying people, many of whom were actively yelling at her that she could not bring a car so close to the ship. Without a hint of care paid to any of the many protesting observers, she parked the car right smack in front of the gangplank.

"Darling, wake up," Eleanor whispered as she nudged her deeply sleeping husband. "Edmund? COLONEL!"

Edmund stirred and struggled to open his eyes.

"Eleanor?" he asked groggily.

"We're at the ship, darling. We need to board, and then you can go right back to sleep."

She squeezed his hand and then got out of the car and skipped around the back to help him out. Kuveni held the door open as he positioned his cane and leaned his entire body weight onto it to stand up, as he had done for many years as a decrepit old man in the 1890s.

He looked around at the frenzied action, and they both startled as the imposing steam-powered passenger liner (far bigger than Eleanor had imagined it—she couldn't believe it was possible the Titanic could have been any bigger) let loose its resounding horn.

"Come on, darling. I think that means it's leaving." Eleanor grabbed his arm, and Kuveni flanked him.

He stopped to look at Kuveni confusedly for a long moment, and then he reached into his pocket and pulled out several shillings that Kuveni had undoubtedly planted there in the first place when she'd laid out his outfit hours before.

"I'm sorry, I almost forgot to pay you," he said as he closed them into her hand.

"Thank you, sir. Mr. Valov said that my job isn't done until I help you get on the boat," Kuveni replied with an admirable impression of a thick Turkish accent.

"Well, jolly good on Mr. Valov," Edmund murmured.

Edmund walked carefully up the awkward gangplank, and several valets rushed to greet them.

"Colonel and Mrs. Marriner," Edmund said with his greatest impression of authority. "I believe you were expecting us in Constantinople. We made a bit of a detour."

One of the valets gestured to his suited superior.

"Colonel!" the man exclaimed with a thick Yorkshire accent, leaving the two porters he was ordering around mid-sentence to greet them. "Your butler warned us you'd be joining us late. Welcome! But what happened?!" He eyed Edmund's hunched-over posture leaning heavily on his cane.

"Oh nothing. I simply... er... fell," Edmund lied. "I will be perfectly well in no time with a bit of rest."

"We were wandering about at the ruins of Ephesus, and it turned out to be more dangerous than we realized," Eleanor elaborated.

She wasn't sure what to think of the man's reference to their butler. Had Mr. Valov really already gotten everything in order for them? Or could this man have just let slip that the spies they had already evaded in Constantinople were hot on their trail? She didn't like the idea one bit, for many reasons. A shooting menstrual pain in her lower back added to her growing annoyance.

"Oh yes. Yes, indeed. Those ruins can collapse quite easily, I've heard. Come. I am Mr. Corrigan, and I am the Chief of Staff here. I will help you to your suite personally." He looked straight at Kuveni. "Thank you kindly, sir, but I can take it from here."

He shooed her away.

Kuveni moved to protest, but then looked down at her youthful male Turkish form and gave up. She knew perfectly well that there was no reasonable excuse for Edmund's local driver to stay with him as he boarded the fancy ship now that the Chief of Staff was taking over his care. She shrugged her agreement, squeezed Edmund's arm in an overly affectionate goodbye, and then threw Eleanor a nod. She mumbled something subservient in Turkish, and left them alone.

"Please, Colonel, follow me," Mr. Corrigan suggested with a bow.

Eleanor held tight to Edmund's arm as Mr. Corrigan led them through the bustling corridor, spreading the waters as his obedient staff rushed out of their way, until they reached a completely modern elevator.

"How marvelous!" Edmund exclaimed. "A lift? On a ship?"

"Here at the P&O Company we don't spare any expense when it comes to our passengers' comfort," Mr. Corrigan said proudly. "I reckon there weren't any lifts on your army transport ships, were there, Colonel?"

"You reckon correctly," Edmund agreed amicably. "It would have been ripe for disaster. I can see the many undisciplined ideas that my young lieutenants would have cooked up for its improper use in my mind's eye right now."

361

Eleanor squeezed his arm, grateful that he was regaining enough consciousness to have a coherent conversation with a stranger. Mr. Corrigan led them onto the elevator, and a young man in an elaborate uniform dutifully closed the iron grate door and pushed the button (his sole purpose on the ship's staff, as far as Eleanor could surmise).

"We will be going all the way to the top passenger floor. Your suite has one of the best views on the entire ship, second only to the captain's quarters," Mr. Corrigan explained. "Your man informed us that you'd be quite late, so we have prepared a light tea service for you in your room. Cocktails will begin at six thirty, and dinner will be served at seven o'clock in the first class dining room, but if you aren't feeling up to it, we can have your meals brought to you. Just give us a ring from the telephone in your suite."

"Our man, Mr. Valov, isn't here now, is he?" Eleanor asked. "We left him in Constantinople... the poor man. He has been exceptionally kind, given that we left him for Smyrna without proper warning. We were on a bit of a romantic adventure, you see, and leaving word with our butler just didn't feel very adventurous."

Eleanor threw in the last bit to support Mr. Valov's intended story of ignorance about their escape in the Grand Bazaar, just in case Mr. Corrigan was an MI-5 spy. She hated that she was suddenly second-guessing a stranger's every mundane move. It was bad enough that she was constantly looking for Yakshas, but Yakshas were friends. Now, enemies everywhere, *that* was already becoming very tiresome.

"No, no. Mr. Valov isn't here. He has been conversing with us from Constantinople," Mr. Corrigan explained. "I assured him that I would take care of all of your needs personally. He sure has your best interests in mind—he's been calling us frequently to check up on whether you've arrived safely. You'd better ease his mind, I reckon, when you have a free moment. The telegraph operator has his information. He is staying at a hotel in Constantinople at the moment, if I'm not mistaken."

Eleanor relaxed a bit. She had hoped that he wouldn't say that Mr. Valov was staying at an ostentatious Ottoman palace on the Bosphorus... Although, if Mr. Corrigan were a spy, surely he wouldn't have admitted that his colleague was staying at the Secret Service Safe House... Eleanor fought back a frustrated growl at her mind's new tormenting trick.

As they reached the top floor, the elevator boy rushed to open the grate for them, and Mr. Corrigan stepped out to make room for Eleanor to escort Edmund through the cramped opening. Eleanor's anxiety kicked up a notch as she noticed Edmund's posture looking decidedly worse than it had when they'd entered the elevator.

"Are you alright, darling?" she whispered into his ear.

"Yes, perfectly fine," he lied. He looked down at Mr. Corrigan and held tighter onto his cane. "I just need a bit more rest, I think."

"Yes, yes, of course. Please follow me." Mr. Corrigan finally moved with the urgency that Eleanor was secretly feeling.

They followed him slowly through several wood-paneled hallways, but as they made their final turn, who did they run into?

"Blimey," Eleanor whispered. Edmund tensed.

"Why, speak of the Devil!" Mr. Ridgeway exclaimed with too much excitement as he and his wife stopped dead in their tracks.

Mr. Ridgeway sported a sling over his suit but looked rather cheerful at their unexpected meeting, while Mrs. Ridgeway looked decidedly wretched. Dark bags under her eyes, disheveled hair, and stained clothes indicated that she had not slept well or taken reasonable care of herself in recent days. Daisy and Lily were nowhere to be seen.

"Come along, George," Mrs. Ridgeway hissed as she grabbed onto his uninjured arm.

"Hello, Mr. and Mrs. Ridgeway. What a surprise to see you here." Eleanor greeted them unenthusiastically on behalf of herself and Edmund.

Mr. Ridgeway stepped back to observe Edmund's hunched posture and cane. "Well, I'll be..." He eyed Eleanor's unusual Roman outfit, pausing for an extra-long moment on her large, sparkling green sapphire necklace.

"The colonel fell at the ruins of Ephesus," Mr. Corrigan explained on their behalf.

"I bet he did," Mr. Ridgeway said as his curiosity morphed into excitement. "Enjoying your touristic honeymoon, I presume, *Colonel.*" He tapped his finger to his nose and winked.

"George!" Mrs. Ridgeway hissed. "Please excuse us." Mrs. Ridgeway yanked him forcefully around the corner, but her voice traveled easily for all of them to hear. "George, how can you possibly find this entertaining in the slightest? Do you know what this means? It means we're in danger again! The girls are in danger! If the colonel is here, who knows who else is on this bloody ship! I told you we should have gone straight back to London!"

"Oh Eloise, stop. You always make everything so bloody dramatic."

"Dramatic?! *I'm* not the one who..." She mercifully dropped into a whisper, and their footsteps finally dissolved as they turned another corner.

Mr. Corrigan looked momentarily curious, and then thought the better of following up. "Here is your room, Colonel."

He pushed open the wood-paneled double doors into an enormous suite, far more luxurious than anything Eleanor could have imagined (especially after her disappointment with the lack of luxury on the Orient Express). A large sitting room filled with intricately carved wooden furniture covered in upholstery embroidered with a menagerie of modern floral forms led into a royal bedroom with yet another canopied bed heaped high with silk pillows. The door was open to a large bathroom, and Eleanor squinted to spy a claw-foot tub just inside.

"Thank you for your help, Mr. Corrigan. I think we will go straight to bed for now."

"Yes... yes, of course," he agreed. "Your trunks are in the closet just there, and those doors there open onto a balcony. The telephone is in the wall by the door. Ring if you need anything." He glanced at Edmund sympathetically, and then closed the door behind him as he scurried out of the room.

"Let's get you to bed." Eleanor immediately began helping Edmund out of his clothes.

He helped her as much as his weakened state would allow, but as she walked him through the bedroom, he hesitated.

"I'm sorry, Eleanor... I know it's rather odd... but I feel the most overwhelming urge to sleep in the bath."

She smiled. It hadn't even occurred to her *not* to set him up for a nap in the bath.

"Somehow, I don't find that very surprising, darling."

Eleanor helped him sit on the edge of the bed and then rushed to turn on the faucet in the bathroom.

"I haven't..." Edmund's face contorted with stress as a deep red blush took hold. "I haven't been... er... sleeping with my elements out in the open, have I? Like I did on our wedding night?"

Eleanor returned to face him as the steaming water began filling the bath. She sat down beside him and took his hand into hers.

"I love you, Edmund. I love all that you are. Mischievous violet blood included."

"Blimey," Edmund whispered, as he recognized that her response meant that he had, in fact, been displaying his thoroughly alien trait in his weakened state.

Eleanor leaned in to gently kiss him on the lips, and as he returned her gesture and wrapped his arms around her, she reveled in a moment of pleasure at his touch that she'd already come to miss. But, as he leaned in for a deeper embrace, he suddenly pulled away, and a strange look crossed his face.

"Do you smell that, dearest?" he asked as he sniffed the air. "It's like spiced wine and Christmas pudding."

Eleanor sniffed around to no avail. "I don't smell anything, darling. Are you hungry? You haven't eaten anything in over a day."

Edmund thought about her question carefully. "No, I have no appetite whatsoever. But... there is something... something unusual that is arousing my senses..."

Edmund sniffed again, and his eyes turned black.

"Blimey, I know what it is..." Eleanor whispered.

"What? What is it, dearest?" Edmund asked innocently, completely unaware that he was demonstrating his demonic trait.

Eleanor ran through her options, but as Edmund looked at her imploringly with his black demonic eyes, she shrugged and gave in. She was not going to put up with hiding *this* from him every month for the rest of their lives together.

"Darling... it is my feminine cycle. I think you are smelling... er... *that*."

"Good lord," Edmund muttered. He stood up and walked straight into the bathroom. Eleanor chased after him, worried that he might spot his black eyes in the mirror and add an even more unpleasant revelation to the many piling up in his weakened state. Instead, Edmund stood in the corner, leaning up against a gilded wall, looking down at his naked body. "I'm sorry, Eleanor. I have no words to properly express my shame."

"You don't need any, darling. We must figure out how to make this work together. Perhaps when you are feeling more yourself we can more actively combat it. For now, you look rather wretched. Why don't you take a nice nap in the bath, and I will sleep out here in the human bed tonight."

"The human bed?" he asked astutely. "As opposed to what?"

366

Anxiety exploded from the pit of Eleanor's stomach as her unintentional use of Mélusine's language got her into trouble.

"I suppose I was thinking of the bath as a different form of bed... a form of bed that is uniquely useful to you, darling. Don't you think that the large bath in our bedroom at home seems a bit like a bed?"

Edmund thought about the idea for the first time. "Yes... yes, I suppose it does..."

"I didn't mean to offend you, darling. I did not mean the distinction in a derogatory way. I am quite happy for you that you have discovered a way of sleeping that is more comfortable than what you were used to before. For now, though, given the circumstances, I will let you rest alone until we are both back to our normal selves."

Edmund moved to protest, and then shrugged his concession. "You are more forgiving than I could have ever imagined, dearest. More forgiving than I deserve... in so many ways, I can't even count them."

"Please don't bother, Edmund. Just get yourself back under control with the mantras Mr. Johnson taught you, and take a nice long rest. I think I will go out to the dining room for dinner, if you don't mind. I'm rather famished myself, and that way you can rest for a while without me. Then, when we're both feeling better, we can figure out how we're going to deal with this next month."

"You are a bastion of reason, my dearest thistle."

Eleanor could hear the emotion in Edmund's voice, but she held her ground to avoid arousing his senses any further.

As he looked back at her, his eyes returned to their human hazel, and Eleanor smiled encouragingly. "You have already made such great progress, darling. I'm sure you can overcome this too. We will come up with a perfectly reasonable plan in no time."

With another encouraging nod from his forgiving wife, he slipped into the sinfully hot water of the steaming bath.

"Shall I fetch you anything while I'm out?" Eleanor asked casually.

"I have everything I need right here," Edmund said as he looked straight at her.

"I'm glad. I'll be back soon. Sleep, darling. I will lock the door to our room and tell the staff not to bother you unless you call for them directly."

She blew him a kiss and closed the door to the bathroom. She gathered a golden key on a small table by the door and locked the door behind her. As she looked down for a place to stash the key, to her great excitement, she noticed two perfectly disguised pockets in her dress.

"How brilliant," she whispered. "Thank you, Kuveni."

"I will keep watch while he rests, Mistress Eleanor. Enjoy your dinner," Kuveni's disembodied voice whispered into Eleanor's ear.

Eleanor looked down at the perfectly intact folds of her Roman dress, but her excitement at the pocket discovery morphed into stress.

It was time, for the first time in her life, for her to face her new high society peers alone.

CHAPTER 23 – REUNIONS

Eleanor shifted uncomfortably as she approached the open doors of the first class dining room. Two tuxedo-clad hosts eyed her flowing Roman dress and her enormous green sapphire pendant (which she had to admit, looked a bit absurd), and rushed to greet her.

"I am Mrs. Marriner," she said, unsure of the proper protocol. "The colonel has decided to stay in tonight, so I will be dining alone."

"Yes, Mrs. Marriner, of course, Mrs. Marriner. Please follow us," the younger of the two said enthusiastically with a thick cockney accent.

She followed him in, hiding her wonder as she glanced around the ornately decorated space. It looked almost like one of Mélusine's creations. She could hardly believe that humans had been able to make any room on a ship look so grand! She smiled to herself. She'd reached the point in her relationship with her supernatural friends at which mundane human success surprised her.

She glanced around the room at the many fashionable diners, many of whom glanced subtly back at her, politely avoiding comment as they assessed her unusual choice in dress. The interest in the expressions of the women indicated that they thought her to be rather stylish, and she relaxed a bit as she spotted several empty two-person tables. *Those* she was very used to occupying by herself.

But, as she followed the hosts and humored them by sitting quite daintily as they enthusiastically pulled out her chair for her, the squeal of a familiar voice brought her immediately to attention.

"*Mon dieu*, look who it is! Ozzy, they made it after all!"

Yvie grabbed Oz's and guided him straight to Eleanor's table, ignoring the snide comments of the British diners who found her outburst to be too enthusiastic... continental, even!

Eleanor jumped out of her seat and engulfed Yvie into a tight hug.

"Yvie! Oz! What are you doing here?!" she asked as Yvie pulled her into enthusiastic cheek kisses. "I thought you were planning on staying in Constantinople for a week!"

"We weren't feeling like exploring anymore after the incident. We were both quite ready to get back home to Perth," Oz admitted as he shook her hand jovially.

"And to be honest, we were worried about you. We were hoping we'd see you on the steamer to make sure you escaped from those brutes in Sofia, and we were simply mad with worry when you didn't board in Constantinople," Yvie explained. "*C'est magnifique*," she added as she felt the delicate chiffon of Eleanor's dress. "*C'est la hauteur de la mode.*"

Eleanor didn't understand her last comment, but it was clear that Yvie was quite taken with the dress. "Oh yes, I ran into an old friend in Constantinople. She gave it to me. It is based on a Roman design. It is rather unique, isn't it?"

"*Oh, je l'aime tellement*," Yvie agreed. "I *love* it. And that pendant, *que c'est beau!*" Eleanor tensed slightly as she fingered Mélusine's talisman. "It glistens so strangely!" Yvie noticed Eleanor's uncomfortable posture and thoughtfully moved the conversation along. "And your hair looks lovely like that too. Like an ancient goddess."

"Thanks," Eleanor said as she fought back her own blush at the complement. "I wore my hair very similarly for our wedding, actually. I haven't been able to get up the courage to cut it short, so I've had to be somewhat creative."

"Don't cut it short!" Yvie exclaimed. "It's so spritely!"

"Thanks," Eleanor smiled. "I think so too, but there are so many derogatory jokes about gingers, I hate to admit that I'm quite happy to be one."

"Anyone who tells such a nasty joke is just jealous of your beautiful hair," Yvie winked.

"Where is Edmund?" Oz asked as he noticed that there was only one place-setting at Eleanor's table.

"Oh, he isn't feeling well at the moment. He's resting in our room," Eleanor said casually.

"I hope nothing too horrific happened to him?" Oz asked.

Eleanor understood exactly the source of his concern. He had seen Edmund heal quite readily from the stabbing wound on his face, and she knew that without context, she too would assume that anything that would debilitate him so thoroughly must be rather gruesome.

"No, no. Nothing particularly horrific," Eleanor reassured him. "We visited the ruins of Ephesus, and he fell through a hole in the rubble. I'm sure he will recover in no time, but he needs his rest for the process to run its course."

Yvie glanced around to make sure no one was listening in. "That must have been quite a fall."

Eleanor lowered her voice. "Yes, at least ten meters into some catacombs below an ancient church. Neither of us noticed it was there until the rocks under his feet gave way. It took him quite the effort to pull himself out afterwards, so he is especially tired now."

She was rather pleased with her believable lie.

"Lucky it was him and not you," Yvie whispered.

"Yes, I suppose it was," Eleanor said distractedly, as it occurred to her for the first time exactly how much more dangerous the world was for her than it was for him. She hoped against hope that she would never succumb to such an accident by his side—it would surely torment him even more than her dying of old age. She pushed the thought aside.

"Will you join us for dinner?" Yvie asked cheerfully.

"I would love to," Eleanor agreed.

Oz gestured to one of the hosts, who led them to a larger empty table without batting an eye.

"May I interest you in a cocktail, Madame? Dinner won't be served for another half hour," one of the waiters inquired, as another boy rushed to collect the fourth place-setting and disappeared into the kitchen. "We have many mild and sweet options for ladies to choose from."

Eleanor couldn't resist rolling her eyes at his unintentional condescension. "I would like a glass of the finest cognac you have, neat."

"And I would like the same," Yvie added.

"Why don't you just make that your finest *bottle* of cognac with three glasses?" Oz suggested.

"Yes, sir!" the waiter agreed.

He scurried off, and Oz laughed jovially. "I reckon you modern sheilas left that bloke a bit gobsmacked just now."

"It is one of my favorite pastimes," Eleanor winked.

Yvie reached across the table to squeeze Eleanor's hand affectionately. "I am so glad to see you well, Eleanor. I will sleep much better tonight."

Eleanor smiled, and then sighed with contentment at the beautiful reality of her new friendship. It had been so long since she'd met a 'body-carrying friend' (one of her sisters' favorite phrases, describing a friend who would carry a dead body in the night for you without asking a single question) that she couldn't even remember the last. Perhaps a few of the nurses in the VAD, none of whom she'd kept in particularly good touch with since the war (except for Anne with her doomed marriage to the freshly impoverished Baron of Heathfield, of course). She sighed disappointedly at Anne's tragic downfall, and then pushed the memory away. Anne had, despite everything, brought her and Edmund together. She couldn't blame her too much for anything else she'd ever done.

A tuxedo-clad elderly gentleman approached their table with a dusty bottle of cognac in one hand and a silver tray with three crystal glasses in the other.

"You ordered the finest cognac on offer, sir?" he addressed Oz entirely, without even glancing at Eleanor or Yvie.

"Well, I can't tell the difference between a fine cognac and a bottle of Kentucky Moonshine, I reckon, but these sheilas always keep me straight," Oz said as he directed the man's attention towards them. "They will be the final decision-makers as to your offering's quality, mate."

The man rolled his shoulders, working hard to hide his surprise and annoyance.

"A. de Fussigny special reserve 1818," he declared as he held the bottle out before Yvie and then Eleanor.

"*C'est magnifique!*" Yvie exclaimed. "My great-grandfather knew Monsieur de Fussigny! Before the war, my family always thoroughly enjoyed his special reserves at Christmas. I believe 1847 was a better year, but I suppose you are rather limited in your supply."

The sommelier relaxed as Yvie demonstrated her competence in cognac selection. He opened the bottle and poured them each a small taste. Eleanor swirled her glass and then took in a long whiff, remembering fondly her first evening with Edmund when they had done the same together.

"*C'est bon.*" Yvie nodded her approval.

"I'll take it from here, mate," Oz said as he gathered up the bottle to fill their glasses himself.

The sommelier bowed, ignoring Oz's uncouth move, and left them alone.

"To the colonel's timely recovery," Oz declared as he held up his glass in a toast.

Eleanor smiled and joined Yvie enthusiastically in clinking their glasses.

She sat back, relished the silky complexity of her sip, and finally relaxed for the first time in many days.

For hours, she dined and drank with her friends, laughing genuinely at Oz's many jokes and remembering Yvie's sharp sense of humor (that always struck most unexpectedly at the perfect moments to cause all of them to explode into laughter), to the great disapproval of the diners at the surrounding tables.

Eleanor didn't care. She loved every second of it.

As the evening continued along amicably, she looked around the room from time to time, observing the other tables and noting that Mr. and Mrs. Ridgeway were not there. At one point, she spied a table in the far corner where three very sour-looking older men whispered heatedly amongst themselves and snapped angrily at the waiters every time they were bothered with minor inconveniences like their food being served. She was ever so glad to be in the company of friends.

Finally, as the crowd thinned out, and they finished off their second bottle of wine on top of the bottle of cognac they'd topped off (rather unexpectedly, given Edmund's absence), Eleanor felt the pull of the human bed, and the desire to make sure that her peacefully sleeping husband was still alright.

"Thank you so much for taking my mind off of unpleasantries," she said as she stood up. "I'd better check up on Edmund."

"Yes, yes, of course. Send him our best." Yvie stood up to pull Eleanor into a tipsy hug.

"Tell him we're expecting his company at his earliest convenience. I still have the story of the kangaroo races to recount, and I'm quite sure his imagination will help me make it a legendary tale," Oz said as he pulled Eleanor into his own tipsy hug.

"I will tell him," Eleanor agreed. "Have a lovely evening, both of you."

She skipped happily out of the dining room, down the hallway, into the elevator, and finally into the hallway leading to her room, but as she approached her door and reached into her secret pocket for the key, the creak of movement and the shuffling of fabric followed by a series of heated whispers brought her right to attention.

She held the key tightly in her fist, placing the sharp edge between her fingers as a makeshift weapon, and then held her breath as she tiptoed to the end of the hallway. She took one moment to compose herself (although, she had to admit later that it didn't even occur to her that the wisest thing to do would have been to simply enter her room and lock her door), and then rushed around the corner with her weapon wielded.

"Ahhhh!!!!" Daisy and Lily screamed in unison. Eleanor almost fell over with surprise.

The two girls stared up at her with wide eyes from their position huddled up against a locked supply closet.

"Good lord," Eleanor murmured as she got herself under control. "My darlings, what are you doing in this dark hallway alone in the middle of the night?"

"We aren't alone, we have each other," Lily squeaked.

Eleanor returned the key to her pocket and slowly approached them. As she got closer, she noticed that Daisy did not look healthy at all. She was pale and sweaty with dark bags under her eyes.

"What's wrong? What happened?" Eleanor asked with her gentlest tone. "You girls can tell me anything, you know."

"But you're a spy," Lily whispered.

"But spies aren't all bad, are they?" Eleanor asked, running with the lies Mr. Valov had told them. "I am a spy for the Empire. Spies for the Empire protect little girls like you."

"Spies are not supposed to admit that they're spies," Lily informed her.

Eleanor smiled. "You're right. I'm not a very good spy. But I'm also a nurse. I helped many people, *thousands* of people, get better when they were hurt during the war. Are you hurt, Daisy?"

Eleanor kneeled down and gently coaxed Daisy's hand out of her lap.

"Oh my, yes, you are hurt, aren't you? Is this from the glass on the train?"

A nasty infection filled with green puss oozed from the palm of Daisy's hand.

Daisy looked up at her and burst into tears.

"Do your parents know about this? Where are they now?" Eleanor asked.

"They're in our room… fighting," Lily whispered. "We left, and they didn't even notice."

"I really should call them. They need to know where you are."

"NO!" they squealed in unison. "Please don't call them! They'll only fight more! Daddy will hit Mummy again!"

"I see." Eleanor gathered her wits. "Well, we need to tend to this wound. Both of you, come with me."

Lily hopped up and helped Daisy, and Eleanor took Lily's hand to guide them back towards her room. As they reached the door, both girls stopped solidly in their tracks.

"Is *he* in there?" Lily asked nervously. "The abominable snowman?"

Eleanor kneeled down to address them face to face. "You saw Edmund do something very scary, didn't you?"

"Yes," they squeaked.

"Do you know what those bad people would have done if Edmund hadn't stopped them?"

"They would've killed us," Lily whispered.

Eleanor's heart broke as she saw the same sadness in Lily's eyes as she had felt herself after her father had killed himself. She saw, in that moment, the tragedy that those two little girls were no longer children, and she almost gave into tears. Instead, she held herself together and focused on her lecture.

"Sometimes good people must do horrific things to help other good people stay safe. Edmund did that on the train, and it was very painful for him. He didn't want to hurt those bad people. But he also didn't want to let those bad people hurt you. Do you understand? Sometimes grown-ups have to make very difficult choices to keep little girls safe."

"But his face... his eyes... he wasn't just a grown-up," Lily argued.

"You're right," Eleanor admitted. Her mind began racing. "You know what he really is?"

"An abominable snowman," Lily replied matter-of-factly.

"He isn't. He told you that to tease you, Lily. He is really an angel in disguise, just like the Bible says."

"An angel..." Lily murmured. "But he killed those people! Angels don't kill people!"

"Angels make the hardest choices on Earth, darling. They are here to protect innocent people. They hate killing, but sometimes they must, and that is what you saw."

The girls both thought about her assertion in silence.

"But you mustn't tell him I told you," Eleanor added quickly. "He doesn't like people to know, because he is in disguise, you see. If people know, then he has failed at his mission."

The girls nodded their solemn agreement, and Eleanor sighed with relief at her triumph.

"I will go inside and make sure he's not up and about. He's resting, you see, after another harrowing rescue. Wait here, and I will let you inside in just a minute, okay?"

Eleanor slipped into the room and closed the door behind her. Without a moment wasted, Kuveni materialized in the form of Kate, clad in a stylish black and silver beaded flapper dress.

"He's still soundly asleep in the bathroom. I will keep the door locked while you bring them in here. Would you like me to help you? You are doing marvelously, my dear. It is as if you've been a part of our clan for centuries."

"To be honest, I could use your help," Eleanor admitted. "I don't feel particularly practiced in using scripture to manipulate people. I've always been patently against it."

"We use what we have for the greater good, my dear," Kuveni reassured her.

Eleanor skipped back to open the door. "Come in, my darlings."

She whisked them inside and closed the door behind them.

"Whoa," Lily whispered. "Your room is much bigger than ours!"

She glanced around the room and landed her attention on Kuveni.

"Daisy and Lily, this is Kate," Eleanor introduced the girls. "Kate is Edmund's cousin."

"Is she an angel in disguise too?" Lily asked.

Eleanor looked searchingly to Kuveni.

"I am, my dearest child," Kuveni agreed. "Now, what is this I hear about an injury?"

Eleanor helped Daisy walk sluggishly across the room to the large sitting area and seated her on an elaborate divan, while Lily followed her sister and plopped herself down right next to her.

Eleanor kneeled down on the floor and gathered Daisy's hand into hers.

"This is a nasty infection. It needs to be cleaned and treated or else it will become very dangerous." Daisy flinched as Eleanor ran her finger gently along the rosy edge of the growing wound on the palm of her hand.

378

"Come, I will clean it for you," Kuveni said as she kneeled down beside Eleanor and took Daisy's hand.

"You're warm," Daisy said as Kuveni held her hand between her palms and whispered a quiet mantra. "But the colonel is cold."

"Angels come in many shapes and sizes, my dear child, and many temperatures as well. We are just as variable as humans are," Kuveni explained as she let go of Daisy's hand and returned it to Eleanor's custody.

"We should take her to the ship's doctor," Eleanor whispered.

"There isn't one, my dear girl. Mr. Corrigan was very unhappy when he failed to re-embark after a sojourn to the brothels of Smyrna."

Eleanor snorted. "Blimey, a lot of help he would have been anyway, the bloody bampot." She took a moment to calm herself. "Do you know if Mélusine's Roman remedy is still in my trunk?"

It was only at that moment that Eleanor realized that her black eye had entirely healed. When she'd looked at herself in the mirror in Smyrna, she hadn't seen any sign of it, but she had been in such a state that she'd forgotten about that plight entirely. She sighed with relief.

"I will check right now," Kuveni offered as she stood up and walked straight to the closet.

Daisy held up her hand, and Lily reached over to inspect it.

"It still hurts," Daisy whimpered.

"Angels cannot heal you, Daisy. They can only provide the resources that human science has realized are necessary to help you heal," Eleanor explained.

"That doesn't make them very magical," Daisy humphed.

"The world is not full of magic, Daisy. You must make your own way. You cannot expect God or angels to step in to help you. It was extremely unusual that Edmund was there to save you on the train, and it is exceptional that Kate has agreed to join me now to help you."

"You asked her to come?" Daisy asked. "For *me*?"

"I did," Eleanor confirmed. "She and I have a very special relationship, one that humans almost never have with such divine creatures."

"But why?!" Lily exclaimed.

"Because Eleanor is the kindest, most loving human who has ever walked the face of the earth," Kuveni answered on her behalf. "God loves humans who are kind more than any other humans, and humans who are kind to the weak? To the ostracized? God loves those humans most of all. Eleanor is a very special human indeed, and you are exceptionally lucky to have encountered her, my children. If only every human were so lucky."

She handed Eleanor Mélusine's Roman leather pouch, and Eleanor dug right in and began massaging the paste onto Daisy's wound.

"I honestly don't know if this will be enough," Eleanor whispered to Kuveni in Gaelic. "The wound is already intensely infected. Their parents should have been keeping it clean from the beginning. I'm not sure what we can do at this point."

"I have thoroughly cleaned it, and Lady Mélusine's remedy should help somewhat. There isn't much else anyone can do for her, is there?"

Eleanor nodded solemnly as she finished up treating the wound.

"Have you eaten, my darlings? You look famished." Kuveni snapped her fingers, and two steaming miniature carpenter's pies appeared on the low coffee table before them.

"Whoa," Lily whispered.

"Really, *Kate*, that was a bit on the nose, even for you."

"They will not tell anyone that they have encountered an angel in disguise, will they?" Kuveni asked as she snapped her fingers and produced two forks and two napkins.

"No, ma'am," they agreed in unison.

Kuveni smiled approvingly. They dug right into their pies as if they had, in fact, been starving for days.

"Eat slower, my dear girls, there is more where that came from if you are truly famished. No one will stand in your way."

"Darlings, how long have you been hiding from your parents?" Eleanor asked sweetly.

"Since yesterday morning," Lily admitted. "Mummy wanted to go back to London, but Daddy said that we had to stay the course. They started fighting, and we ran away. I don't think they've noticed, though. They don't notice when we disappear most of the time."

"How sad," Kuveni murmured.

"I'm sure they've noticed. You must have them worried sick," Eleanor countered.

"We went back earlier tonight because we were hungry and Daisy's hand was hurting more. But Daddy already told her she had to be a big girl and bear it like Queen Victoria would, so she was afraid he'd be cross if he saw that she wasn't bearing it like Queen Victoria," Lily explained.

"Sounds like a winner…" Kuveni muttered.

"And they were fighting again," Daisy added. "When they fight, they yell at us if we try to interrupt them."

"I see." Eleanor thought through their options.

Kuveni lowered her voice and switched back into Gaelic. "My poor boy will not dare to come out of the bathroom tonight, Eleanor. He was far too distraught to risk feeling aroused by your condition again. If you would like to invite the girls to sleep in here, I will warn you if he begins to stir."

Eleanor nodded her solemn agreement.

"Would you girls like to sleep in here tonight?" Eleanor asked them cheerfully as she returned to English.

"Where is the colonel?" Lily asked nervously.

"He is sleeping in the bath," Kuveni replied nonchalantly. "Angels like to sleep in all sorts of strange places. I prefer sleeping in the sea myself."

"Are there angels in the sea below us right now?" Lily asked.

"There very well might be," Kuveni replied.

"Okay then," Lily agreed.

"Come," Kuveni urged them. "I will help you into the bed."

Eleanor watched as Kuveni lifted each girl onto the comfortable bed, and then she glanced over to the hard divan in the seating area and sighed her concession.

"Eleanor, aren't you going to sleep here too?" Lily asked. "And Kate? Mummy always sleeps with us when we're scared… at least she used to, before she and Daddy were fighting so much."

"Yes, my darlings, we will sleep right beside you," Kuveni agreed as she crawled onto the bed next to them. "We will keep you safe until morning."

Eleanor reached down and unlaced her Roman sandals, and as she approached the bed, she noticed that it looked especially large… much larger than it had earlier in the evening. Kuveni winked, and Eleanor, still clad in her comfortable Roman silk, climbed under the covers next to them.

Kuveni pulled a silk sheet up to cover the girls, and then snapped her fingers, and the lights went out.

"Good night, my sweet children," she whispered. "Sleep well as the angels watch over you."

As Lily nestled into her nook, Eleanor pushed back a pang of melancholy at the extreme unlikeliness that she'd ever have a child of her own. She pushed the thought away, wrapped her arm around the poor girl, and slept.

Eleanor awoke in the dark to a child squirming.

"Eleanor? Kate? Daisy is shaking," Lily whispered. "She's really hot. I think she has a fever."

Kuveni snapped her fingers, and the lights came on. "It is just past four o' clock in the morning," she whispered.

"I don't know what else to do," Eleanor whispered back. "She's entering into shock from the infection. At this stage, there is usually nothing to be done."

Lily whimpered.

"I don't want to jump to any conclusions," Eleanor reassured her half-heartedly as she gathered Daisy's hand into hers to inspect it again. She grimaced at the ugly, green-puss-filled wound and felt her forehead. "She certainly has a fever."

"Do you think your Australian friend might have any ideas?" Kuveni asked.

"It is possible. I'm sure he saw his fair share of wicked infections on the front." Eleanor hopped out of bed. "Do you know where his room is?"

Kuveni dissolved herself, but Lily did not make any comment, as her attention was focused entirely on her quivering, unconscious sister.

Kuveni reappeared. "Come. I will take you to the doctor now."

She gathered Eleanor, Daisy, and Lily into her arms, and with a moment of dizziness, they were standing in a dark hallway outside of a closed, locked door.

Kuveni released Lily and Eleanor from her grasp into a standing position as the lights turned on. She held Daisy in her arms, whispering reassurances into her ear.

Eleanor banged on the door, and a loud clomp echoed from inside the room, as if a lamp had just fallen off of a bedside table…

"They were asleep. I decided not to take any chances," Kuveni whispered.

Eleanor banged loudly again with her fist. "Oz? Yvie? We need your help. It's an emergency!"

Yvie cracked open the door and blinked uncomfortably at the blaring electric lights in the hallway, hiding what was undoubtedly her naked body behind the shelter of the door to peer at all four of them.

"Is Edmund alright?" she asked groggily.

"Edmund is perfectly fine. Daisy is not." Eleanor gestured to the poor child who was now shaking violently in Kuveni's arms.

"Please, help my sister!" Lily begged desperately.

"Give us one tiny minute."

She closed the door, and Eleanor listened as they awkwardly danced around, putting their clothes on. Without a moment wasted, Yvie pulled the door open.

"Tell us," she said as she whisked them into the room.

She looked at Kuveni's strangely familiar form, and then pushed away the frivolity of her curiosity to focus on Daisy's dire state. Kuveni laid Daisy on a divan that was very similar to the one in Eleanor's room, and Lily sat down right next to her, placing her hand on her sister's sweating forehead.

"She's sick, isn't she? Really, really sick," Lily asked miserably.

"Yes, darling. She's very sick." Eleanor switched immediately into her professional demeanor as she addressed Yvie. "Daisy's cut from the glass on the Orient Express is infected. I think she's septic. I cleaned the wound last night and applied a paste, but now she's in shock. She's gotten markedly worse in the last fifteen minutes. Do you have any ideas about how to treat her?"

"Ozzy, bring the medical bag," Yvie called towards the bathroom.

Oz rushed out of the bathroom in his flannel pajamas towards the closet and gathered up a leather medical bag to join them on the floor by the divan.

"Let's use the Duchesne mold," she said as he placed the bag on the floor and began rifling through it on her behalf. "When I was a girl, my father knew a man who studied infections. He submitted his findings to the *Institut Pasteur*, but they didn't pay him any mind, the rascals. He was right, though. Mold fights bacteria and wins. I always carry some with me. It has been useful too many times already."

Oz handed her a vial of white powder, and she set about rubbing it into the wound. Daisy whimpered, but Yvie paid her no mind as she pushed it as deeply into the wound as she could manage. When she was finished, she measured out a small serving into the palm of her hand and forced it into Daisy's mouth. Daisy coughed and gagged, and Kuveni stealthily produced a bowl of ice cream that she collected from the floor beside the divan, just outside of Oz and Yvie's view, and immediately began feeding it to Daisy.

"Eat this, darling girl. It's yummy chocolate," Kuveni whispered to Daisy as she finally calmed down and opened her eyes groggily.

For many patient minutes, Kuveni fed her the entire bowl, coaxing the bitter antibiotic powder down along with it. When she was finished, Daisy lay down with her head in Lily's lap and returned to sleep. Eleanor felt Daisy's forehead.

"How remarkable. The fever is already lower," she said with wonder.

"Really?" Yvie asked. "It works, but it doesn't usually work that fast."

"There was willow bark extract in the ice cream," Kuveni admitted. "I believe that reduces fever, does it not?"

"Brilliant," Eleanor whispered. "You are absolutely right. I wish I'd thought of it earlier."

Kuveni smiled and produced another bowl of chocolate ice cream just outside of Oz and Yvie's view and handed it to Lily. "There, there. You deserve some ice cream too, my dear child, for taking such good care of your sister."

Eleanor stood up, and Oz and Yvie followed, while Kuveni remained focused on the girls.

"Do I dare ask how you were tasked with this crisis in the dead of night without those bludger parents paying any mind to their own ankle biters?" Oz whispered with obvious anger at the Ridgeways' irresponsibility.

"I found the girls hiding from their parents in the hallway by my room, and I took them in," Eleanor whispered. "I agree. The whole situation is absurd. Her wound has obviously not been tended to since you treated it on the train days and days ago. I'm sure you told them they had to keep it clean and bandaged."

"Oh, we told them," Oz hissed angrily. "Over and over and over again. That Ridgeway bloke just doesn't listen!"

"We should demand that they come here now. They must come and comfort their children!" Yvie exclaimed.

"A lot of comfort that pommy bastard will be," Oz muttered.

"You know what he told that poor lass? He told her to bear it like Queen Victoria would!" Eleanor worked hard to keep her

386

voice down. "And there's more… the girls told me they were afraid Mr. Ridgeway would hit their mother again if they returned. Who knows how far that goes. That's why I didn't call them as soon as I found the girls."

"*C'est honteux*," Yvie muttered. "It's shameful."

"I'm sorry to ruin your night," Eleanor said as she took a step back and observed their disheveled pajamas.

"Please, do not think twice about it." Yvie pulled Eleanor into an affectionate hug. "We are happy to help."

"You saved that girl's life, Ellie," Oz seconded. "She would have died without Yvie's treatment. It is a crying shame that the rest of the human race can't use it too. We saved hundreds of people with it in the army hospitals during the war, and still no one believed that it was anything more than an old wives' tale."

Kuveni finally stood up as Lily's head fell heavily onto the edge of the divan in a deep sleep. She walked slowly to join Eleanor, demonstrating an unusual reticence. "Both girls are sound asleep now. The second ice cream had a sleeping tonic in it."

Eleanor could tell that Kuveni had not entirely thought through her plan when she'd whisked them to the Helmsworth's door. Eleanor didn't have a clue how she was going to keep Oz and Yvie from asking Edmund about his mysterious female doppelganger, and she was quite sure that Kuveni didn't either.

"Where did you get ice cream in the middle of the night?" Yvie asked as she eyed Kuveni with more focused curiosity.

"I thought you'd been in the army hospitals long enough to know not to ask," Kuveni shot back, parroting the phrase they'd told Edmund and Eleanor in confidence on the Orient Express.

Eleanor threw her an annoyed look at her needless demonstration of her Yakshini lurking.

"Kate is Edmund's cousin," Eleanor explained. Her mind rushed to fill in a reasonable story. "She was already in Turkey when we arrived in Constantinople, and after Edmund fell through the ruins in Ephesus, she joined us in Smyrna to make sure he was alright. She's a bit of a big sister, really, and he doesn't like her reporting back to the family, so he would be very unhappy to know that she weaseled her way onto this ship during our honeymoon. Wouldn't he, Kate?"

Kuveni couldn't hide her smile at Eleanor's increasingly skilled lies.

"Guilty as charged," Kuveni agreed. "He doesn't like to be coddled, you see, but he really did need some help with this particularly difficult recovery. I promise I will be leaving you at the next port of call, and my darling Edmund won't know a peep of it... That is, with your discretion." She looked to Oz and Yvie.

"Yes... yes, of course..." Oz agreed distractedly.

"What is it, my dear mate?" Kuveni coaxed. Eleanor smiled as Kuveni used Oz's slang oddly with her posh English accent.

"It's just... never mind. Mum's the word." He suddenly looked mad at himself.

"Oh, I see... You aren't sure if I know of Edmund's many special talents," Kuveni said casually. "Don't worry about it for one tiny minute. Edmund and I are both uniquely talented. It runs in the family."

"Huh..." Oz grunted.

"We thought that perhaps... perhaps his... eh... *talents* were a result of the chemicals in the war," Yvie admitted.

"He is far more interesting than some poor victim of an army experiment," Kuveni informed them. "I'd best not get into the details. You have seen that he is an honorable man, and I trust that you understand how much the world needs powerful honorable men to counteract the many powerful despicable ones."

"Yes, we know that very well," Oz agreed.

Kuveni smiled. "Eleanor tells me that you have been consummate allies in keeping our family's secrets. I would appreciate your discretion on this point as well."

"Yes... yes, of course," Yvie agreed.

"Of course," Oz seconded.

Eleanor glanced over to the sleeping children and sighed apologetically. "I don't know what to do now. I don't want to just leave you with this burden, but I think it's best for everyone if we let them get some rest before we submit them to their worthless father's judgment. What do you think?"

"We can take them for now," Yvie agreed. "I will need to give Daisy another dose of the medicine in the morning anyway. She will need to take it consistently for several days to keep the infection under control. I can't say that I trust the Ridgeways to do much of anything at this point. They could have prevented this completely by following the orders we already gave them."

"I will help however I can. Perhaps with two nurses and a medic on their case, we can keep them in line," Eleanor suggested.

She took Kuveni's hand, but as she led her past the girls towards the door, Lily stirred.

"Eleanor, you aren't leaving, are you? Kate? Please stay!" she implored meagerly. "We need the angels in disguise to watch over us!"

Eleanor threw a searching look to Oz and Yvie.

"Stay," Yvie offered. "Sleep on the bed with us. It will feel like the VAD dorms again."

"Sleep," Kuveni suggested. "I'll watch over them from the chair, and you should rest, Eleanor. You have hardly slept a wink, and dawn is coming soon."

"It stays quite dark with the shutters closed. We can sleep late into the morning," Oz suggested. "We are both quite tired ourselves still."

Kuveni took the seat next to Lily and began gently stroking her hair until she sighed contentedly and nestled back into her position on the couch with her sister.

Yvie climbed into the middle of the large bed and gestured for Eleanor to join her on the left while Oz lay down beside her on the right.

Eleanor giggled. "Can you imagine what a scandal it would have been if they'd caught a man in your bed in the VAD dormitories?"

"That's why the men had to work so hard not to get caught," Yvie winked. "Ozzy had his fair share of close calls, didn't you?"

"I would have done almost anything for an extra few hours with my Yvie," he confessed.

Lily sighed as Kuveni turned out the lights, and together, like one big happy family, they slept.

Eleanor awoke to the sound of Lily whispering to Kuveni. She hopped off the bed as quietly as she could, and glanced across the room to the sitting area, which was only illuminated by a few flickering candles on the low coffee table. Lily was sitting up, and Kuveni was feeling Daisy's forehead as the girl gazed up at her with glassy eyes.

"What time is it?" Eleanor asked Kuveni, who looked as awake as ever.

"It is already past two o'clock in the afternoon," Kuveni whispered. "The Ridgeways are wondering where they are, but they haven't mustered the wherewithal to admit to anyone that they lost track of them."

"Bloody bludgers," Eleanor muttered.

"Indeed. But I think it is a good time to bring their attention to their shortcomings, as soon as Oz and Yvie are awake."

"Yes, you're right," Eleanor whispered. "But before we wake them up, I'd like to sneak a bath."

"Good idea," Kuveni agreed. "Go refresh yourself, my dear. I will stay with Daisy and Lily. Your dress will be clean and unwrinkled when you're ready for it."

Eleanor squeezed Kuveni's hand in thanks, and then scampered to the bathroom. She had to admit, it had been far too long since she'd enjoyed a proper bath... since Paris, in fact.

She turned on the faucet and slowly undressed herself, enjoying the rich sensation of the steam filling the room, and stopping for a moment of curious inspection at the perfectly clean magical Yakshini panties Kuveni had provided. Of all the Yakshini inventions she'd stumbled across, that one was by far her favorite.

She placed them neatly on top of her folded dress and then sank down into the hot water, letting her mind wander to what her sleeping husband might be dreaming about at that very moment. She hoped the commotion hadn't disturbed him too much. She pushed back a pang of anxiety at the danger they might face if he wasn't back to his strongest state soon, from Surpanakha... from revolutionaries... from his own friends and colleagues in the army that he'd dutifully served for decades... She pushed the frustrating thought away and focused on the peaceful sound of the water pouring from the faucet onto her body, refreshing it more and more every minute.

She lay in the bath for longer than she'd intended (perhaps a new vice she'd learned from her gentle husband), and as she heard the noises of Oz and Yvie moving around, she sheepishly collected herself and dried off with one of their clean towels.

When she re-emerged, all of the shutters were open, and Oz, Yvie, and Lily were all sitting cheerfully at a round dining table just inside the balcony, while a warm, gentle afternoon breeze wafted in, whipping the white linen curtains. Before them, an enormous Yakshini feast was already well underway, as each of them happily ate individually-portioned carpenter's pies. Fresh berries, carafes of milk and coffee, and a beautiful plate of pastries including Kuveni's canelés, pains au chocolats, and colorful petits fours were presented on silver platters atop a neat white tablecloth. Daisy was sitting on the divan, looking much better than the night before, finishing off her first bowl of chocolate ice cream. Kuveni sat beside her, holding a glass of chocolate milk as her next offering.

Eleanor blushed with embarrassment. "I'm sorry for imposing on your bath."

"Oh, think nothing of it!" Yvie exclaimed. "Come! Join us! Kate called room service, and they brought us this lovely feast!"

"Did she now?" Eleanor raised her eyebrows skeptically as she glanced over to Kuveni.

"Enjoy it," Kuveni urged her. "When you're done eating, it will be time to call the Ridgeways over."

"No!" Lily squealed. "Don't call them! We want to stay here forever! Then they'll never fight again! You don't fight, do you? You're too nice to fight!"

Yvie threw Oz and Eleanor a resigned look, and Eleanor took a seat beside Lily at the table and took her hand.

"Darling, you can't stay here. Your parents miss you. They must be worried sick, and it is their responsibility to see to your needs. Now, we will be here with you when they come, and we will help them understand that *none* of this is your fault. Do you understand? *None* of it. You were very brave to accept my help last night. It saved your sister's life. You must hold onto that bravery, and remember that you made the right decision, no matter what they say to the contrary. Okay?"

Lily nestled into Eleanor's arms and began to cry. Eleanor squeezed Lily and let her sob, without voicing a word of protest as the little girl wiped her mucus and her tears on the delicate layers of lavender chiffon (to Yvie's silent horror), until Lily's sniffles subsided.

"Darling, everything will be okay," Eleanor reassured her. "No matter how bad it feels now, you are strong enough to get through it. My father died when I was just a lass, and I thought the world would end, but it didn't. I got through it, I went to school, I became a nurse, and now I have lived a lovely, happy life for many, many years. I never could have imagined how lovely my life would be back then when I was crying just like you are. I had my sisters to confide in, and so do you. It will all be okay."

"And you married an angel in disguise," Lily sniffled.

Eleanor smiled. "Yes, I did that too. I was happy before I met him, and even happier after. There are many things in this world that can make us happy, Lily. So many things that you haven't experienced yet, but be a good girl, and they will come to you in their own time. And if your father scares you again while you're on this ship, you come to me, okay? Come straight to my door, and I will help you. Aye?"

"Aye," Lily agreed.

"Kate, may I have more ice cream please?" Daisy asked Kuveni with more manners than Eleanor had seen her display since their initial meeting.

Kuveni leaned down, blocking Oz and Yvie's view, and then gathered a new bowl of freshly created ice cream up from the floor.

"What a coincidence, my darling child, there was another bowl of ice cream just waiting for you right here!"

Eleanor smiled, and Lily finally relegated her sniffles and returned to her carpenter's pie. Eleanor took a deep breath, poured herself a large cup of coffee, and gathered a canelé and a pain au chocolat onto her plate.

"Where are we?" she asked as she gazed past Yvie to the brown water and sunburnt yellow hills beyond.

"We're in the Suez Canal. It's Egypt on both sides," Oz replied as he returned to devouring his carpenter's pie.

Eleanor finally relaxed into mundane conversation as she finished off her first two pastries and collected two more canelés. "Have you ever been to Egypt? I've always wanted to go. We talked about stopping on our way back from India, but we decided to postpone the decision until the end, in case we're too tired."

"Yes, we went there on our honeymoon, actually. It was quite the adventure! Ozzy almost traded me for a camel accidentally!" Yvie said excitedly.

"Really, how?!" Eleanor exclaimed.

They fell into another one of Oz's colorful tall tales, and as Eleanor drank down her third cup of coffee and felt her residual menstrual pains dissolve, she glanced over to Kuveni, who offered her a sly wink.

Lily and Daisy listened quietly while the adults continued on their jovial conversation, until the coffee was gone, and Eleanor had eaten far more than her fair share of Kuveni's delicious pastries.

"This feast was far better than dinner last night, wasn't it, Yvie? Maybe we should eat in our room for every meal," Oz said as he stood up and stretched, patting his full belly with satisfaction.

Eleanor threw Kuveni a nervous look, but Yvie came to her rescue. "Now, now, Ozzy. I'm sure the cooks on duty have everything to do with it. Perhaps a better staff boarded in Port Said."

"Peew-tetreh," Oz said with a wink.

"It's *peut-etre, mon amour,*" Yvie corrected him.

"Say vray," he agreed. "That means, 'the wife is always right,' for those of you who don't speak fluent French."

"Oh, Ozzy, don't tease," Yvie giggled.

Oz smiled, took a deep breath of warm, dry air, and then sighed unenthusiastically. "It's time for all of us to face the music, I reckon."

Lily tensed as he walked across the room to the phone by the door.

"G'day mate… Yes, thank you for the scrummy meal… Yes, three of us will dine together in the dining room tonight as well, unless the colonel has recovered properly, then it might be four… But that's enough of the niceties, I'm afraid. Mr. Corrigan, you'd best bring the Ridgeways over to our suite. We have two precious items of cargo they are very likely missing. Tell them to come straightaway. No dawdling now… Thank you kindly, mate."

Kuveni stood up and made her way towards the door. "I'd best be on my way. I think you can handle everything the girls need from here. I will be preparing myself to disembark at the next port of call. Good luck, mates. Eleanor, I will be in touch to make sure

Edmund's recovery has finished up as expected. My darling children, cheer up and listen to everything these wise adults tell you."

"Thank you for your help, Kate," Eleanor said with a wink.

"My pleasure, as always, my dear. It was lovely meeting you both." Kuveni waved to Oz and Yvie and spirited herself out the door with great haste, closing it behind her.

"I'd better get properly dressed before they arrive," Oz said as he gathered his clothes from the closet and disappeared into the bathroom.

"Me too," Yvie said as she gathered a simple periwinkle blue silk dress from the closet and changed into it right in front of the girls.

Eleanor helped her tame her short brown hair with a matching headband covered in delicate silk flowers, and as she finished up, a knock at the door brought Lily straight to her sister's side on the couch.

"*On y va.*" Yvie shrugged unenthusiastically. "Let's get this over with."

Oz rushed out of the bathroom to beat them to the door. They stood beside him, and with one look of team cohesion at their unpleasant task, Oz pulled open the door.

"Precious cargo?" Mr. Ridgeway asked confusedly without even a polite hello. He eyed Yvie and Eleanor, and Mrs. Ridgeway muttered her disapproval under her breath. Mr. Corrigan stood behind them silently assessing the scene.

"The most precious, one might say." Oz gestured for them to enter, and as Mrs. Ridgeway's eyes fell on her whimpering daughters, she burst into tears and rushed to gather them into her arms.

"Where have you been?!" she exclaimed with a combination of love and anger. "I've been going mad with worry!"

"What is going on here?" Mr. Ridgeway asked with booming anger. He could not hide his embarrassed blush, and Eleanor disliked him even more than she ever had as she recognized the obvious truth that he was attempting to disguise his personal shame in anger.

"I found your daughters huddling in the hallway in the dead of night," Eleanor explained flatly. "Daisy's hand was badly infected and had clearly not been tended to in days. You are extremely lucky that there were three medical experts on this ship to help her out."

"Three?!" Mr. Ridgeway exclaimed indignantly. "You are nothing but a lady spy!"

"I am a nurse, Mr. Ridgeway, and I have been for twenty years," Eleanor countered with obvious annoyance. "And your daughter would have died last night if we hadn't stepped in."

"Died?! Oh, hogwash. No one's ever died of a little cut," Mr. Ridgeway said haughtily as he eyed Mr. Corrigan.

"You couldn't be wronger about that, Mr. Ridgeway." Oz straightened his posture and spoke with the most commanding tone Eleanor had ever heard him use. "I have seen many thousands of men die from similar injuries. That is why I told you many times that you needed to keep it clean and bandaged. I see you've taken my advice for your own bullet wound. Did you not think that your own child deserved the same courtesy?"

"Oh Daisy, dearest, why didn't you just tell Mummy?" Mrs. Ridgeway inspected the ugly wound and kissed Daisy on the forehead. "Why, she's still feverish!"

"She is much better than she was last night. If it weren't for the medicine Yvie gave her, we would have called you to see to her deathbed," Eleanor replied.

"Why didn't you call us? Why didn't you call as soon as you found them?" Mrs. Ridgeway's dismay morphed into anger.

"Your daughters begged me not to," Eleanor shot back. "They told me they didn't want you to fight anymore." She threw an especially accusatory look towards Mr. Ridgeway, holding her tongue as to not get the girls in more trouble with their admission

396

that he was beating Mrs. Ridgeway. "Have you noticed that your daughters have been hiding from you since you boarded the ship? Did you even notice that they hadn't eaten anything or returned to your room in *two* days?"

"Why... why... I... I..." Mrs. Ridgeway's anger morphed into anguish, and she burst into tears. "This is all your fault, George. All of it! We should have bloody gone back to London the moment we arrived in Constantinople! Stay the course, you demanded. Stay the bloody course! For what?! We're visiting *my* bloody brother!"

"It is not my fault that our daughters have no discipline, Eloise. It is your responsibility to teach them to be good, obedient girls. What is it you've been doing all this time while I've been slaving away at work? Not mothering them properly, that's for sure." His voice burgeoned into a shout, and Daisy and Lily burst into tears simultaneously.

"Perhaps, mates, we don't have to explain to you why your daughters begged us not to call you last night. I can see that we were right to give them some peaceful time to rest without you spewing vitriol from all directions," Oz said sharply.

"I'm sorry," Mrs. Ridgeway cried as she gathered her daughters into her arms. "Mummy's so, so sorry..."

"Mr. Corrigan, might I see you for a moment in the hallway?" Eleanor asked as an idea crossed her mind.

Mr. Corrigan followed Eleanor out of the room.

"Is there an empty first class room on this ship?" she asked.

"There are several," Mr. Corrigan agreed.

"I want you to make one available to Mrs. Ridgeway and the girls. Charge it to us. Tell her whatever you need to tell her to convince her to use it. I didn't call them last night because the girls were afraid that their father would beat their mother again."

"Good lord," Mr. Corrigan murmured. "Of all the dishonorable things..."

"I agree. So, can you help me with this? They mustn't know the idea came from me, nor that I had anything to do with it. Do you understand?"

"Quite right," he said as he put his finger on his nose.

Eleanor smiled. "Thank you, my friend."

"There are many who should be thanking you, I can see," Mr. Corrigan replied.

"They can thank me when Daisy is out of harm's way, but I'm not sure there's much anyone can do for the rest of them once she's recovered. That is the ugly way of things, isn't it?"

Mr. Corrigan nodded his agreement, and Eleanor pulled the door open again.

"I will leave you now," she declared. "I must return to my ailing husband."

Mr. Ridgeway snorted, and Mr. Corrigan couldn't hide a look of shocked disgust at his unsympathetic reaction.

"Oz, Yvie, I will endeavor to meet you for dinner, but don't wait for me if I'm late. I'm not sure what Edmund will want to do. Give me a ring if you need my help."

"No worries, mate."

"Mr. Ridgeway, you'd better treat your family properly. My husband is rather outraged by injustice, and I don't know what he might do if he gets wind of some innocent children being tormented by their father's temper." Mr. Ridgeway looked legitimately concerned for the first time since his arrival. "Daisy and Lily, mind Oz and Yvie... and your mother. Oz and Yvie will see to your medical care." She winked to Lily, reiterating her secret offer of refuge, and then saluted and left them alone.

She took a deep breath as she walked straight down the hallway, realizing for the first time that she had no idea how to get out of the labyrinth, since Kuveni had transported them straight to Oz and Yvie's door in the dead of night. She wandered about the identical hallways confusedly for many minutes until she finally reached an elevator, and with the help of the same dedicated button-pusher she'd seen the day before, she finally made it back to her room.

She closed the door behind her and took another deep, calming breath, pushing back her many emotions at the train wreck of a family she'd just encountered far more intimately than she'd wanted to. Her heart ached for those two girls, but she sighed and pushed the thought away, as she often did when she encountered patients whose tragedies were too overwhelming to contemplate for too long. She could take certain reasonable actions to ease their suffering, but at the end of the day, their fate was theirs. That was just the way of the world.

She glanced over to the closed bathroom door, debating whether or not to check on Edmund, and then she thought the better of it. He still needed his rest. And so, she took off her Roman dress and hung it neatly in the closet, changing into a more casual pair of white linen trousers and a light blue chiffon blouse with a matching wide-brimmed hat to lounge about on their balcony for a few hours of lazy silence. She grabbed a small notebook and a pencil from her suitcase and skipped with refreshed energy towards the balcony. The idea of sitting in relaxed silence was overwhelmingly appealing.

She opened the shutters and took in a deep breath of warm, salty sea air, gathering her feet up onto the chaise longue, and sighing with satisfaction as a carafe of fresh watermelon juice appeared on the table beside her along with a glass of perfectly round ice.

"Thanks, Kuveni," she whispered. "For everything."

"It is my pleasure, Mistress Eleanor," Kuveni's disembodied voice replied.

Eleanor poured herself a drink, positioned her notebook on her knees, gazed into the distance at the arid, yellow desert stretching as far as the eye could see, and relished her first relaxed moment of silence since her wild marriage adventure began.

CHAPTER 25 – MR. CORRIGAN'S ACCIDENT

Eleanor was scribbling silly limericks, pausing every few lines to glance at the hazy brown sunset, when the creaking of the floorboards and the shuffle of fabric in the room distracted her.

She turned around to spy Edmund slowly approaching her, clad in his black silk pajamas. He walked without the cane, but his gait was still slower than normal.

"Good morning, darling." Eleanor stood up to greet him with a genuine smile of relief. "Good evening is more accurate, of course. How are you feeling?"

She kissed him gently on the lips, and he relished the sensation, but then pulled away self-consciously.

"Much better, dearest, thank you." Edmund sat down on the empty chaise across from where she had been lounging. "Don't let me distract you. You looked like you were deep in thought."

"Oh, I've just been jotting down silly limericks."

"I didn't know you wrote poetry!" he exclaimed.

"Poetry is certainly a stretch to describe it," Eleanor laughed. She pointed to her most ridiculous of verses:

There once was a colonel named Ed
Who never liked sleeping in bed
But a warm steaming bath
Quite an inkling he hath
For a wet rest to clear his nice head

"Ed, is it?" Edmund asked with a bemused smile.

"I told you they were silly, and making rhymes is really much harder than it seems." Eleanor was glad that he didn't seem to be offended. "It is a pastime I've done for years to occupy my mind, keeping it away from unpleasant thoughts."

Edmund looked pained as she said it.

"I didn't mean about you, darling."

He raised his eyebrows skeptically.

"Really, I didn't. We will figure out these mundane trivialities. I was distracting myself from thinking about Daisy and Lily. I've had a rather difficult time with them. They remind me of me when I was their age; although, even with his tragic faults, my father was far better than theirs is."

"Has that Ridgeway chap been giving you trouble?"

Eleanor could tell that Edmund was pushing back his instincts to rush right out and demonstrate to the brute the error of his ways. Part of her wouldn't have been upset if he had, but then she took a deep breath and remembered how much she loved her gentle soldier's exceptional self-control.

"Not me personally, no." Eleanor answered before his basest protective instincts became aroused. "I found Daisy and Lily in the hallway by our room last night when I returned from dinner. Daisy's wound from the Orient Express was dangerously infected. There were many hours when it seemed like Daisy might die from the ailment."

"Good lord," Edmund murmured. "Was that the commotion I heard in our room last night?"

"It was. I let them sleep here for a bit, before it was clear how dangerous Daisy's condition really was, and then I took them to... Actually, I don't want to tell you where I took them yet. I think it will be a nice surprise for you, when you're ready to explore beyond our room. In any event, I didn't sleep in our room last night. I slept with the girls to keep an eye on them. Daisy was doing much better by morning."

"Why didn't you just send them back to the Ridgeways? If they were my children, I would have been worried sick."

"I know exactly what you mean," Eleanor shrugged. "They begged me not to call their parents because they were afraid their father would beat their mother again. They've been hiding from him for two days in various nooks about the ship."

Edmund's eyes turned momentarily black at the idea, and he whispered a quiet mantra, relegating his vengeful instincts.

Eleanor sighed resignedly. "I can't say it was the biggest surprise. We both knew that man was bad news the moment we met him, and he has only proven himself to be a dastardly ignorant villain ever since. I told Mr. Corrigan to book a separate room where Mrs. Ridgeway can go with the girls if she needs to. I told him to put it on our bill. I hope that's alright?"

"You don't need to ask my permission to spend money, Eleanor," Edmund said seriously. "What's mine is yours. I mean that in every sense of the phrase, and I can't think of a better use of our copious funds than that."

Eleanor leaned forward and lured him into another kiss. "I love you, Edmund. I'm so glad I married you. Every time I learn something new about you, I love you even more."

Edmund moved from his chaise longue to hers to gather her into his arms for a stronger embrace, but as their passions began to grow, he pulled way with a miserable look on his face.

"I'm sorry. We shouldn't. I can still smell..." He closed his eyes and whispered his mantra, and then reopened them with their human hazel. "I don't believe for one second that you love every new thing you learn about me, Eleanor. At least you shouldn't."

"Hey," she protested as she stroked his cheek affectionately. "Didn't you love me more when you learned that my father shot himself? That I was a rotten little bastard who rode stolen horses against their owners' express orders for the undisciplined fun of it? Who ran away from home as a child to prove to my mother that she had no vision?"

"I wouldn't put it like that..." Edmund argued. "But I suppose I must admit that I did love you more when I learned those things... because I knew more about you. I knew why you were so beautiful. I had more evidence for what I already knew— that you were the strongest person I'd ever met in my century on Earth."

Eleanor smiled. "So why is it so hard for you to believe that when I learn the things that you dislike most about yourself, I love you more, Edmund?"

He thought about her clever (and truthful) point for a long time. "My darkest secrets are darker than yours, Eleanor. Even I don't want to know about them."

"Do you think that I want to think about the fact that my father shot himself? That he didn't care enough about us to face the music like a man? Or, even better, that it never occurred to him that his selfish farce would end as it did, and that *we* would be the ones to pay the price? What does that say about me, Edmund? That cheeky bastard is half of who I am!"

"You are nothing like that man," Edmund countered.

"The irony is that I am," Eleanor admitted. "I don't even want to think about it myself, but deep down I know that it's true. I'm a lot like him. My irreverence, my tenacity, even my fiery hair. They're all from him. No matter what I ever do, I will still be a walking, talking testament to Robby MacLeod. It's really bloody awful sometimes."

"I love all of those things about you," Edmund said as he felt one of her fiery tendrils with his fingers.

"So do I." Eleanor finally cracked a smile. "It's rather confusing. I suppose those characteristics are balanced in me by a certain type of hearty sensibleness that I inherited from my mother. For all her faults, I must thank for her that. They make everything I inherited from him a benefit instead of a curse. I think… I think perhaps that something similar might be true for you."

Eleanor knew that the statement landed her solidly in dangerous territory, but her irreverent tenacity wouldn't let her stand down.

"What do you mean by that?" Edmund asked, clearly startled by her assertion.

"I think, darling, that your humanity balances many of the foreign characteristics that torment you. I think that your mother's genes give you a certain strength… a strength that perhaps Mr. Johnson doesn't even have. Perhaps that's why he taught you to cling to your humanity when you're struggling against your dark urges. Have you ever considered that?"

"No, I can't say that I have…"

"Tell me this honestly, Edmund, no matter how unpleasant the answer is: What does the scent of my cycle do to you? How does it make you feel?"

Edmund took in a deep whiff, and closed his eyes again as he contemplated the idea.

"It arouses me." He cringed. "It makes me want to ravage you."

"And that's it? That's all it does to you? It doesn't make you want to drink my blood or eat me or feed me to the sharks?"

Edmund smiled at her silly exaggeration. "It does none of those things."

"Darling, it arouses me too. This is an entirely human conundrum you're facing. During this time of the month, I am very conscious of what's happening to me. It keeps my mind preoccupied, and often I feel especially aroused about nothing in particular."

Eleanor leaned forward and enticed him into a tender embrace.

"But, Eleanor… surely we mustn't," Edmund protested half-heartedly.

"Not if you don't want to," she agreed as she let him pull away.

"It's not that…" Edmund's eyes turned black as his entire body perked up at the prospect. "It's just… are you certain? Are you certain that you'd like to try it?"

"Darling, I've done it before. It is a bit messy, I will admit, but we have plenty of towels. We should, I think, use the bed, though. I don't want to tempt fate by trying it in the bath."

Edmund hopped up and pulled her into his arms with more enthusiasm than she'd seen since their wedding night. He escorted her as hastily as his sluggish body would allow to the bed, and helped her undress. She neatly folded her special Yakshini underwear as he gathered several fresh towels from the bathroom, and then she slipped off his silk pajamas and invited him into the bed.

She felt his heart racing as he entered her, and she kept her gaze locked on his black eyes as their passion mounted. He had a certain vigor to him in his altered state, a vigor that she found strangely captivating. He was a bit rougher than normal, but still remarkably controlled, and she reveled in the unusual sensations.

"Ravage me, Edmund," she whispered.

He growled as he kicked up his vigor another notch, and together, they set about exploring the most pleasant of many options for dealing with Eleanor's monthly feminine cycle.

When they were finished, Eleanor slipped out of the bed, grabbed her Yakshini panties and the wet towels, and scampered to clean herself in the bath while Edmund rested in the bed with satisfied sighs.

406

"How are you feeling?" she asked when she returned and nestled into the nook of his arm to place her head on his cool chest.

"Relieved," he admitted. "You have more faith in me than I have in myself, Eleanor. I suppose that has always been the case."

"I've told you many times that I have impeccable judgment. Maybe one of these days you'll believe me." She began running her fingers along his chest in gentle tickling patterns.

Edmund kissed her forehead. "You make my life so beautiful, my dearest thistle. I never dreamed I'd meet someone like you. I never dared to dream that someone like you existed at all."

"Oo! Speaking of wonderful people, how are you feeling, darling? Are you up for going to dinner? I have a wonderful surprise for you. I think we might be able to make it late if we hurry."

"I'm not sure if it's a good idea... I'm still not back to my strongest self."

"I see... so you're like the rest of us slow, weak humans at the moment?" Eleanor teased him. "You seemed perfectly strong and fast just now."

"I suppose I need to be properly motivated." He smiled as he gave in.

"Oh darling, you must trust me. This surprise is sufficiently motivating. I *promise*." Eleanor hopped up and pulled him up into her arms. "Chop chop, Colonel! We're late!" She slapped his bum naughtily as she shooed him into the bathroom. "I'll select the most appropriate suit for you. It's so lovely and warm outside. I suppose that's how it will be from now on as we get closer and closer to the tropics."

She rushed into the closet and dug through his trunk, pulling out a perfectly-tailored white linen suit that must have been made for him in anticipation of the warmer leg of their journey. She laid it out on the couch and then dug through her own trunk excitedly for another perfectly-curated warm-weather outfit. She pulled out a green silk flapper dress with an elaborate floral design embroidered into the fabric with black sparkling sequins and beads.

She squeezed into it and rushed to check her hair, which was maintaining Kuveni's Roman design with unusual fortitude, and then she hastily put on some perfunctory makeup, while Edmund dressed himself up in his new suit.

"This is rather comfortable, isn't it?" he said happily as he pulled on the jacket. "I don't know what I'll do with myself in the tropics without a wool army uniform. It will be a completely new experience! I suppose I should be wearing a tuxedo to dinner, but I'm not feeling up to the stiff collar."

"Come on," she said excitedly as she grabbed his hand. "They wouldn't dare turn away Colonel Marriner on his first night of recovery."

She guided him out of the room, leaving the door unlocked, and retraced her steps straight to the elevator. He looked around the ship with freshly observant eyes, and held her hand, rubbing her palm secretly with his finger.

As they approached the open double doors of the first class dining room, Eleanor was practically bursting with excitement.

"Welcome, Colonel!" one of the hosts greeted them. "Your party has already begun eating. Please follow me!"

"My party?" Edmund asked curiously.

Eleanor watched his face as they followed the host, waiting for the moment when his eyes would light up with recognition.

"Strewth, you're a sight for sore eyes, mate!" Oz exclaimed as he noticed their approach.

Edmund grinned and squeezed Eleanor's hand excitedly. "This is a wonderful surprise, dearest. I'm glad you let me experience it in its full glory."

He let go of her hand to shake Oz's in both of his.

"Glad to see you're on the up and up, Colonel. We were worried about you!" Oz said as Yvie joined them to offer Edmund her traditional French cheek kisses.

"Come. We had them seat us at a table for four in the hopes that you'd feel well enough to join us." Yvie gestured to the waiters, who swiftly set two extra place-settings.

"I was telling them about your unfortunate accident, Edmund. About how you fell through the ruins at Ephesus into some catacombs below an ancient church," Eleanor explained proactively to get him straight into her cover story.

"Oh yes. Don't go spreading it around." Edmund added, taking her pass and running with it. "It was a clumsy move, if I do say so myself. But Eleanor was most supportive of my recovery. I'm still not entirely back to normal, but I'm most of the way there now."

"We are ever so glad to hear it," Oz said as they each took their seats and the waiters rushed to pour them some red wine.

Eleanor lowered her voice. "How are the Ridgeways?"

"As good as can be expected, I suppose," Yvie shrugged. "I gave Mrs. Ridgeway the medicine along with very specific instructions. We are planning to stop by their room after dinner to make sure they are complying with our orders. If they stop the medicine too early, the infection might come back even worse. I've seen that happen many times now, and the second time around, the medicine never works."

"Those poor girls," Eleanor murmured, and then she cheered herself up, refusing to let the Ridgeway's problems sully her otherwise pleasant evening. "Oz, I believe that you owe Edmund a story about selling Yvie to a camel trader in Egypt on your honeymoon."

Oz grinned, and dove right into the story, telling it with twice the drama (and the number of camels) the second time around.

They sat together in jovial conversation for hours enjoying each other's company, as Edmund picked unenthusiastically at his food, to Oz and Yvie's unspoken attention, until they were enjoying a final pot of tea, and Mr. Corrigan, looking rather tired, approached their table.

"I just wanted to let you know, Mrs. Marriner, that Mrs. Ridgeway and the girls are sleeping in the room you provided for them tonight. I'm not sure what the right protocol is for keeping you informed, but they are in room number twelve on the fifth floor. Normally I would never report anything so private, but I understand that Dr. and Mrs. Helmsworth were planning to check up on the girls."

"Thank you for the update, Mr. Corrigan. I'm certain that it is in everyone's best interest for us to keep an eye on Daisy's recovery," Eleanor reassured him, offering him a merciful excuse to not publicly state the other reason the girls were likely seeking refuge in a separate room from their father.

Mr. Corrigan bowed, but as he left them alone and walked across the dining room towards the kitchen door, Eleanor heard a subtle crack, and as he and several other people looked up to identify the source, a large crystal chandelier fell from the ceiling, landing right on top of him.

"Good lord!" Eleanor and Edmund exclaimed in unison.

"Strewth!"

"*Mon dieu!*"

Oz and Yvie rushed to his side. Eleanor ran after them, and Edmund, tired after his long night and not yet fully recovered, made his way more slowly to the scene.

Several of the waiters rushed to help Oz lift the heavy object off of Mr. Corrigan's limp body, and Eleanor and Yvie immediately began taking his vital signs, while Oz leaned down to listen for breath.

"He's alive," Oz reported.

"His pulse is slow but recovering," Eleanor seconded.

"The back of his head is bleeding. He probably has a concussion," Yvie added.

"Look here, his collar bone is broken as well. There and there." Eleanor pointed. "It looks like the cuts are minor, though."

"Mr. Corrigan?" Oz called. "Mr. Corrigan, can you hear me? Try to open your eyes if you can hear me."

Edmund watched helplessly as his three companions used their medical expertise to tend to the ailing man, but as Mr. Corrigan continued to remain unconscious, Oz finally decided to make the next move. "Let's get him to a private place where he can rest. We'll keep a close eye on him there."

Edmund moved to help him pick Mr. Corrigan up, but Oz brushed him off. "We don't need two injured men, Colonel. You are still on the up and up, and you should keep it that way. These fine men will be perfectly sufficient. Won't you?"

The waiters rushed to help him, and Edmund begrudgingly gave in. "Get yourself to bed and rest, Colonel. We will see to Mr. Corrigan, and we will keep you updated."

"Let me know if I can help," Eleanor said as Yvie followed the men out of the dining room.

"We will!" she called. "Oh, Ellie, follow up with the Ridgeways, will you? Daisy must have her dose of the medicine tonight!"

"Alright!" Eleanor called.

Edmund looked down at the remnants of the chandelier, and then up to the place where it had fallen. He kneeled down and gathered the broken chord in his hand.

"It's frayed." He squinted to inspect it in the dim light.

"Someone did this on purpose," Eleanor whispered as she inspected it with her own eyes. "And their timing was absolutely impeccable."

"You don't think it could have been Mr. Ridgeway, do you? As retribution for his wife and daughters switching to another room?"

Eleanor thought carefully about his assertion. "I don't think he has the skill to do something like this. Do you? He was a chemist during the war. You saw how clumsy he was on the train. I'm not even sure how they did this. They must have frayed the chord

411

perfectly for it to stay attached to the ceiling with no sign of an electrical problem, and then they did something else at the very last minute to cause it to fall… but why?"

"Good lord. I hope this isn't another mystery to solve," Edmund sighed. "Solving mysteries is not really my cup of tea."

"I know, darling. I know," Eleanor commiserated. She stealthily placed the frayed chord in her pocket, and then wrapped her arm around his and guided him towards the door. "Let's go check up on Daisy, and then get to bed. I have a sneaking suspicion that we will need all the sleep we can get before this mystery gets any deeper."

Edmund sighed with stress. "Happy honeymoon, dearest."

"I am happy, Edmund," Eleanor replied truthfully.

"So am I," he agreed as he squeezed her arm.

"Onward, husband!" Eleanor declared. "Together we shall save the day!"

CHAPTER 26 – WATCHING OVER

"Please, Edmund, follow my lead," Eleanor said as they reached the door of the Ridgeways' safe haven room. "And do not argue with the children if they refer to you as an angel." She cringed as she revealed the detail that she knew he would not be the least bit happy about.

"An angel?".

"They were going on and on about you being an abominable snowman, darling. I think we both know who's to blame for that one. And so, I told them you were an angel in disguise." Edmund tensed, working hard to control his annoyance, and Eleanor pushed forward. "Darling, they understand angels. The reference makes it easy for them to believe that no matter what they saw you do, you are still a good person. Do you know of any other explanation a small child would be able to comprehend?"

"I suppose I don't. But, dearest, this is not a farce I am prepared to perpetuate. What about Mrs. Ridgeway? Am I to tell her I'm an angel as well?"

"She will believe what she wants to believe, darling, no matter what you say. My guess is that she will understand and appreciate that your little farce is for the children, while assuming that you are the result of some sort of army experiment, which is, by the way, what Oz and Yvie assumed. Do you like that explanation better?"

Edmund thought about the prospect. "Not really. I suppose I don't like any explanation. They are all similarly inaccurate or incomplete."

"Well, at least you are aware of your own limitations on the matter now," Eleanor winked. "Now, my angel in disguise, we have some children to check up on."

"But, Eleanor... tell me truly... *you* don't believe I'm an angel, do you? Please tell me you don't..."

"Darling, that was no angel who ravaged me earlier tonight," she whispered mischievously.

Edmund finally smiled, relegating his nerves, and Eleanor took his hand into hers, rolled her shoulders, and knocked loudly on the door.

"Mrs. Ridgeway? It's Eleanor. We've come to check on Daisy. Dr. Helmsworth is otherwise occupied," Eleanor called.

"Dr. Helmsworth?" Edmund whispered.

"If you're an angel, he can be a doctor," Eleanor winked. "He knows more about medicine than any civilian doctor I've ever met. It's not his fault the war got in the way of him finishing medical school. Anyway, can you imagine what kind of cockamamie wives' tales they would have taught him at a rural medical school in Australia?"

"I hate to think of it," Edmund admitted.

"Mrs. Ridgeway?" Eleanor called.

Squealing and clomping inside the room indicated that the children were, in fact, inside. Eleanor tried the door handle, realized it was unlocked, and pushed it open. With one look from her position huddled on the floor crying in the corner of the room, Lily jumped right up and ran into Eleanor's arms.

414

"Mummy's gone mad!" Lily exclaimed.

On top of the bed, Mrs. Ridgeway was fully dressed, high-heeled shoes and all, standing over Daisy, who was screaming and kicking her away.

"Take the bloody medicine!" Mrs. Ridgeway screeched as she tried unsuccessfully to force a dose of Yvie's bitter powder into Daisy's mouth, spilling it all over the bed as Daisy fought back.

Eleanor rushed to break up Mrs. Ridgeway's attack on her sick daughter.

"Eloise, stop it this instant!" Eleanor ordered sharply.

Mrs. Ridgeway broke out of her stupor and collapsed onto the bed beside Daisy in tears.

"Good lord," Edmund murmured at the train wreck unfolding before them.

"I tried!" she exclaimed. "I tried to follow their orders. Really, I did! But these girls just won't listen!" She threw a terrified look at Edmund. "Really, I tried. I swear, Colonel!"

Edmund threw Eleanor a searching look. "I am not here to punish you, Mrs. Ridgeway."

Mrs. Ridgeway did not look like she entirely believed him.

Lily looked up at him, and instead of fear, a look of utter relief crossed her face. "Please help us, Edmund. Can I call you Edmund? Or should I call you something else? They call the angels by their first names in the Bible, don't they?"

"You may certainly call me Edmund," he agreed diplomatically.

Eleanor coaxed Daisy out of her position with her face hidden under the pillows, tucking her into the bed and feeling her forehead. She still had a mild fever.

"Daisy, darling, how are you feeling?" Eleanor gently gathered up Daisy's hand to examine its progress. "You are looking a bit better, but you will need to take your medicine, or you will feel very horrible again. Even worse than you felt last night. Don't you want to feel better?"

"But it hurts!" Daisy cried. "The medicine tastes too bad! It hurts my throat to swallow it, and then it hurts my mouth, and then it hurts my tummy!"

"I see." Eleanor climbed onto the bed and stroked Daisy's hair soothingly until Daisy relaxed. "Have any of you eaten anything tonight?"

Mrs. Ridgeway nodded in the negative as she gave into silent tears, observing her daughter's calm reaction to Eleanor's alternative tactics.

Eleanor looked across the room to Lily holding onto Edmund's leg as he stood by the door. "Edmund, darling, can you call room service from the phone by the door? I think the Ridgeways need some dinner. Ask them to bring meals for three, plus all of the desserts on the menu, and double the ice cream, if they have it. And two very large glasses of milk."

Edmund gently coaxed Lily off of his leg. "Perhaps you would be more comfortable on the couch?"

She obediently followed his advice.

As he called in the order, Eleanor continued to stroke Daisy's hair soothingly. "Medicine often tastes bitter," she explained to the child and Mrs. Ridgeway simultaneously with the same tone she used to calm her patients (and her husband) after the peak of their shell-shocked episodes. "It is not uncommon for it to hurt your tummy. But if you eat it with food, especially tasty food like ice cream, then your tummy doesn't even know it's there, and it can do its work. Did you like the ice cream you ate last night and this morning, Daisy?"

Daisy nodded her agreement.

"There was medicine in that ice cream. We will put your dose of medicine in the ice cream again tonight, and if they don't have any ice cream, we will put it in something even tastier. I know they have chocolate cake. I ate it just an hour ago. Do you like chocolate cake?"

"Mm hmm," Daisy sighed with relief.

416

Edmund finished up his order and sat down on a chaise opposite Lily, but she quietly crawled out of her spot to sit next to him.

"They said they would be here as soon as they could manage it. Mr. Corrigan is apparently doing better, but he hasn't woken up yet. Oz and Yvie are staying with him," Edmund said as Lily nestled her head into the nook of his arm, throwing herself against his upper body in several attempts to find a comfortable position.

He looked to Eleanor for guidance, but she only shrugged.

"You're warm now," Lily pointed out. "Not cold like you were before."

"I have many temperatures," he explained vaguely.

He gathered up a large pillow and placed it on his lap so that Lily could lie down. She took his offer and nestled in, and he stretched his arms out across the back of the chaise, unsure of what else to do with them with the resting child in his lap.

"I'm sorry," Mrs. Ridgeway finally whispered. "I'm a hopeless mother, and I always have been, and *twins*. Good lord, Eleanor. You cannot imagine how difficult it was having twins and being alone all day every day while George was at work. We didn't even have a nanny! He said that it was my womanly duty to earn my keep by raising them up all by myself!"

"Eloise, your daughters have ears." Eleanor worked hard to curtail the sharp tone of her voice as Eloise demonstrated a similar quality to one that had always infuriated her about her own mother. "They are not infants anymore. They understand everything you say, and they absorb it. That includes everything that you and George say and do to each other."

Eloise only sobbed quietly.

"We're not here to judge you," Eleanor said calmly. "Although, while we're on the topic… your girls are very good at communicating, Eloise. Did it even occur to you to ask Daisy why she didn't want to take the medicine?" Eloise stared up at the silken canopy with silent tears. "They can help you, if you let them. Daisy, will you help Mummy? Will you tell her why you are being disobedient from now on? Will you give her a chance to convince you to be obedient before you run away from her or do any other loud, wild protestation?"

"Yes, Mummy," Daisy agreed.

"Me too, Mummy," Lily called from the couch.

"And Eloise, you must try to reason with them," Eleanor advised. "Chasing them around, screaming at them, and trying to force them to do something they don't want to do is not going to work. They are already big enough to fight you off, and can you imagine how those tactics will play out when they are even a little bit bigger? You aren't going to be able to force a teenaged girl to do anything. You must help them choose the right path for themselves, and you must start now."

"I am not in a position to help them," Eloise said dismally. "I have horrible judgment myself. Lily would rather cuddle up to a stranger who killed five men in cold blood right before her eyes than to her own worthless father."

Edmund shuddered at her reference, and Eleanor threw Eloise a furious look of disapproval. "Ears, Eloise. They have ears. We all have ears, for that matter."

"I'm sorry, Colonel," Eloise whispered. "I didn't mean anything by it. You saved our lives that day. It was bound to be bloody with those murderous bolshies killing a priest."

"Mummy, sometimes angels have to kill, but they don't like it one bit," Lily informed her matter-of-factly. "Isn't that right, Edmund?"

"Yes. Yes, that is right," he agreed. "That's why it's important for humans to avoid bloody fighting in the first place, so that the angels don't have to kill. If those men had made their demands just with words, no one would have been killed."

"No one would have listened to them," Eloise pointed out. "Men only kill when they believe they have no other choice."

418

"If only that were true," Eleanor said wistfully. "I believe you are sadly mistaken, Eloise. Many men jump to arms before it is necessary. Your husband is a prime example."

"No one listened to those revolutionaries anyway," Edmund added. "And now at least twelve people are dead, and your children know what death looks like. All of it was for nothing, and worthless suffering is certainly enough to make the angels weep."

A knock at the door released them from their increasingly uncomfortable conversation.

"Come in," Edmund called.

Two waiters pushed in a room service cart covered in silver platters.

"Just leave it, and we will tend to it ourselves," Edmund suggested. "Send Mr. Corrigan our regards."

"Yes, sir." The boys bowed and scurried out of the room, closing the door behind them.

"Are you hungry?" Edmund asked Lily as she sat up and began sniffing the warm food's aroma.

"I suppose," she conceded. "I don't like to eat when Daisy is sick. My tummy always hurts when she doesn't feel well."

"Well, Daisy is going to eat too, isn't she?" Eleanor said cheerfully as she hopped off the bed and approached the cart.

She half-expected to see three heaping carpenter's pies as she pulled off the silver covers, but instead, three servings of the same beef wellington they'd eaten at dinner with mushy green beans and peas in the English style awaited them.

"Mmm... beef wellington!" Eleanor exclaimed disingenuously. "And look, chocolate cake!"

Lily finally stood up to join Eleanor in assessing her options, and Eloise reluctantly joined her, leaving Daisy alone in the bed.

"Three pieces of chocolate cake *and* vanilla ice cream! How lucky you are! We didn't have vanilla ice cream when we ate in the dining room, did we, Edmund?" Eleanor exclaimed. "Daisy, darling, would you like to start your meal with dessert? Only sick little girls get to eat dessert first."

"Okay," she agreed as she sat up.

"Would you like to do the honors?" Eleanor asked Mrs. Ridgeway. Eloise was at a loss as to what she might possibly mean. "The medicine," Eleanor whispered. "*Now* is the best time to put the medicine in the ice cream."

Eleanor could see a well of tears ready to burst. "I'd already forgotten!" Eloise wailed. "I'd forgotten about the medicine completely! I'm a terrible mother!"

"Blimey," Eleanor whispered. "Watch how I do it, and then you can do it next time, alright?"

Eloise wiped her tears and took in a sniffling, resigned breath. She handed Eleanor the vial of powder, already half-empty thanks to her unwise waste of the substance that was still littering the bed where Daisy was lying, and Eleanor worked it into the ice cream with a spoon, placed the ice cream in a big bite of chocolate cake, and carried it over to feed to Daisy in bed.

"I wish I could eat dessert first!" Lily declared.

"There, you see, Daisy. You have a special privilege that even Lily doesn't have. Now open up for chocolate cake and ice cream," Eleanor said as she brought the bite to Daisy's mouth and fed it to her.

Daisy's face contorted as she swallowed. "It's still bitter. Kate's ice cream was better."

Eleanor hoped that Edmund wouldn't smell her pang of anxiety at Daisy's unintentional revelation of Kuveni's presence. "Well, now you have an entire piece of chocolate cake to wash it down with. How about some milk, too?"

She gestured to Eloise, who ignored her until she realized that Eleanor was telling her to gather the milk from the room service cart.

"Oh for god's sake, Eloise. Pay attention," Eloise muttered to herself as she rushed to comply. She brought the glass of milk to Daisy's side and held it while Daisy ate a few more bites of cake.

"That's better, isn't it?" Eleanor asked as Daisy thirstily drank down the entire glass of milk. "Now, why don't you wait for a few minutes to make sure your tummy is feeling alright, and then you can have more food. Any food you want."

Eleanor squeezed Daisy's uninjured little hand and then escorted Eloise back to the room service cart.

"Eleanor... please forgive my ignorance... but shouldn't Daisy be eating healthy food?" Eloise asked timidly.

"At the moment she is weak. Her body needs anything she can keep down to help it fight off the infection," Eleanor explained. "And now she has Yvie's medicine to help. Did your mother not let you eat whatever you could stomach when you were sick as a child?"

Eleanor thought back fondly to the only times her mother coddled her as a child. She'd resented her mother for years for the unpleasant truth that she'd often wished she was sick in order to gain her mother's tender support... She pushed the thought away.

"My mother died in childbirth," Eloise admitted. "I have no bloody clue how to be a mother. I've never seen anyone do it."

Suddenly, Eleanor's harsh judgment of Eloise's many shortcomings melted into pity.

"You should eat too. You're looking malnourished and exhausted," Eleanor advised. "Have you been sleeping?"

"I've only slept a few hours since the incident on the train. My mind won't let me forget the images." Eloise glanced at Edmund as she spoke.

Eleanor rubbed Eloise's back. "That is very common for people who have experienced a trauma like you did. But you must rest, Eloise. An insomniac mind breaks down. It makes the symptoms worse. I have helped many thousands of soldiers combat similar symptoms after the war. If you want, we can stay with you in here tonight, if it will help you sleep better. Edmund will make sure we don't have any uninvited guests…" She hoped that Eloise understood that she was referring to George, and that perhaps she would understand the importance of such subtlety in front of the children. "Unless you think Edmund's presence will disturb you more. You can be honest with us, Eloise. He will not take offense."

Eloise glanced over at him, and he offered her a timid, reassuring smile.

"Yes. Please stay," she decided. "It is not the colonel who frightens me. His actions were entirely logical, given the circumstances. My mind keeps anticipating that more Bolsheviks will burst through the door any second."

"Then we'll stay. Edmund and I have both slept quite soundly in the last few days. We will keep watch until morning, and when you're awake, we will go back to our room."

Eloise fought back another round of tears and pulled Eleanor into a weak hug. "No one has ever cared this much about me. I've longed so desperately to not feel so alone."

"Eat," Eleanor said gently.

Eloise gathered her wits and collected a plate to eat on the couch opposite Edmund, and Lily followed her and sat down right next to her mother. Eloise threw Eleanor a surprised look, and Eleanor offered her a supportive smile.

"Lily, you like sitting with Mummy, don't you?" Eleanor asked.

"When she's not mad," Lily replied honestly as she began eating the puff pastry of the beef with her fingers.

"Darling," Eloise hissed as she glanced at Edmund and Eleanor with embarrassment. "Use a fork and knife."

"But I don't know how!" Lily argued.

"Very good!" Eleanor exclaimed. She applauded, and Eloise and Lily both looked at her confusedly. "Lily, did you just tell

Mummy why you were being disobedient, just like you promised you would?"

Lily's face lit up with excitement at her unintentional good deed.

"Eloise, Lily just explained to you *why* she was acting that way. Now you can teach her what she needs to know."

Eloise set about showing Lily how she wanted her to eat. With a few minor mistakes, Lily proudly began emulating her mother.

Eleanor sat down beside Edmund, and he took her hand tightly into his.

"I love you so much, Eleanor," he whispered into her ear.

Eleanor sighed with many mixed emotions as she nestled into his arms.

They sat quietly for a long while as Eloise and Lily finished up their food, and Eloise made her best attempt to feed Daisy some beef wellington, until all three of them gave into exhaustion.

Eloise took Lily into the bathroom to help her wash up, and then Eleanor tucked them in beside Daisy, and switched off the light.

"Might we leave one on?" Eloise asked. "The darkness torments my mind."

Eleanor switched on the bathroom light. "How about that? You can see everything in the room, but it is not so bright as to keep you awake. Shall we try it?"

"Thank you, Eleanor. You really are angels in disguise, aren't you?" Eloise asked weepily.

"One doesn't have to be an angel to be kind, Eloise," Eleanor said gently. "But we will be right here all night all the same."

Eleanor joined Edmund on the chaise and placed her head on the pillow in his lap. "Is this alright, darling? Or do you need to lie down yourself?"

"I'm perfectly fine, Eleanor. I've had plenty of time to rest."

And together, with two kind angelic guardians watching over, the tragic Ridgeway girls slept.

Eleanor awoke in the middle of the night to a loud banging on the door.

"Eloise!!! What in god's name is this foolishness?!" Mr. Ridgeway's livid voice boomed. His slurred words indicated that he was well-lubricated with drink. "Eloise Ridgeway, you come out of there this instant, or I'll ring your bloody neck, you hear?!"

Eleanor scrambled out of Edmund's lap, and Edmund stood right up while the girls and Eloise all whimpered.

"Stay right where you are. I will deal with him," Edmund addressed them with feigned calm authority.

Eloise moved to protest, and then she gathered her girls into her arms. "Do what you must, Colonel."

"Remember your mantras, darling. Keep yourself under control."

He took a deep breath as he approached the door. He whispered his mantras and swung it open. Eleanor stood many feet behind him, watching carefully for any signal that Edmund might miss about Mr. Ridgeway's next foolish move.

Mr. Ridgeway stumbled backwards with shock at the unexpected twist.

"Colonel?" he asked as he leaned up against the wall to steady himself. His face was red, his eyes glassy, his sling with his injured arm dirty, and his shirt stained with sweat. "I'm… I'm… I'm sorry, I must have gotten the room number wrong…" Mr. Ridgeway paused as he contemplated the unexpected circumstances. "I'll ring that waiter's neck when I get my hands on him," he muttered to himself. Then he switched into an attempt to act casual. "I didn't intend to disturb you, Colonel. You know how it is on these ships. All the bloody halls look the same. Rather like a train, I reckon." He exploded into awkward, nervous laughter.

"And what exactly were your intentions, banging on anyone's door with such threats in the middle of the night?" Edmund asked sharply.

"I… I… I was looking for my wife! My daughters! I was worried about them!" Mr. Ridgeway's attempt to casually brush off his abusive tirade dissolved into desperation.

"Well then, let me ease your mind, Mr. Ridgeway. They are perfectly fine, and they will be even more fine after many more hours of safe sleep without a drunken fool to keep them awake."

Mr. Ridgeway's fear morphed into anger. "They *are* in there?! Eloise? What is *wrong* with you?" He turned his attention on Edmund. "You can't keep my children away from me. They're mine!"

"I most certainly can," Edmund countered. Eleanor shivered as a wave of power emanated off of him. "And they are not your slaves. They belong to no one. Now, you will return to your room now, and we will deal with this like civilized British citizens in the morning when you are sober."

Mr. Ridgeway took one look around the empty hallway, and then rushed straight at Edmund. Eloise screamed, and Eleanor held her breath as Edmund dodged Mr. Ridgeway's clumsy drunken attack and gathered him into a simple chokehold, pulling him into the room and slamming the door behind him.

Mr. Ridgeway squirmed and grunted, but Edmund held him steadfastly in his grip.

"Eleanor, why don't you take Eloise and the girls to their room," Edmund suggested. "I will join you shortly."

"Please don't kill him, Edmund!" Lily exclaimed. "Please don't kill Daddy! He'll get better, I promise! We can help him get better!"

Edmund looked deeply pained. "I am *not* going to kill him." He looked straight at each of the Ridgeways as he spoke. "Your father and I are going to have a little chat, and then I will lock him in here until morning so that he can sober up, and you can get some rest."

Eloise helped the girls out of bed, and Mr. Ridgeway wriggled like an ornery toddler trying to get out of Edmund's grip as they passed.

"Come along, girls," Eloise whispered as she threw her husband a look of distinct disdain.

Eleanor followed her out. "I will get them settled in."

"We're in room ten on the third floor, Colonel," Eloise added.

Edmund nodded his agreement. Eleanor closed the door behind them, but all four of them stopped in the hallway to listen.

"What is *wrong* with you?" Edmund booming voice resonated through the door. "Have you so little sense that you would destroy your family? The most precious gift you have ever been given? You would terrorize your wife and your children for the sport of it? Get it together, man! Where's your bloody honor?" Mr. Ridgeway's protestations were muffled. "I don't care about excuses! I will be back in the morning, and you'd best be sober, or you will find out what the British Army does with despicable, abusive scoundrels. Do you understand? That is 'I understand, *sir*'!"

Eleanor couldn't help but smile. She had a sneaking suspicion that Edmund had given that brand of speech many times before, and after their weeks of focused attention on his superhuman qualities, the reminder of his many decades as an exceptional human leader was nice.

He left Mr. Ridgeway alone, locking the door from the outside, and then he stopped to take in his audience. A deep red blush worked its way onto his face.

"I did not intend for you to listen to that," he said self-consciously.

"Edmund, do you think Daddy will find his bloody honor?" Lily asked innocently.

Edmund sighed with resignation and kneeled down to address her eye to eye. "I will do what I can to help him try, but people must find these things for themselves, Lily. No one can make them do it. But you must always remember that you are not responsible for his actions, and it is not your responsibility to make him a better person. All you can do is make yourself a better person, a stronger person, who will succeed and live a happy life no matter what he does."

"But how can I do that if Daddy is a despicable scoundrel?"

"You can," Eleanor interjected. "Just like I did."

"I didn't even know my father," Edmund added. "I grew up in an orphanage."

"But what about Kate?" Lily asked. "Didn't you grow up with Kate? She said she was like your big sister!"

Edmund threw Eleanor a look of intrigue, and Eleanor's heart almost exploded as he stood back up to address her.

"You talked to Kate? Kate Marriner? She was here, on this ship?" He glanced back and forth between Eleanor and Lily questioningly.

Eleanor could see his mind moving a mile a second to process the implications. What the implications were to him, she couldn't even guess.

"She gave us chocolate ice cream!" Lily exclaimed. "It was much better than the ice cream we ate last night."

"Kate was here, and you talked to her too, Eleanor?" Edmund pressed.

"Yes, Edmund, darling, she was here. Let's talk about it later," Eleanor evaded. "Let's get the Ridgeways settled in, and then we can return to our room and discuss it."

Eleanor took Lily's hand, and Eloise carried Daisy, as the group made their way to the elevator and finally to the Ridgeways' original room.

"Thank you so much for your help." Eloise looked around her messy room with bewilderment. "We should be fine on our own for the time being."

"You must make sure that Daisy takes her medicine in the morning," Eleanor ordered sternly. "You have seen how to successfully get her to do it now without a fight."

"Yes... yes, of course..." Eloise murmured.

"Get some rest," Eleanor advised more gently. "You should sleep as long as you can, and we will be around tomorrow to check in on you."

"Good night, Eleanor! Good night, Edmund!" Lily pulled each of them into a hug. "You're the best angels in the world!"

"Good night," Eloise whispered as she looked to each of them self-consciously as she closed the door.

Eleanor sighed with stress and resignation. "Let's go back to our room, darling. We can talk there."

Eleanor's mind raced as she contemplated how she was going to explain her blatant lie about Kate as they made their way silently back to their room. She could tell Edmund was upset. Upset at her. For the first time in their relationship, he was genuinely and rightfully upset at her for her dishonesty, as he should have been all along.

She cringed as Edmund closed the door behind them, but before he said a word to her, he picked up the phone and dialed the operator.

"Yes, this is Colonel Marriner. I'd like to speak to the Chief of Security right now... There is a drunken fool in room ten on the fifth floor. He is locked away where he can't do any harm, and he is to stay that way until I say otherwise, do you understand? He is not to be let out if he calls for assistance. You can tell him that the British Army thanks him for his support. Thank you."

He hung up and took a deep, calming breath as he prepared for his uncomfortable confrontation.

"Eleanor, why didn't you tell me that Kate was here?"

Eleanor wasn't prepared for such a direct question.

"She came to check up on you after your turmeric reaction. She asked me not to tell you, darling. I wasn't sure what to do."

Edmund paused to contemplate her statement. "I don't understand. I don't understand why they are toying with me in this way. Toying with you. How wretched for them to put you in such a position. Asking you to lie to me. I don't like it."

Eleanor couldn't believe he was letting her off so easily. "I don't like it either, darling. I hate being in that position. But I honestly don't know what to do. They tell me these things that they don't want you to know, and I'm not sure, darling, if they are right or wrong."

"Do you think... Do you think that they've always done this? Checked up on me without my knowledge? But now you, dearest, are here when they come?"

"I think it is a likely possibility," Eleanor agreed.

Edmund seemed to be cataloguing something in his head... his memories, perhaps, of other odd instances, even turmeric reactions, when Kuveni and Mélusine had stepped in.

"Would you have been happier if I'd told you that Kate had come while you were asleep and then skipped off before you could talk to her?" Eleanor asked, genuinely unsure of his answer.

Edmund thought carefully about her question. "I would have felt similarly to how I feel now, I suppose. But you would have felt better not being forced to choose between keeping her confidence and keeping mine."

"Please, don't worry about me, Edmund. Really, I'm a big girl. But tell me honestly how you really feel. If they do something like this again, what would you like me to do? Do you want me to tell you, even when they ask me not to?"

Edmund pulled her into his arms and kissed her gently.

"I trust you, Eleanor. I trust your judgment. Do what you think is right. They don't tell me anything they don't want me to know anyway. It's not as if I can force the matter. I think that perhaps stubbornness is a trait that I share with them."

"And with me," Eleanor smiled as she relaxed. "I love you, Edmund. I hope that you can forgive me for every loving lie I'm ever forced to tell you."

"I forgive you for every indiscretion that my wretched circumstances submit you to, dearest. I have no one to blame but myself... and Mr. Johnson, I suppose. Although, blaming one's father is a bit clichéd, I think. I'd rather just bear the brunt of the responsibility myself."

Eleanor guided him to the bed and enticed him into a deeper embrace.

"Would you like to prove to me one more time before the sun comes up that you're not an angel?"

Edmund's eyes turned black at the prospect, and he licked her lips in response.

And so, as her beautiful divine demon set about gently ravaging her, Eleanor reveled in her husband's exceptional forgiveness until long after the sun came up.

CHAPTER 27 – UNEXPECTED VISITORS

Eleanor had been lazing about in bed for hours watching the sun rise high in the sky through the open shutters while Edmund slept soundly by her side, when a knock at the door finally wrested her from her wonderfully relaxing morning.

"Just a minute," Eleanor called.

She hoped that it wasn't another crisis from the Ridgeways, as she'd left the 'do not disturb' sign prominently on the door, and the staff so far had been nicely respectful of her wishes.

Edmund stirred and took in a deep Rakshasa breath as he opened his eyes.

"Good morning, dearest," he said happily as he pulled her into his arms for a morning kiss. "I haven't slept that well in a human bed since… well, ever, I think. Did you sleep alright?"

"Yes, perfectly well," Eleanor said distractedly, wondering if the person who had knocked had passed. Another knock answered her question. "I hope it isn't the Ridgeways. I could use a day without thinking about their plight."

She got up and slipped on her red kimono, and Edmund followed, hopping around the room as he put on the black silk pajamas that Eleanor had enthusiastically helped him take off in the heat of passion the day before.

Eleanor swung open the door, and Edmund's eyes lit up.

"Well, aren't you a sight for sore eyes! Come in!" Edmund pulled Mr. Valov into the room and closed the door behind him. "You must forgive our mess. We've been staying in, and you, more than anyone, know what pigs we can be."

Mr. Valov smiled and shook Edmund's hand amicably, but Eleanor spotted him subtly looking around the room, doing a quick survey... of what, she wished she knew.

"If you give us just a few minutes to tidy up, we can call for some breakfast! Are you hungry? Speaking of which, how did you get here?" Edmund spoke with the enthusiasm of someone who had just surprisingly run into an old friend.

"There will not be any breakfast, Colonel. It is almost three o'clock in the afternoon," Mr. Valov said distractedly as he eyed the pile of stained towels in the bathroom. "I flew from Constantinople to Aden and boarded there. We left Aden early this morning, and from here we will have four days at sea before we reach Bombay. Is everything alright?"

He addressed his question to Eleanor.

"Yes, yes. Things couldn't be better." She knew exactly what was bothering him, but was unwilling to acknowledge it in front of Edmund. "Well, for us at least. The Ridgeways are another story, but we can fill you in over tea. Perhaps you can call for some while we get dressed? Edmund, darling, I think I'd like to take a quick bath. Can you get it started for me?"

"Yes, of course, dearest," Edmund agreed. She loved seeing a happy spring in his fully recovered step.

As soon as Edmund entered the bathroom, he noticed the pile of stained towels and shut the door.

"What happened?!" Mr. Valov hissed with his natural British accent as soon as Edmund was out of earshot.

432

"Absolutely nothing of consequence. It is my time of the month." Mr. Valov stared blankly at her, and she rolled her eyes. "It is my feminine cycle. We enjoyed ourselves anyway, and hence, the mess."

Mr. Valov stopped to think through the idea. "People do that? Never mind. I don't want to know. Please, Eleanor, be careful."

"I don't need anyone lecturing me about what I should and shouldn't be doing with my husband, Mr. Valov. Least of all you."

"Yes... yes, of course. Please forgive me. I won't say another word about it. But... he was fine? He didn't... er... become something darker than normal?"

Eleanor raised her eyebrows.

"Never mind. I'm sorry," Mr. Valov reiterated. "How is he recovering?"

"I think he's back to his old self. He was still a bit sluggish when we went to dinner last night, but he was wonderfully vigorous by morning." Mr. Valov shifted uncomfortably. "Did you sort everything out in Constantinople?"

"Yes and no." Mr. Valov dropped into a whisper. "That's why I went to great effort to meet up with you here. There is something afoot. MI-5 has not let go of the trail, but I couldn't get any information about their next move. I think... I think I'm out of the loop, Eleanor. I couldn't even get details from my superiors. This is a very dangerous situation. If my superiors will not keep me up to date, it means that I am under suspicion too."

"Then why'd you come?" Eleanor exclaimed.

Mr. Valov glanced nervously at the bathroom door.

"I came to warn you. It is more important than ever that Edmund not reveal his talents. I think it is very likely that you are being watched."

"Bloody hell," Eleanor hissed as she looked around the room with fresh eyes and a blush worked its way onto her face.

"I didn't mean right now," Mr. Valov reassured her. "I checked the security of the room as soon as I boarded the ship. It's clean. There are no peepholes or the like, and this is the only balcony on this side of the ship other than the captain's, and he was out cold drunk when I boarded at eight o'clock this morning."

"Is that wise?" Eleanor asked.

"Is it wise for the captain to be out cold drunk at eight o'clock in the morning?" Mr. Valov asked rhetorically. "Of course not! But what do you expect from these greedy private companies? They always hire the cheapest help! And he's *French*," he rolled his eyes, "so it shouldn't be surprising. At least he didn't have a mistress in there with him."

Eleanor was a bit taken aback by Mr. Valov's cynical tone. She was still quite used to his jolly, easygoing personality, and it only occurred to her at that moment that *everything* about the man she knew was a farce. She was worldly enough to realize that anyone clever and cold enough to rise through the ranks of the most powerful intelligence organization in Britain must have had a certain shrewdness, and suddenly she didn't like the idea one bit.

Mr. Valov must have sensed her reaction, and he softened his demeanor. "I'm sorry, Eleanor. The captain has put everyone on this ship at risk with his irresponsible behavior, but it is a common problem. We must focus on the things we can change… And so, we must focus on protecting Edmund's secrets. When you are in public, he must act perfectly normal no matter what happens around you. Has he given anything away yet?"

Eleanor relaxed a bit, but kept her observation about Mr. Valov's shrewdness top of mind. "Nothing. He has been rather skillful at keeping his secrets so far. He even kept himself under control when he was managing that Ridgeway bastard in the middle of the night."

Mr. Valov looked unhappy with the intel.

"I'll let Edmund tell you that story over tea. It is only a mundane distraction, I think."

"Fine. But be careful, Eleanor. I will have tea with you, and then I am going to finish my survey of the ship. Do *nothing* to help me, understand? In fact, in public it would be even better if you act annoyed that I have gone off and disappeared on you, the worthless butler that I am. Suspect everyone."

"Great. I was just trying hard to get my mind to stop doing that," Eleanor humphed.

"You will get used to it, Eleanor. It will be a great asset when it has become a natural part of you."

Edmund opened the door with only a clean towel around his waist. "It's all yours, Eleanor."

She rushed past him, but he caught her in his arms for a surprise embrace, and she noticed a mischievous twinkle in his eye as he slapped her naughtily on the bum. Despite Mr. Valov's dire warning, she was rather excited that Edmund was in such a good mood. She hoped dearly that it wouldn't get either of them in trouble.

"Well, Mr. Valov, perhaps you can help me choose an appropriate suit for a lovely warm afternoon like this one," Edmund suggested as she closed herself into the bathroom. "I've been meaning to thank you for your help with this latest debacle. I understand you helped Eleanor whisk me out of harm's way…"

"Oh, Colonel, really it was nothing…" Mr. Valov switched immediately into Czech, and Edmund joined him. Eleanor wondered if Edmund had even noticed the transition.

She looked around the bathroom for the pile of stained towels, opening the cupboards to no avail. With a gentle breeze, Kuveni was standing before her in her preferred chubby form, and a fresh stack of clean towels was folded on the counter by the washbasin. Kuveni pulled her into a motherly hug, and then ran her hands across Eleanor's frizzy, wild hair, smoothing it into a manageable state.

"Oh, Mistress Eleanor, how I love you," she whispered. "I took care of the towels for you. My beautiful boy folded them neatly and put them in the cupboard under the sink, but we needn't have the housekeepers find them. I must admit that you had more faith in him than I did, and I'm ever so happy that everything worked out... but, we won't speak of such things again... Now, our virtuous spy is correct. There are a number of spies on this ship, but I have secured your suite. No one can see or hear anything from the outside. You can use this as your safe haven."

"Do you know who the spies are?" Eleanor whispered.

"All of the old human men look the same to me," Kuveni shrugged. "They think of themselves as very important, and they act very grumpy. There is at least one American and two Brits, along with a few minions who report to them—all men—and they are here to see whether the claims about Edmund's talents are true. They are the ones who dropped the chandelier on that poor Mr. Corrigan. They thought Edmund would blur to the rescue after his jovial conversation with him in the lift, and now they are regrouping on their next plot, which will be more sinister, I suspect. They haven't stated yet what exactly it will be. One of the Brits is not convinced the rumors are true, the other two are willing to do whatever it takes to find out."

"Blimey," Eleanor whispered.

"Edmund is dressed and calling for room service now. I'd best be going. I will continue my efforts invisibly. None of their special gadgets can compete with one motivated Yakshini." Kuveni winked, and then dissolved.

Eleanor sighed with stress, and then slipped into the bathtub to let the hot water relax her. She washed her hair thoroughly for the first time since the day before her wedding, noticing in passing that it wasn't the least bit dirty (thanks to Kuveni, she was sure), and then she lay about lazily for a bit, while Edmund's jovial laughter kept her quite certain that he was enjoying his time alone catching up with Mr. Valov. She was curious what Mr. Valov's complicated cover story would be, and finally she let her curiosity pull her out of the bath and back into the real world.

She dried herself off, pulled her hair into a simple ponytail, and did some minor makeup. She inspected the perfectly clean

Yakshini panties Kuveni had given her before she put them back on, and then scampered in her kimono straight to the walk-in closet where she closed herself in to decide on her next tropical outfit.

As soon as she was clad in a relaxed, low-waisted cotton dress in olive green and ivory with adorable matching sandals, she took a deep breath and readied herself to dive into Mr. Valov's web of lies.

The two men were seated at a round table just inside the balcony, identical to the one in Oz and Yvie's room, sipping tea from a silver platter, and drinking dainty glasses of sherry. A large pile of tea sandwiches and pastries were awaiting her consumption on a tiered plate.

"You're a vision, dearest!" Edmund said happily as she sat down beside him.

"Thank you, darling. I feel much better. I love the bath, don't you?"

Edmund smiled. "Indeed, I do."

"Aren't you going to eat, Colonel?" Mr. Valov asked curiously as he watched Eleanor pile her plate high with sandwiches, while Edmund only sipped his tea.

"I have yet to regain my appetite after my little incident. I'm sure it will return any day now. It always does," Edmund replied casually. "But, you must tell Eleanor now what you told me about your adventure in Constantinople!"

Mr. Valov jumped right into an elaborate cover story while Eleanor and Edmund listened. They sat for hours as the sun became yellow and dropped low in the sky, and Eleanor noticed every so often that Mr. Valov gave away subtle signs of stress as Edmund kept him fully engaged in their conversation. Finally, as the sun dropped below the horizon, Mr. Valov stood up.

"Colonel, it has been a pleasure catching up, but you two had better get dressed for dinner, and I'd better get myself settled in. I am staying in a second class room on the second floor, in case you need me."

"Yes, yes. Of course." Edmund blushed as he realized that he'd been keeping Mr. Valov for too long, but Mr. Valov only smiled and made his own way to the door.

He pulled a pocket-watch out of his breast pocket. "You should really hurry. Dinner begins in fifteen minutes. I already told them to reserve a table for you to eat with the Helmsworths."

"Jolly good, Mr. Valov, thank you!" Edmund slapped his back.

"It was my pleasure as always, Colonel." Mr. Valov bowed and left them alone.

Edmund paused in deep thought, watching the door.

"What is it, darling? Did you hear something?"

"You don't think… You don't think that Mr. Valov is one of Mr. Johnson's spies, do you? One of those agents we were talking about last night who reports back to him without my knowledge. That would explain a lot, wouldn't it?"

"It would," Eleanor agreed. She had absolutely no idea what to say to him. It was exactly the explanation she had jumped to herself in the beginning.

"I mean, really, Eleanor. Aden is a very hard place to get to by land or air. Even with his contacts in the Czech legions, he would have had to procure a very precarious airplane passage to get here in such a short amount of time. But if Kate got here, then surely she had the means, and perhaps Mr. Valov would have had the means too…"

Eleanor was taken aback by his astute observation.

"Darling, how would you act differently if Mr. Valov were one of Mr. Johnson's agents?"

"I suppose I would demand that he tell me all that he knows, and he would reply with the same stubbornness I've come to expect from them. I would eventually give up on trying, and come to depend too heavily on him. I would expect his help at every turn and become a worthless, lazy lout."

438

Eleanor couldn't help but laugh at his melodramatic characterization. "Really, darling? A worthless, lazy lout?"

Edmund cracked a smile. "Perhaps that's an exaggeration. But I do not want to fall into the same trap I fell into in the trenches, Eleanor. I waited and waited for Mr. Johnson to come, and he didn't. I don't know how I would have acted differently if I hadn't expected his intervention, but certainly I would have done something better. I will not fall into the same trap again."

"You are very wise, darling. I think it's best to keep our awareness raised, and to continue to make our own decisions, no matter who is in our midst. If we make our own fates, then we will have only ourselves to blame... or to thank. We've done quite well making our own decisions so far, don't you think?" She winked as she pulled him into a gentle embrace.

"Yes, we have," he agreed as he squeezed her bum.

They almost lost themselves in the moment, but Eleanor reluctantly pulled away.

"I am rather hungry. Shall we continue this later, after dinner, darling?"

Edmund followed her into the closet.

"I suppose I have no excuse not to wear a tuxedo to dinner this time. I'm fully recovered, I think. It seems rather mad to wear such heavy fabrics in the tropics, but I suppose we'd best keep up appearances." Edmund gathered his tuxedo that was hanging nicely in the closet. "I think women's fashions are much more comfortable in this climate." He eyed a new Roman dress that had not been hanging in the closet when Eleanor had dressed herself earlier after her bath. She smiled as she inspected the unusual cuts and folds in the rich green silk. She made a mental note to thank Kuveni for it later.

"I'm quite glad that the tables have finally turned. Now if we can just remove high heels from the picture, women will finally have the upper hand," Eleanor winked.

"You are doing your part, I see," Edmund pointed out jovially as he pointed to another pair of flat, laced golden Roman sandals.

"I do what I can." Eleanor reveled in the moment of mundanity as they dressed together in the closet.

"You look very dapper, darling," she said as she finished up helping Edmund tie his bowtie.

He pulled uncomfortably at the stiff collar and then shrugged and pulled her into a gentle embrace. "And you look especially lovely in that green. It goes so perfectly with your eyes, dearest. And with that pendant I bought you in Constantinople. It really is stunning. Are you sure it was paste?"

"I don't think you had enough cash on you to buy a real one, darling. I think you gave it all up to that pimp at the Moulin Rouge in Paris."

She winked, and he smiled.

"That feels like a lifetime ago, doesn't it? I can hardly believe it was only a few days."

"A little bit over a week, to be precise," Eleanor corrected him. "Come on. Let's go eat."

When they arrived at the dining room, there were no hosts to seat them. The waiters were rushing about in a disorderly panic, while several large tables of loud Italians laughed and shouted tipsily.

Eleanor spotted Oz and Yvie, who stood up to greet them.

"We thought you'd never make it! We had half a mind to escape back to our room, away from this wild ruckus," Oz said as Yvie pulled them each into French cheek kisses.

"What's going on?" Eleanor asked as one table exploded into a chorus of jeers.

"They boarded in Aden. That's all we know. The staff is in an uproar, but with Mr. Corrigan still indisposed, they don't have any clue what to do about it. They are very apologetic to us, for what it's worth," Yvie whispered.

Edmund and Eleanor followed them to their table, and Yvie poured them tall glasses of red wine from the second open bottle on the table.

"We've been waiting for service for almost an hour," she explained. "They dropped off the bottles as a peace offering with their first apology."

"How is Mr. Corrigan?" Eleanor asked as she thought back angrily at the revelation that the poor man was a victim of his own government's shenanigans.

"He's recovering, but he's still in bed. A nasty concussion, I'd say. I've ordered him to stay on bedrest for now," Oz reported.

"And how are the Ridgeways?" Eleanor decided to get all of the bad news over with at once. "I should have checked in with them. We didn't realize how late it was when we woke up."

"No worries, mates," Oz reassured her. "We stopped by around noon. Daisy is recovering nicely. The three of them had already called in room service when we stopped by, and Mr. Ridgeway was nowhere to be found. I assume we have you to thank for that, Colonel? They said you'd locked him into another room last night when he showed up to make a scene?"

Edmund nodded. "I told security not to let him out. I suppose I should deal with that sooner rather than later." He eyed the tipsy Italians. "Although, I think that perhaps one fewer drunken fool wandering about will be better for everyone. There was plenty of food in the room when we left him there last night."

"I wouldn't hurry, if I were you. The girls are better off the longer they can go without him around," Yvie said with annoyance. "Shameful, he is. Just shameful. I will never understand how God can bless a scoundrel like that with two beautiful children when so many people can't have children at all."

Eleanor noticed that Oz squeezed Yvie's thigh supportively under the table, but before she could let her mind wander to her own uncertainty, Mr. Valov interrupted them.

"There you are!" he exclaimed as he practically ran right up to their table. "Why, thank you, Colonel. I don't mind if I do!"

To everyone's surprise, he casually gathered up an empty chair from a neighboring table and took a seat right next to Edmund.

Mr. Valov poured himself a glass of wine and laughed jovially, while they watched his odd spectacle with silent confusion.

"Really, Colonel, I cannot keep being a gossip. But, since you asked…" He threw them each a look indicating that they needed to play along with his farce. "You are in the company of many famous people tonight! How lucky you are to spot such stars! I heard from a Hungarian waiter that the Italians are traveling with Beniamino Gigli himself, the famous opera tenor, who is on his way to tour India, and then, of course, there is the famous actress Ava May with her entourage over there."

He pointed to a woman who was, indeed, dressed to the nines and surrounded by an adoring entourage. Eleanor recognized her as one of the many fashionable women who'd appreciated her Yakshini Roman dress upon her entrance two nights before.

"And then, of course, you certainly have already recognized those famous men over there." Mr. Valov glanced towards the table of the three grumpy older men that Eleanor had noticed in passing. "Those are some real heroes, Lieutenant Helmsworth. Colonel Marriner surely already recognized Colonel Snell, but your discretion, Colonel, was not necessary." He paused to make sure they understood the gravity of the intel. "Colonel Snell is a household figure now as the head of MI-5. His picture was in the paper many times with his many triumphs against German Intelligence during the war. He is sitting with General Kettering, whom you must know at least by reputation, Colonel. I believe you provided him with some testimonials for the historical volumes he was writing on the World War? And, of course, they are seated with some important American, I'm sure. No one knows who he is, but he is in good company."

"Thank you for the gossip, Mr. Valov. You have set our minds at ease," Edmund replied, clearly overwhelmed by the implications.

"My pleasure, Colonel. I know how you like to stay in the know. Now, don't go telling Signore Gigli that I told you who he was. I have it on good authority that he refuses to perform as a party trick. Only vast opera houses will suit his tastes..." Mr. Valov trailed off as he glanced out the window at the twinkling lights of a nearby city on shore. "Colonel, you know this route well, don't you? From your days in the Colonial Army?"

"Yes, Mr. Valov, I do," Edmund confirmed. Eleanor could feel him tense with Mr. Valov's change in tone.

"Does the route normally follow the coastline of Arabia for so long? We left Aden ten hours ago at full steam."

Eleanor followed Edmund as he stood up and walked to the window. A seaside village with twinkling lights and square mud houses built up against a craggy coastline looked lovely under the bright blue light of the full moon, but Eleanor's anxiety kicked up as she noticed a look of distinct panic entering Edmund's expression.

Oz and Yvie joined them, followed by Mr. Valov.

"We are not on course," Edmund whispered. "Ten hours out of Aden in a ship this fast should not have us anywhere so close to a coastline. And that, Mr. Valov, is most certainly not Arabia. It looks... it looks quite a bit like Africa, actually. Perhaps Somalia?" Edmund shifted uncomfortably at the inconvenient observation. "We are too far to have taken a detour towards Berbera in British Somaliland. We must be father than that by now. We've been going at full speed all day?"

Oz nodded his agreement.

"Has anyone communicated a change in course?" he asked the group at large.

"Not that we've heard," Oz replied.

"No one has said a word about it," Mr. Valov seconded.

"We must get to the bottom of this now. If we are hugging the coast of Somalia, we are in enemy territory. We won't return to safe waters until we reach Kenya… That is, *if* we reach Kenya. There is something dangerously amiss."

Edmund was not at all enthusiastic about his own suggestion as he glanced across the room at the table of military intelligence leaders whom Mr. Valov had so bluntly unmasked. Eleanor knew that Edmund understood the implications, even if he didn't have the full context. Those men, under no circumstance, could learn of his talents.

"Colonel, you must be careful," Mr. Valov warned.

"We must all be careful," Edmund countered. "It is very likely this ship has been commandeered."

"What do we do?" Oz looked to Edmund.

"We must start with the appropriate protocols," Edmund decided resignedly.

He took a deep breath and walked straight across the room, past the belligerent Italians who had started pounding their hands on the table while one of their compatriots chugged several tall glasses of beer in a row.

He stopped as he reached the table of the three secret intelligence leaders, and Eleanor's heart almost exploded as Mr. Valov threw her a desperate look. Oz ran after him to participate in whatever his unspoken plan was.

Edmund stood up straight and saluted, and Oz followed his lead.

"General Kettering, I am Colonel Edmund Marriner. I believe, sir, that this ship is not on course."

The two other men at the table threw each other annoyed glances at Edmund's blatant recognition of his superior officer, while General Kettering glanced curiously at Oz.

"Lieutenant Jack Helmsworth, sir. Royal Army Medical Corps, 22nd field hospital, Reims—retired, sir."

"As you were, gentlemen," General Kettering said casually. "Colonel Marriner, yes, your testimonials about your command in the trenches were most useful to my project. I've been meaning to set up a meeting to thank you in person. Perhaps we will talk about it at a more convenient time when you've returned to London. You are on leave, are you not? For your honeymoon?"

Edmund couldn't hide the fact that he was taken aback by the general's nonchalant response to his report of dire danger.

"I am, sir. Thank you, sir. But if you will look out the window, you will see that we are traveling very close to a populated coastline. Clearly, we are off course. What are your orders?"

General Kettering glanced past Edmund, but the lights of the city that had aroused their attention had passed, and all that was visible was the bright reflection of the inside of the dining room.

"I daresay, Colonel, that you are addicted to your work!" General Kettering laughed heartily. "Enjoy yourself! There is absolutely no need for you to be in an uproar. How about I check up on the captain and the course, and you go back to that lovely wife of yours. She was very captivating when she entered the dining room the other night. Like a Roman goddess... or perhaps a Druidic one with that ginger hair. You are a lucky man."

Edmund looked suspiciously to the other men seated at the table and then back to General Kettering. After a long, awkward moment of contemplation as Edmund spied another cluster of lights out the window, he shrugged his acceptance of the situation. Certainly, they were in on whatever was going on, and Edmund had just confirmed it.

"If those are your orders, sir?" Edmund asked for confirmation.

"Indeed, they are, Colonel. Enjoy yourself!"

Edmund saluted again, and Oz followed him as he ignored the Italians who had recently launched into a loud, drunken song, and returned to the rest of their group who were still huddling by the window.

Mr. Valov didn't dare look in the direction of the leaders he'd outed. "Colonel, is everything alright?" he asked innocently.

"We must check the bridge," Edmund whispered. "Eleanor, you and Yvie should go back to our room. Mr. Valov, Oz, and I will join you shortly."

Eleanor grimaced at the patronizing suggestion. "Oh, for god's sake, Edmund. We most certainly will not!" Edmund was taken aback by her strong reaction, but she didn't let him get a word in. "You need our help! Yvie and I both know how to fight, and none of us have any idea what we're up against yet. The last time I checked, *you*, darling, weren't in a position to be hopping about saving the day by yourself, for *many* reasons."

She eyed the spies, and Edmund glanced around at their group readying himself to argue, but as Eleanor threw him a furious look, he finally gave in. "Fine. Time is of the essence. Do any of you know how to get to the bridge?"

"I reckon we do, don't we, Yvie? It's the last stop on the lift before we get to our floor. Follow me." Oz led them swiftly out of the dining room.

The group ran at their fastest inconspicuous speed to the elevator, and then followed Oz straight onto the bridge. A young officer sat alone at the helm, reading a magazine with his feet up on the control panel. He did not bother to improve his position as they approached him.

"Where is the captain?" Edmund demanded.

The officer shrugged, barely looking up from his reading.

"*Où est le capitaine?*" Yvie demanded.

The officer rattled off an unenthusiastic response as Edmund and Yvie engaged him in French, until Edmund growled with frustration. "This boy knows nothing."

He looked out the window and pointed at another close by seaside town, explaining in French with a fresh batch of calm authority why the boy should be worried. The boy only shrugged and pointed to a closed door across the room.

446

Edmund ran straight over to it and pushed it open. As the rest of the group rushed to follow him, Edmund stumbled backwards, closing his eyes and whispering his mantras. Eleanor knew exactly what Edmund's strong reaction meant, but she waited strategically for the others to discover it on their own, and gathered Edmund's hand tightly into hers.

The captain lay face down on the floor with a bottle of liquor beside him. Oz kneeled down and turned him over, and Yvie gasped as his dead corpse gave off a putrid scent.

"*Mon dieu*, he has been dead for hours!" Yvie whispered.

"He didn't die of drink, that's for sure," Oz said as he examined the man's broken neck.

"The break is clean. Someone skilled did this," Eleanor said as she kneeled down beside them for her own examination. "What's this?" Eleanor noticed a note in the man's stiff hand. She pried it out of his rigor mortis grip and handed it to Yvie. "I think it's in French. What does it say?"

Yvie's expression was puzzled and then concerned as she read it.

"What is it, Yvie?" Oz pushed.

"It is phrased strangely. There isn't a perfect translation of the word *coquin* in English... perhaps it is like a rascal, but it often has a kinky connotation... more like 'naughty boy.' So, it says something like, 'I was a naughty boy who spied where good boys shouldn't.'" She looked to Oz. "What do you think it means?"

"Sounds fair dinkum strange to me. This man didn't break his own neck like this," Oz said as he examined the broken spine again. "Do you think he was a spy?"

"It is strange... the verb was not *espionner*." Yvie read through the note again. "To spy on state secrets, we would use the verb *espionner*, but this note says *épier*, which means to spy, but it can also mean to... eh... 'peeping-tom,' you'd say Ozzy? So, it could say, 'I'm a kinky boy who peeped where good boys shouldn't.' It changes the meaning entirely."

"Blimey, we don't have time for this," Eleanor muttered. "There is something much bigger than this man's death happening here. It is obviously a piece of a larger, more dangerous puzzle."

"What do you reckon we should do, Colonel? Should we tell the general?" Oz asked as he stood back up and surveyed the room.

"No…" Edmund said unsurely. "Not yet. He had quite a clear view out of the window by his table. Surely he saw what we saw, and yet he didn't care. He ordered us not to look into it, in fact… He must be in on whatever this plot is, and that means… I don't want to think about it. It means that some of the highest-ranking officials in the government are complacent with whatever is going on here. With the captain's *murder*. We need a plan."

"Our room is just down the hall," Eleanor suggested. "I didn't realize we'd been staying so close to the bridge, but I suppose we haven't spent too much time exploring the ship. The door looks just the same as all the others!" She pushed back a burst of embarrassment that the ship's bridge crew may have overheard their loud night (and morning) of passion.

The group rushed down the hallway, straight to their room. Eleanor slammed the door, and Mr. Valov went straight to the balcony and closed the doors and the shutters.

Edmund took a deep breath, and began reasoning out loud. "The ship is off course, flanking enemy territory. The captain has been murdered. The head of MI-5 and an army general are relaxing as if they are on holiday together, while a troop of Italian revelers destroy the first class dining room right before their eyes… What could it mean?"

"You don't think that it could all be an elaborate trap, do you?" Oz asked.

"A trap?" Edmund asked.

Oz shifted uncomfortably and lowered his voice. "A trap for you, Colonel. For a man with your unusual… er… talents." Edmund's posture deflated at the idea. "Do you remember last night when that chandelier fell on Mr. Corrigan? We all heard the chord snap many seconds before it fell. Even he heard it; we saw him look up before it fell. And now we are off course with the head of MI-5 here for no apparent reason, on the same ship with us… with *you*… after what happened on the Orient Express… It just makes me wonder… I suppose that's a bit paranoid…"

Eleanor threw a surprised look to Mr. Valov at Oz's astute observation.

"It is suspicious…" Edmund trailed off as he thought through the implications. "Mr. Corrigan's accident, and maybe even the dead captain, I could imagine some over-enthused spies orchestrating, but taking an entire civilian ship full of innocent people into enemy territory… I can't believe that anyone in the British government would do something so dangerous just to entrap me… Dearest, do you think it's possible?"

Yes! Of course, it is!!! Eleanor reined in her screaming mind to produce a feigned calm response. "I wouldn't like to think so, darling, but we can't ignore the possibility."

Eleanor thought more carefully about the situation as she tamed her emotional response. Even with what Mr. Valov had told her, and what they had combatted in Constantinople, she too had trouble believing that they would sink to such depths—an entire passenger liner! In Constantinople, no innocent people had been put in danger with their spying shenanigans, but there were hundreds, maybe thousands of people on the ship at that very moment. Somalia was famously dangerous. The Somali rebels had fought against the British for years, as had the Italians…

"The Italians!" Eleanor exclaimed. "The ship is suddenly crawling with Italians! Don't the Italians have territory in East Africa? In Somalia, in fact! They must have something to do with it! You heard how bad those drunkards were at singing. There is no way that the entourage of a famous opera singer would dare to sing so poorly in public. Don't you think? In fact, those men didn't seem like they'd be the entourage of an opera singer at all. They weren't even wearing tuxedos!"

"If Italians have silently hijacked the ship, then why would General Kettering not care?" Edmund asked. "You don't think... no. No. It couldn't be true."

"What, darling?" Eleanor encouraged him.

"There have been various traitors in the ranks for decades. You don't think that General Kettering could be on the side of the Fascist Italians, do you?"

"While he's entertaining Colonel Snell? The head of MI-5? He'd have to have a kangaroo loose in the top paddock!" Oz exclaimed.

"Unless they're working together," Yvie interjected.

"But why here and now, unless it has something to do with you, Colonel?" Oz began pacing. "It would have been fair dinkum bad trot for them if the legendary hero of the 23rd regiment just happened to be on board for their coup."

"They must have known I'd be here." Edmund flipped open one of the shutters to glance out across the moonlit water to shore. "I had to submit my itinerary when I applied for my leave." He closed it up and turned back around to address the group. "It is a trap. A wretched, shameful, treasonous trap."

"Bad trot, mate," Oz whispered. "What should we do?"

"Well, I suppose there's only one real solution." Edmund sighed with resignation. "I'll go confess my many secrets, and get them to turn this bloody boat around. When everyone is safe and sound, I'll escape from their clutches and meet up with my wife somewhere down the road. Mr. Valov, can you take care of Eleanor for me in my immediate absence?"

Mr. Valov was speechless, and Eleanor almost laughed until she realized he was serious. "Edmund George Marriner, that is the worst idea I've ever heard in my life!"

Edmund was startled, and she was glad. She didn't even care that her shrill tone made her sound exactly like her mother.

He worked hard to keep his wits about him as he addressed her before the group. "Dearest, I can't put any of you in harm's way. There are innocent women and children on this ship. It is very dangerous for everyone that we are skirting the coast of Somalia like this. There are rebels and pirates in these waters, and it is deep into Fascist Italian territory on shore. If I can get them to turn the boat back towards British Somaliland, or even Bombay, then everyone will be safe without any bloodshed. I will not let my secrets put more people at risk. I should have just declared them to the world years ago, and many thousands more men would have lived."

Eleanor worked hard to rein in her sharp tone. "Darling, what makes you think that you would be able to convince someone who is willing to sacrifice thousands of British citizens to unmask one heroic colonel to do anything rational at all? And what makes you think that you even could escape from their clutches? They know what you can do. You showed them exactly what your strengths were on the Orient Express. They will not just let you escape."

As Edmund's expression descended from concern into misery, the door swung open, and Kuveni burst into the room in the form of Kate, bearing a large suitcase in her left hand. She shut the door behind her and dropped the suitcase on the floor. The beads and sequins of her elaborate black and silver flapper dress jangled as she rushed across the room, gathering Edmund and Eleanor into a group hug.

"Never fear, my darlings. Big sister is here!"

"Kate?!" Edmund exclaimed.

Eleanor was too relieved by her intrusion to worry about the dangerous level of meddling that had just commenced.

"Oh, don't act so surprised, my dear boy. I know that those dear-hearted Ridgeway girls gave away the secret of my little visit to you. I came to check up on you after your incident, and what did I find?"

Edmund looked as curious about the answer to her rhetorical question as Oz and Yvie were.

"A mess of trouble, that's what!" Kuveni exclaimed. "I was going to disembark as soon as I made sure you had recovered, but there was just too much to keep me busy. The situation was so dire that intervention could not be avoided, and so here I am to keep you out of irreversible trouble. I mean *really*, Edmund. Give yourself up to a troop of murderous spies? What happened to that wonderful imagination of yours?!"

Edmund was too bewildered by her presence to answer her.

"Never you mind. I realize that when those we love are in danger, we often have irrational ideas. The key is to not let those irrational ideas distract us from the better ones. Now, let me tell you what I've learned with my skilled spying." She glanced over at Mr. Valov. "There are *two* plots afoot, and a terrible two plots they are. Both of them are ripe for disaster when they come together as a pair. Perhaps I should start with the pirates."

"The pirates?!" Eleanor exclaimed.

"Exactly," Kuveni winked. "It is not an everyday problem that would warrant my overt meddling, you know. Now, the pirates are a combination of Italian hooligans employed by Mussolini's government on a mercenary basis and Somalian separatists. The Italians have provided the arms and set the new destination coordinates without a peep of protest from the bridge crew... I will get to that foolishness in a minute... We are headed towards Mogadishu full steam ahead, where they plan to unload the enormous cache of weapons in the hold of the ship before they capture everyone on board and auction each of you off to the highest bidders. They are especially excited about the children, as they will fetch the highest prices."

"Good lord," Edmund murmured.

"Why would there be an enormous cache of weapons in the hold of a passenger ship?" Eleanor asked.

"The P&O Company manages transportation and logistics for many things. Passengers and weapons included..." Edmund trailed off. "I thought they only did that during the war, though. Why would they need to be transporting weapons now?"

"Darling, the British government is already mobilizing for another war," Kuveni said gently.

"With whom? The Germans can hardly feed themselves!" Edmund exclaimed.

"Have you not been paying attention to Mussolini's politics? He is consolidating power and making alliances. Why, my dear boy, do you think the Italians have provided weapons to some random

Somalian separatists? It is the same story as it was two thousand years ago, in the exact same places! The Romans meddled with the ancient Somalis over the same bloody trade routes!" Kuveni paused for a moment to collect her thoughts. "My point is that these things often unfold over years, not just days or weeks. And, like it was during the Roman Empire, the politics of this particular corner of the world have far-reaching consequences. The Italians and the Somali separatists plan to sell and distribute the weapons to various anti-Imperial causes. There are quite a few enthusiastic buyers already lined up, including Kenyan, Irish, and Hindu nationalists. Now, I do not blame those buyers for wanting the British Raj out of their hair one bit—it's always rather unfortunate when an outside force is pillaging your homeland for their own profit—but that is not the point, my friends."

"What is the point?" Mr. Valov asked testily. Eleanor watched him curiously as he reacted to Kuveni's cutting statement against his empire.

Kuveni smiled confidently. "My dearest virtuous butler, why do General Kettering and Colonel Snell not care in the slightest that a treasure trove of weapons is about to be handed over to the enemy? Do you think, Mr. Valov, that they don't know what's happening?"

"They must," Oz interjected. "We've been skirting the coastline of Africa for hours."

"And they do, my dear boy!" Kuveni agreed excitedly. "Those fools believe that the ship going off course—that the entire silent takeover by the Italians—is a plot orchestrated by their American colleague's team of spies. And he, my friends, believes that this whole debacle is a plot by the British. Both of them commanded the bridge crew not to argue with any strange orders, and so when the Italians showed up and told the young Frenchman at the helm to set a course for Mogadishu, he shrugged his agreement and complied! And so, you see, these fools who have bet everything simply to catch a talented colonel in his moment of heroism have allowed their greatest enemies to win at a far more important game without a peep of protest."

"Blimey," Eleanor whispered.

"And so, Edmund, darling, handing yourself over and confessing your darkest secrets to those fools will do absolutely nothing to save this ship. It will, however, put you in a position in which you cannot come to the daring rescue of the seven hundred and forty-two passengers who now need our help."

"What do we do?" he asked miserably. "I can't just go around killing scores of men with my bare hands to take the ship back. That will give our spies exactly what they're looking for, and it will indulge my darkest tendencies in a way that is dangerous for *everyone*." He looked self-consciously to Oz and Yvie.

"You're right." Kuveni forcefully took his hands into hers. "But you are not alone, my dear boy. We are all here, and we are going to save the ship together."

Edmund was not convinced, despite her personal gesture. "Let's say we indulge this ill-fated idea to fight them off. How exactly do you propose we do that? We don't even have any weapons."

Kuveni grinned and rushed to gather up the suitcase. She glided across the room to the round dining table, pushed the remnants from their earlier tea service right onto the floor to make room, and opened it right up.

"Strewth!" Oz exclaimed as Kuveni nonchalantly reached into the suitcase and began handing out military-grade guns.

"Where did you get those, Kate?" Edmund asked nervously.

Kuveni laughed. "Edmund, my dear boy, with everything you know about me, do you believe for one moment that I will tell you an honest answer to that question?"

She handed Eleanor a pistol, and Eleanor checked the cartridge and then practiced her aim, responsibly pointing the gun towards a painting on the far wall without a human in sight.

Edmund couldn't hide his surprise at her shocking comfort with the weapon. "Dearest, I didn't know that you knew how to fire a gun!"

Eleanor smiled slyly, relishing one of many moments in which she could surprise her old-fashioned, chivalrous husband with her modernity.

"Darling, I lived in a war zone that was crawling with horny soldiers for four years. Carrying a gun and knowing how to use it was a daily necessity."

Kuveni handed another pistol to Yvie, who followed Eleanor's lead, demonstrating the same comfort that Eleanor had, to the men's surprise.

"These modern sheilas never cease to amaze you, do they, mate?" Oz winked as he collected the largest gun from Kuveni's suitcase alongside a cache of ammunition. He began handing out extra cartridges, and Eleanor put several into her pockets.

As his human companions armed themselves, Edmund looked more and more dismayed. His dismay morphed swiftly into panic. His eyes turned black, and he began hyperventilating.

Eleanor put the pistol in her pocket and rushed to his side to rub his back as he leaned over with his hands on his knees to catch his breath.

"We can't do this, Eleanor. *You* can't do this. It's going to be too dangerous," he implored desperately between shallow breaths. "You have nothing to protect you! I can't lose you, Eleanor! I will crawl into a dark abyss and die a thousand painful deaths if anything happens to you! Do you understand, dearest? I will *die* if something happens to you!"

Eleanor threw a searching look to Kuveni.

"Edmund, my dear boy, Eleanor can take care of herself." Kuveni joined Eleanor in rubbing Edmund's back. "She is a modern woman."

"Many modern men had their heads blown off right beside me," Edmund countered dismally. "My despair is not about a backwards army man insisting on being a white knight to some distressed damsels." He looked to both of them as he said it. "Pirates and spies and separatists are *dangerous*. To all of you. Oz and Mr. Valov included. None of you should be risking your lives when *we*, Kate, will be perfectly fine taking on the enemy ourselves, if you do, indeed, share my talents."

Kuveni was obviously taken aback by his reasonable point.

"But, Edmund, my dear boy, if we hop about this ship bringing swift death to the twenty-eight enemies we must fight, everyone will know our family secrets. I thought that you understood the requirement for discretion for people like us who are dangerously different."

"Oz and Yvie know the truth. So does Mr. Valov. And Eleanor. And Charlie and Debbie and Howie MacLeod. And Edward bloody Rutherford!" Edmund exclaimed. "Not to mention some very traumatized passengers on the Orient Express… and apparently, everyone who was there when I rescued all those men from the mustard gas attack against the 23rd bloody regiment! And *everyone* in the army medical corps! And now that worthless Ridgeway chap and his entire family have weaseled their way into the club, and I believe you're well-acquainted with them, *Kate*? If that abusive wanker knows my bloody secret, then why shouldn't the whole world know it too? Let's just get it bloody over with!"

Oz and Yvie threw each other a nervous look, as if they had accidentally stumbled upon an old family argument unfolding before their eyes.

Kuveni was unfazed by his outburst. In fact, she looked rather proud. She reached forward and stroked Edmund's cheek affectionately. "I will never be more grateful to anyone than I am to the virtuous souls in this room who have so thoroughly led you to believe that the entire human world knowing our secrets is a fine idea, Edmund. It is only through their incredible kindness and acceptance that you have any inkling in your mind right now that such a plan is remotely reasonable. But, Edmund, my dearest boy, Eleanor, and Oz, and Yvie, and even your virtuous butler are not normal. There are many dangerous humans who will do horrible things to you and to others if they know our secrets. At least three of those men are on this boat right now. Perhaps I should have just killed them myself and gotten it over with…"

But, as Edmund struggled for a response, and Eleanor contemplated whether or not Kuveni meant her statement, the door burst open, and Mélusine, in the form of Lord Blakeney, sporting a tamer, more fashionable black tuxedo rather than her standard ridiculous purple suit and carrying a suitcase that matched Kuveni's, rushed inside, slamming the door behind her.

"Edmund, this is absurd. You will not reveal our secrets to the head of British Intelligence," she said matter-of-factly.

He stumbled backwards. "*You* are one of us?" Edmund asked as he threw Eleanor a stunned look.

She was so surprised by Mélusine's blatant revelation, that she had no response at all.

"Mon chéri, it should have been patently obvious that I was distinctly different." Mélusine spoke with an accent that mirrored Edmund's, rather than the absurd, affected accent of the Scarlet Pimpernel. "Did you really not notice my outrageous anachronisms? You certainly noticed that my alias had already been sullied by some worthless human writer."

"Eleanor said you were in the Secret Service," he whispered.

Mélusine threw Mr. Valov a taunting look. "What a useful story that is. We can cover so many of our oddities with such excuses. It makes one wonder if there even is a Secret Service at all, or whether it is entirely *us* making an unwise ruckus in the human world." She threw an angry look at Kuveni. "Now, mon chéri, you must understand before we go any further that I am not the same as you. I am more like Kate than I am like you, and she is a distinctly different beast. Our talents are different, *tu comprends?* So, I don't want you getting any ideas."

Edmund glanced awkwardly at Oz and Yvie.

"Oh, mon chéri, don't be afraid! If you were happy telling the head of British Intelligence all about our many talents, you should have no qualms at all with my unexpected revelation before your forgiving friends!"

Edmund moved to argue, and then resigned himself. He looked around at his audience, thought carefully about his response, and gave in. "Who are you, really?"

Mélusine was clearly annoyed by his choice of question. "You may call me Percy, mon chéri."

"But that is not your name," Edmund countered.

"I have many names," Mélusine shot back. "I do not have a Christian name because I was born a Roman." She looked over to Oz and Yvie who were silently holding hands as they watched the spectacle unfold. Mélusine softened her demeanor. "But I was Sir Percy Blakeney, mon chéri. I saved many thousands of innocent people from the guillotine using that name, including Yvie's great grand-mother, if I'm not mistaken? Countess de Saint-Cyr?"

"*C'est vrai*, she was my great-grandmother!" Yvie exclaimed. "But how do you know who I am?"

"I know many things, ma chérie. My point, Edmund, was that Sir Percy Blakeney was one of my many personas that worked its way into legend, just as many of yours will someday. That is what they do with us. They exaggerate the stories of our triumphs and our follies, and eventually the truth dissolves into a sea of lies, just as it does with folklore and religion. That is why we must keep our talents away from those dangerous men who are hunting us. If we are going to save all of these people and keep our talents a secret, we will need these valiant humans' help."

"If you're not human, what are you?" Yvie asked timidly.

"We are angels in disguise, ma chérie." Mélusine glanced over to Edmund, who looked rather unhappy with the idea. "It is as good an explanation as any, Edmund. Angels do not have to go around quoting scripture and enticing lost souls into giving their

meagre wages to a corrupt human institution in the name of *God*."
She rolled her eyes with annoyance at the idea. "We help humans
when destiny decrees it. Today is one of those days, and destiny
has decreed that we won't do it alone. Now come, look at what
I've brought for you."

She gathered up the suitcase and whisked it over to the table,
dropping it right next to Kuveni's suitcase full of weapons.

She ripped it open and gathered up one of many white silken
garments that looked quite a bit like long underwear. She handed
the first to Eleanor for inspection, and Eleanor held it out before
her curiously.

"It is a Roman design," Mélusine explained. "The fabric is
woven so tightly that a modern weapon will not be able to
penetrate it. This is yet another invention that the human race lost
when that empire fell, and a useful one it was. You must put it on
under your clothing, so that it sticks tightly to your skin."

Eleanor attempted to push her finger through it, and Edmund
picked one up and tried unsuccessfully to do the same.

Mélusine eyed their test results approvingly. "Now, the catch
of this marvelous invention is that it does not allow the ideal
freedom of movement, so the sleeves stop before the elbow, and
the legs stop before the knee. You should all keep in mind this
armor's limitations as you prepare yourselves for the unpleasant
tasks at hand."

She handed one each to Yvie and Oz, conspicuously
overlooking Mr. Valov, and then handed the last one to Edmund.

"You'd best wear one too, mon chéri. This one is your size. It
will keep you from being taken temporarily out of the field, and it
will serve as a perfect excuse for any demonstration of unique
heartiness that you happen to display before our foolish audience."

Edmund handed his extra armor to Mr. Valov, and Mélusine
watched him take it with a look of disapproval in her expression.

"Perhaps you two should change in the bathroom," Kuveni suggested to Eleanor and Yvie as they looked down at their silk evening gowns, contemplating their next move.

They obediently headed towards the bathroom.

"Are you just going to watch us undress?" Edmund asked with a hint of annoyance at Kuveni.

"Darling, I was there when you were born. You have nothing I haven't seen before," Kuveni replied.

Eleanor couldn't help but smile at Kuveni's embarrassing motherly response.

"I have changed a bit since then, you know," Edmund countered.

"Fine, fine. Embrace your human modesty. I will join the ladies in the bathroom," Kuveni conceded, throwing a look of minor jealousy at Mélusine, whose male presence did not arouse Edmund's modesty.

"Aren't you going to wear them too?" Edmund asked as he noticed that Kuveni and Mélusine were the only ones without the Roman armor.

"Mon chéri, as I already told you, we are not the same as you. It will only get in our way. Besides, it is most important for you to escape from this little escapade unmasked, and for the rest of your friends to escape unscathed. We are only a legendary side-note."

"Edmund, darling, don't argue with Percy. He always wins, no matter how infuriating his arguments are," Kuveni advised as she joined Eleanor and Yvie in the bathroom and closed the door.

"Are you really angels in disguise?" Yvie asked Kuveni timidly as soon as they were alone.

Kuveni smiled. "We are, my dear girl. Edmund has not yet accepted his destiny as a member of our little tribe, but in truth, we are more angelic than any other creature on Earth."

"*Mon dieu*," Yvie whispered.

"Never fear, my dear girl. We are very good-humored!" Kuveni reassured her. "That is, unless someone crosses us by being a worthless, harmful, selfish scoundrel…" Yvie did not look reassured. "But you and your virtuous husband are not at risk of that, Yvie." Kuveni pulled her into a motherly hug, and Yvie threw a bewildered glance to Eleanor. Kuveni pulled away and straightened the many folds of Yvie's dress. "In any event, you must understand that even we have our limitations, and we are not omnipotent. The armor is necessary to keep you safe. What injuries nature imparts, we have no power to mitigate, so you must take care of yourselves."

Kuveni began helping Eleanor and Yvie undress to put the Roman armor on underneath their fashionable silk evening gowns.

"Will this armor really work?" Eleanor asked as she wiggled awkwardly to squeeze her legs into the tight fabric.

"It will," Kuveni confirmed. "The bigger problem will be the parts of you that are not covered by the armor, but I have a few tricks up my sleeve to help with that too. I shouldn't get into the details. But, even with our help, it is pivotal that you avoid as much danger as you can. We must get everyone out of this without our enemies learning any more about our family secrets. Understood, Eleanor? The safer you keep yourself, the safer Edmund will be, in more ways than one."

"Aye," Eleanor agreed as she refocused on squeezing into the tight fabric.

When she was finished, she put her Roman dress back on over the armor, checking that the pistol was in position in her large pocket. As Eleanor noticed that her sleeves were suddenly longer (just long enough to cover all hints of the armor), Kuveni inspected her approvingly. Yvie stared at it, and as she finished putting her dress back on, she glanced down to spy Kuveni's tasteful additions to her dress as well.

"*Mon dieu*," Yvie whispered. "How fantastical."

"My dear girl, just wait until you see what else we can do," Kuveni winked.

Without any warning, Kuveni burst open the bathroom door, and Edmund scrambled to pull up his trousers.

"Now, now, we don't have any more time to dilly-dally!" Kuveni exclaimed.

Edmund finished buttoning up his trousers, but as he observed Eleanor and Yvie's bare forearms, he fell immediately into another panic attack.

"We can't do this. You can't do this! This armor won't do anything to protect your heads! Your arms! I won't do it!"

Mélusine approached him and took his hand into hers. She closed her eyes and pushed a hefty dose of euphoria straight into him. "Relax, mon chéri. Everything will be okay," she whispered.

Edmund looked around at his audience, landing his attention on Eleanor.

"I wish I could believe that," he countered miserably. "I have heard it falsely far too many times in my life, and the stakes are higher than they've ever been."

Mélusine gathered him into a motherly hug. "Trust us, Edmund. We will keep all of you safe."

Kuveni approached and took his shaking hands into hers. She leaned forward and whispered into his ear. "Edmund, my dearest, most beloved child, think of your most special talents—the talents that your boyhood dreams never even fathomed—and multiply them as far as your imagination can climb, and *that* is how powerful we are."

She ignored a disapproving look from Mélusine and let go of him, placing her right hand out palm-up before him. With her other hand, she gracefully waved her fingers as if she was playing an invisible instrument until a small cyclone of dusty particles appeared, swirling slowly into a finite shape, just as if she were a wizard conjuring an object from the great beyond. A pleasant breeze accompanied her magic until a sword was fully formed in her hand.

"Good lord," Edmund murmured.

464

"*Mon dieu*," Yvie whispered with wonder at the sight.

"This is your favorite weapon, is it not?" Kuveni asked as she closed it into Edmund's hand.

He held it out and swung it around, marveling at its solid state.

"It is," he agreed, working to hide his bewilderment.

"And why is that?" she pushed.

"Because it intimidates my enemies into avoiding the misfortune of engaging me in the first place. It saves more lives than it takes."

Kuveni pulled him into a tight hug and whispered into his ear. "My beautiful boy, we could not help you in the trenches because you had to learn the true hellish nature of war for yourself, but you know it now. You do not need another reminder. And so, we will do now what we wished so dearly we could have done then. We will save everyone together." Kuveni kissed him on the forehead. "Trust me, Edmund. I have taken a great risk to be by your side today. Together, we will make it worth the sacrifice."

Edmund nodded his reluctant agreement, as Eleanor took his hand tightly into hers.

"Now, before we head into battle, I have one more thing to show you, mon chéri," Mélusine said as she glanced around the group. She landed her attention on Mr. Valov. "I need a volunteer. How about you."

Mr. Valov avoided eye contact as she approached him.

"Come, Edmund, I want to show you something that will be useful to you from now on."

Edmund hid his nerves and offered Mr. Valov an apologetic glance as he obeyed and took his position beside her.

"With our unique strength, it is quite easy for us to knock out an adversary without killing him, mon chéri. You simply need to find the right position with your hand, always between the neck and the collar bone…" Mr. Valov gulped as she ran her hand along the area she was describing. "And then apply just enough pressure that it cuts off the blood-flow and causes a shock to the system."

She pressed down, and Mr. Valov collapsed unconscious onto the floor.

"Percy!" Edmund exclaimed disapprovingly as he kneeled down to check on Mr. Valov's entirely unconscious state.

"I'm sorry, mon chéri. It needed to be done."

Mélusine did not look the least bit sorry, and Eleanor wondered what ruthless espionage she had witnessed for her to eliminate Mr. Valov from their team so aggressively.

"We could have used his help! He killed six men on the Orient Express!" Edmund exclaimed. "We need all the help we can get!"

"You needed a demonstration of the technique, and now you've had one," she countered. "The point, mon chéri, is that you don't have to kill these men with your bare hands in order to neutralize them. You can knock them out instead and save the killing for the ones who deserve no mercy."

"Still, *Percy*," he rolled his eyes as he said her false name. "He didn't volunteer to be attacked." Edmund moved Mr. Valov into a more dignified position.

"Well, now that he's out, he will be out of harm's way, and we will not have to worry about him. The fewer people we need to protect, the more successful we will be."

"How long will he be out?" Eleanor asked.

"Many hours. They always are with this technique. It is usually enough for us to do what we need to do and get out of the limelight. He'll probably have a wicked headache when he wakes up, but *c'est la vie*. Now, *allons-y*. We don't have much time. The pirates have been working on breaking their way into the hold to collect more weapons, and they've almost succeeded. Now, Edmund, you and Oz must secure the bridge, and I will assist you. I trust that between you two, you can figure out how to turn this ship out to sea, away from the African mainland. Kate will join Eleanor and Yvie to stop the pirates *before* they get their hands on more weapons."

"And what weapon will you be using by our side to perpetuate our farce, Sir Percy?" Edmund asked with a combination of nerves and cheek.

Mélusine looked around the room, surveying Kuveni's open suitcase of weapons, Edmund's sword, Oz's pistol, and then landing her gaze on the cane that Edmund was no longer using, tucked between the bed and the nightstand.

In a blur, she pried it from its position and swung it around, challenging Edmund and his sword with an exaggerated flourish.

"A cane is the ultimate gentleman's weapon," she said with the affected accent of the Scarlet Pimpernel. "It takes them by surprise every time."

In a series of moves too fast for Eleanor to follow, Mélusine used the cane to disarm Edmund, landing him in her grip with his sword in her hand.

Mélusine laughed at her triumph and let Edmund go with an exaggerated bow. She didn't hide her proud smile. "Never fear, mon chéri, I am on your side. Now, shall we go vanquish some pirates?"

"We must, mustn't we?" Edmund conceded. He couldn't hide a fresh look of respect in his expression for her admirable fighting skills.

"Time is of the essence," Kuveni pushed forward.

Edmund pulled Eleanor into a passionate embrace, and she could feel his heart pumping.

"Eleanor, my life will be over if something happens to you," he whispered desperately into her ear.

"Same goes for you, Edmund." She kissed him gently. "Remember your mantras. Be as human as you can be, and keep yourself alive, Colonel. We have a honeymoon to get back to."

Edmund kissed her again, and Oz and Yvie rushed into their own passionate embrace, licking each other's tongues in a decidedly French style until Kuveni cleared her throat loudly.

"Come, mes chéris. It is time to become legends again," Mélusine declared.

And with one final glance at the messy room, the cache of unused weapons, and the sleeping spying butler, the posse of virtuous heroes set forth to save an unsuspecting ship from a perilous pairing of pirates and fools.

CHAPTER 29 – PIRATES AND FOOLS

Eleanor had never seen Kuveni look so determined as the service lift slowly worked its way towards the bottom level of the cargo hold. Her own nerves were raging, and she wondered if Kuveni could sense her pumping adrenaline.

"Didn't the path to the lift seem strangely empty for this early in the evening?" Eleanor observed. "We didn't see a single passenger on our floor."

"My dear girl, you and Edmund are the only passengers on your floor! That's why it's called the captain's suite," Kuveni explained. "But that was not the only reason for our unobstructed passage. Our spying friends have been quietly putting the ship on lockdown for hours, since even before dinner. They are trying to minimize the number of witnesses to their sinister plan after the scores of people in the first class dining room witnessed their attack on Mr. Corrigan. For once, though, their foolishness will be a blessing for us. It means we will have a smaller audience witnessing our talents in the height of battle."

"Battle…" Eleanor murmured. "I didn't want to think of this little endeavor like that."

"We will do our best to keep it from becoming an accurate description," Kuveni reassured her unconvincingly. "But that is certainly the expectation that has kept your husband on the edge of a shell-shocked episode, Eleanor. He is doing remarkably well given the circumstances, and now we must give him an experience that will help him out of his hell, not send him right back into it."

"Aye," Eleanor agreed as the lift reached the very bottom floor.

"Darlings, stay behind me, and keep your pistols poised. I will be your shield while you shoot at the pirates. I recommend aiming for their shoulders and legs. They are not the heartiest of warriors, and I've never found mercenaries to be particularly motivated in the face of a real fight. One or two minor injuries will likely scare the others off," Kuveni advised.

Eleanor and Yvie threw each other a determined glance, and without another word, Kuveni pushed open the iron grate and stepped into a hallway lit by flickering electric lights. At the very end, a group of disheveled Somalis and stumbling, sweating, intoxicated Italians were shouting at each other as they attempted unsuccessfully to kick open the stubborn door to the cargo hold.

"My dearest pirates, it is time for you to surrender!" Kuveni called.

Yvie threw Eleanor a nervous look at Kuveni's unexpected revelation of their presence to their otherwise preoccupied adversaries.

The entire group turned to look at them, and then burst out laughing at the sight of three beautiful women in stylish evening attire daring to challenge them.

The pirates licked their cracked lips and high-fived each other as they let the women approach.

"Really, darlings, that was very unwise of you," Kuveni informed them as they reached the increasingly excited group.

470

The sweaty, intoxicated Italian leader lunged forward and pulled Kuveni into his arms. He hissed something snide in Italian at her, and Kuveni threw Eleanor and Yvie an anticipatory nod.

With one effortless movement, Kuveni ripped the man's arms off of her and slammed her hand onto the same pressure point Mélusine had shown Edmund.

As the man collapsed unconscious onto the ground, his companions' hoots and jeers dissolved into stunned silence. Before the pirates could gather their slow wits, Eleanor and Yvie both grabbed the closest men and kneed them each in the groin.

Two men swung clumsily at Kuveni, and she redirected their efforts against each other. An excruciating pop rang out as their skulls collided, and they collapsed unconscious onto the ground. As the three unconscious bodies littered the area in front of the locked door of the cargo hold, the rest of their crew finally processed the shocking truth that three modern sheilas were successfully defeating them.

With grunts, growls, and some drunken machismo shouting, the men redoubled their efforts, this time without holding back. One grabbed Kuveni's arm, and she threw him onto the floor and squeezed his pressure point with the heel of her shoe.

Yvie chased after a straggler who pushed her up against the wall in an effort to escape towards the elevator. She let him pass, and then ran after him, pummeling him from behind, wrapping her arms around his neck, and wrestling him to the ground. She grabbed her high heeled shoe and slammed it onto the same pressure point Kuveni had used, but the man only reached up at her, trying to cop a feel. Eleanor rushed to her side and slammed her hands onto the shoe, and together they produced enough pressure to knock the scoundrel out cold.

The last conscious pirate lunged at Eleanor, and she hopped up and channeled all of her anger at the wretchedly foolish situation into her arm. As her fist made contact with his jaw,

Kuveni rushed towards them at her fastest human speed and squeezed him unconscious with a pinch of her fingers.

"Men. They bring it upon themselves every time," Kuveni declared as she brushed off their sweat from her hands. "Now come, my darlings, we must use our upper hand to help our men on the bridge. Their approach will not be as easy as ours was."

They ran straight to the elevator.

"I'm glad we didn't have to shoot them," Eleanor admitted.

"I am too," Kuveni agreed as she took her guarding position in front of them. "But prepare yourselves. The next round will not be so easy."

They stood in silence as the elevator slowly cranked its way up a seemingly endless number of floors.

Eleanor's heart jumped into her throat as the sound of muffled shouting and gunshots penetrated into the elevator shaft. She took a deep, calming breath and gripped the pistol, readying herself to shoot.

When the elevator reached the bridge floor, Kuveni held out her arms, blocking Eleanor and Yvie with the flowing beaded sleeves of her dress as she pushed open the grate.

Yvie ducked, and Eleanor flinched as a fresh round of gunshots rang out from dangerously close to their position. Terrified Italian shouting followed.

"Stay behind me," Kuveni whispered over her shoulder.

Boom.

Boom.

Boom.

They followed Kuveni as she walked slowly through the corridor, collecting a rash of bullets in her form.

As she reached each pirate, Kuveni ripped the guns from the men's hands and dissolved them into thin air, following up each triumph with a quick knock-out until they reached the door to the bridge, and each and every pirate was unconscious, littering the corridor.

"My darlings, are you alright?" Kuveni turned around, completely unscathed, without any evidence of the bullets she'd absorbed on their behalf.

"*Mon dieu*," Yvie murmured.

"That was fifteen pirates in all. There are thirteen more to go," Kuveni whispered, ignoring Yvie's wonder at her miraculous condition.

"Where did the bullets go?" Eleanor asked as she felt Kuveni's perfectly intact beaded dress with her hand.

"I dissolved them as soon as they entered my form," Kuveni explained. "They went to the same place where I put the guns— out into the air around us. Now, come. We must be more careful on the bridge. There are spies watching, and we'd best intervene before Edmund gives himself away. It will be a miracle if he hasn't already."

Kuveni waited for Eleanor and Yvie to nod their agreement, and then she pushed open the door to the bridge, slamming it behind them as soon as they were inside.

Edmund and Oz stood at the helm next to the same boy who hadn't cared earlier when they'd pointed out that the ship was off course. This time, the boy was unconscious in his chair, pushed off of to the side of the control panel with his magazine on his lap. Mélusine stood in front of the wide-open window where shattered glass littered the floor, holding Oz's gun and listening intently. Four unconscious Italians slept soundly on the floor, and their guns were stacked neatly in the corner.

"Dearest?!" Edmund exclaimed as he noticed their arrival and rushed at his fastest human speed to gather Eleanor into his arms for a passionate embrace. "That was fast!"

"They didn't think three women would put up much of a fight. We proved them wrong." Eleanor couldn't hide her smile of pride at their easy triumph, and Edmund pulled her into his arms for an even more scandalous kiss. She felt the same lightheadedness that she'd felt several times before when he was in a particularly passionate mood, and she leaned into his arms to let him steady her.

"What's next?" Yvie asked as she approached Oz. "Kate knocked out several pirates in the hallway just now."

"Yes, they've been trying to get onto the bridge since we commandeered the ship a few minutes ago. We locked them out, but there are more who have been shooting at us through the window. Percy has been shooting back," Oz explained.

Eleanor finally ripped herself away from her intensely relieved husband, and they both wiped the remnants of her red lipstick from their lips as they refocused on the crisis at hand.

"We've just figured out how to work this control panel," Edmund said as he cleared his throat and guided her to join him beside Oz. "We're turning the ship back towards British Somaliland now, but we will still be in enemy waters for several hours before we get there."

Boom.

Boom.

Boom.

Edmund pulled Eleanor into his arms protectively as a fresh round of fire broke out between Mélusine and the pirates outside.

Oz gathered Yvie into his arms, but Kuveni positioned herself between them and the line of fire, reaching her arms up to let her flowing sleeves protect them. As Eleanor spied Kuveni's fearful expression, for the first time, Eleanor found Edmund's protection of her more useful than offensive.

Boom.

Boom.

Boom.

"Got him!" Mélusine exclaimed triumphantly.

"That leaves only eight," Kuveni said as she relaxed and joined Mélusine to assess the situation just outside the window.

"The worst eight, I think," Mélusine replied. "I think the leaders sent the thugs to do the menial tasks while they kept their best men readied in position for a fight. This sniper has been much more skilled than the others we disabled."

"Was the helmsman a traitor?" Kuveni asked curiously as she eyed the unconscious boy. "I did not get that sense from him."

"No, he just annoyed me," Mélusine shrugged. "The lazy lout would have let the Devil himself take over this ship without a peep of protest."

As Edmund reluctantly let Eleanor out of his arms, the sound of heavy footsteps in the hallway beyond brought them each to attention. Mélusine handed Oz's gun to Kuveni and gathered up her cane from the floor. She rushed across the room at her fastest human speed and readied herself to engage their next enemy.

"Colonel?" a familiar voice called through the door.

Eleanor felt Edmund tense as she let out a long, annoyed sigh.

"Colonel? Please let me in! I want to help!" Desperation rang out in George Ridgeway's voice.

"Help indeed," Kuveni scoffed. "Edmund, we must get this worthless bugger out of our hair as soon as possible."

"*Sacre bleu*, we don't have time for this!"

Mélusine ripped open the door, grabbed Mr. Ridgeway, pulled him inside, and pushed him up against the wall, holding him up by the neck with the cane.

"You are not welcome here! Now crawl back under the rock where you came from."

"Who...who... who are you?" Mr. Ridgeway stuttered as he eyed the scene.

"I'm the Scarlet bloody Pimpernel, and you are one slothenly, drunken, abusive swine if ever I've seen one. Now *allez!*"

"How exactly did you escape from your captivity, Mr. Ridgeway?" Edmund asked suspiciously as he glanced out the window, without budging from his position by the helm. "I gave the Chief of Security explicit orders not to let you out."

"I climbed out through the balcony! Down onto the deck two floors below!" Mr. Ridgeway's tone was strangely high-pitched, as if he wasn't entirely sure where his story was going. "I knew we were traveling too long along a coastline! Something had to be done! You have to admit it, Colonel! You must have been the one who knocked out those bolos in the corridor. I can't say I understand one lick why you didn't just kill them." Mr. Ridgeway squirmed, and Mélusine tightened her grip until his voice was reduced to a pained rasp. "I'm sorry! I didn't mean it! You're too important for me to challenge anything you do, Colonel! So, I've come to help! Tell me what you want me to do, and I'll do it! For king, for country!"

Edmund straightened his posture, squeezed Eleanor's hand, and approached Mr. Ridgeway, while Mélusine maintained her grip. He leaned in uncomfortably close to Mr. Ridgeway's face to declare his orders.

"Mr. Ridgeway, I want you to head straight back to your wife and your daughters, and I want you to stay with them, humbly, apologetically, and valiantly, until the danger on this ship has passed. You will be the husband and father that they deserve, and you will help them get through this crisis like the honorable man that you should already be. You will go now, without one more word of protest."

"But…"

Edmund leaned in until his face was only inches from Mr. Ridgeway's.

"Without *one* more word of protest," he reiterated.

Mélusine slowly let Mr. Ridgeway down, and he felt his neck, straightened his wrinkled collar, rolled his shoulders, looked upon his disapproving audience, and sighed his defeat loudly.

"You will regret this, Colonel. All of you will regret it," Mr. Ridgeway declared.

He ripped open the door and slammed it behind him.

"I hope that's the only one of my orders that he disobeys," Edmund muttered.

"He is out of our hair. That is what matters most right now," Kuveni reminded him. "Now we must secure the rest of the ship. There are eight more pirates lurking. We must neutralize all of them before the unsuspecting passengers will be safe."

Edmund returned to Eleanor's side and took her hand. "What do you think we should do, Kate?"

"We should corner them and knock them unconscious. Only then will we be able to deal with the other thorn in our side." Kuveni eyed an ugly painting on the far wall behind which, Eleanor realized, their uninvited observers must be lurking. "Oz and Yvie, you should stay here and make sure the ship remains on course. The rest of us will go after the pirates. With four of us and eight of them, they will not last long."

"Do you know where they are?" Eleanor asked.

"I've seen several pass by as I've been toying with the sniper," Mélusine interjected. "I believe they are doing various surveys of the ship to make sure that none of the passengers have realized what's going on. Once they discover that we've taken back the helm, they will not be pleased."

"We should take them on while they're not together. It will be easier and safer to neutralize them in small groups," Edmund strategized.

"*On y va.* Let's go down to the main deck," Mélusine suggested.

Kuveni handed Oz back his gun. "Stay away from the window, and keep the door to the bridge locked. You must keep this ship on course to safe waters, and we will not be here to help you fight off any more enemies." She threw a knowing glance to Yvie.

Kuveni rallied Edmund and Eleanor, shoving them forcefully towards the door.

"Where's your weapon, Kate?" Edmund asked as Mélusine positioned her cane, Eleanor took the pistol out of her pocket, and he squeezed the handle of his sword.

"I've always preferred to use my bare hands," she replied. "Being a woman often allows me to get close enough to take my enemies by surprise. Never underestimate the power of being underestimated, Edmund."

Mélusine pushed open the door, and together they ran past Kuveni's unconscious victims, straight into the elevator.

"Eleanor, how on earth did you defeat those pirates so fast? Really?" Edmund asked as soon as the lift was clunking its way downwards. His posture softened as he noticed a cut and a bruise on her fist, and brought her hand to his mouth to kiss it. "You're injured."

"Darling, I will be perfectly fine. I didn't even notice it."

"Mon chéri, you mustn't let yourself be distracted by unimportant details. There is more to do, and Eleanor is a worthy partner. She is worthier than any human we could have ever chosen to stand by your side, in this way and every other."

Edmund stopped to contemplate the odd statement, and Eleanor held her breath, hoping simultaneously that Mélusine hadn't just given away her close connection to them and... that she had. Then her interminable farce would finally be over...

Instead, he honed in on another detail of her statement. "Did you think you would choose a woman to stand by my side? That you'd arrange a marriage for me as if I were some royal prince?"

"No, mon chéri. It is strictly forbidden for any of us to meddle in others' personal affairs. It always ends in misery. Doesn't it, *Kate*?"

"Eight more," Kuveni changed the subject as the elevator reached the main deck. "We only need to neutralize eight more, and everyone will be safe. Edmund, remember there are some powerful spies watching. We must be more careful than ever not to give ourselves away."

Eleanor felt his pulse racing as Edmund held her hand tightly in his.

Kuveni and Mélusine positioned themselves in front of Edmund and Eleanor as the elevator clunked to a stop at its destination. Mélusine pushed open the grate, and they followed her as she stepped out into the warm, salty, moonlit night.

"Mes chéris, keep your eyes and ears open. The sniper changed his position several times before I got him. Keep your attention on the crow's nest and the steam funnels up there." She pointed to the massive metal drums that released the steam from the ship's many boilers. "As well as the areas immediately around us, and I will do the same."

Eleanor wrestled her hand away from Edmund's as she positioned her pistol, ready to shoot.

Her heart raced, and she hoped that Edmund wouldn't be distracted by the scent of her heightened fear, as the tranquility of the full moonlit night and the gentle ocean breeze made her feel like there was something ominously amiss more and more with every quiet step they took.

They wandered about the deck for an excruciatingly long time without a soul in sight, and Eleanor wondered if her gentle husband had even noticed the oddity that there were no passengers out and about, despite the fact that it could not have been much later than ten o'clock in the evening.

"Where do you think the pirates might be?" Eleanor finally whispered to Kuveni. "You don't think they've gotten into the cargo hold, do you?"

"Certainly not. I locked down that floor when we left it. No one will get in or out until I let them," Kuveni whispered back. "But it is curious. I don't like being constrained like this one bit. I've lost track of all of our enemies without being able to spread myself around to do a sweep."

Eleanor let her mind entertain the odd idea that being solid for a few hours felt like a constraint to Kuveni.

But, before Eleanor's wandering mind lulled her into a false sense of security, shouting rang out from just around the corner, and Kuveni and Mélusine both rushed at their fastest human speed to beat Edmund and Eleanor to the scene. They disappeared around the corner, but Edmund stopped and threw Eleanor a desperate look as he stood straight up against the wall, working to get his anxiety under control.

"Darling, I'm right behind you. We will do this together," Eleanor whispered as his breathing exploded into another round of hyperventilation.

Boom.

Boom.

Boom.

Gunshots rang out.

More shouting.

Two excruciating crunches.

Mélusine shouted something angrily in Italian.

Boom.

Boom.

Boom.

She heard the thuds of several bodies collapsing unconscious.

Kuveni spat something snide in Somali.

"That was eight!" Mélusine exclaimed.

Boom.

"*Mon dieu*, did we miscount?" Mélusine hissed.

The gunshots echoed from higher in the sky.

Boom.

Boom.

Boom.

"Blimey, I think it's another sniper. I think he must be standing on the platform around one of the funnels," Eleanor whispered.

Edmund closed his eyes and whispered his mantras desperately as Eleanor readied herself to join in the fight.

"Edmund, neither Kate nor Percy have guns. We need to help them."

Boom.

More shouting.

Mélusine swore in French.

Kuveni responded in Latin.

Boom.

Boom.

Boom.

"Edmund, now! We have to help them!"

Edmund opened his eyes and continued his mantras as he nodded his silent agreement. A look of fresh vigor and determination entered his expression. Eleanor wondered if perhaps his darkest urges had just been awakened; if perhaps whatever had led him to enjoy killing his enemies on the Orient Express was working its way to the surface at that very moment. A fresh sense of urgency bombarded her at the thought.

"Come on!" Eleanor hissed.

She followed him around the corner where several unconscious pirates' bodies littered the ground, flanked by two dead ones bleeding out all over the wooden flooring of the deck.

Edmund whispered his mantras more vehemently.

Boom.

He threw himself in front of her.

The bullet bounced off of the Roman armor and landed on the ground with a subtle clank.

She looked straight up at the crow's nest, aimed the pistol, and pulled the trigger.

Boom.

Kuveni and Mélusine both looked over to watch her smoking gun as a man dressed entirely in black fell from his position in the crow's nest at least ten meters onto a platform below.

"Nice shot, my dear!" Kuveni exclaimed.

"I thought you said there were only twenty-eight to begin with!" Mélusine hissed.

"There were!" Kuveni exclaimed. "I don't understand where the extra man came from! Perhaps he was a sleeper? Perhaps many of the passengers are really pirates, and they didn't give away a peep about it when I was doing my survey!"

"That means that we have no idea how many more we have to fight! It could be hundreds!" Mélusine exclaimed. "*C'est un disastre encroyable!*"

As soon as she declared the dire news, frenzied footsteps, shouting, and whimpering rang out, and lo and behold, three gun-wielding Italians escorted Mr. Ridgeway and his trembling wife and daughters onto the deck.

"Please don't hurt us!" Mrs. Ridgeway begged. "We don't know anything about anything! Please, just let the girls go!"

"Edmund!" Lily exclaimed. "Edmund, please help us!"

"You will give us the ship now, or these English *cazzoni* will die!" the most brutish of the Italian mercenaries, who reeked of alcohol and sweat, declared with a thick Italian accent.

Eleanor raised her gun and aimed it straight at the man. The man chuckled at her brash feminine cheek, and then looked puzzled as Edmund straightened his posture and raised his sword (rather pointlessly, Eleanor had to admit).

"Agree, Edmund," Eleanor whispered in Gaelic. "We can buy time by escorting them to the bridge. We will defeat them there with Oz and Yvie's help."

"*Silenzio!*" another mercenary screeched as he pointed his gun straight at Eleanor's chest.

"Fine. We will take you to the bridge. Follow us now," Edmund said with his greatest impression of calm authority.

"What?!" Mr. Ridgeway exclaimed indignantly. "No! I will not let this Italian scum dictate anything! For king, for country!"

"Daddy, no!" Daisy squealed.

"Don't unmask the angels, Daddy! God will be very cross with you!" Lily screamed.

Mr. Ridgeway rushed forward and tried to grab the gun from his closest captor.

Eleanor looked up as two more pirates appeared on the closest balcony above them, pointing their guns at Mrs. Ridgeway and the girls.

Mr. Ridgeway's captor wrestled him off, ripping at his slinged arm until he screamed with agony. The man threw him onto the ground and kicked him in the stomach. Blood began leaking through his sling from the partially healed bullet wound that had just opened back up.

"You never learn, George. Do you?" Mrs. Ridgeway muttered as the mercenary kicked him in the stomach a second time, and he coughed up blood. As George wheezed with pain, the mercenary returned his attention (and his pointed gun) to Mrs. Ridgeway and the girls.

"Any more English tricks?" the mercenary leader hissed as he aimed his gun at Edmund.

Eleanor glanced around, her mind moving a mile a minute to formulate any reasonable plan. But, as soon as she spied a potential exit for them in the dark shadows between the two steam funnels, two more pirates dressed entirely in black revealed their position on the platform at the top of the closest steam funnel.

As they aimed their guns at Eleanor and Kuveni, Eleanor could not deny that the group was entirely surrounded.

Once again, the situation was completely and utterly hopeless, and Eleanor did not have the faintest idea how they were going to get out of it without any of Edmund's secrets being revealed. She half-hoped that Mélusine would just give up, snap her fingers, and dissolve all of their adversaries into thin air.

Boom.

Boom.

The two gunmen on the lower balcony collapsed.

Boom.

Boom.

Blood splattered onto Mrs. Ridgeway and the girls as the two pirates closest to them collapsed with ugly chest wounds. Edmund closed his eyes and whispered his mantras, while Daisy and Lily burst into tears.

"Mummy?" Lily squeaked as she held up her bloody hands. "This is *his* blood! It's the bad man's blood!"

"Sshhh," Mrs. Ridgeway whispered as she wiped their hands clean with her dress, ignoring the fresh blood on her own face and in her hair. "Sshhhh. Let the angels save us, darling. We must be silent for the angels to save us."

The mercenary leader looked around with panic and surprise as he realized that he was the lone standing combatant on the deck.

Boom.

Boom.

One of the gunmen on the funnel's platform collapsed, and the other rushed for cover behind the funnel.

Oz and Yvie stood on the captain's balcony, each aiming their smoking guns at the two remaining pirates.

"Blimey, you're both bloody good shots," Eleanor murmured.

Despite his unenviable position, the remaining mercenary maintained his stance with his gun pointed at Edmund.

"You are surrounded," Edmund informed him. "This is your last chance to surrender."

The man grinned cheekily and aimed his gun at Eleanor. "I will take that doll with me."

Her fiery rage burst its way to the surface, and in a split-second judgment, Eleanor decided that she was not going to let that bastard get away with anything, least of all taunting her tormented husband with a petty threat against her life.

Without a hint of regret, she pulled the trigger.

Boom.

Boom.

As her gunshot rang out, so did his.

Edmund jumped in front of her, but his chivalrous move came milliseconds too late. She stumbled backwards as the stinging pain of the mercenary's bullet bouncing off Mélusine's Roman armor underwear traveled through her. After a moment of shock, waiting for the excruciating pain of a mortal bullet wound to reach her senses, she shivered and took in a deep breath of relief as she watched the bullet land on the ground below her. She could feel a fresh bruise pulsating painfully from the point on her chest where the bullet had made contact, but she didn't care at all.

"I knew Eleanor was an angel too!" Daisy exclaimed.

"By god, the colonel is not the only one!" Mr. Ridgeway hissed as he struggled to stand up. "She's bloody bullet proof!"

"Eleanor!" Edmund exclaimed. He lowered his voice as he observed the hole in her dress and her unscathed body with a combination of residual panic and fresh wonder. "Eleanor, my speed didn't work. I must not be fully recovered yet!"

"And a lucky duck you are for it, too, darling. I'm perfectly fine. The armor deflected the bullet. Now I just need to catch my breath."

She leaned over with her hands on her knees, trying to slow her dangerously racing heart. She refused with all her might to let her mind run through what might have happened without Mélusine's armor.

She looked up into Edmund's black eyes.

"Return to your mantras, darling. I will be just fine."

Edmund obeyed as he positioned himself behind her, ready to block any more unexpected attacks.

As Eleanor looked up at the scene, the mercenary leader was unconscious and bleeding on the ground. She couldn't tell from her angle where her bullet had hit him, and she didn't care. He was out of the way.

Oz held his gun aimed at the funnel where the remaining known gunman awaited behind the shelter of the enormous steel drum. Yvie kept her gun pointed at the scene, readied for any more pirates to jump out of the woodwork, while Mélusine stood with her eyes closed, seemingly in deep thought.

Mr. Ridgeway gathered up the gun of the closest dead mercenary, but as Eleanor cringed, awaiting another declaration about king and country, Mr. Ridgeway did something entirely unexpected. As Eleanor thought back on the moment years later, she could never fully believe how seamlessly the man earned his rank as the most despicable she'd ever encountered… more despicable, she was sure, than any of the murderous pirates they'd already defeated.

George Ridgeway straightened his posture and aimed the gun at his wife.

"George? George Ridgeway, what in god's name are you doing?" Eloise asked with a quiver in her terrified voice. "George, have you gone mad?"

"Daddy, what are you doing?!" Lily squealed.

Eleanor glanced up to spot Yvie aiming her pistol right at Mr. Ridgeway's head. A burst of anxiety exploded in her gut as she envisioned the horrific scene that would unfold in front of those two little girls' eyes, and she nodded subtly, hoping that Yvie would take her cue to wait.

"George, there is no need for any of this. You still have the chance to be the hero," Eleanor called. "Show your family what kind of man you can be."

"That is exactly what I'm doing," Mr. Ridgeway declared.

His hand was shaking as he held the gun tightly in his grip.

Lily gathered Daisy into her arms, and they both stepped in front of their mother.

"Daddy, please," Lily implored. "Please find your bloody honor."

Eleanor's heart broke as the girl parroted the orders Edmund had declared to the drunken fool the night before.

At the reference, Mr. Ridgeway ripped Lily away from her sister and into his arms, taking her hostage while he maintained his position, pointing the gun at his wife.

"The angels won't let you, Daddy. The angels won't let you hurt us again," Lily whimpered.

"I'm counting on it," Mr. Ridgeway muttered.

In that moment, Eleanor noticed the same mad desperation in his eyes that she'd seen too many times before in the homicidal maniacs she'd treated throughout her years as a nurse in the godforsaken lunatic asylums.

"Stop me, Colonel. I dare you. We both know what I saw on the bloody Orient Express. Do what you have to do to stop me! Hop over here in the blink of an eye, tear my head right off with your bare hands if you must, show the world what kind of soldier you really are! Then Colonel Snell will know who the real liar is, and the Empire will have the weapon it deserves."

"Colonel Snell? What is he talking about?" Eleanor whispered.

"I have no bloody clue," Edmund murmured. "Madness. It's all madness."

"For king, for country," Mr. Ridgeway declared.

Boom.

Lily and Daisy shrieked in unison, while Mrs. Ridgeway let out a blood-curdling scream.

George Ridgeway collapsed onto the ground, and Lily squirmed out from under him as a large gunshot wound in his upper right chest bled out all over the ground.

"Mummy, this is *his* blood! It's Daddy's blood!" Lily wailed as she held up her freshly bloody hands again.

Still shaking violently, Mrs. Ridgeway gathered Lily into her arms alongside Daisy and began silently wiping her husband's blood off of her daughter's hands.

Eleanor looked up. Yvie held the smoking gun with a look of simultaneous relief and dismay painted across her face.

"Colonel?" George Ridgeway rasped as blood filled his mouth. "Colonel Snell? Where are you hiding? You said all the guns had blanks. You said no matter how it looked, no one was really getting hurt!"

Eleanor rushed to examine his dire wound, while Edmund stood in position with his eyes closed, whispering his mantras. Kuveni and Mélusine rushed to Eleanor's side.

"Where is Colonel Snell?" Mr. Ridgeway asked Eleanor confusedly. "He said nothing would happen to them! To me! He said this was all part of his plan, for king, for country!"

Mélusine stood up to survey the scene.

Boom.

Eleanor flinched as another gunshot rang out, this time from the crow's nest.

Boom.

A second shot rang out from Oz and Yvie's position, and Oz stood with his smoking gun still aimed at the shooter as another man dressed in all black fell from the crow's nest onto the platform below.

Edmund opened his eyes with a look of agony painted across his face, and she spied a fresh bloody hole in the lower half of his right trouser leg. He went momentarily limp until he sucked in a deep, calming breath and pretended with all his might that he had not just been shot in the calf. His mantras burgeoned to a volume that was barely quieter than a shout, but she was grateful that they'd managed to switch themselves into the odd hissing language that he sometimes used when his brain was most addled.

Eleanor threw a desperate look to Kuveni, who whispered a quiet charm, and Eleanor glanced over to catch Edmund's trouser leg repairing itself into a perfectly clean, perfectly untouched condition, paired with a new bullet on the ground below him.

"You stay with this fool. I will help Edmund," Kuveni whispered into Eleanor's ear.

Kuveni rushed over to escort him to a staircase where he could sit down.

"This… wasn't… supposed… to happen," Mr. Ridgeway rasped between shallow breaths. Eleanor knew exactly what the grotesque gurgling of blood in his lungs meant. "They were never… supposed to be in any danger… Colonel Snell swore it! Eloise? Eloise, please!"

Mrs. Ridgeway did not come to his side. She only held her girls tighter.

"Mummy loves you," she cried as she kissed Lily and then Daisy. "Mummy loves you so, so much."

"Eloise… I never… would have… hurt you. You know that, right?" George's voice dissolved into pained, bloody, gurgling coughs.

"Just as you've always said, George. I know nothing," Eloise spat.

"Even if that gun had been filled with blanks, you would have terrorized your wife and your children, just to prove that you are not a mad fool?" Eleanor leaned down and whispered into his ear. "You failed, George Ridgeway. You have failed at everything that ever mattered. I hope you take that to your bloody grave."

Mr. Ridgeway wheezed, choking on blood, and then he closed his eyes, and took his last breath.

Edmund continued on with his mantras, while Kuveni sat beside him stroking his back and whispering reassurances into his ear.

"Colonel, you will explain yourself this instant!" a familiar voice shouted.

Eleanor startled, and Edmund looked around, continuing his mantras with even more urgency.

General Kettering kicked open a slatted supply closet door from the inside and pushed Colonel Snell right out into the open. Their American colleague slinked out behind them, as they revealed their hidden position from which they had apparently watched all of the carnage unfold.

"I... I... I don't understand what happened here!" Colonel Snell stuttered like a school child caught in the act of mischief. "Major Jackson, what were you thinking?!" he addressed the confused American. "There weren't supposed to be any real bullets!"

"What was *I* thinking? This was all *your* plan! All we did was drop the goddamned chandelier!" the American shouted back.

"But all we did was lockdown the passengers and tell the staff not to intervene with your bloody plan!" Colonel Snell exclaimed. "Are you telling me that none of these gunmen were yours?!"

"Of course they weren't! We wouldn't sacrifice good men just to test out a cockamamie theory about a magical soldier!" Major Jackson rebuked.

"But they are magical!" Colonel Snell exclaimed. "Both of them! They're bullet proof! Do you know what this could mean for us in the next war! We will be unstoppable! Those Fascists won't know what hit them!"

He rushed towards Eleanor, and she stood up and faced him indignantly with her head held high. She glanced over to Edmund and Kuveni, and then ripped open the front of her evening gown to reveal the Roman armor.

"We are not magical," she said flatly. "We were wearing bullet-proof fabric. It's an old Scottish technique that we only pull out of the closet when we're going into battle against pirates and fools. It still hurts like hell, though. You can see that my husband's bruises have knocked him right out of contention." Colonel Snell looked over at Edmund skeptically. "You will notice the bullets on the ground where we were shot. The armor deflected them."

Major Jackson walked over to where Eleanor had been shot and collected the bullet. He held it up in his hand.

"Jiminy Cricket, it's true!" he exclaimed, without any regard for the somber scene of devastation around him. "That'll be mighty useful the next time we face those goddamned Krauts, won't it?!'"

Colonel Snell reached forward to finger the fabric on her chest, and Eleanor slapped his hand away.

"You may examine it when I am not wearing it," she said sharply.

An expression of intense embarrassment worked its way onto his face. It morphed into dismay, and then into fear as he glanced down at the dead body of his foolish dead civilian shill, over to Mrs. Ridgeway and the young girls who had just witnessed their father killed before their eyes, and finally back to General Kettering whose face was bright red with rage.

"'Trust me,' you said. 'I have discovered a weapon that will save the bloody empire. That will make our foes tremble, and never dare to challenge us again, you said!'" General Kettering boomed as he loomed over Colonel Snell. "All I see here are civilian casualties of the greatest folly I have ever witnessed in my career! I will have your head for this!"

"But... but... it wasn't my folly! It was the Americans! Where did you even get all of these men?!" Snell looked accusingly to Major Jackson.

"Eight of these men are mine. *Eight*. None of them fired a single shot. That woman knocked them out with her feminine death grip before they even had a chance to do anything, ya hear?" He pointed accusingly at Kuveni. "Now, what were you doing with those snipers in the crow's nest, Colonel? No bullets, you say? Explain to me what the point of a sniper is if they don't have any bullets! And clear as day, those snipers were shooting with bullets."

"We needed proof!" Colonel Snell exclaimed. "The snipers weren't shooting to kill!"

General Kettering looked like he might explode with anger. "You assigned *snipers* to shoot at innocent British citizens? At a ranking officer in the British Army?! At a bloody war hero with so many medals for valor that he can't even fit them all onto his uniform?! What were you *thinking*?!"

"They were under strict orders not to kill!" Colonel Snell looked down at his feet as the full weight of his folly finally registered in his otherwise empty head.

General Kettering walked up to the unconscious body of the mercenary Eleanor had shot. "Who is this man? Is he one of yours?" he addressed Major Jackson.

"I have never seen him before in my life," Major Jackson replied.

General Kettering moved his attention to Colonel Snell.

"He is not one of ours," Colonel Snell replied, finally demonstrating a hint of humility.

"Are you two telling me that neither of you take credit for these drunken thugs?"

"*Vous êtes imbéciles*! They are pirates, you fools!" Mélusine finally interjected. "They are the Somali separatists and Italian Fascist mercenaries whom you *let* commandeer this passenger liner! Do you not understand what almost happened here?! If we hadn't saved you—if Edmund and Eleanor and Oz and Yvie had not fought off *twenty-eight* bloody pirates—every civilian on this ship would have been sold into slavery in Mogadishu, and the scores of British weapons in the hold would have been handed over straight to your enemies."

"Pirates!" Major Jackson exclaimed. "This isn't the goddamned Caribbean! None of these men even have an eye patch!"

"In a few hours they'll wake up, and you can ask them about their business yourselves," Eleanor said flatly.

"That will not be necessary," General Kettering intervened. "Colonel Snell, Major Jackson, you two will gather all of these unconscious men into the brig. When you are finished, you will clean up this mess. Every aspect of it, you hear?"

Colonel Snell saluted his acknowledgment, avoiding eye contact with everyone but General Kettering.

"Now, Colonel Marriner, I must offer you and your wife my deepest apologies, and thank you for averting one of the greatest maritime debacles in British history." Kuveni helped Edmund stand as General Kettering approached him, taking on the brunt of his weight as he balanced against her. He held in a pained grunt as he shook General Kettering's hand.

"I am grateful that it wasn't our entire military who lost their bloody minds tonight," Edmund replied as he glanced over at Colonel Snell.

"No, Colonel. There were two valiant soldiers who kept us on course... you, and Lieutenant Helmsworth."

"I reckon there were some modern sheilas who deserve as much credit as we do," Edmund corrected him.

"Right, yes, of course." General Kettering offered Kuveni a cursory glance, but then returned to his original point. "I'd offer you and Lieutenant Helmsworth a commendation, Colonel, but this entire incident will be classified at the highest levels. Rest assured, though, you will both be rewarded."

"I don't need a reward, General. I just need some rest," Edmund said as Kuveni redoubled her efforts to prop him up.

"Yes, yes, of course. Now is not the time to discuss such trivialities. Thank you for your service, Colonel. I look forward to our meeting under better circumstances. Perhaps then you can provide me with a sample of your wife's highly useful fabric. It could save many lives. For now, I will take command, as I should have done before this folly even began. You'd best escort your wife back to your room. The ship will be on lockdown until we can eliminate all of the evidence. It should go without saying that you are to speak of this to no one." He looked around to each and every conscious member of his audience. "Speak of it to *no one*. Do you understand? This never happened."

He glanced over to Mrs. Ridgeway, and Eleanor rushed over to help her and the girls up.

"Mrs. Ridgeway, my deepest condolences. Your family will be richly compensated for this loss," General Kettering said stoically. "I will be in touch later to explain your options. Rest assured, your lives will be more than comfortable from now on."

Daisy and Lily held each other's hands while tears streamed down their faces, but Mrs. Ridgeway had no words. She was trapped in shocked silence as she stared past the general to the bloody, dead corpse of her foolish husband.

"Eloise, perhaps you'd like to go back to the room we booked for you," Eleanor whispered into her ear. "Try to rest. Try to get the girls to rest. I'm sure that Kate will be by shortly to bring you some food." She glanced over to Kuveni who nodded her agreement. "This was a great tragedy, Eloise. It is natural for you to be in shock. We will be here, and we will help you."

She glanced down at Daisy and Lily, and then pulled them into her arms. She fought back a wave of her own tears as she remembered the horrific moment when she learned of her father's doomed fate.

"You will get through this, my darling girls. I promise. It doesn't feel that way now, but you must believe me. Alright?"

Lily and Daisy squeezed her as tight as their little arms could squeeze.

"Kate will be by soon, and I will stop by in the morning. Aye?" Eleanor said as she wiped away the girls' tears and offered them a sad smile.

"Aye," they squeaked.

"There are more pirates just outside the locked door to the cargo hold. You'll gather them into the brig if you know what's good for you," Eleanor addressed General Kettering.

"We plotted a course out of Italian Somali territory, back towards Berbera about an hour ago," Oz called from his position on the bridge's balcony. "Someone should make sure we stay on course this time."

"I will see to it personally," General Kettering declared as he threw one final glance of furious disapproval at Colonel Snell.

Mélusine joined Eleanor and whisked her over to Kuveni and Edmund's position by the stairs. She took in one deep whiff, and then sighed with resignation. "Oz, perhaps you and Yvie can meet us in Edmund and Eleanor's room. These two have some bruises from the bullets that could use some medical attention," she called.

Oz and Yvie nodded their agreement, and with one last look at the scene of utter devastation, the angels in disguise left the foolish humans to clean up their own bloody mess.

CHAPTER 30 – AU REVOIR OR ADIEU?

When the group arrived at Edmund and Eleanor's room, Oz and Yvie were already waiting inside, and Mr. Valov was sitting at the table beside the Yaksha suitcases of weapons and armor, smoking a cigarette and drinking a fresh glass of cognac. An ashtray overflowing with finished cigarettes and ash indicated that he had been awaiting their return for quite some time.

Kuveni and Eleanor whisked Edmund inside, and Mélusine slammed the door behind them.

"That Roman armor worked like a charm!" Oz exclaimed. "I could hardly believe my eyes when those bullets bounced off of you!"

"It does have its limitations," Kuveni said as she helped Edmund into the bathroom.

Eleanor helped him lift his leg up onto the corner of the bath, while Kuveni pulled up the cuff of his right trouser to reveal the nasty bullet wound underneath. His Rakshasa plasma wriggled around it, attempting unsuccessfully to rebuild his missing human flesh.

"Good lord, darling. I thought the bullet just grazed you! This must have been absolute torture to endure for the last half hour!" Eleanor exclaimed.

"It has been rather painful," Edmund admitted. "But I did a valiant job of hiding it, I hope? Do you think they suspected anything?"

"You were wonderful, darling. Really. I can't believe you pulled it off." Eleanor kissed him on the forehead.

"It was like you had centuries of practice, my boy," Kuveni winked.

Edmund grimaced with another burst of pain, and then moved to reach in and pull the bullet out with his fingers, but Eleanor rushed to stop him.

"Edmund, darling, we have a medic here. You do not need to rip it out with your fingers. I think it will hurt much less if Oz does it, don't you?"

Oz and Yvie approached tentatively, and Kuveni moved out of their way to make room.

"Strewth," Oz whispered as he leaned in to take a closer look at the alien sight. "I've never seen anything like it in my life."

Edmund blushed self-consciously. "Please do not trouble yourself. I am excessively experienced in getting bullets out of my flesh all by myself. It is a great rarity for me to be surrounded by so many people while I'm in a grotesque state like this... In fact, it has never happened before in my century on Earth."

"Your *century*..." Yvie murmured.

"You don't show it, mate," Oz said with wonder. "I think maybe your tall tales have a lot more truth to them than mine do!"

"I have no doubt." Edmund smiled as he let the pleasure of his revelation distract him momentarily from his pain. "Why, Oz, did I ever tell you about the time I fought off pirates alongside the Scarlet Pimpernel?"

"I'll one up you, mate. Did I ever tell *you* about the time I fought off pirates alongside two modern sheilas with wickedly good aim and some very talented angels in disguise?" Oz countered amicably.

Edmund looked down at his alien plasma hovering in his gaping wound. "I suppose I don't have a better explanation for you about all this, but you shouldn't expect divine intervention from me. You'll be dastardly disappointed."

"I've never been a praying man," Oz winked. "Except when I'm praying to the porcelain god after a rotten night at the boozer."

Edmund relaxed at Oz's casual reassurance, and reached towards the bullet again, readying himself to use his fingernails to rip it out.

Yvie squealed, while Oz gently put his hand on Edmund's to stop him. He shivered but said nothing about Edmund's especially frigid temperature. "No need, mate. Let me do it for you. Ellie, do you have a medical bag? I'll need some forceps."

Before Eleanor could respond, Kuveni whispered a quiet mantra and produced a pair of forceps in her hand. She presented them to Oz without offering a word of explanation. He took them with a polite nod and no questions, and kneeled down to get a better look at the wound.

"That is an ugly one, isn't it? You must have nerves of steel. Hold on tight, mate, I'm going in."

Edmund grunted and hissed as Oz poked and pried, letting out a final roar of pain as Oz broke it out of the stubborn Rakshasa plasma and held it up to the light.

"Yup, that's a doozy. I got all of it, though. Came out in one clean piece."

He dropped it into the washbasin, and Yvie gathered up a clean, wet washcloth to treat the wound, but Edmund held her off. Instead, everyone watched as Edmund's Rakshasa plasma set about hastily finishing off its healing work.

His pained grunts continued quietly as everyone, even Eleanor, watched with fascination while his violet plasma rebuilt his flesh and then absorbed all evidence of blood and gore right into his perfectly intact leg, dissolving itself back into his new skin.

Oz handed the forceps to Yvie, and she cleaned them off with hot water in the washbasin, but as she looked for a place to store them, Kuveni took them back and put them away in a hidden pocket in her dress. Eleanor watched curiously as every trace of their bulging presence disappeared into Kuveni's form.

"How are you feeling, darling?" Eleanor asked as Edmund put his leg back down onto the floor and pulled down his trouser cuff. He noticed the perfectly clean, perfectly intact fabric with no trace of a bullet hole and glanced at Kuveni, but didn't say a word.

"I'm perfectly fine now." Edmund pulled her into his arms for a gentle kiss. "As good as new, like always." He looked self-consciously to Oz and Yvie.

"I reckon I'll never see anything like that again," Oz said cheerfully. "I hope my surgery didn't hurt too much."

"It was much better than it normally is. Thank you," Edmund said, working to push back his timidity. He let go of Eleanor to take Oz's hands into his. He squeezed them gratefully. "I have so much to thank you for, I will have to take some time to think about the long list and give you a proper speech before you disembark."

"No worries, mate. I reckon we owe you our lives again. All of you, really." Oz looked to Kuveni and Mélusine.

"Think nothing of it, my dear boy!" Kuveni declared cheerfully. "All in a day's work! Now, I think Edmund and Eleanor will need some time alone to unwind after this wretched ordeal."

"Sounds like a good idea to me," Oz agreed.

"We will see you tomorrow," Yvie said as she pulled Eleanor into a friendly French farewell. "We will plan to stay on board all the way to Perth, assuming this ship returns to its route."

"Thank you," Eleanor whispered.

"It was a pleasure fighting by your side, Ellie," Yvie winked. "We modern sheilas have to stick together."

Edmund and Eleanor walked to the door of the bathroom to offer Yvie and Oz a friendly wave, but Edmund leaned himself heavily on the doorframe.

"Are you really alright?" Eleanor asked concernedly.

"Perfectly fine," he lied.

She raised her eyebrows skeptically. "I know you too well for you to get away with those kinds of lies now, Colonel."

"I suppose I'm feeling a bit lightheaded still. I think I'll take a few minutes to wash up."

"Shall I help you?" Eleanor asked.

"No. Really, dearest, I'll be fine in a few minutes. I'm sure of it," Edmund refused. "But I'd like to say goodbye before the rest of you leave, if you don't mind waiting?" He addressed Kuveni and Mélusine.

"Take your time, mon chéri. We will be here," Mélusine reassured him.

Eleanor stepped onto her tiptoes to kiss him on the cheek, and then left him alone as he closed himself into the bathroom.

As soon as the door was closed, Kuveni dissolved.

"Where'd she go?" Eleanor whispered to Mélusine.

"She went to survey the ship to make sure our triumph was complete. She's been itching to disperse herself for hours. This little sojourn has kept her in her corporeal form longer than I've seen her hold it in years."

Eleanor eyed Mr. Valov suspiciously. "Should we say anything in front of him?"

"Indeed, *Lord Blakeney*," Mr. Valov said with a hint of annoyance with his native British accent. "What exactly did I do to deserve to be taken off the roster?"

"Mon chéri, I think perhaps you've lost your spying touch. Did you not realize that General Kettering was here to assess your loyalties for himself? It only took me a few minutes of lurking to uncover that pertinent detail."

"General Kettering..." Mr. Valov whispered.

"He is the leader of MI-3, is he not?" Mélusine asked. "It is his organization that is in charge of maintaining loyalty within the ranks—yours and Edmund's, as it turns out."

"Is he?" Mr. Valov asked with genuine surprise. Mélusine was not convinced by his supposed innocence. "Truly, I didn't know that he was involved in intelligence at all! I suppose it makes sense, though. I always thought it was odd that a general would be puttering around writing historical volumes. This changes everything..." He began cataloguing some sort of list in his head.

"So, mon chéri, you are welcome. By knocking you out of contention, you were nowhere to be seen during this debacle. You can tell your superiors whatever you want about what exactly you were doing, but with my thoughtful help, you were not at any risk of giving away that anyone knew anything about your real mission."

Mr. Valov's demeanor softened at the development. "If ever you're in need of a human career, look me up. I'm sure I can find a position for you at the highest levels of British Intelligence."

"Ha!" Mélusine laughed. "A position worthy of the Scarlet Pimpernel himself, no doubt."

"A position worthy of a Yaksha." He eyed Mélusine for her reaction as he baited her.

"Nice try, my spying friend," she winked. "But your cleverness cannot compete with my two thousand years of experience."

With a pleasant breeze, Kuveni reappeared by their side.

"All of the pirates are accounted for in the brig. All of the spies are being reprimanded at this very moment... except for you, of course, Mr. Cumberland. I believe you might see a commendation coming your way soon... Oh, my dearest boy is ready to return to us..." She snapped her fingers, and a small Yaksha feast replaced the suitcases on the dining table.

Edmund pushed open the door with his shirt unbuttoned and his tuxedo jacket and bowtie over his arm. He tossed them onto the couch and walked towards the group, fully recovered with a spring in his step. He gathered Eleanor into his freshly warm arms for a passionate embrace, and then pulled away to observe the feast with momentary curiosity, landing his attention on Kuveni and Mélusine.

"Dare I ask where this came from?"

"We daren't give you an answer," Kuveni sighed apologetically.

He turned his attention to Mélusine.

"I should be rather ashamed that we spent so much time together in the last few months, and I didn't realize you were... related to me?"

Mélusine smiled. "Not by blood, mon chéri. We are related in many ways, but not like that."

"Mr. Johnson said almost the same thing," he said quietly.

"Mr. Johnson and I have known each other for a very long time, Edmund. Almost two thousand years. It is why he sanctioned my meddling in this little affair, but not Kate's. He has known her for even longer than he's known me. Long enough to know that she doesn't have the self-control that I have when you are in danger. If ever the topic comes up, I would appreciate it very much if you would be discreet about her presence here these last few days."

"I get to keep a secret from Mr. Johnson?" Edmund asked with childlike enthusiasm.

Kuveni stroked his cheek affectionately. "Edmund, my dear boy, you will be doing me a kindness so great that you cannot comprehend it."

Edmund pulled her into a familial hug. "I will do whatever I can to repay you, Kate. I cannot thank you enough for keeping everyone safe. This is the first battle I have ever fought that has not left me… shall we say, in a shameful state."

Kuveni squeezed him until he looked like he might burst. "Oh, how I love you, my beautiful boy."

When she finally let him go, he approached Mélusine to shake her hand. He held onto it for an extra-long moment, assessing her curiously.

"You and Kate do not feel exactly the same. You feel… more familiar. You feel, in some way, more similar to Mr. Johnson. Are you sure we aren't related? You aren't… you aren't my brother, are you?"

Mélusine smiled sadly. "I am not your brother, Edmund. But there are connections that are more powerful than blood. I cannot wait until the day when we can really know each other. That day is not here yet, but when it comes, it will be glorious."

"I will wait impatiently," Edmund conceded.

"You have many more pleasurable things to occupy you until then, mon chéri. Love is a rare and beautiful gift. Do not waste one moment of it worrying about us… and on that note, we should be going. It is not healthy for us to meddle like this, and we will not be doing it again. You must fight your own battles from now own, alongside your wild Scottish thistle."

Mélusine pulled Edmund into a motherly hug and then kissed his forehead. Before Edmund had a chance to comment on the odd gesture, Mélusine gathered Kuveni's hand into hers and guided her assertively to the door.

"We will check up on the tragic Ridgeway girls before we go," Kuveni informed them. "You two should rest and relax. You have a honeymoon to return to, and you haven't even reached the shores of India yet. May your adventures be more romantic and less dangerous from now on."

"Do you think that's even possible?" Eleanor laughed. She realized as soon as the words came out of her mouth that they weren't particularly funny.

Mélusine shrugged. "Ma chérie, we must let destiny decide. For now, you should celebrate the beautiful triumph of light over darkness. It is not every day that a battle like this is won with so few casualties. May it be the first of many."

Edmund waved wistfully. "*Adieu, mes amis.*"

"No, no, mon chéri. Never fear. It is only *au revoir*," Mélusine corrected him amicably.

Kuveni blew them each a kiss, and Mélusine offered them an affected bow worthy of the Scarlet Pimpernel. With one long sigh of resignation, Kuveni closed the door.

Edmund stared at it for a long moment, lost in thought.

"What is it, darling?" Eleanor asked curiously.

"Do you think… Do you think they're an item?" he finally posited.

Eleanor burst into laughter, and after a moment of contemplation, Edmund followed. They laughed heartily at the idea (why exactly Edmund found it so funny, Eleanor was not entirely certain), and Mr. Valov stood up, ready to offer his own goodbyes.

"I will leave you two for now. Enjoy your evening. I will check up on the progress of the ship's recovery. It is a shame that the hundreds of passengers will never know who it was who saved them from a fate worse than death, Colonel. You will just have to celebrate your secret triumph tomorrow with the Helmsworths."

"That sounds like a jolly good idea, Mr. Valov. Jolly good, indeed!" Edmund agreed cheerfully.

"Sleep well. Recover. And I will see you both in the morning." Mr. Valov shook Edmund and Eleanor's hands, and then offered them a polite bow as he left them alone in the room, closing the door behind him.

Edmund took Eleanor into his arms and then whisked her into a romantic dip. She squealed with the thrill and licked his tongue naughtily as he stood her back up, stealing a final, delicious nibble.

He became pensive as he looked around the messy room. "I don't know what I have to say about all this. You were so wonderfully strong, Eleanor. Stronger than I could have ever imagined. I have never felt like I wasn't alone in battle. Never. Not even with Edward Rutherford by my side. But, you, dearest... you were marvelous. You gave me the strength to carry on so many times. Over and over and over again, just as you have since we met. I would never have been able to do any of this without you. Having you in my life is such an intensely good fortune, I still worry sometimes that I will wake up and it will all have been a dream."

"This is entirely real, Edmund. Every moment of it." Eleanor enticed him into another embrace. "I marvel every day at uncovering your unique strengths, you know. I often find it hard to believe that a man like you exists at all, and that you chose to put up with a wild Scottish thistle! What were the chances?!"

"It is the greatest privilege of my life to have a wild Scottish thistle by my side, Eleanor. You make me believe that somehow there is meaning in all this, even in the darkest struggles."

Eleanor took his hand and guided him to the bed. She stepped out of her ripped Roman dress, and Edmund ran his fingers along her nipples through the tight fabric of the Roman armor.

She sighed with satisfaction as he leaned down and kissed her neck, helping her out of the uncomfortable garment until she let out a louder sigh of relief. He worked his way down to her bare breasts while she helped him undress, until they were both wonderfully naked in each other's arms.

"I love you, my dearest wife," he whispered as they lay down next to each other.

"I love you, my darling husband," she smiled back.

And together, as their ship chugged along full steam ahead towards friendly waters, and seven hundred passengers went about their business without any inkling of the true peril from which they had narrowly escaped, in each other's loving arms, the angels in disguise celebrated their greatest glorious triumph yet as man and wife.

EPILOGUE

My greatest hope, Ellie, is that through this story you will gain some sense of the wonderful firecracker that your mother really was, and the incredible degree to which her kindness and tenacity made Edmund into the father you have loved so much your whole life.

For me, this portion of their story reiterates how important the people you choose to engage with are to your happiness, and to your sense of self-worth. Your father thinks back on this period in his life as one of his favorites, not just because of your mother, but because of the many 'body-carrying' friends that they made together. This was, as you might have guessed, the only time in his life until last year when so many people knew his secrets.

He associated his great fortune with your mother's presence, and she was certainly due quite a bit of credit for her contribution, but as I look back on their memories, I think that (like always) he is drastically underappreciating his own role in his transition. Eleanor certainly lured him out of his shell, but he had to go out on many uncomfortable limbs to push himself along the way. I'm quite sure, dearest Ellie, that your mother wanted you to fully understand that, so that you too will find the courage to push yourself. It took your father 105 years to do the same, so you still have fifteen years to outpace his development if you start now ;). Don't worry, though. I won't push you on behalf of your mother, and neither will he. You have to find your own path. We just want to remind you that you do not have to do it alone.

On that note, I should make it clear that your father has read this manuscript. Last week, as soon as I finished it up, I thought it was only fair to let him censor it before I sent it to you, given how incredibly personal it is. He blushed intensely as he read it, but in the end, he gave into your mother's wishes and approved every word of it for you to read. He really is a good sport—the best I've ever met.

As soon as he finished reading it, he suggested that I take one of his own memories to share with you as an epilogue. It is a memory of an experience that you two shared many years later, and that I know from your memories always puzzled you. He wasn't willing to give you the full context back then because it was too painful, but he is ready now. I have decided to use both of your memories together to tell the little tale, in the third person, since it I found the dialogue came out rather confusing when I wrote it to you in the second person.

I will warn you: The memory is equal parts sorrow and joy. If you are reveling in the happiness that they shared during this beautiful age of innocence in their lives, you may want to wait to read this passage. I will leave the decision up to you.

In the meantime, I am already working on the next installment of their adventures in India. If you thought fighting pirates and spies alongside the Scarlet Pimpernel was wild, just wait for what's coming next. ;)

With all my love,
Supriya

510

May 1947, Corpus Christi College, Oxford

It was the end of Edmund's freshman year at Oxford.

For eight months, he had been reveling in the unexpected joys of his return to vigorous youth after the fire in Basingstoke the prior year had swiftly cured his years of painful aged decline in a few minutes.

The allied world was still reveling with their great triumph in the second world war, and all of Britain was buzzing with a form of intense excitement and relief quite unique to that era.

Ellie was at art school in London, living in the same flat where Edmund had spent so many delightful times with her mother—the flat he'd been avoiding since his transition back into a young man, out of fear that Mrs. Collins, the nosy old gossiping neighbor, might recognize him and send out the signal to all of the superstitious grannies of London that there was a de-aging demon afoot.

On her own, with her father consumed by the many exciting distractions of his first year of university (the least of which was his recent rise to Oxford fame as the best cricket bowler anyone had ever seen), Ellie was slowly and secretly coming to terms with the shocking truth of her father's foreign nature—a truth that the fateful fire had finally revealed to her after nineteen years of the most painful lies he had ever told in his life.

She hadn't entirely forgiven him yet for her childhood of lies, especially for what they had meant for her during her years of introspection on the unexplained violet metallic plasma that had surfaced once many years earlier when she'd fallen from a high branch of one of the many ancient linden trees in the woods of Basingstoke. When the traumatizing incident had happened, she hadn't dared to tell her overprotective father, out of fear that he might lock her away like Rapunzel where she'd never be hurt again, but with her silence came her fear. Her fear of what it might mean for her... of being something utterly alien, her theory of which, it turned out, was uncannily correct.

The extended time away from each other was strange for both of them after nineteen years together as a family. It was almost as strange as their new relationship as relatives of seemingly similar age. When they were honest with themselves, both of them were rather relieved to be living apart, away from the awkward assumptions from all who encountered them that they were a young married couple, an assumption that was particularly difficult for Edmund to bear, given his daughter's unusually strong resemblance to her mother.

And so, while Ellie slaved away at her first year's final project in photography, Edmund woke up long after noon on a particularly warm Saturday in his dormitory bed. He was not alone.

For one beautiful twilight moment as he worked his way into the waking world, he felt a warm body in his arms, and he was back. Back to the happiest time in his life, when his wild Scottish thistle would nestle into his nook and run her warm fingers in gentle patterns across his cold chest. He opened his eyes and startled at the blonde girl beside him in bed. Multi-faceted guilt bombarded him as he took in his loud, awakening Rakshasa breath.

She was the first woman he'd slept with since Eleanor's death. The first woman he'd touched in twenty years. He looked upon her sleeping face and naked body, contemplating the complicated implications of his hasty choice the night before to give into his youthful urges (with the responsible protection of a condom despite her use of a diaphragm, so as to not risk the faintest chance that he might kill her with pregnancy).

Their rowdy night at the spring formal the night before had bewitched him into believing for a few beautiful hours that he was, in fact, just a normal university student, and now he didn't have the faintest idea how he felt about it. Part of him was relieved. He had lived for so long in the constant presence of Eleanor's ghost that even a few moments of feigned normalcy were a rare and beautiful gift. The other part of him was screaming in his head with rabid, self-effacing guilt. Guilt at betraying Eleanor. Guilt at giving into his youthful urges. Guilt that he had done so without revealing to his unsuspecting girlfriend that he was, in fact, not at all who she thought he was.

She stirred, and he pushed his raging emotions momentarily aside.

"Good morning, Edmund," she yawned dreamily.

"Good morning, Edith," he replied as he kissed her forehead. "How are you feeling this morning?"

"Just swell!" she exclaimed as she sat up and looked around the sun-drenched room. The white linen curtain rustled in the gentle afternoon breeze. "Golly, Edmund, I think we must have slept past noon!"

He reached over to the nightstand to gather up his old pocket watch. "Blimey. It's half past one. I was supposed to meet the chaps for a pre-game feast two hours ago. I hope they don't think I've gone AWOLL before the big game tonight."

A mischievous grin spread across Edith's face. "Maybe I can offer you a different kind of feast."

He blushed at her suggestion, but gathered her into his arms anyway.

"Gee, Edmund, where'd you learn that trick, anyway? I've never heard of anything like it! If more girls knew about it, they'd have a whole new take on life!"

"I'm glad you enjoyed it," Edmund said as he ran his finger along her naked breast.

"But, really, Edmund. How'd you learn something like that?" she pushed.

"I've had a lot of experiences, Edith. Just like all the other soldiers," he explained vaguely.

"I bet you learned it in France!" Edith exclaimed. "When you were a spy in the war!"

"I wasn't a spy." He had lost count of the number of times he'd uttered that same sentence in the seven months since they'd met at a fancy dress party hosted by Edith's college, Lady Margaret Hall.

"That's what spies always say, you know," she brushed him off as she searched around the bed for her bra. "Besides, if you weren't a spy, what other top secret mission would you have been up to, speaking every language in all of creation? You know, the girls at Lady Margaret think you were a code breaker, but I told them that Winston Churchill would never have relegated the best athlete on the planet to a boring desk job like that."

"No comment, like always." Edmund shrugged as he pulled on his boxer shorts from the floor.

Edith had been needling him since their first official date to reveal what he'd been up to during the war, and every time they'd gone through the conversation, he'd felt guiltier and guiltier about leaving her in the dark. After all, her friendly needling wasn't entirely a unique personal deficiency. All of the girls seemed especially preoccupied by seducing the most interesting war heroes they could get their hands on. He wondered secretly to himself sometimes if the real reason behind their interest wasn't the intrigue at all, but the fact that the most well-traveled soldiers had come home with quite a useful plethora of new skills in bed.

Despite her annoying habit, though, Edmund had always liked Edith's tenacity. As one of the only Americans he'd met at Oxford, she had a certain energy about her, a certain irreverence and distaste for the stodgy manners of the old-school Brits that he found freeing (and somewhat reminiscent of Eleanor—a detail that he never fully admitted to himself). Despite her silly slang, she was unquestionably brilliant, and it had been no small feat that she had earned herself one of the only women's spots available at Oxford. It was these redeeming traits that he now focused on as he thought back on his questionable choice the night before. He still didn't know what he thought about it.

Edith finished dressing herself (seemingly forgetting her prior suggestion of returning to their sexy games, to Edmund's relief) and took Edmund's hand into hers.

"Honey, it was a thoroughly enjoyable night. I hope we can do it again soon, but I think there are some very worried cricketers wondering where their bowler is…" She trailed off as she noticed his wedding ring on his right hand. He had moved it from his left just before he'd started college, and no one had ever dared to ask about it.

He followed her attention, and shifted uncomfortably as she coaxed his hand out of its position in his lap for a closer inspection.

"That sure looks like a wedding ring," she fished.

Edmund's heart and mind raced against each other as he contemplated his options for a response.

"That's because it is." His heart almost exploded as he said the words. She looked at him with a certain seriousness that he'd never seen before in her expression. "I am a widower, Edith."

She sat completely still with silent shock for an excruciatingly long pause as she contemplated his statement. "That's not a very funny joke, Edmund Marriner."

Edmund straightened his posture and took the ring off. He handed it to her and pointed to the engraving on the inside that he and Eleanor had chosen at the silversmith in Edinburgh two decades earlier.

"It says, '*Ars longa, vita brevis, E&E gu bràth.*'" He only let her examine it for a few seconds and then took it back from her and let out a subtle sigh of relief as he returned it to his finger. "'Art is long, life is short. E&E Forever.' Her name was Eleanor MacLeod, and she was Scottish. The first phrase is in Latin, and the last phrase is in Scottish Gaelic."

"You poor thing!" Edith exclaimed. "Edmund, why didn't you ever say anything? Did she die in the Blitz?"

"It don't like to talk about it," he said quietly. "No one needs to know my tragedy. I can forget my sorrow sometimes when no one around me knows about it."

"But... but... honey, you must be so lonely!" Edith exclaimed.

She pulled him into a kiss, but he pulled away.

Somehow, his relevation did not have the relieving effect he'd hoped it would. In fact, he suddenly felt worse. He couldn't pinpoint exactly why, but a troop of angry butterflies exploded in his stomach. A pang of dangerous desperation bombarded him.

"Edith... Edith, I am lonely. I have been for a long time."

"Oh, honey!" She stroked his cheek affectionately.

He felt even worse.

"You don't need to be lonely anymore. Edie is here for you!"

She leaned in for another kiss.

He pulled away.

"Edith, I have to tell you something. I haven't been entirely honest with you."

Edmund took a deep, calming breath and stood up. She watched him with nervous curiosity as he pulled out the top drawer of his writing desk and placed it on his blotter. He tapped on the back left corner of the bottom of the drawer until a secret compartment opened, and he pulled out a stack of incriminating photographs that had survived the fire in Basingstoke, packed away safely in his undergound lair.

He straightened his posture and readied himself for his last desperate move in his unfocused effort to relieve the storm of confusing emotions that were pummeling his weary being.

He shuffled through the pile, and then, as his heart almost exploded, he closed his eyes, whispered his mantras for the first time in more than a decade, and handed her the entire stack.

"Are these your parents, honey? They look so happy!" Edith exclaimed as she squinted to examine the wedding photograph.

Edmund said nothing. Instead, he began pacing as he waited for her to get impatient (as she always did), and explore the rest of the stack.

"By golly, you sure look like your grandpa!"

She held up the picture of him riding the camel in the Colonial Army in India in 1895. Her enthusiasm morphed into puzzlement as she reached the set he had taken starting in the 1860s when he'd decided to monitor his aging process with the modern technology of the era. When she reached the 1850 daguerrotype, she paused for a longer moment of inspection, finally holding it up to compare to her terrified boyfriend. She turned it over to read the description, hand-written in Edmund's artistic, old-fashioned cursive. She thumbed through the stack again, pausing for a long moment on the photograph of him receiving his Victoria Cross from the king, and finally returning to the wedding picture.

"You sure have strong genes in your family, don't you, honey!" she exclaimed. "How nice that you have all these old photos. We don't have any that old of my family. They were all destroyed in the great Chicago fire... Edmund, honey, what's wrong?"

As Edith looked up at him searchingly, Edmund got a hefty taste of his own rich, spicy Rakshasa fear, and before he could close his eyes and whisper his mantras to get himself back under control, a fresh whiff of Edith's fear joined up with the dangerous bouquet.

"Edmund?" She stepped away from him. "Edmund, what's wrong with you?"

He turned away from her and took several deep breaths. They did not calm his raging nerves. His eyes were undoubtedly trapped in their demonic black, but thanks to Eleanor's (and many others') silence on the matter, Edmund still had no idea about his frightening manifestation of his darker struggles.

"They're me, Edith. All the pictures are me. I'm older than I look. I married Eleanor MacLeod in 1923."

"But... but... but that's crazy, Edmund! No one lives that long!"

He turned around, and she whimpered. "Edmund, what's wrong with you? You're scaring me. You're not... you're not a vampire, are you?"

Edmund walked straight into the sunlight streaming in through the open window.

"I am *not* a vampire, Edith. I'm just very old. I'm really very ordinary other than that. I'm sorry I lied to you."

Another fresh batch of fear wafted off of her as she eyed the door. Edmund did not understand why she was so acutely afraid. He knew that his age was a surprise, but he hadn't intended to offer up any more of his alien traits. In fact, he was intensely disappointed by her brilliant mind cooking up such an absurd explanation for his unusual age. He'd expected more from her... he'd expected... Eleanor. At that moment he fully comprehended the depths of his foolishness. How could he have ever believed that any woman in the world could be half as perfect as Eleanor?

"What are you?" Edith asked as she took a step towards the door.

"I can't give you a satisfactory answer to that question. I am not entirely human, Edith. But I'm not evil. There are a few others like me, and we've all done many things to help innocent people throughout the centuries. Just because we're different, it doesn't mean we're dangerous."

"Not entirely human?" Edith murmured. "But... but... how could you do this, Edmund Marriner? How could you sleep with me without telling me that you're... you're... you're a creature?"

"We've been courting for months, Edith. The timing seemed right," Edmund said flatly as his fear morphed into frustration. "And I'm not a *creature*. I'm really very ordinary."

Her reaction reminded him far too much of his traumatizing first wife, Alice. He had been so careful to only consider girls who were brilliant and not the least bit religious, and yet, here they were.

"It's not like we just met at a party, Edith. We've known each other for seven months, and I'm the same person I've always been. There is just more context that I didn't tell you. Based on your reaction now, I think you've answered your own question. I didn't tell you because I was afraid of this exact scenario."

"So you only got up the nerve to tell me after you took your spoils?" Another burst of acute fear wafted off of her as she let herself challenge him.

"Do you think it's any different for girls who sleep around with their coveted war heroes? They get a surprise in the morning too, you know. And the following week. And the following month. You're really very lucky that I don't have a single vinereal disease to share with you."

"Edmund Marriner, that was a horrible thing to say!" Edith momentarily got over her fear to chastize him. "You shouldn't say anything at all about war heroes!"

"I was a war hero, Edith. In World War One. I was an allied commander in the trenches of Belgium against the same bloody Krauts for four hellish years. That's why the king was giving me that medal in the picture."

Edith thought about his point, and then let her cheek get the best of her. "Well, at least these war heroes aren't lying about their *species*. For all I know, I just slept with a Martian! Or... or... a *demon*!"

Edmund was taken aback by her cruelty. He had feared her cold reaction to his revelation, but he hadn't expected it. As he'd toyed with the idea over the prior month, he'd envisioned her acting like the many understanding humans who'd supportively loved him even after they'd seen him kill men with his bare hands. He'd hoped with all of the freshly recovering soldiers hopping about that he would benefit from the same worldliness this time around, and then a lightbulb went off in his head. There was one major difference: Eleanor. Other than Edward Rutherford stumbling upon him healing in the trenches, Eleanor had been there *every* bloody time someone had learned his secret. Eleanor was the missing piece. Eleanor helped them accept him. *Eleanor* made his life beautiful and honest and true.

As Edmund looked down at the stack of pictures in Edith's hand with his wedding photograph right under her thumb, an overwhelming urge to protect them came over him, and in a blur, he was standing uncomfortably close to her, prying the photos out of her hand. She squealed with fearful surprise.

Edmund blurred to his desk drawer and put them back into the secret compartment, but as Edith made a beeline for the door, he blurred in front of her, blocking her path.

"Edith, you can't tell anyone what I just told you. Many people will be in danger if you tell *anyone*. Do you understand? Not the girls at Lady Margaret, not a single professor, not the hair dresser, or your sisters or your parents. No one! Do you understand what happens in this world to people who are different like I am?" Edmund worked his hardest to calm himself, but his mind focused entirely on Ellie. He had put Ellie in danger with his incredible foolishness, and he hated himself for it.

"Please, just let me go, Edmund." Tears of fear poured from her eyes. "I promise... I promise I won't tell. Just let me go!"

He noticed her trembling with fear, and his posture deflated.

"I'm not a monster, Edith. I'm just an ordinary man with a few unusual talents. There is no need to be afraid of me. I won't come by Lady Margaret again. I expect you'll be keeping your distance from my haunts from now on too."

Edith nodded her agreement, ripped open the door, and slammed it behind her.

"It's about time, Edith! It's really bad form to distract the star of the team when he has an important match, you know. We've gotta beat Cambridge tonight! Now go in there and tell Edmund that he's late for the pre-match practice!" Storey, one of his college mates, called from the hallway.

"You tell him," Edith mumbled as her footsteps dissolved down the stairs.

520

He took in a momentary breath of relief. At least she hadn't run through the hallways screaming his secrets at the top of her lungs to all who'd listen.

"Ed?!" Storey called. "Edmund? Coach Wilson was asking about you."

"I'm taking a breather, mate," Edmund called. "If you want a star bowler tonight, you'd best leave me be. Tell them all that I'll see them at the pre-game warm-up at seven."

"Coach Wilson's not going to like that," Storey called.

"I don't bloody care!" Edmund roared.

"Alright, mate. I'll tell him," Storey whispered.

Edmund tasted a puff of residual fear through the door as he listened to Storey's footsteps dissolve down the stairs.

He stood for a long moment of silent contemplation, and then his full anguish hit him. Suddenly, he felt as if he'd been shot in the chest. His grief over Eleanor's death exploded, consuming him more than it had in years. He worked hard to silence his violent sobs as violet tears burst from his eyes.

He looked around his small dorm room desperately for anything that could rescue him from his dangerous spiral. He spied the illicit telephone under his bed that Storey had helped him set up a month into the school year when his status as the best bowler in history had earned him the generous support of many of his clever classmates.

He rushed to his bed and ripped the phone out of its position. He dialed Edward Rutherford.

"Hello? This is the Rutherford household." Margaret's grating voice answered the phone.

"Hello, may I speak with Edward, please." Edmund could barely get the words out without giving away his miserable state. He was quite sure there was still a quiver in his voice.

"May I ask who's calling?" Margaret said sharply.

"It's... Ed..." Edmund paused as his overtaxed mind struggled for a believable alias. "It's Col... Major Edward Shoe." He slammed his hand against his forehead at his idiocy as he spied the shoe in the corner that had served as his uninspired muse.

Margaret paused for a long moment, and then covered the mouthpiece of the phone in an attempt to muffle her voice.

"Shanti, don't run in the house!" she screeched.

"But Grandpa told me to chase him!" a young girl's voice argued.

"He did not!" Margaret argued. "Lying might be alright in India, but it isn't alright in England, you hear?"

"I'm not lying!"

"Edward Rutherford, you get in here this instant! Edward? You're not hiding in the pantry again, are you? I told you not to play with Shanti in the house!"

Edmund's heart soared for one beautiful moment until Margaret ruined it.

"I'm sorry, Major, was it? He'll have to ring you back. Where can he reach you?"

Edmund looked down at his illicit phone and realized that his farce had ended. He could not tell Margaret Rutherford that Edward should return the call of one Major Edward Shoe. He wouldn't have the faintest clue who it really was.

"I will ring some other time," Edmund said as his tears returned full force.

"Suit yourself," Margaret said unapologetically as she slammed down the phone.

Edmund looked around his room, and an intense form of loneliness he had never felt before in his life overwhelmed him. It was as if he was desperately homesick for a life that would never be again, and this time, for the first time since Eleanor's death, he did not have Ellie to distract him.

He picked up the receiver and called her.

"Hello? This is Ellie Marriner speaking."

"Ellie? Ellie-bean?" He knew she could hear the anguish in his voice.

"Dad? Dad, what's wrong?" Ellie lowered her voice.

"Ellie..." His mind raced. "Ellie, can you come? Can you come to Corpus Christi?"

"Dad, what happened? Were you injured?"

"No... no, I'm fine."

"You don't sound fine."

"I told Edith. I told her some things... some things I shouldn't have told her. She didn't take it well."

"Blimey," Ellie whispered.

"I'm sorry, Ellie. I'm sure you're busy."

"I'll be on the next train. Do you need me to bring you anything from the flat in London?"

"I just... I just need to see you, Ellie-bean. I don't want to be alone."

"I'll be there as soon as I can. It will take me some time to wrap up what I was working on for my final project. The timing of the chemicals in the dark room has to be perfect or I'll lose everything, but I should be able to leave in about half an hour."

"I love you, Ellie-bean."

"I love you, Dad. I'll be there soon. Hang in there."

Edmund put down the phone, and another round of tears flowed. This time they came with a combination of relief, joy, and melancholy.

He returned the phone to its hidden position under his bed, closed the window, and gathered up his wedding photograph from the stack in the drawer. The happier one, the more impromptu picture with their silly romantic dip that Illa had taken on that fateful day had been destroyed in the fire in Basingstoke—he'd kept it by his bed since her death. All he had left was the formal one he'd stored for safe-keeping in his lair. At least he had one, he reminded himself. And he had Ellie—the brightest light in his dark life.

He gripped the photograph as he sat cross-legged on the floor in the style of his youth in Hyderabad.

You fool. You betrayed Eleanor. What did you think would happen? Think of how devastated she would be if she knew you'd forsaken her! You killed her with your ignornance. Every moment of your misery cannot begin to compare with the agony she suffered at your hands! The dark voice in his mind tormented him.

He stared at the picture of his wild Scottish thistle and sobbed silently for hours.

"Edmund?"

He startled and wiped his eyes as Ellie pushed open the door to his dorm room. She observed his position on the floor and the familiar photograph in his hand, and closed and locked the door behind her. She sat right down next to him, mirroring his position as she had so many times as a child when she would join him in his library to read side by side.

She handed him a dusty bottle of cognac, but he put it down beside him on the floor and pulled her into a tight hug.

"I love you, Ellie-bean. Thank you so much for coming."

She let him squeeze her until he finally ripped himself away. Another fresh batch of violet tears were pouring down his face, and he quickly wiped them away. He picked up the dusty bottle of cognac to inspect it.

"It was Stanley's idea. He thought that you might be missing fine spirits worthy of your adult palate," Ellie explained.

"Stanley..." Edmund murmured.

Edmund let his mind momentarily wander to think fondly about their butler who had served their household for decades, since before Ellie was even born. He was one of the last people who had stumbled across Edmund's secret, and whom Eleanor had been alive to indoctrinate. He had kept Edmund's secrets dutifully from Ellie for too many lonely years, and Edmund had missed his thoughtful help quite a bit throughout his freshman year.

"Stanley's here, by the way. He thought you wouldn't want your formal butler to come into the dorms in front of the other students, but he accompanied me on the train, in case you needed his help. He told me to ring him at some pub in town if we need him. Do you need his help, Dad? What exactly happened? How much danger are we in?"

Edmund popped open the bottle of cognac and took a long swig.

"I don't know," he admitted. "I showed her the pictures and told her that I was a bit older than I look, and then she accused me of being a vampire."

Ellie raised her eyebrows in a gesture that looked so hauntingly similar to Eleanor. "I thought you said she was brilliant."

"I don't understand it." Edmund took another long swig. "She came all the way from America to study astronomy at Oxford. She must be bloody brilliant, right? She never sounded particularly brilliant, but I always attributed it to the American accent. I suppose she had her moments of insight, but it was almost as if... as if she was trying not to seem too intelligent. Many of the girls are like that here, so I assumed she must be putting on appearances. Now, I just don't know. How could I have been so foolish?!"

Ellie was at a loss. Coaching her father in the dynamics of college relationships was not something she had ever contemplated before. She had been strictly avoiding any inkling of interest from boys her whole life, terrified secretly even before she knew her father's secrets that she might die in childbirth like her mother had.

"You must have found something to like about her, right? You've been dating for months. I've never known you to have the patience to put up with someone you don't like for very long, and I don't believe for one second you would have spilled your secrets to a girl you didn't even like."

Edmund thought carefully about her astute assertion. "I told her in a moment of desperation, I suppose. I wanted so dearly to be honest. But you are right. I did like her. I think... I think I wasn't ready, though, Ellie. All I can think about now is your mother and how I've betrayed her."

Ellie took his hand tightly into hers. "I'm sure that Mum would not have wanted you to live your life alone for eternity, Dad. It's been twenty years. I think it's okay to move on... Maybe you should just avoid vapid American blondes from now on." She winked, but he was not convinced.

"I've been such a fool," he whispered.

"Do you think she's going to tell anyone what you told her?" Ellie asked seriously.

"I made her swear she wouldn't. She agreed... but she was under duress, Ellie. At least she felt like she was. She was bloody terrified of me. I'm not even sure why. She didn't even see the violet blood."

Ellie worked hard to hide the fact that she was hurt by the whole idea. Her father had seen fit to reveal to his college girlfriend what he had worked so hard to hide from her throughout her entire life.

"Why'd you even tell her?" she asked with a sharper tone than she'd intended.

"We've been courting for months, Ellie. It seemed like the appropriate time." After his hours of personal castigation, he could not bring himself to admit to her his ultimate betrayal of her mother.

"Months! You kept your secrets from me for years!" Ellie exclaimed.

"I'm sorry, Ellie-bean," Edmund said miserably as he took a smaller sip, savoring the rich flavors of the rare vintage in an effort to calm himself. "I've already told you how sorry I am for lying to you for all those years. I was so bloody afraid that you'd leave me. I could bear for Edith to leave me, but not you, Ellie-bean. You're the only light in my dark life."

"You should have known that I wouldn't leave you, Dad."

526

"I should have," he agreed. "I should have had more faith in you, Ellie. You are so much like your mother. You are so much better than everyone else. Perhaps... perhaps it was your kindness that led me to foolishly believe that Edith would be the same. But she has reminded me of the common limitations of normal humans. You and your mother are entirely exceptional."

"If you're not entirely human, I'm not either, you know." Ellie reminded him of a detail she had pointed out many times throughout the prior year.

Edmund pulled her into another hug and kissed her forehead. "I'm so sorry, Ellie-bean."

"That wasn't meant as a criticism, Dad. It is what it is. If you're a Martian, I'm a Martian. I'm working on getting used to it, but it means that neither of us are alone now."

"I love you, Ellie-bean," Edmund said weepily.

They sat side by side for many minutes while he slowly sipped the cognac. He offered her a swig, and she refused, instead glancing around his small spartan room.

"This dorm sure is a far cry from what you're used to, isn't it?"

Edmund smiled. "It is. I must admit that I miss the peaceful silence of the country, and of our lovely life together in Basingstoke. But there is an energy about this place. There is always something absurd happening around me. It makes me feel more human than I ever have in my life. It's a sensation I'm appreciating quite a bit."

"They certainly appreciate you. It was like a citadel getting in here to visit the great Edmund Marriner. If Storey hadn't recgonized that I was your sister, I'm not sure I would have gotten in at all!"

"I'm glad he was there to help." Edmund finally felt himself relax at the mundane turn of the conversation, and he took in a deep, final sniffle. "The big game against Cambridge is tonight.

There have been all sorts of rivalrous shenanigans afoot, so everyone has been on alert against intruders."

"Doesn't it seem odd that all these men who were fighting for king and country last year are hopping about like mischievous monkeys, obsessing over petty rivalries?" Ellie asked.

"I think they need the absurdity just as much as I do. These petty obsessions occupy their minds and help them build a new life away from their tormenting memories. Your mother helped me do that after the first world war."

A chorus of jeers echoed up the staircase from the lounge below, indicating that perhaps another round of mischief had just come to a head. Edmund glanced up at the yellow, late-afternoon sun.

"I'd better get moving soon before they think I've been kidnapped by the enemy."

Ellie looked at her watch. "It's four o'clock. When do you have to be there for the match?"

"I told them seven. Is it really only four o'clock? I felt like I was sitting here relishing my misery for much longer than that."

"I suppose it was the opposite of time flying when you're having fun," Ellie quipped, hoping to keep him from descending once more into his melancholy.

Edmund hopped up from the floor and reached down to offer her his arm. He pulled her up in one swift movement and gathered her into a final hug.

"Thank you for coming, Ellie-bean. I don't know what I would have done without you. I was feeling lonelier than I ever have in my life."

Ellie squeezed him. "I've been missing you too, Dad."

"Do you have time to stay for the match?" Edmund asked. "I'm sorry to have distracted you from your final project. I hope I didn't ruin anything for you?"

"No, no. I actually just finished. I'd love to stay for the match. That is if there's room for me. I suspect all of Oxbridge is gathering. The train station was a mess."

"I suspect you're right," Edmund agreed. "But I'm certain that the greatest bowler Oxford has ever known can procure some prime seats for his guests of honor. Perhaps we should go say hello to Stanley?"

"Let's join him at the pub," Ellie agreed. "I'm sure you need to fill up before the big game anyway."

"I haven't eaten since yesterday evening," Edmund admitted. His stomach growled loudly at the idea.

Ellie smiled at his return to normalcy, and then noticed his poorly buttoned shirt. She pointed to his error, and he blushed intensely, fixing it without offering an explanation. When he was finished, he placed his precious photo with the rest, closed them into his secret compartment in the drawer, and returned it to its stealthy position.

"Do you think that's safe? Did Edith see you do that?" Ellie asked with a pang of anxiety.

Edmund thought carefully about her question. "You're right. I'd better move them to a new hiding spot. But I don't want to carry them around with me. I'll lock the door while I'm out, and then I'll find a new spot for them after the match tonight. I don't think she's going to tell anyone, actually. And to be honest, I don't think she'd get much traction even if she did. No one here is the least bit interested in anything that might take me off the cricket team, my status as a half-human creature of mystery included."

"I still can't believe Mr. Johnson wouldn't tell us what we are. We have a right to know!" Ellie humphed with annoyance at the idea. "But he didn't argue when I asked if we were Martians."

"I know he didn't, Ellie-bean. But he is very good at withholding truths he doesn't want us to know. I wouldn't take his silence as a confirmation. Shall we?"

He followed her out of the room, locking the door behind him. They swiftly made their way down the stairs, past a large group of jeering boys who were brainstorming their retaliation plans as they inspected the lounge's couches that had recently been covered in some sort of bright green slime, and into the courtyard garden that was usually more charming without the copious decoration of toilet paper that had appeared some time during the night.

As they made their way to the imposing gate, two beautiful, well-dressed blonde girls who looked slightly too old to be students were arguing vehemently with the guard.

"Look, ladies, I can't let you in. No one without a valid Oxford student card can come in or out until Monday. Chancellor's orders," he reiterated as he glanced back with annoyance at the vandalized garden.

"How did you get in?" Edmund whispered.

"I waited for a group of students, and then laughed with them as if I was part of their group as we passed the guard." Ellie smiled with pride at her triumph. "Then I ran into Storey who whisked me right inside."

"Brilliant, Ellie-bean." Edmund squeezed her hand supportively.

As they passed the gate, one of the two beautiful blonde girls reached forward and grabbed Ellie's hand.

"Eleanor?" she asked questioningly with an air of hope in her voice.

Her sister looked at Edmund, squinting at him with an odd look on her face. "Edmund? Colonel Edmund Marriner?"

Edmund and Ellie both felt their hearts jump into their throats.

"Colonel Edmund Marriner was my father, yes," Edmund said as he eyed the guard.

The women followed his gaze, and realized their error. As Edmund looked them up and down, trying to figure out how he knew them, he realized that they were twins.

"I'm sorry, we're being very rude confronting you like this, Edmund. I am Daisy Ridgeway." She reached out her hand, and watched Edmund's expression for some hint of recognition.

"I'm Lily Ridgeway," her sister said as she held out her hand to Ellie. "We met Edmund and Eleanor Marriner many years ago... on a boat that was hijacked by pirates on the journey to India. Perhaps he told you the story? It did not make it into the news."

Ellie looked nervously to her father.

"Daisy and Lily Ridgeway," he murmured as his memories from the incident rushed back. "Good lord, it's hard to believe it's been that long... Come with me."

"Edmund, only students are allowed inside," the guard protested.

"Neville, they're my guests," Edmund said authoritatively. "If you want Oxford to win the match tonight, you'd best let them pass."

Edmund felt slightly guilty about using his celebrity in this way, but he had more important things on his mind. Neville begrudgingly let the girls pass.

"Follow me," Edmund said as he took Ellie's hand and held it tightly as he led Daisy and Lily back into the dorm and straight up into his room.

They looked to each other with excitement and nerves as he locked the door behind them.

"Why are you here?" he asked. Ellie had never seen him so flustered.

Daisy cleared her throat. "We saw your picture and your name in the paper in an article about the cricket match. We had to see if you were... you."

"We wanted to thank the angels in disguise who saved us," Lily added. "We never got a chance to say goodbye to them back then. We had to disembark in Berbera to follow our father's coffin back to Britain. But we hoped... we hoped that maybe there was some chance that you were the Edmund Marriner we knew. I suppose it was a foolish notion. You look much younger than he looked, but we saw things back then... things that made us believe that anything was possible."

"We hoped that Eleanor was still around too. It's so lovely to see you together still!" Daisy swooned. "I knew you were both special! And Kate, oh Kate! We hoped so dearly to see Kate again!"

Edmund looked to Ellie, who was at yet another loss at how to proceed.

"I'm not Eleanor MacLeod. I'm her daughter," Ellie replied awkwardly.

"Yes... yes, of course," Lily agreed disingenuously, obviously assuming that Ellie's response was the same farce as Edmund's had been.

Edmund thought for a long moment about what to do, and then he walked straight to his hidden drawer and pulled his pictures out again. Ellie could not believe that he was going to reveal his secrets so casually after the disaster he'd just overcome.

He held out the wedding picture and showed it to the girls, and then he handed them the stack and waited for them to peruse it. They paused for an extra-long moment on the picture of him in the Colonial Army, appearing a similar age, and then they held it up to compare.

"I knew it!" Lily exclaimed. "I told you, Daisy! I told you it would be worth coming over here to find out! We've been arguing about it for weeks, you know," she confided as if they were old friends. "We've been driving Mum mad with our banter."

Edmund smiled. Somehow with the decades that had passed, she still sounded like the little girl he remembered. He was intensely relieved that her father's tragedy had not quelled her outgoing nature.

"I am Edmund Marriner. I am the one who helped you on that boat in Somalia. But Ellie here is our daughter, Eleanor's and mine. Eleanor died in childbirth in 1926, but Ellie looks quite a bit like her. She inherited many wonderful qualities from her mother, the least of which is her exceptional kindness."

Both girls looked up at him with a look of utter devastation on their faces, and Edmund worked hard to push back his emotions.

"It happened a long time ago. Ellie has been here ever since, giving me a reason to live in her mother's absence." He squeezed Ellie's hand.

"I'm sorry," Lily whispered. "Eleanor was the kindest, most beautiful person." She looked to Ellie. "Your parents saved us in so many ways, and we were just strangers—two rambunctious, ill-tempered little brats, in fact."

"You were just children, Lily," Edmund said kindly. "All children run around like wild beasts from time to time. Ellie did her fair share of it herself. I would ensnare her into a match of cricket in the garden until she ran out all of her energy. If your parents had done the same, you wouldn't have needed to play tag on the Orient Express."

"We did meet an abominable snowman that way," Lily winked.

"Indeed, you did," Edmund smiled.

Ellie was barely following their conversation. Among his sea of lies, Edmund had never revealed to her the small detail that there were people in the world who already knew his secrets. People who had known them since before she was even born.

"Colonel... Edmund... I know you're probably busy getting ready for the big game, but we were planning on having an early dinner in our garden. Our house is just over by the Christ Church gardens, and Mother is heading back to Eastbourne tomorrow after many weeks with us. I know she'd be overjoyed to see you."

"You live here in Oxford?" he asked with surprise. "Together?"

"We have for several years," Lily confirmed. "My husband was a student when the war broke out. We stayed anyway, after he was killed in action in Normandy." She didn't make eye contact as she revealed the sad fact. "General Kettering's compensation for our father's tragedy has kept us very comfortable all these years. We haven't had any problem with expenses. But, please, Edmund, join us! Say hello to Mum. It will prove to her that our weeks of arguing about coming to find you were worth something."

Edmund looked at his watch. It was half past four. Then he looked up at their faces, beaming with hope and anticipation.

"Yes... Let's do. Thank you for the invitation!"

Ellie could not hide her shock at his response.

"Dad! Are you sure that's wise?"

"I am, Ellie-bean," he said as he squeezed her hand.

"This is going to be so lovely! Mum will be floored, and we have another surprise for you. It's Lily's surprise, really. Just wait until you see!" Daisy exclaimed.

Edmund returned his incriminating photographs to their hiding place once more, this time without any of the misery he'd had the first time, and with a quick lock of the door, he and Ellie accompanied the Ridgeway girls out of the college and down several winding streets that were filled with tipsy, silly-costume-clad relevers, many of whom stopped to enthusiastically offer Edmund supportive high-fives.

"Are we going to win tonight, Edmund?" a pirate, a turtle, and a bishop each stopped him to ask as soon as they noticed his height and realized he was their famous star bowler.

"I have no doubt in my mind," he replied jovially each time.

They burst into cheers and took more swigs from their paper bags.

"Something absurd every day," he reminded Ellie with a wink.

As they walked, she finally understood exactly why he was enjoying his time at Oxford so much. She had never seen him so happy, despite the dismal beginning of his day.

In truth, the contrast between his earlier misery and his present contentment was so vast because he was operating on a noticeable adrenaline high that he had only felt a few times in his life, and by the time they reached the door of the Ridgeways' enormous mansion, he was feeling positively giddy.

"Come on. Mum is probably in the garden already. There are a couple more people I'd like you to meet," Lily said excitedly.

Ellie threw Edmund a nervous look at the prospect of more people, and Edmund agreed with her caution. He hoped dearly that he hadn't just walked into some sort of sinister trap.

They walked through the old-fashioned manor house that was certainly hundreds of years old, perhaps belonging to one of the university's many famous graduates at some point in history, following Daisy and Lily out to a vast open yard backing entirely onto the Christ Church gardens beyond. Not a single house other than theirs had a view onto the private space, and Edmund felt a pang of nostalgia for Basingstoke.

A familiar middle-aged woman was sitting at a well-decorated outdoor dining table heaped high with food, while two young children, a boy and a girl, each with golden blond hair, chased each other and squealed.

"Edmund! Eleanor! I have some very special people for you to meet!" Lily called.

Edmund and Ellie looked to each other with surprise as the two blond children ran to greet them.

"Edmund Ridgeway-Jones, meet Edmund Marriner. Eleanor Ridgeway-Jones, meet Ellie Marriner. The Marriners are your namesakes."

Little Edmund and Eleanor Ridgeway-Jones politely shook the hands of their guests.

"Wow, you're cold!" Edmund Ridgeway-Jones exclaimed. "Are you really the famous bowler? I'm named after the best bowler in the world?"

"Indeed, you are," Edmund agreed cheerfully.

"You are named after my mother," Ellie clarified for little Eleanor. "You and I both are."

"Are you really angels in disguise, just like Mummy says you are?" little Eleanor asked.

"I suppose in some ways we are," Edmund agreed.

Ellie could not believe her ears. Her father had already told her vehemently many times that he would never, ever perpetuate an angel farce to explain his unique abilities. In truth, Edmund thought back so fondly on the way Eleanor had used the excuse to relieve the young girls of their fears of their father, that he didn't have the heart to ruin the decades-old farce now.

"You most certainly are," the middle-aged woman said as she joined them. "Eloise Ridgeway... Colonel?" she asked as she looked him up and down with a combination of puzzlement and wonder.

"It is a pleasure to see you again, Mrs. Ridgeway," he said as he shook her hand politely. "I'm sorry that Eleanor and I couldn't do more for your situation when we were on that boat in Somalia. But I'm glad to see that you have all made the most of your circumstances after such a senseless tragedy."

"Good lord, it really is you," she murmured as she pulled her hand back and shivered. "Colonel, I do not have words to express my thanks."

"You do not need to thank me."

"Then come, join us!" Eloise pushed forward. "We have plenty of food, although, if we'd known you were coming, we would have bought out the entire grocery."

"I'm sure this will be perfectly delicious," he said as his stomach growled.

"Aww," little Edmund whined. "Can't we play just one little round of cricket?"

Edmund's eyes lit up at the exciting prospect. He looked around the entirely private garden, and an even more bewitching prospect crossed his mind. He glanced at Ellie and smiled mischievously.

"Yes, I'd say we have time for a little round!" he agreed. "I'll bowl, and who'd like to be the batsman?"

Little Edmund and little Eleanor both clapped excitedly, while Ellie watched them prepare for their game with utter disbelief. She had never seen her father be so outgoing.

Little Edmund picked up the bat, and Edmund winked at Ellie as he prepared himself for a revelation that he had been pointlessly avoiding since she'd learned his secret.

Edmund bowled, and little Edmund hit the ball high into the sky. In a blur, Edmund ran to the edge of the garden and waited patiently for the ball to fall right into his hands.

"Whoa!" Little Edmund exclaimed.

"Blimey, Dad. I didn't know you could do that!" Ellie exclaimed. "No wonder you're the star player!"

He blurred back to greet her, ball-in-hand.

"I don't use that particular talent on the field. I had plenty of practice hiding it when we played together in the garden when you were a child. I'm sorry I didn't reveal it to you sooner. It was just... you were just getting used to things. I didn't want to push you... I hope it's not too shocking for you now."

Ellie looked over to the other adults, none of whom seemed shocked by the revelation.

"They've already seen it," Edmund said as he followed her gaze. "I'm glad they can see that it's useful for something other than battle."

"Battle?!" Ellie exclaimed. "What battle?!"

"It's a long story," Edmund demurred. "Would you like to play cricket with your father at full-throttle?"

"I'd love to, Dad," Ellie agreed, letting her excitement at the prospect push her past her bewilderment at yet another superhuman ability her father had skillfully hidden from her.

He pulled her into a hug. "I love you, Ellie. I dreamed of this moment your whole childhood. I can't believe it's finally here."

That was the moment when he realized how Mr. Johnson must have felt during their beautiful wedding cricket game. A wave of forgiviness washed over him as he fully comprehended for the first time the striking parallel between his self-imposed silence with Ellie, and Mr. Johnson's silence with him.

"I love you, Dad," she whispered into his ear.

He squeezed her once more and then pulled away and grinned with anticipation. He handed her the ball to bowl and took his position as the only fielder, while little Edmund handed the bat begrudgingly to his sister.

"Let's play!" Edmund declared.

And so, under the warm late-afternoon sun, in the private garden of the family he had saved with his wild Scottish thistle decades earlier, Edmund and Ellie Marriner reveled in the beautiful honesty of their relationship for the first time.

Eleanor MacLeod watched from her silent position nestled deep inside the soul of her daughter, overwhelmed with relief and joy that the moment she'd been longing to see for twenty long years had finally arrived.

~TO BE CONTINUED~

GLOSSARY OF HINDU REFERENCES

Hinduism, the world's oldest continuously practiced religion, is an exceptionally diverse collection of philosophies and rituals practiced by over one billion people globally. There is no single institution and no single written text that defines the 'rules' of Hinduism, and thus it varies widely in practice and belief across the world.

While there is a pantheon featuring a plethora of gods and goddesses with various regional names and stories, there are also numerous sects who worship Vishnu (Vaishnavism), Shiva (Shaivism), Shakti (Shaktism), and combinations/permutations of these major gods and goddesses, and their manifestations (including avatars), as representations of the one supreme being.

The vast and fascinating complexity of Hinduism cannot be captured in a short glossary, and it is not the author's intent to do so. This glossary is meant to give the uninitiated reader some basic context for references throughout the Ashley Mayers universe. Further research is recommended for those interested in digging deeper.

Agni (uh-**gnee**) – 'Fire' in Sanskrit, Agni is also the god of fire and the conveyor of sacrifices to the gods. It is Agni's role in the Hindu pantheon that is invariably linked with the many rituals, both daily and for special occasions, that require a *yajna*, or sacred fire.

Artha (**ahr**-tah) – One of the four aims of human life in Hindu philosophy, sometimes 'meaning, sense, or purpose,' *artha* generally focuses on the 'means to live the life you want,' including but not limited to wealth, career, and financial security. It can perhaps be thought of as 'why you do work.'

Asura/Asuri (ah-soo-ruh/ah-soo-ree) – Originally a term used to describe divine, powerful beings, good or bad, the term later came to represent primarily darker powered beings in Hinduism and is sometimes (but not always) synonymous with demons. Rakshasas are sometimes described as one type of *Asura*. *Asuri* is the feminine form of *Asura*.

Avatar (ah-vuh-tuhr) – In Hinduism, an avatar is a deliberate descent of a deity to Earth. The term is most commonly used to describe incarnations or manifestations of Vishnu, but has been used with other deities, including Shiva, Ganesh, and Shakti. The lists of avatars and consensus around them is dubious. Some sects believe that Shiva, as a formless entity, will never have an avatar, while others believe that Hanuman is an avatar of Shiva. The lists of Vishnu avatars range from ten to twenty-five avatars, and some characters in epics are referred to as 'partial' avatars, such as Rama's brother, Lakshmana, sometimes being considered 'one-quarter Vishnu.' One major thematic element throughout the Ashley Mayers universe explores what exactly it means (and doesn't mean) to be an avatar.

Ayodhya (ah-**yoh**-dyuh) – An ancient city located in Uttar Pradesh in Northern India that remains inhabited today, Ayodhya is considered to be the birthplace and ancient kingdom of Rama. In modern times, tragedy and controversy, fuelled by Hindu/Muslim animosity, have plagued the city after a violent uprising in 1992 that led to the destruction of the 16th c. Babri Mosque, which many people believed was built upon the site of Rama's original temple.

Bhoomi (**boo**-mee) – The embodiment/personification of 'Mother Earth.' Bhoomi is referred to as the mother of Sita, and at the end of *the Ramayana*, when Sita's suffering becomes unbearable, she returns to her 'mother,' being swallowed by the earth.

Ceylon (say-lon) – The historical, British colonial name of modern-day Sri Lanka, Ceylon is a key setting in *the Ramayana*, as the home of the Rakshasa king, Ravana, who kidnaps Sita and takes her back to Lanka to woo her (while she is imprisoned).

Chiranjivi (chee-ruhn-**jee**-vee) – Seven immortals in Hinduism who remain on Earth to lead humans in various paths of righteousness. In this series, we have two: Vibhishana, Hanuman.

Dasara (**Duh**-suh-ruh) – Otherwise known as *Dussera*, *Dushera*, or *Vijayadashami*, depending on the region and language, Dasara is a holiday at the end/culmination of Navaratri, the nine-night autumn festival devoted to the Goddess. Dasara traditions vary across India, ranging from sacred dances of Garba and Dandiya in the north, to a candlelight vigil and elephant parade in Mysore in the south, a city that considers itself the namesake of the Goddess in her defeat of the demon Mahishasura (sometimes referred to as *Mahishasura-Mardini* from the Sanskrit holy mantras). It coincides with the culmination of Durga Puja in Bengal, and always involves great cheer, festivities, and often fireworks and light shows.

Devi/Deva (deh-**vee**/deh-**vah**) – 'Heavenly' or 'divine' beings in Hinduism, *Devi* can be synonymous with 'god' or 'deity' but primarily refers to powerful beings who are 'good,' and can sometimes be contrasted with the 'evil' *Asura*. However, the designations of 'good' versus 'evil' are far less clearly defined in Hinduism compared to Judeo-Christian religions, and so, for example, Kartikeya, the god of war, is still considered a *Deva*. In Hinduism, an *Asura* can ascend and become a *Deva*, with Vibhishana being a prime example, demonstrating that birthright is less important than actions on Earth to define one's character and virtue.

Devi Mahatmya (deh-**vee** muh-**hat**-myuh) – The *Devi Mahatmya* is a religious text (from the *Markandeya Purana,* one of eighteen primary religious texts in Hinduism) devoted to the Great Goddess (Shakti). It recounts her manifestation on Earth in the warrior form of Durga to protect the innocent by defeating the shapeshifting buffalo demon Mahishasura, and her subsequent return of balance and virtue to the world. A text revered by Hindus across many sects, the *Devi Mahatmya* serves as a primary text for Shaktist Hindus, who believe that the Goddess is the Supreme Being. It serves as the inspiration for the festivals of Navaratri, Durga Puja, and Dasara/Vijayadashmi.

Dharma (**dahr**-muh) – One of the four aims of human life in Hindu philosophy, with many meanings, *dharma* is roughly translated as virtue, morality, righteousness, obligations, and correct conduct. The Hindu epics, *the Ramayana* and *the Mahabharata,* both demonstrate that there is often no single clear path to *dharma,* as various 'right' paths often conflict and need to be prioritized, with each difficult choice producing complicated consequences and satisfying drama.

Diwali (Dih-**vah**-lee) – Also known as Deepavali in many South Indian languages, Diwali is one of the most important festivals across Hindu tradition, and celebrates the triumph of light over darkness, knowledge over ignorance, and hope over despair. Based on the Hindu calendar, the festival of lights typically falls between mid-October and mid-November each year, and its observance dates back to ancient times. The rituals vary across the many cultures who celebrate the holiday, but it is generally consistent that people light candles and offer prayers to Lakshmi.

Durga (door-**gah**) – A principle form of the Goddess (Shakti), who manifests physically in many different forms depending on the task at hand, Durga is also called Maa Durga or the Holy Mother (not to be confused with the Christian/Catholic Holy Mother Mary). The primary hero of her own epic, the *Devi Mahatmya,* Durga is most famous as a warrior for justice who wields the power of the entire pantheon, coming to Earth with many arms and weapons to defeat the shapeshifting buffalo demon, Mahishasura. Her triumph in defeating an insidious, ever-changing manifestation of evil can be viewed as a model of perseverance that can be applied in everyday life. Every year her triumph is celebrated during the festivals of Navaratri ("Nine Nights," each celebrating a manifestation of the Goddess), Durga Puja (five nights celebrating her defeat of Mahishasura, primarily celebrated in Bengal), Dasara (the culmination of Navaratri celebrated across India), and Diwali (the Festival of Lights, celebrated across the Hindu world and by other related religions). As the Great Goddess, she is sometimes referred to interchangeably with Parvati, wife of Shiva, and she is sometimes said to manifest as Lakshmi and Saraswati in their roles as the primordial energy that animates the universe. Across most sects,

Durga is worshipped as the underlying creative, preservative, and destructive energy of the universe (Shakti), who exists as a formless entity always, and sometimes takes form within the gods or goddesses, to fulfill tasks on behalf of the universe.

Durga Puja (door-**gah poo**-ja) – A five-night festival primarily celebrated in Bengal, Durga Puja coincides with the festival of Navaratri in other parts of India, all in celebration of the Great Goddess (Shakti), manifested as Durga for her defeat of the shapeshifting demon Mahishasura. Known for its *pandals* (elaborate temporary altars to the Goddess), Durga Puja is celebrated with costume, dance, food, special rituals, and bright firecrackers, making the streets of Calcutta one of the liveliest (and most crowded) places in the world to experience the frenetic energy of the Devi in one of her most beloved forms.

Garuda (**guh**-roo-duh) – The 'mount' of Lord Vishnu, Garuda is a large bird, sometimes a humanoid bird, who flies Lord Vishnu around. Sometimes represented as a large phoenix, eagle, or kite, Garuda also exists in Buddhist mythology.

Hanuman (**hahn**-oo-mahn) – Rama's right-hand man and a beloved star of *the Ramayana*, Hanuman is a Vanara, a monkey-like humanoid race who fought by Rama's side in his attack against Ravana in Lanka. In *the Ramayana*, Hanuman uses his flying ability to track and eventually make contact with Sita while she is incarcerated by Ravana, but she refuses to go with him back to Rama. Various interpretations of this interaction range from it exemplifying Sita's purity through her refusal to be in another man's arms, even to be rescued, to a valid observation that had Sita agreed to go back to Rama with Hanuman, the entire war between Rama and Ravana might have been avoided. Hanuman is consistently referred to as one of the *Chiranjivi*, representing loyalty, courage and devotion.

Harihara (**hah**-ree-**hah**-ruh) – A combined form of Shiva and Vishnu (Transformation and Preservation), Harihara is sometimes used to explain/describe the complementary nature of the two gods as aspects of one supreme being. The symbolism evokes the necessary balance (and tug-of-war) between the two primary aspects of existence, each keeping the other in check.

Hiranyakashipu – (**hee**-ran-**yaak**-shih-poo) – A demon evil enough to warrant the Preserver of the Universe coming to Earth (as Narasimha, the fourth avatar of Vishnu), Hiranyakashipu gained a boon from Lord Brahma so that he couldn't be defeated by man or beast, thus requiring Lord Vishnu to take a more clever form, in his case, as a half-man, half-lion, to defeat him.

Lakshmi (**luhk**-shmee) – The female aspect of the Preserver of the Universe, often referred to as the goddess of prosperity (material and spiritual), and the wife of Lord Vishnu, Lakshmi (or Laxmi), is one of the principal goddesses of the *Tridevi*, or 'Trinity of Goddesses.' She is said to be the life-force of Lord Vishnu and is worshipped during the major festival of Diwali every autumn. As the wife of Rama, seventh avatar of Vishnu, Sita is an avatar of Lakshmi.

Kali (kuh-lee) – Hinduism's primary apocalyptic demon—not to be confused with Kali, a fierce incarnation of Shakti (spelled the same in English but not in Sanskrit)—this demon is often depicted with a dog's head. He is said to fan the flames of human greed, violence, and iniquity during *Kali Yuga* ('The Age of Vice'), an era that many Hindus believe describes the modern world. It is sometimes said that Ravana is an incarnation and/or devotee of the demon, Kali, and that Lord Vishnu will incarnate in his ultimate avatar form, Lord Kalki, to defeat Kali and bring the worlds into *Satya Yuga* ("The Age of Truth").

Kali/Kaali (Kah-lee) – A fierce incarnation of the female life-force of the Transformer of the Universe, Kaali (often spelled Kali in English, but too easily confused with the demon Kali), is one of the most misunderstood incarnations of the Goddess. Often referred to as the goddess of time, and represented with blue or black skin, her tongue out, standing on the dead body of her husband, Shiva, wearing a skull necklace and holding a severed, bloody head, she is often thought of as a ghoulish character by those who don't know any better. However, the symbolism of the imagery of her standing on Shiva's body is meant to represent that she is his life-force, and without her, he is lifeless. The life-force of change is fierce, and the ravages of time often frightening, which are two reasons why she is depicted in such a monstrous style. She is, however, a natural manifestation of the destruction required for our ever-changing universe to exist.

Kalki (kuhl-kee) – Lord Kalki, 'Destroyer of Filth,' the tenth and final avatar of Vishnu (the Preserver of the Universe), is believed to be the only avatar who has not already been on Earth. Legends tell of him being born in Shambhala, a mythical place of great spiritual power north of Tibet, a place of great interest to the sages when the stories were written, due to its association and proximity to the homeland of the invading Khans. While references to Lord Kalki can be conflicting, it is consistent in texts that Lord Kalki will come to Earth to defeat the demon, Kali, and restore balance and order, bringing humans back to the path of virtue, and ushering in the Age of Truth.

Mahagauri (Maa-huh-gau-ree) – A manifestation of Maa Durga (considered her eighth of nine manifestations by some sects), Mahagauri is worshipped on the eighth night of the festival of Navaratri in some parts of India. She is said to be "the fair one," with a fair complexion, who offers forgiveness and protection to all of her followers.

Mantra (mahn-truh) – Words or sounds, often repetitive, that are used in prayer.

Moksha (**mohk**-shuh) – One of the four aims of human life in Hindu philosophy, meaning 'release' or 'liberation,' *moksha* primarily refers to release from the reincarnation cycle of birth and death on Earth.

Naraka (nah-**rah**-kuh) – In Hinduism, Naraka, or the underworld (somewhat similar to Christian purgatory), is a temporary place for expiation of sins to be endured between a soul's mortal death and its return to Earth. There are many different forms of Naraka, each featuring colorful punishments that are related to a person's sins, such as murderers being eaten alive by Rakshasas. As positive and negative actions do not 'cancel each other out' in Hinduism, a soul can repent through their punishment in Naraka and enjoy the peace of *Svarga* (a heavenly place), both before their return to Earth.

Narasimha (**Nur**-sim-**haa**) – Regarded as the fourth avatar of Vishnu, Narasimha is a manifestation of the Preserver of the Universe who comes to Earth as a half-man, half-lion to defeat the demon Hiranyakashipu, who has immortality against "all men and beasts." He is considered a protector of the innocent and warrior for justice, as well as an example of one of Lord Vishnu's many clever responses to the inconvenient ancient boons held by his enemies.

Navaratri (Nuv-**rah**-tree) – Otherwise known as "Nine Nights," Navaratri is the primary festival of the Goddess and takes place at the beginning of autumn, typically three weeks before the festival of Diwali. Traditions and details of each night's symbolism differ across regions and sects, with fasting and the wearing of special colors to honor various manifestations of the Goddess being common across regions. In Gujarat, sacred dances known as Garba and Dandiya, enact Durga's battle and defeat of the demon Mahishasura.

Parvati (**pahr**-vuh-**tee**) – The wife of Shiva and one of the three chief goddesses of the *Tridevi* or 'Trinity of Goddesses,' Parvati is the benevolent female aspect of the Transformer of the Universe, and is often referred to as the goddess of power, love, fertility, and devotion. She is also sometimes referred to as an aspect or alternative name of Durga (the root form of creation, preservation, and annihilation), Shakti (the cosmic energy that underlies all life in the universe), and 'one thousand' other names/personas. In the Shaivism sects, Parvati is considered an inextricable force, without which, Shiva (and therefore God) would cease to exist, for it is her life-force that gives them both power and energy. Parvati is the benevolent form of Shiva's wife (a complementary aspect to the fierce form of Kali), and the mother of their two sons, Ganesh and Kartikeya.

Puja (**poo**-ja) – A prayer or offering, puja describes the manifestation of worship and reverence in Hinduism. Often involving offerings of light (candles or diyas), flowers, water, or food, along with prayers (often in the form of mantras), puja rituals are an important aspect of religious life for most practicing

Hindus, and are particularly common and elaborate on holy days, during festivals, and to celebrate major life events such as weddings, funerals, and baby-namings.

Rakshasa (**raahk**-shuh-suh) – Shapeshifting demons in Hindu mythology, Rakshasas have been referred to with various characteristics throughout Hindu and Buddhist literature. Ravana, Vibhishana, Surpanakha, and Kumbhakarna are Rakshasas in *the Ramayana*. Due to the varying (and often conflicting) representations of Rakshasas throughout the literature, this series has expanded on the mythological depictions with far greater detail than has been generally used in the past. While there has been a parallel drawn between some vampire representations and Rakshasas, they are not considered to be the same, in the mythology or in this series. The origin of Rakshasas on Venus was entirely invented by the author, upon the suggestion of Neha, as she was writing her own story.

Rama (**raah**-muh) – The main protagonist of *the Ramayana*, Rama is generally considered to be the seventh avatar of Vishnu. Often referred to as 'the ideal king' and 'the ideal husband,' despite the miserable ending of his wife, Rama is still a beloved figure in modern Hinduism. While there is significant debate about whether Rama should be considered infallible, this series explores the dichotomy between the divine and human aspects of his character, in line with major historical representations across the Hindu world, including the iconic version by the ancient Sanskrit poet Valmiki, that demonstrate his crooked path to virtue in great detail. The festival of Diwali, one of the most popular Hindu festivals celebrated by hundreds of millions of people every autumn, celebrates the triumph of light over darkness, as embodied by Durga's triumph over Mahishasura, and Rama's triumph over Ravana.

Ramayana, the (**raah**-mah-yuh-nuh) – One of the most well-known and beloved of the ancient Hindu Sanskrit epics, *the Ramayana* follows the many triumphs and tribulations of Rama, the seventh avatar of Vishnu, and Sita, his wife and the avatar of Lakshmi. While the epic covers a range of stories and characters, the primary conflict centers around Rama's battle with Ravana, the Rakshasa King of Lanka, after his capture and incarceration of Sita. While there are many versions of *the Ramayana* referenced across Southeast Asia including in India, Nepal, Thailand, Cambodia, and more, the most famous version is credited to the storyteller Valmiki. *The Ramayana* of Valmiki contains seven *kandas* or 'books.' The seven-book structure of *The Sita Chronicles* is meant to be a nod to the original epic.

Ravana (**raah**-vuh-nuh) – The main antagonist of *the Ramayana*, Ravana is the Rakshasa King of Lanka. He is said to be a devotee of Shiva, and to have received the 'nectar of immortality' as a boon from Lord Brahma that allows him to withstand any injury from any creature, other than a human. Lord Vishnu comes to Earth as the human, Rama, to take advantage of this epic loophole.

Sanskrit (**sahn**-skrit) – The primary sacred language of Hinduism, it has many forms and served as the foundation for many modern languages in Southeast Asia. Its role in spreading Indic culture throughout the region can generally be compared to Latin's role in disseminating and communicating literature, religion, and secular education throughout Europe for the two millennia spanning the Roman Empire to the end of the 18th century AD.

Saraswati (sah-ruh-svuh-**tee**) – The female aspect of the Creator of the Universe, Saraswati is also considered the goddess of knowledge, music, arts, learning, and wisdom. Saraswati is the wife of Brahma, and one of the principal goddesses of the *Tridevi*, or 'Trinity of Goddesses.'

Satya Yuga (**saht**-yuh **yoo**-guh) – 'The Age of Truth,' *Satya Yuga* is said to be the peaceful era that will return to Earth after the Preserver of the Universe vanquishes Kali, ending Kali Yuga (the 'Age of Vice').

Shakti (**shuhk**-tee) – The Great Goddess, the primordial cosmic energy of the universe, and the personification of the 'divine mother,' Shakti has many manifestations, including the *Tridevi*, Durga, Lakshmi, Saraswati, and Parvati. She is said to manifest on Earth as the embodiment of creative power and fertility, and of life itself. Some sects believe that Shakti is responsible for all creation and is the agent of all change, as it is her energy that animates everything in the universe, including the gods. In Shaktism and Shaivism, Shakti is worshipped as the animating energy of the Supreme Being.

Shiva (**shih**-vuh) – One of the primary deities of Hinduism, and one of the *Trimurti*, or 'Trinity of Gods,' Lord Shiva is considered to be 'the Destroyer,' 'the Transformer,' and 'the Regenerator.' He is represented by hundreds, possibly thousands, of different epithets. He is often represented as conflicting personas: He can be 'fierce' or 'benevolent,' and he is portrayed as a 'householder' with his wife, Parvati, and their sons, Ganesh and Kartikeya, but he is also portrayed as an ascetic yogi (chaste and focused on solitary prayer)— two lifestyles that are mutually exclusive in traditional Hindu society. Shiva's wife, Parvati (also referred to as Durga, Shakti, Kali, and many other names), is considered to be his life-force. In Valmiki's *Ramayana*, Ravana is a follower of Shiva, and Shiva is said to have given him a divine sword with the stipulation that if he uses his sword for unjust purposes, it will be returned to 'the three-eyed one' (Shiva himself). Shiva is often considered to be 'formless,' and it is common to worship him through the formless idol of a 'lingam' (internet image search recommended).

Sita (**see**-tuh) – The main female protagonist of *the Ramayana*, Sita is Rama's wife and an avatar of Lakshmi. Often referred to as 'the ideal wife' for her desire and ability to make the deepest personal sacrifices on behalf of her husband, Sita's tragic suicidal ending is controversial in modern academic discussions of the ancient epics.

Sugriva (soo-**gree**-vuh) – The king of the Vanaras (non-human intelligent primates who can fly), Sugriva's support is crucial to Rama's defeat of Ravana in *the Ramayana*. It is with Sugriva's army that Rama attacks Lanka. Many discussions around historical validity of *the Ramayana* have centered around the assertion that Rama led Sugriva's army over a formerly existing land bridge from mainland India to the island of Sri Lanka, as NASA images show that a series of lightly submerged sandbar islands do appear to have, at some point in the past, connected the two land masses.

Surpanakha (**soor**-puh-nuh-khuh) – The sister of Ravana, Vibhishana, and Kumbhakarna, Surpanakha is a primary female antagonist in *the Ramayana*. She is often considered the catalyst of the main events of *the Ramayana* (often taking the blame for Ravana's despicable actions). Surpanakha's story is also complex, as one of her primary scenes in the epic is when she falls in love with Rama. When she is rejected and humiliated by Rama, Rama's brother, Lakshmana, permanently maims her by cutting off her nose with a divine weapon. Surpanakha's hatred of Sita and her anger at Rama's rejection is a driving force of her character's antagonistic actions later in the story and in this series.

Tridevi (tree-**deh**-vee) – The 'Trinity of Goddesses': Saraswati ('the Creator'), Lakshmi ('the Preserver'), and Parvati, ('the Transformer'), serve as the female aspects and underlying energy of their male, godly counterpart husbands. Together they create balance between the three main aspects of existence. Each one individually, and the group as a whole, manifest Shakti's energy as is necessary to participate in worldly endeavors on behalf of the gods and goddesses, usually to support the cause of righteousness and restore balance.

Trimurti (tree-**moor**-tee) – The 'trinity' of Hindu gods: Brahma ('the Creator'), Vishnu ('the Preserver'), and Shiva ('the Destroyer' and 'the Transformer'). Together, the trinity complements each other, representing a descriptive model of various aspects of life on Earth.

Valmiki (**vahl**-mih-kee) – The most widely attributed author of *the Ramayana*, he is credited with inventing the poetic structure of epic Sanskrit literature, somewhat akin to Homer's role in codifying ancient Greek verse. In Valmiki's *Ramayana*, he participates as a character in his own work, being said to have taken Sita in after her trial by fire when Rama banished her to the jungle to raise their twin sons alone. Valmiki's own voiced admonishment of Rama's behaviour in the final chapters serves as a valuable, if controversial, reminder of the story's main point of demonstrating the complex and imperfect paths to *dharma* (virtue), along with its tragic consequences.

Vanara (**vaah**-nuh-ruh) – An ancient race of nonhuman, intelligent primates, the Vanaras are supporters of Rama and serve as his primary troops in his battle against Ravana. Sometimes referred to just as 'monkeys,' other times referred to as 'half-man, half-monkeys,' the literature is not consistent in its depiction of Vanaras. Hanuman and Sugriva are the most famous Vanaras, from their important roles in *the Ramayana*.

Varuna (vuh-**roo**-nuh) – The god of water and the celestial ocean, Varuna was the original chief god of the Vedic pantheon and later appeared throughout Sanskrit literature, primarily as the ruler of the sea. He plays a secondary role in *the Ramayana*, and is often referred to as a symbol of *rta*, an ancient vedic concept believed to encompass cosmic order and divine balance or justice.

Vibhishana (vee-**bhee**-shuh-nuh) – The youngest brother of the villain demon king, Ravana, Vibhishana is an important ally of Rama in *the Ramayana*. In *the Ramayana*, Vibhishana attempts to convince Ravana to return Sita to Rama, but his efforts are not successful. He then joins Rama and provides important intel that leads to Ravana's eventual defeat. Rama crowns Vibhishana the King of Lanka after Ravana is dead. Vibhishana's role in *the Ramayana* is a complex one, as he betrays his family and his race in order to follow a path he considers to be more dharmic. Still, there is no perfect path towards *dharma* (righteousness), and so, he is also considered a traitor. Vibhishana is one of the *Chiranjivi*, one of the seven immortals of Hinduism, who are said to remain on Earth to this day to guide humans on the path of righteousness.

Vishnu (**vih**sh-noo) – One of the primary deities of Hinduism, Lord Vishnu is considered to be 'the Preserver of the Universe.' Lord Vishnu is one of the *Trimurti*, or 'trinity' of Hindu gods, along with Brahma and Shiva. Together with his wife, Lakshmi (or Laxmi), who is considered his life-force, Lord Vishnu is mentioned throughout numerous Sanskrit texts and is worshipped as the supreme being by the Vaishnavist sects of Hindus. Rama is generally considered the seventh avatar of Vishnu among the *Dashavatara* ('ten avatars of Vishnu'). Some Hindu texts/sects refer to more avatars of Vishnu, including Mohini, a female avatar.

Vishrava (**vih**sh-**rah**-vuh) – The father of Ravana, Vibhishana, Kumbhakarna, and Surpanakha, he is described as a powerful rishi or 'seer.' He is said to have left his wife, Kaikesi, the mother of his four Rakshasa children, to return to his first wife after he became unhappy with Ravana's conduct.

Ya Devi Sarva Bhuteshu (**yah** deh-**vee** **sar**-vuh bhoo-teh-**shoo**) – The beginning of the *Devi Suktam*, one of the primary prayers/mantras to the Goddess (often sung in worship), these Sanskrit words celebrate the Goddess's embodiment of power, peace, knowledge, and many other necessary and beautiful aspects of existence in the universe, allowing the worshippers to feel the Shakti, or energy, of the Goddess within themselves, while bowing (figuratively or literally) to the greatness of all that is.

Yajna (**yahg**-nyuh) – 'Sacrifice, devotion, worship, or offering,' it refers to any ritual done in front of a sacred fire, often with mantras.

Yaksha/Yakshini (**yahk**-shuh / yahk-**shee**-nee) – A powerful nature spirit with shapeshifting abilities, generally considered to be the caretakers of Earth. The feminine form of a Yaksha is a Yakshini.

Yama (**yah**-muh) – The god of death, lord of justice, and the gatekeeper of the underworld, Yama is one of several deities who participates in the management of the afterlife. The gatekeeper of Naraka (roughly Hindu 'purgatory'), Yama is said to be one of the judges of human life/morality and 'the first mortal to have died.'

Pronunciation Key:

Rather than using the international phonetic alphabet that is not commonly used by the average reader, these pronunciation notes use references to common sounds in American English, more similar to a foreign language guide for casual travelers. Note that an "h" does not represent an aspiration in this transliteration; it is used to demonstrate various vowel sounds in English. Also note that the consonants have been simplified for an English speaker and do not fully represent the nuanced differences in the Sanskrit alphabet, such as aspirated v. non-aspirated consonants, that a native Hindi speaker would recognize.

Ah – as in "car" and "hard"
Aah – hold "ah" as in "car" and "hard" longer
Uh – as in "under" and "bus"
Ih – as in "in" and "interest"
Eh – as in "extra" and "**e**xcellent"
Oh – as in "over" and "ornate"
Ee – as in "cheese" and "beast," note that this does not indicate an elongation
Oo – as in "choose" and "I do," note that this does not indicate an elongation

This series is dedicated to the Goddess who resides in all of us.
May she give us the energy, inspiration, and perseverance to triumph
over all that holds us back, no matter what forms our enemies take.
"We are told too often what we can't do."
May we do it anyway.
Jai Mata Di.
~Ashley Mayers

www.ingramcontent.com/pod-product-compliance
Lightning Source LLC
Chambersburg PA
CBHW032255020726
47495CB00001B/113